Readers have fallen in love with

The LOST SONG *of* PARIS

'A fantastic read. I was gripped and enthralled. Wonderful storytelling'
Jill Mansell

'Fascinating, moving, romantic and utterly gripping. I couldn't stop reading'
Katie Fforde

'Readers will adore walking through occupied Paris in the footsteps of the brave. A fabulous story'
Mandy Robotham

'A tense, heart-in-mouth story about courage in occupied Paris, and secrets'
Gill Paul

'Takes you right into the beating heart of occupied France [and] shows us the best and worst of what it is to be human, and the redeeming power of love . . . heart-wrenching'
Jane Bailey

'Sarah writes with a lyrical beauty which is testament to her former career as a musician. This is a novel you should not miss and is impossible to put down'
Caroline Montague

Discover why real readers adore
The Lost Song of Paris

'Heartbreaking . . . One of the best books
I have read this year'
☆☆☆☆☆

'Truly riveting . . . A heartwrenching story of love
and the bravery and danger of those involved in espionage.
A must-read in historical fiction'
☆☆☆☆☆

'I was totally enthralled in the story and couldn't
put it down'
☆☆☆☆☆

'Kept me turning the pages wanting to know what
happens next'
☆☆☆☆☆

'Gripping . . . I loved the dual timeline'
☆☆☆☆☆

'I loved this book – a perfect summer read'
☆☆☆☆☆

'A great novel about the war . . . highly recommended'
☆☆☆☆☆

'Wow, what a story. War, secrets, love, intrigue, music,
and lives lost'
☆☆☆☆

Praise for Sarah Steele's
evocative and heart-wrenching novels

'I felt so passionately involved in Flo's journey.
A GORGEOUS read'
***Prima*, Book of the Month**

'An engaging novel, strong on character and place,
that kept me wanting to know more'
Daily Mail

'A lovely read, with the descriptions of the
60s jet-set particularly evocative'
Heat

'A gorgeous, tender debut'
Kate Riordan

'I loved reading the entwined stories. This book is
warm and true, and it pays tribute to the heart and
backbone of women who support each other'
Stephanie Butland

'*The Schoolteacher of Saint-Michel* really draws
the reader in. The storytelling is masterful, as are all the
subtle touches that convey the sense of place; and . . . the
bedrock is Sarah's nuanced, unsentimental portrayal
of warm, compassionate female friendships'
Felicity Hayes-McCoy

Sarah Steele trained as a classical pianist and violinist before joining the world of publishing as an editorial assistant at Hodder and Stoughton. She was for many years a freelance editor, and now lives in the vibrant Gloucestershire town of Stroud.

Keep up with Sarah on Twitter
@sarah_l_steele

and on Facebook and Instagram
@sarahsteeleauthor

Or visit her website at
www.sarahsteeleauthor.co.uk

Also by Sarah Steele

The Missing Pieces of Nancy Moon

The Schoolteacher of Saint-Michel

The Lost Song *of* Paris

Sarah Steele

First published in 2022 by Headline Review
An imprint of HEADLINE PUBLISHING GROUP

First published in paperback in 2023 by Headline Review

002

Cataloguing in Publication Data is available from the British Library

ISBN 978 1 4722 9428 9

Typeset by EM&EN
Printed and bound in Great Britain by Clays Ltd, Elcograf S.p.A.

Headline's policy is to use papers that are natural, renewable and recyclable
products and made from wood grown in well-managed forests and other
controlled sources. The logging and manufacturing processes are expected
to conform to the environmental regulations of the country of origin.

HEADLINE PUBLISHING GROUP
An Hachette UK Company
Carmelite House
50 Victoria Embankment
London EC4Y 0DZ

www.headline.co.uk
www.hachette.co.uk

To all my music teachers

and musical friends

over the years

Prologue

London, 1 March 1941

She pulled a packet of cigarettes from her handbag and sat on the edge of the bed, crossing her long legs and loosening her silk scarf. As she inhaled the unfamiliar English tobacco, she longed for the Gauloises that reminded her of the backstreet Paris bistros she had left behind only days ago. She kicked off her shoes and rubbed her tired, stockinged feet. Even if the price tag was hefty, the rayon stockings she had managed to find on a market stall were a vast improvement on the Elizabeth Arden leg-dye sold to Frenchwomen for thirty francs a bottle.

The ribbed counterpane, pockmarked with cigarette burns and the same dirty green as the river that ran through this city, felt rough under her hand as she thought back over the few days that had brought her to this dingy corner of London. The passage across the demarcation line into Free France had been eased by her connections in high places in Paris, but she still ached from the journey across the Pyrenees and into Spain in a truck with poor suspension, dressed in scruffy borrowed clothes and bearing the identity card of a secretary at the car-parts company she claimed to work for. Once she had packed the papers necessary for her meeting, the small suitcase now locked in the wardrobe had not allowed for changes of clothing, and so she had taken care to keep the red Molyneux suit clean. She had no intention of turning up to the next morning's meeting looking like one of the refugees who had fled Paris nine months ago.

Brown, bucolic oil paintings meant to cheer only depressed her further, and the tray bearing a plate of congealed meat-matter and unrecognisable vegetable mush remained where the maid had left it. As though she could forget, criss-crossed tape across each tiny panel of the sash window was a stark reminder that London was in the thick of a sustained bombing campaign by the German Luftwaffe. She had seen for herself the blown-out windows of department stores, naked, dismembered mannequins strewn across the pavements; women staring into the distance atop the smoking piles of brick and metal that had once been their homes.

She checked her pocket for the paperback book she was supposed to carry with her the next day, then loosened the belt of the jacket and undid its centime-sized buttons, pressing flat the pleats of the matching skirt. The red suit had been a bold choice, with its matching Rose Valois tipped fedora, but she was used to wearing beautifully crafted clothes as armour.

She stubbed out her cigarette in a chipped Welcome to London glass ashtray and switched off the tasselled bedside lamp before wandering across to the window. No doubt the old dragon on the front desk would soon be knocking on doors to tell the guests to close the blackout curtains. Why Herr Hitler would want to bomb this eyesore of a building, she had no idea, but she went to take one last look at London before shutting herself off from the night outside.

As buses carried away the last office workers on the dark, rain-slicked street outside, a low drone gradually crescendoed and half a dozen Germany-bound RAF Beaufighters came into view above the anti-barrage balloons keeping vigil over the city. The dreaded Moaning Minnie sirens began their warning cries and beams of light raked the sky, searching for incoming bombers – spotters on the coast must have seen the first wave of the Heinkels that flew nightly over the Channel. London was even more frightening than she had imagined it might be. Soon the uniformed and the displaced would be the only ones walking the streets, she thought, as she watched the lone figure of a serviceman walk purposefully along the pavement, the bowl of his pipe glowing in the darkness.

Parents began to hurry pyjamaed children towards the Underground station, gas masks hanging around their necks, and she wondered if the hotel guests were meant to be making their way to the shelters. The concentration of bombing had mainly been in the East End and docks area during the last couple of nights, but there was no predicting where would be targeted next.

She heard the rumble of approaching aircraft and looked up in time to see a German bomber caught in a roving light beam. The shrill scream of whistles punctuated shouted warnings from air-raid wardens as shells burst across the city. A series of swishing whines filled the silence between bursts, until glaring flashes a few streets away blinded her briefly. She held her hands over her ears against the deafening bang but could not block out the crash of the bedside lamp falling to the ground, the screams from the street outside, the wail of fire engines streaming across the city.

'Everyone down to the basement,' a voice called out in the corridor outside, as a frenzied knocking began at each door and her fellow guests made their way downstairs. She could go nowhere without the suitcase hidden inside the wardrobe, but as she went to fetch it, she remembered she had locked the wardrobe door. '*Merde*,' she muttered. She hadn't risked her life just for the information hidden in the case to be destroyed in a bombing raid. She rifled through her handbag and was just starting to panic when she remembered that the maid coming in with the supper tray had knocked over the chair where the bag had sat – the key must have fallen out. As she knelt on the floor, brushing her hand across the patterned rug, behind her the windows suddenly blew inwards as a deafening explosion rocked the building. Instinctively, she pulled her hands over her head and curled into a foetal ball, and glass splinters sprayed the room as a prelude to the thick dust and hot, foul smoke that quickly worked their way into her lungs.

The creaking of the broken skeleton of the house became more agonised, and she knew she would have to abandon the case, but as she stood unsteadily, already she could see the ribs of the ceiling above beginning to bow. The bomb's point of impact must have been close by. Flames were visible through the widening cracks in the ceiling and chunks of masonry had fallen from above, blocking the door and her safe exit.

Her only choice now was to jump, and, coughing against the acrid fumes, she tied the silk scarf over her mouth and fought to open the glassless skeleton of the heavy sash window, stuck together with many layers of paint, its chequerboard of wooden struts like prison bars between herself and safety. She grabbed the dressing-table chair, smashing it repeatedly against the stubborn timbers of the old Georgian window until she was able to make enough room to squeeze through and perch on the wide window ledge outside. It was chaos in the street below, the pavement piled with the rubble of the upper floors. There was no point in calling for help: no one would hear her above the fire-engine bells and cacophony of the continued raid.

For a moment she closed her eyes and imagined she was sitting on the diving board at the Piscine Molitor, the sun beating down on her bare shoulders and the sound of Parisians at play beneath her. All she had to do was jump.

Part One

1

London, June 1997

Amy pulled herself upright, heart racing from the traces of her nightmare. A year later and still she endured in her sleep the images she managed to push away during the daytime distractions of running a home and her small daughter alone, and the work that gave her a haven of peace and order in the chaos of her new life.

She heard soft breathing beside her and turned to look at her daughter's long, apricot-coloured hair spread across Michael's pillow, her freckle-sprinkled cheeks making her even more like a miniature version of her mother. Amy knew she would have to address Holly's refusal to sleep in her own bed at some point – she was five years old and Michael had been gone nearly a year – but it gave them both comfort to curl around one another, shored up against the darkest part of the night.

'I don't want to go to school, Mummy,' Holly said, rubbing her eyes.

'You have to, sweetheart.' Amy kissed the top of her head. 'And I have to go to work.'

'But I've got a tummy ache.'

Every day began with the same conversation. Amy knew it was heartache not tummy ache making Holly want to hide from the world, but the world had moved on, and their little family was expected to move with it. She had sat in meeting after meeting with Holly's teacher, agreeing they should find something that gave the little girl joy, invite other children to play even though Holly ignored them when they visited. She just wanted Amy. All the time.

But Amy was the one who had struggled with parenting, while Michael took to it like a duck to water. When he wasn't in rehearsals, he could be there during the day, changing the nappies, helping out at playgroup, being at the school gates while Amy went to work. Topping and tailing Holly's day when Michael had evening theatre performances had been the perfect division of labour, but the last year had thrown the routine and the rule book out of the window.

And so she could only imagine Michael's knowing smile as she abandoned healthy cereal in favour of the sugary hoops Amy loved, swapped homemade lunchboxes for defeatist processed snacks. 'You don't get to leave us, then make me feel bad about lowering my standards,' she said under her breath, having finally backed down on chocolate milk instead of fruit juice, in exchange for Holly agreeing to put on her school uniform.

She looked at the kitchen clock. Seven thirty a.m. and already she was exhausted. A day at work would be a breeze in comparison.

'Well, if it isn't Holly Novak,' Claire said in her soft Irish brogue as she opened her front door. 'Going to walk to school with us today?'

Holly hid behind Amy's legs, rubbing her threadbare toy rabbit against her nose.

'We might leave a bit early and walk through the park . . .' Claire said, her head on one side, her dark bob hanging asymmetrically.

Amy knew that smile: the one Claire used when she tried to persuade Amy to come for a drink, to the cinema, to open up and just have a bloody good cry.

Amy felt the little girl unstiffen slightly and recognised an opportunity to get away without a scene. 'Will you feed the ducks?' she asked Claire.

'Definitely. And there's toast with chocolate spread on the kitchen table.'

Amy sighed. 'Frankly, if there's a mountain of Magic Stars on the table, she can go for it.'

'Magic Stars?' Holly said quietly, moving around to lean against the front of Amy's legs.

'Fill your boots, love,' Amy said, kissing the top of Holly's head as she slid her hand out of her mother's and slipped past Claire towards the kitchen, where Claire's daughter Susie and another neighbour's little boy were running around frenziedly, their school uniforms supplemented with Disney dresses and nativity-play leftovers. 'Thanks for this, again. I don't know what I'd do if you didn't help with the school run now Michael's not here.'

'Ah, and how those other mums miss him at the school gate. They've easily gained at least half an hour of their day back, without him talking at them.'

Amy smiled. 'Why say in two words what you can say in two paragraphs? He really was made for performing. Anyway, thanks. I mean it.'

'You're welcome. I, like Michael, don't have a grown-up

job, and I'm not in work till ten.' She looked down at a streak of butter smeared on her Japanese linen smock. 'And I'll need till then to get cleaned up.'

'Remind me why I didn't get a job in arts admin too?'

'Because you bloody love what you do, and there's only just enough jobs for drama-school dropouts like me as it is. She'll be fine,' Claire said, seeing Amy's concern as Holly hung back from joining the other children. 'Time for a quick cuppa?'

Amy shook her head. Apart from the fact that she had a long day ahead, she wasn't in the mood for the soul-searching that would be the price of a mug of English Breakfast. 'Better get going.'

'Come for supper next Friday, then? Don't panic – David's cooking, so you won't get beans on toast. We've got a few people coming over. Might do you good to talk to new people.' Claire glanced at Amy's tired long black jersey skirt and Doc Martens, the scruffy ponytail barely containing her long, strawberry-blonde hair. 'Maybe dress up a bit . . . you've let your game slip, my friend. Holly can sleep over so you can have a drink. What do you say?'

'I don't know . . .' Amy knew Claire was only trying to help, but she wasn't ready to be thrown back into Chiswick society quite yet.

'It's not all couples,' her friend added. 'And,' she went on, 'I'm not trying to set you up with anyone.'

'Better not be.' Amy smiled. 'I'll think about it,' she said.

'OK. Have a good day. Find out interesting stuff.'

Amy peered along the hallway, knowing she would have to trust that her daughter would have an OK day at school and she herself a good day at work, finding out interesting stuff – Claire's daily parting joke was a succinct but fairly accurate summary of Amy's working life as an historical archivist.

She watched Holly hovering on the edge of the boisterous kitchen activity, holding back as she glanced at her mum, wanting to join in but not remembering how. Amy felt for her mobile phone in her pocket, fighting back the temptation to telephone work and claim her own tummy ache. Instead she turned away, brushing tears from her eyes as Claire closed the door behind her.

'You've seen the list, then?'

Amy looked up from the typed memorandum she'd been reading over the first coffee of the day, as Eleanor came to sit beside her in the busy staff room, her long Perspex earrings rattling gently.

Twice yearly, the Cabinet Office released swathes of declassified files into the public domain, and once the Collections Care department had assessed, repaired and catalogued them, staff were able to call up and examine these fresh windows on recent history. Amy ran her eye down the run-of-the-mill government papers released under the thirty-year rule and those held back until the death of named persons, or for which specified amounts of time had elapsed. Some of the new releases from the security services dated back to the Second World War, and Amy wondered whether she could clear her diary for the day. She had a university seminar to prepare and some notes to make for a meeting about an upcoming museum exhibition, but there was nothing that wouldn't wait.

Eleanor tapped her glasses against one name on the list. 'I never thought I'd see that one before I retired.'

'None of us was ever sure she even existed,' Amy replied. 'Are we any the wiser as to her identity?'

Eleanor shook her head. 'Not yet. Collections Care haven't found anything in there to identify her, but obviously we'll go through the file with a fine-tooth comb.'

'Just to have concrete proof that she wasn't an invention designed to put the wind up the Germans is enough for now.'

'We'll cancel our catch-up later, shall we?' Eleanor said. 'I've a feeling you'll be busy today. Do you want me to handle that radio interview this afternoon?'

'Would you?' Amy said, remembering she was due at Broadcasting House after lunch to record a short piece on a Special Operations Executive agent about whom a major new film had been made.

'Leave it to me.'

'You don't want to check this file over before me?'

'No, this is your baby. You put so much work into planning that exhibition about female agents before . . .' She hesitated.

'It's OK, Eleanor, and being back at work is really helping.' Amy appreciated the kindness of the older woman who had employed her five years earlier, possibly seeing a younger version of herself in Amy's dedication to finding the human stories behind the facts.

'Good.' Eleanor hesitated. 'I know things have been tough, but I'd love to see you fly with this stuff again. This might not have been a career you'd planned to get into, but you're bloody good at it.'

'What do you mean?'

Eleanor smiled. 'I did read your CV, you know. People don't spend three years at music conservatoire in order to become historians.'

Amy was surprised. She'd been employed on the back of the History degree she had taken after her need for an abrupt change of direction, the Masters in records management she had been recommended to pursue. She had thought her background was truly that – in the background, where it belonged – and had been careful to avoid sharing with Eleanor some of the more painful twists and turns of her path away from music. Amy never wanted anyone to think that her work was a consolation prize – it was a passion, a vocation she felt privileged to have found. 'You know I love my job?' she said.

'Of course. I just want you to find your spark again.'

Amy was tired of people knowing what was best for her. Eleanor, Claire, Holly's teachers . . . even Michael's parents constantly weighed in about how Holly should spend more time with them and give Amy the break she really didn't want.

'Thanks,' she said, 'but I'm fine, honestly.'

She watched Eleanor walk away, feeling suddenly incredibly exposed by the reference to her earlier life. If Michael hadn't tried to drag it up again, maybe they wouldn't have argued that last day, and they might still have the rest of their lives to look forward to together. Instinctively she rubbed at the scar on the palm of her hand, the old tic that always surfaced alongside memories of her former life.

Amy already had a long-term life partner when nearly twenty years ago she let her guard slip in a smoky pub and fell in love with the shaggy-haired drama student who happily accepted that he would always come second. Music was such an ingrained part of Amy that it was like her twin, her head and her hands full of tens of thousands of notes that poured from her for hours each day. The fact that Michael supported her so wholeheartedly, would regularly sit in the corner of a practice room pretending to learn lines late into the evening so that she would not have to walk home alone, only made her love him more. Instead of sulking in her shadow, he had been proud of her elevated status at the performing arts school where they had been undergraduates together, as she scooped up prizes and awards both at home and internationally. Her waif-like Celtic beauty had no doubt played some part in the feelers put out by a small independent label hoping to feature her strawberry-blonde locks and delicately freckled complexion in their marketing campaign for a recording of little-known twentieth-century French piano music. It had taken years to learn to leave all this behind and make a new life, and the conversation with Eleanor had unsettled the fragile equilibrium through which she navigated each day.

Amy made herself take some deep breaths before she ordered up the files that had sat dormant on a dusty Foreign Office shelf for decades. Already she found her mind shifting away from her own life towards the secrets she might uncover about one of the most successful yet enigmatic spies of the Second World War.

She was about to meet Agent Colette.

2

Amy loved the peace of the staff reading room, where her colleagues pored over files or worked quietly at microfiche readers. This was the beating heart of their profession, the direct interaction with voices from the past. This was where she understood why she had been steered towards history as an alternative career.

She was a musical storyteller, her professor had told her, and after the accident, he had tried to persuade her to transfer to the conservatoire's orchestral conducting course, where her talent could be applied on a larger scale. Amy had been adamant, however, that if she couldn't play as she used to, then music would no longer be part of her life. He had understood, suggesting instead that perhaps in studying history she could exercise her curiosity about hidden narratives. It had been a stroke of genius, and one that had allowed Amy to find a new passion.

Although she missed the buzz of performing, the direct communication with the past through documents, private letters and government papers was thrilling. Every noisy, bloody and epoch-defining event in recordable history could be found within the miles of shelving that housed the archives, be it a police report on a Suffragette rally or the minutiae of colonial handovers in the Far East, the details of a Royal wedding or papers relating to the formation of the National Health Service.

Her pulse quickened as she opened the plain box file in front of her and saw the folder inside, 'SECRET' stamped in bold red ink beside another stamp bearing the release date of the file. Taped to the front was a piece of paper with the hand-typed name of the subject:

Agent 'Colette', SIS Section VIII, French Division

Amy could still not quite believe she was looking at the physical proof that Agent Colette had not only existed but had been an active part of the Secret Intelligence Service's resistance activities. Her work had been so undercover that she had become almost mythical, her correspondence with London so need-to-know that even some members of Churchill's War Cabinet were unaware of her. It was said she had provided information that led to the destruction of German armament factories and coastal defences, as well as delaying the deployment of lethal long-range missiles that would have lengthened the German grip on mainland Europe.

Whereas the Special Operations Executive had been disbanded at the end of the war and many of its agent records eventually made available, Secret Intelligence Service personnel files from World War Two were notoriously thin on the ground, much of the collection still held by the Foreign Office under the post-war reclassification of the agency into the more commonly recognised MI6. For a file such as Agent Colette's to become accessioned was a rare and important event.

Amy carefully untied the fabric tape wrapped around the thick folder and opened out the envelope leaves. Atop the official letters and memorandums, reports and accounts was a cellophane wallet containing a photograph of a woman in a flimsy couture gown, a background of mirrors and chandeliers framing her slender neck, immaculately styled blonde Hollywood hair and tear-shaped face, with its slightly wistful smile and the disarmingly direct gaze of her huge eyes. Amy wondered how anyone so beautiful could have operated undetected for so long, but maybe her beauty had dazzled the enemy into seeing only what they chose to see.

One by one, Amy removed the treasury tags from each document. The first few tissue-paper-thin sheets were reports from other agents in the field, recommending 'Colette' for active duty. An officer named 'Kestrel' had written to Sir Richard Tremayne, the Chief Staff Officer of Training, suggesting his unnamed asset could take over operations in Paris and that SIS should arrange formal training for her. A high-level contact in Paris had expressed an interest in working with her, on the condition of absolute anonymity. There followed various communications in which plans were outlined for her transportation to London, and a few panicked messages when her initial meeting in Whitehall in March 1941 was delayed due to a bombing raid. All references to her real name had been redacted in thick black pen.

Reports on Colette's subsequent training in Morse and unarmed combat followed, along with doctors' reports on her recovery from a head injury during the bombing, and a psychiatrist's assessment of her suitability as an agent. Amy examined receipts for clothing – 1 silk blouse with seams in the French style, 1 set underwear, 1 red suit, repaired – and for the Colt .38 revolver issued to her. Alongside three million French francs in cash, false identity papers and the means to disguise herself, she had of course also been issued her radio set and crystals.

Colette had returned to Paris in June 1941 with her affairs in order: letters from the accounts department confirmed that her monthly salary of thirty pounds and five shillings be paid directly to a school in Surrey Amy knew to have cared for Jewish children who had escaped from Europe. A copy of her will stated that her estate should be shared between her cousin, whom she had named as executor, two other friends and the daughter of a family called Goldmann. A copy of the Official Secrets Act had been signed in an undecipherable script in the presence of Chief Staff Officer Sir Richard Tremayne, and there followed an RAF form outlining the details of her return flight to France and successful parachute drop.

Months' worth of reports from returning agents, including Kestrel, cast light on the activities of Agent Colette, and occasional correspondence between herself and her case officer Verity Cooper revealed a demonstrable fondness. 'My dear godmother . . .' Colette's notes always began, and records of gifts between them, transferred via the Lysander shuttle plane service, outlined a love of small luxuries such as soap and perfume, tea and stockings – a bunch of French irises had even found their way across the Channel at one point. Letters to and from Tremayne and the War Office testified to successful missions carried out by Bomber Command on the strength of evidence passed along Colette's network.

Nothing in the file related to events after January 1944, but as Amy turned over the last sheet of paper she saw an envelope addressed to Flight-Lieutenant Alec Scott, 614 Squadron, in the same hand as Colette's own signature. A note clipped to it read, 'To be delivered in the event of death.' The envelope had already been sliced carefully open by the conservators, and

Amy took out the folded piece of paper, laying it on the table in front of her.

The opening sentence was a handwritten plea for understanding from a woman forced to abandon the man she loved so that she might fight for her country. As well as the familiar, uncomfortable sense of trespassing on long-preserved intimacy, Amy was struck by the visceral, too-close-to-home shock at reading an unspoken goodbye, and she quickly folded the letter with shaking hands, unable to banish the sudden ghost of her own unspoken goodbye and the pain its memory caused. The last time she had seen Michael, he had left the house too angry for breakfast. Too angry to kiss and make up. Too angry to turn round and say goodbye, and she had been too angry to say 'I love you.' Or even 'Goodbye.' She felt tears prick at her eyes, and quickly rubbed them away, looking around in the hope that none of her colleagues had witnessed her rare display of grief. Staying strong was how she managed to get up each day, how she managed to work, parent, eat, breathe, but something about this letter had unsettled her.

As she replaced the letter in the envelope, forcing herself back into historian mode, she couldn't help wondering why it had never been delivered. Had Colette and her pilot enjoyed the reunion that Amy and Michael were denied? Surely the occasional happy ending was possible?

Amy had seen enough for one day and was too fraught to do professional justice to Colette's papers. She suddenly needed to be with Holly, who would have finished school and be at Claire's by now. She needed to go home and find a quiet place where she could release her grief safely. She placed the file on her allocated stretch of shelving, gathered her belongings and headed out of the building into the fresh air rippling the shallow lake that softened the edges of the Brutalist building.

She had a feeling that discovering Agent Colette's story would be a challenge in more ways than one.

'Oh, Amy, I'm sorry,' Claire said, pushing a box of tissues across the crayon-strewn table.

'No, I'm sorry. You must think I'm stupid, sobbing like this about some letter written fifty years ago. And only one line of it! It just really got to me. I thought I could handle it, but . . .' She trailed off, dabbing a tissue against her wet cheeks.

'Don't worry. You are allowed to let it out sometimes, you know? And besides, I could tell something was up the minute you walked through the door.' Claire squeezed her friend's hand. 'It's not just about the letter, is it? You haven't ever really talked about what happened with Michael that morning before he left – it's no wonder this has upset you.'

Amy blew her nose and smiled. 'Damn, you're good.'

Holly had turned away from the television in the corner of the room to watch her mother. 'It's fine, sweetheart,' Amy said. 'Something at work made me sad.' She turned back to Claire. 'Does she always just watch telly when she's here?'

Claire shrugged. 'Sometimes she plays with Susie, but only when I don't push it. Anyway, it's *Blue Peter*. Edifying as well as entertaining. And she'll know how to make you a coathanger cover when she gets home.'

'Perhaps I should ask Susie round to play more often.'

'Ask *me* round more often, and I'll bring her with me. How about that?'

'*Touché*.'

'I only want to help, you know? David and I hate seeing you like this. It's no way to exist.'

'Unless you can bring Michael back, I'm not sure there's anything anyone can do to help.'

'I can make five-year-olds eat green vegetables, but I'm not a miracle worker. There must be something that would bring your spark back. What about that piano Michael got you?'

Amy shook her head. 'That's the last thing that would help. It's what caused the argument in the first place.'

Claire slapped her forehead. 'Jeez, I'm an eejit. Well, how about joining a running club?'

'Now you really are being ridiculous.'

'You could come to yoga with me?'

'I'm so tense, I'd snap.'

'Take up golf.'

Amy laughed. 'That would be the day I give up entirely.'

Claire sat back, running her fingers through her dark, shiny hair that was just beginning to show a sprinkling of grey. 'Then what about this spy woman you were telling me about?'

'Agent Colette?'

'That's her. You say you don't know why the letter wasn't delivered to her pilot?'

'I assume it's because they found each other and there was no need.'

Claire leaned forward on her elbows, narrowly missing a piece of cold buttered toast. 'Exactly. You only assume. What if you were to find out for yourself?'

'I don't know. It's none of my business.'

'Except that it completely is your business. Literally. You're . . .' She sat back, searching for the words, then stared at

Amy. 'You're a history detective. Aren't you even a bit curious about what's in the rest of the letter? Don't you want to know what happened to the spy and the pilot? It's like some war film without an ending. I'm on tenterhooks – read it for me, if not for yourself.'

Amy hesitated. Of course she was curious, but the letter had shocked her with its immediacy and sense of loss, and she hadn't allowed herself to think further than cataloguing the contents of Agent Colette's file. It was true, though: the letter wasn't just a piece of paper; it was part of a love story between two very real people who had endured very real danger and enforced separation.

Claire took her hand. 'Come on – it might even help, finding a bit of closure for someone else.'

'And you'll never give up, will you?' Amy said, squeezing Claire's hand in return.

'Never, my friend. So you may as well give in. Read the rest of the letter or I will never give you another day's peace.'

It was late afternoon, and there was a definite Friday feel to the staff reading room as weekend plans were whispered and seats vacated in favour of an early train home. Amy had spent the afternoon making preliminary notes on Colette's recruitment and pre-engagement papers, pointedly avoiding looking at the letter tucked in the back of the file. As she came to pack up for the night, however, she couldn't help being drawn to the envelope once more. Claire was right: the unfinished nature of an unsent letter was tantalisingly open ended, and she looked once more at the name written on the front. What if Alec Scott were still alive? What if his family needed the sort of closure this letter might bring?

Avoiding reading the letter was helping no one, and so Amy rode on the coat-tails of her curiosity, opening the letter once more before she could change her mind.

The opening was no less powerful, no less emotional than she remembered, and the rest told of a woman who had been forced to keep her identity from her lover, but who longed for the opportunity to explain actions that may have seemed suspicious to anyone unaware of her agent status. Had Alec ever discovered the truth? Or had he died believing the worst of her?

Amy headed back to her desk and rang the number of an ex-colleague now working at the MOD. 'I don't suppose you have access to Air Force personnel post-1919?' she asked. 'I want to track down the next of kin for . . .' She looked once more at the envelope. 'Flight-Lieutenant Alec Scott. He was with 614 Squadron in April 1941.' She waited patiently, eventually smiling as she received a response. 'Really? That would be amazing. Yes, just fax it over.'

A few moments later she was holding a piece of paper: 'Mrs Verity Cooper,' it read, '72 Chalcot Crescent, Primrose Hill.'

There was something familiar about the sister's name. Where had she seen it before? Amy riffled through her notes, and there it was. Flight Officer Verity Cooper, case officer to Agent Colette and now apparently sister to Colette's lover. Had Verity Cooper known she was a third side of the triangle linking an RAF pilot, a French spy and an SIS officer?

Amy had begun all of this simply to reunite a family with a wartime story that had remained untold, but now it seemed she had stumbled upon something far more complicated. She grabbed a copy of *Kelly's Directory* and ran her finger down pages of Coopers until, incredibly, she stopped at a W. and V. Cooper of Chalcot Crescent. It had to be the same household. There, hidden in plain sight, was the woman who helped train and organise Allied spies until the German retreat in occupied France in the summer of 1944. And yet where Vera Atkins of the Special Operations Executive had retained a reputation that outlived the war, SIS personnel such as Verity Cooper were notoriously difficult to research after the war had ended. Amy had seen photographs of female staff leaving Bletchley Park for the last time and wondered how easily these women would swap Enigma coding for housekeeping bills. Had one-time Flight Officer Cooper been one of those who had slipped into the fifties advertising idyll of the satisfied housewife?

She picked up the telephone again and dialled Claire's number. 'I've found his next of kin,' she said. 'She's still alive.'

'Then what are you waiting for?' Claire yelled across the sound of boisterous Friday-night letting-off-of-steam. 'Phone her up.'

Verity Cooper was likely to be an elderly, fragile lady who would not take kindly to shocks being delivered by telephone, and so instead Amy sat at her desk and typed a letter in which she explained that papers relating to the family during World War Two had come to light. If Mrs Cooper would like to discuss this further, Amy would be very happy to meet with her.

As she walked back across the river towards home, oblivious to cyclists and weekend-hungry drivers, Colette's words clung to Amy like a heady scent, the power of her love for Alec undiminished by time. What were you meant to do with love when it could no longer be received? Amy so often found herself overwhelmed by her feelings for Michael, only to know they had nowhere to go, no one to receive them. Would she ever find a way to negotiate life without the pain of his loss?

3

Verity Cooper would not like to discuss this further, Amy soon discovered. A curt reply by post from Mrs Cooper's daughter stated that her mother was unwell and, further, unwilling to discuss family matters. Mrs Penny Marshall thanked Amy for her thoughtful offer of a visit and wished her well.

Amy should have been happy to leave it at that: she had been politely yet firmly turned down. End of story. Except that it wasn't. Disappointed that the trail had gone cold so quickly, she penned a brief reply to Penny, explaining that she merely wanted to pass on a copy of the contents of an undelivered letter. She included her work telephone number, in case Mrs Cooper should change her mind.

Amy had done everything she could, and it was with some relief that she focused on other work projects, and feeling guilty about ducking out of the dinner invitation, allowed herself to accept an invitation from Claire for a special screening at the BFI. The theatre still felt too close to Michael's world for comfort, but cinema was a step removed, even if Claire's choice of a black-and-white war film was all too obviously aimed at encouraging Amy's investigation into Colette.

A week later a phone call came through from Penny Marshall, a no-nonsense middle-aged woman who told Amy that Verity Cooper had been particularly tetchy since hearing about the letter Amy had found. Penny was concerned at her obsessive poring over old photographs of her late brother, Penny's uncle, which in turn was driving up her blood pressure. A can of worms had been opened, it seemed, and so Amy had better show the contents of the letter to Mrs Cooper, so that they could all relax a little. Mrs Cooper would expect Amy for tea on Monday.

Four days later, Amy stepped out of the lift at Chalk Farm Tube station and made her way towards the pretty Georgian enclave of Primrose Hill and the terraced crescent that was home to a retired intelligence officer. Defiantly shabby, its front door a drab brown and windows dressed with lace curtains rather than acres of Osborne & Little, the Cooper home stood out amongst its smart, pastel-stucco neighbours. A For Sale sign suggested that Amy had arrived just in time.

'You must be the historian.' A fresh-faced woman around the same age as Amy's mother opened the door, her bobbed grey hair pulled back in an Alice band.

'Archivist, but yes, I suppose so. I hope it's not inconvenient?' Amy peered along the tiled hallway at the boxes stacked high.

'Honestly, there's no such thing as convenient these days. Have you ever moved someone after sixty years in the same house? Well, don't! Especially if they won't see why they can't keep seven tea trays and twelve umbrellas. Our granny flat in Shropshire is about an eighth the size of this place, so you're doing me a favour by keeping her occupied while I sneak some bags to the charity shop. I'm Penny, by the way. I'm sorry if I seemed unenthusiastic in our correspondence, but Mother's on the other side of a nasty chest infection. It's made her rather grotty, I'm afraid, and she's not a great one for visitors at the best of times, but until she sees this wretched letter she'll be insufferable. Just don't wear her out.'

'Thank you.' Amy followed Penny through the house, the empty hooks and bright rectangles of colour on the sun-bleached floral wallpaper suggesting a shedding of the house's custodianship. 'Did you grow up here?' she asked.

'Yes, except when my brother and I were evacuated to Shropshire during the war.'

'Your parents stayed in London?'

'Dad was in the Navy, but Mum stayed. She had a secretarial job at the War Office.'

'A secretary?' Amy said, holding back what she knew of Penny's mother. In her experience, people chose to keep these things private for good reason.

'I don't imagine it was terribly exciting, but she wanted to do her bit, I suppose.' Penny stopped just as they were about to pass through into a small conservatory where an elderly lady sat in a rattan chair, her back to them as she stared out to the garden. 'You don't mind my asking what's in this letter, do you?'

'I don't want to say too much until I've spoken with your mother, but it appeared in a recently declassified file.'

'A file? Like a government file?'

'Nothing to be alarmed about. I'm just hoping to tie up a loose end.'

Penny smiled. 'I can't imagine my family has any deep, dark secrets. Apparently my uncle was a Battle of Britain pilot – not that I really remember him – but that's as far as it goes. We're terribly boring, I'm afraid.'

So the case officer involved in one of the most successful agent networks in wartime Europe had simply shrugged off her uniform and returned to everyday life as though it had never happened. 'There's no such thing as a boring family, in my experience,' Amy said, smiling.

'Perhaps. Anyway, you go through. I've left a tray of tea in there, and while you're chatting I'll slip out.' She frowned. 'You won't keep her long, will you? She gets awfully tired.'

'Of course not.'

Penny left Amy in the garden room, where the one-time spymaster sat silently, the fingers of one hand scratching at the arm of the chair. 'Mrs Cooper?' Amy said quietly as she came to sit in the chair opposite, trying to reconcile this elderly figure dressed in a well-serviced tweed skirt and cashmere twinset, a red and gold silk scarf tied at her neck, with the woman who had sat in Cabinet meetings and trained countless spies. 'Flight Officer Cooper?' Amy tried, and the old lady snapped to attention.

As she stared back at Amy, her shoulders set themselves a little straighter and her back a little stiffer, in keeping with the fiercely lacquered grey hair. 'No one has called me that for years,' she said. 'You must be the archivist.'

'Amy Novak. I'm honoured to meet you. Of course I've come across you from time to time during my work, but . . .'

'But I did a good job of covering my traces.'

Amy glanced towards the hallway, where she could hear Penny banging about. 'Even with your own family?'

'Especially so. There is much I prefer to forget about those days.' As the old lady paused, the sounds of nearby London Zoo cut into the silence. 'They turned Primrose Hill into allotments during the war,' she said suddenly. 'They'd send dung across from the zoo. People used to boast that an elephant had fertilised their Sunday lunch.'

'You remember how it was here during the war, Mrs Cooper?'

'Mrs Cooper was my late mother-in-law. Please, call me Verity or you might conjure up her restless, cantankerous soul, and then we shall all be in trouble.' Verity trained her steely-grey eyes on Amy. 'If you found that letter, you already know I spent little time here during the war. At least, after 1941.' She held out her hand. 'You said you would bring a copy?'

Amy reached inside her battered satchel and pulled out a photocopied sheet. 'Here.'

As Verity took the paper from her, Amy looked away. She suddenly regretted bringing such distress to someone already suffering the upheaval of leaving her home. Verity glanced briefly at the letter before handing it back to Amy. 'Thank you,' she said quietly.

'You don't want to keep it?'

Verity shook her head. 'I read the original over fifty years ago, at the end of her active service. I just wanted to be sure it was the same letter and had not been returned to her.'

'I'm sorry to ask, but do you know why it was never delivered to your brother?'

'He went missing in action. What was the point?'

'I'm sorry. That must have been terrible for you.'

Verity tutted. 'How would you know how it must have felt? You young people think you know everything, but you have no idea.'

'Maybe not,' Amy said, realising she had touched a raw nerve, 'but if there's one thing I do understand, it's losing someone you love.' She reached for her handbag. 'I've upset you. Perhaps I should go.'

'Perhaps you should. You have done what you came to do, and I have looked at your letter. There is no more to say.'

'I'm sorry to have disturbed you. Thank you for your time, Verity.' Amy stood, and was about to hold out her hand to shake Verity's, when she reminded herself that she was in the presence of possibly the only living person who might be able to tell her who Colette had really been.

Verity hesitated. 'It is I who am sorry – a word I rarely say, I'm told. I was rude. Tell me, who did you lose? A parent? Grandparent?'

Amy shook her head. 'My husband.'

'You are too young to be a widow, as so many of my generation were.'

Amy sensed a softening of the brittle shell and chanced a question before her opportunity disappeared. 'Verity, do you know who that letter was written by?'

Verity snapped her gaze towards Amy. 'Agent Colette, of course.'

'That was her code name. No, I mean, who it was really written by.'

'I have already said I do not wish to discuss this. These matters belong in the past.'

'And yet still they find us.' Amy dug in her bag and pulled out the copy of Colette's letter once more. '*My darling Alec*,' she began reading hesitantly, then looked up at Verity.

The old lady held a hand up to stop her, but let it fall in her lap. 'Finish if you must. It will change nothing. It will not bring him back.'

Amy paused, giving Verity the chance to stop her, but the old woman had sat back, eyes closed, ready to listen to the words that had travelled across half a century, and so she went on.

My darling Alec,

Leaving you is the hardest thing I have ever done, and if you receive this letter, I have gone to my death with the fire of your love burning brightly inside me.

You may hear some terrible things about me, but to explain would put myself and others in danger. I beg you to trust that I am doing everything I can to help end this awful war, and that I am the woman you fell in love with.

If one can still believe there is such a place as heaven, I will wait there for you.

Your own

S

For a moment all was silent, bar the trilling of a bird in the garden and the distant hum of traffic, until eventually Amy spoke. 'Mrs Cooper, who was "S"? Who was Colette?'

Verity shook her head. 'I promised I would never say.'

'Promised whom?'

'I was SIS. I signed the Official Secrets Act. There are things even my own husband never knew.'

'But her file has been declassified. It is only a matter of time before someone discovers who she was.'

There was a missed beat, in which Amy knew she had an opportunity, and so she waited.

'Maybe, but it will not be I who divulges it.'

'Will you at least tell me how you came to know her?'

'Why does it matter so much to you?'

'Because . . .' Amy was not sure when exactly she had come to the point when she couldn't go back, but she knew she had reached it now. 'Because I believe she was misrepresented in her real life, whatever that was. She was trying to tell your brother not to believe rumours about her. I saw some of your correspondence with her – do you not want to put straight the record of an agent you were clearly very fond of?'

'It is not that simple.' Verity hesitated. 'My family knows nothing of my war work. I have always wanted it kept that way. If they knew what had happened to Alec, and my part in it . . . If anyone found out how I treated that woman . . .'

'But she was your agent. You took great care to protect her.'

'Agent Colette, yes. Yes, I did. But the woman who wrote that letter . . .'

'I'm sorry, Verity. I don't understand. They are the same woman.'

'I know that now. But it was not always so.' She sighed. 'In war, we do not always make the right decisions, but I did my best, for the best reasons.'

'You've lost me, I'm afraid.'

Verity looked at Amy. 'I have told no one what happened with Alec and that woman. Not a soul, for all these years. Why should I talk to you now?'

'Because I think that whatever you did has weighed on you heavily for a long time. Because I think deep down you want to tell someone. And because Colette deserves the truth to be told.'

'And because I am old, there may not be many more opportunities?'

'I didn't say that.'

'But it's true.' She held out her hands, examining the liver spots and pronounced veins that marked the decades. 'Old age. It is cruel, but it is also very freeing in some ways. Maybe you are right. Maybe telling my story – Alec's story – will help to dissipate the cloud that has hung over me all these years.' She looked up. 'But this is off the record, you understand? I do not want anyone to know I have spoken to you about this – even my family.'

'Of course.'

'Very well. And I if choose to stop, then you must respect that.'

'Verity, I'm grateful for anything you can tell me about her. You are completely in control of how much you divulge, I promise.'

Verity took a long, deep breath. 'Then I suppose I had better begin at the beginning.'

'And where is that?' Amy asked.

'Right here, in London. Bombs were dropping all over the place, my children were in the country and my husband at sea, and my brother was staying with me whilst on leave.'

'And when was this?'

'March the first, 1941. The night that changed everything.'

4

London, 1 March 1941

From the pain in his shoulder and his hip, Alec guessed the blast had propelled him backwards into the doorway. Idiot, he scolded himself. Why hadn't he left the club earlier? Said no to that second whisky with Bunny Warren?

Gradually the ringing in his ears subsided and was replaced with the sound of collapsing brickwork, the continued aerial battery of the streets beyond and the shouts of firemen fighting to put out the blaze threatening to engulf the buildings across the road. He'd thought he'd already seen hell, thousands of feet up in the air, where German bullets strafed his squadron and pilots from both sides fell burning into the waiting depths of the English Channel. But it seemed hell had many faces, and as his eyes adjusted to the smoke and flames, the dust and beams of torchlight, he knew he had just discovered a new version.

He stood carefully, checking each limb for injury and finding only a few scratches from broken glass, although his RAF uniform was grey with dust, blood and dirt congealing on the scar tissue of his cheek. He kicked aside bricks and hot, gnarled metal to emerge on to what was left of the pavement, where a street sign opposite told him he was on Baker Street.

It had been more than one bomb, he realised. A few hundred feet away a bus had been upended into a fresh crater, and tin-hatted wardens attempted to haul passengers out of the back door, whilst the conductor sat on the ground, his head in his hands and ticket machine still strapped to his chest. As the metal screamed against its precarious mooring, a burst water pipe added to the carnage.

Already an ATS canteen van had arrived to dole out tea, blankets and smiles to the displaced and their rescuers, and through the smoke and raging fires, he saw several ambulances. These requisitioned vans were driven by volunteers as diverse as duchesses and drapers, hairdressers and housewives. One had already stopped, its driver assessing the bodies lined up on the pavement and deciding whether she would be driving to the mortuary or the hospital, whilst others worked their way through the chaos around the bus-filled crater.

Fire engines had managed to get through to the blazing buildings further along, where trailer pumps released jets of water and uniformed figures crawled over debris, pulling survivors from the crushed terrace. He held his arm across his nose and mouth, picking his way through fractured furniture and charred, smouldering beams, offering his help to an air-raid warden. The man told him to check for any sign of life in front of the damaged buildings across the road, but to be quick, the whole bloody lot would be down in a minute. The roof of one had taken a hit, its core imploded, leaving exposed a ladder of fireplaces and a patchwork of singed, shredded wallpaper, a tilted painting stubbornly hanging above a mantelpiece. Next door the shabby façade of the Claremont Hotel clung on, despite deep cracks and the fire raging within its upper floors.

Its metal sign hung forlornly from the final L of its name as a human chain helped its bewildered residents emerge from the cellar and through a gap left by the splintered front door.

An elderly woman in a housecoat and slippers stumbled past Alec, blood running from a wound on her temple as she called out a man's name. 'Help me,' she said. 'My husband's under here.'

Alec called for a blanket for the woman and glanced around, spotting a few feet away the elderly wedding-ringed hand reaching lifelessly from the mangled wreckage. 'Take her away,' he said as an ARP warden joined him. 'She's looking for her husband,' he added quietly, gesturing towards the semi-buried body. 'For God's sake don't let her see.'

Alec began gently pulling bricks and plaster away, wiping the filthy sweat from his brow with his shirtsleeve and looking up to see whether the smoke-filled skies were clear of further attacks. The Germans had gone for now, although they could easily be back later, this first rash of incendiaries and bombs merely the hors d'oeuvre to a long night of sustained raids.

A torch beam glanced across the blackened brickwork of the hotel, and he looked up in time to see something move on one of the upper floors. He asked the warden to flick the light across the burning building once more.

'Bloody hell, there's a woman up there,' someone shouted.

As the wind changed direction, taking the smoke northwards along the street, they suddenly had a clear view of a woman in red gripping a window ledge on the first floor, ready to jump as from behind her smoke billowed through the smashed window.

'Wait!' Alec shouted. But the sound of his voice was lost in the clanging of back-up fire engines screaming up the street.

He looked around, saw one of the refugees from the basement and snatched the blanket from around her shoulders. 'Take two corners of this,' he shouted to the warden. 'We'll catch her.'

They stumbled across the wreckage, kicking aside a broken pram and an upturned, scorched armchair, the warden tripping and landing heavily on his knees in the dusting of broken glass.

'Come on, man.' Alec waited impatiently for the warden to right himself. They could not afford to hang around if they were to reach the woman before the flames licking at the room behind her either engulfed her or forced her to take her chances.

And then it was too late. The woman dropped to the ground in a flash of red, landing on the rubble nearby like a rag doll.

Alec scrabbled closer, rough stone and jagged metal shredding his hands and knees as he reached her side and took her wrist, relieved to feel a faint pulse close to the surface. She could have been sleeping had it not been for the weeping gash along her blonde hairline. She was around his age, he guessed, dressed in a red tailored suit that had taken its fair share of damage during the fall.

Finally the warden waved an ambulance through, and two uniformed women leapt out carrying rolled-up stretchers. 'Over here,' he shouted above the scream of water pumps and groaning architecture. 'She jumped from an upstairs window,' he explained as the ambulance driver pulled aside the woman's jacket to check she was breathing.

'Molyneux. Lucky lady,' her co-driver said in clipped Mayfair vowels, glancing at the label. 'Long time since I've seen anything that classy in London.'

'Make yourself useful and unroll that stretcher,' the driver snapped. 'We're not at a fashion show.' She checked the woman's limbs and, seeing nothing obviously broken, looked at the blood leaking into her dark-blonde hair. 'Head wound. We're going to have to take her in. You support her head, sir, while we roll the stretcher underneath her.' She looked at him and sighed irritably. 'You're going to have to let go of her hand, you know.'

5

A breeze roused her from a deep sleep and as she tried to capture the tendrils of her evaporating dreams, she found only a heavy emptiness. She turned her head away from the bright, milky sunlight pouring through latticed windowpanes, light curtains dancing in the draught.

She tried to raise herself to a seated position in the narrow metal bed, but the stiff sheets and grey woollen blankets were tucked too tightly around her, and as she pushed her shoulders up from the bed, a searing pain in her head halted her. She lifted a hand, finding a dressing bound to her forehead, gradually becoming aware of more pinpoints of pain in her hip and shoulder.

With no recollection of where she was or how she had come to be here, she looked around. A clipboard hung at the end of her bed, and a red suit was folded across the back of a chair. To her right, a thin curtain veiled her from what she now saw was the rest of a hospital ward. Through the sound of banging trolleys, of uncontained pain and stoical banter, she made out the soothing tones of medical staff and frightened cries of fellow patients.

She began to panic: there was somewhere she should be, something she had forgotten, but nowhere in her confused mind could she recall what it was. All she remembered was a corrugated green bedspread, the soft light of a tobacco pipe bobbing along a darkened street. She tried to search further back but found only blanks where she expected memory.

A ferocious thirst overtook her, and she leaned across to the jug of water, pouring herself a glass and drinking deeply, her dirt-grimed hands shaking.

The curtain drew aside and a nurse in a stiff starched cap, a long apron over her blue puff-sleeved dress, smiled at her. 'Come around, then, have we?' The young woman stood at the side of the bed, taking her wrist and looking down at the watch pinned to the chest of her apron.

'*Qu'est-ce qu'il m'est arrivé? Où suis-je?*'

'What's that, love? Spanish? French? You'll have to start again in English.' She dropped her patient's wrist and scribbled something on the chart hanging from the end of the bed. 'Looks like we couldn't get your name last night. You were in a bit of a state. How about telling me now? In English, if you can.'

English? Why was she not in Paris? Why couldn't she remember something as enormous as an overseas journey? Had something happened to her country? There was a war, she remembered now, but her countrymen were fighting for . . . for what? She could not recall.

'So, your name . . . ?' the nurse said, her pen poised over the notes.

Her name . . . A man's insistent, almost angry voice came to her, telling her she must not tell her name to anyone, and yet she could not remember it, her identity hovering just out of reach. Why was her identity secret? What had she done to find herself here? 'I'm sorry,' she said, surprised and relieved to find herself able to speak the same language as the young woman. 'I do not remember.'

'Well, at least you speak the King's English. Any idea where you live? Here in London, is it? Or are you visiting?' Getting nowhere, she tried another tack. 'How about next of kin, that sort of thing?'

'I am French. I'm sorry, but I do not know why I am here.' She was, she realised with some terror, adrift from her identity and her home, and so she shook her head.

'What do you do? For a job, like? Or have you got a husband looking for you?'

'I am . . .' What was she? Everything was such a muddle, but how could she forget such an important piece of information?

'Not to worry, ducks. You've had a nasty bump to the head. The doctor says here on your notes it might affect your memory short term, but no real harm done.' She frowned.

'What is it?'

The nurse shook her head. 'Just a note saying we're not to discharge you without letting some office in Whitehall know first. Someone obviously knows who you are.'

'You can tell me who this is?'

'Sorry, love. It's not written down here.'

Somehow this information unsettled rather than comforted her, and she determined that when she was well enough, she would slip away quietly. 'But I will remember?'

'All in good time,' the nurse said gently, seeing her tears. 'We'll have you out of here pronto – need your bed for the next lot.' She leaned across and plumped the pillows, straightening the sheets. 'Want you looking smart, don't we? There's a gentleman waiting to see you. The second so far today: aren't you the popular one!'

Did she know anyone here? Was he the reason she was so anxious about an appointment she felt she was missing? 'Who was this other man?'

'Left no name. Short, stocky, thick tortoiseshell glasses. Looked a bit dodgy, if you ask me. This one, though . . .' The nurse winked. 'A pilot. Proper looker, he is. Now let's look at you,' she said, smoothing her patient's hair. 'That's better. And you send your friend my way if you don't want him!'

He sat up suddenly at the sound of a voice close by, aware he must have dozed in the uncomfortable wooden chair in the hospital corridor.

'She's awake, sir. A bit groggy, but you can see her now.' The nurse watched as Alec scrambled to his feet. 'You family?'

'A friend, you could say.'

'Don't suppose you can tell us who our mystery guest is? It's just she's having a few problems with her memory.'

'I'm afraid not. I was in Baker Street last night when the bombs hit, but she wasn't conscious. I just came here . . .' He hesitated. Because he hadn't been able to get her out of his mind? Because letting go of her long, slim hand and passing her over to the ambulance drivers had been almost impossible? 'I wanted to make sure she's all right, I suppose. Have the doctors assessed how badly hurt she was?'

'She's had a bit of head trauma, which has affected her memory, and she's got a few scratches and bruises, but she'll be fine. Out in a few days, probably.' She looked him up and down. 'Not had time to go home and change, have we?'

He looked down at himself. His CO would hit the roof if he saw the state of the precious RAF uniform, the once-white shirt bloody and dirty, trousers torn at both knees and tie long since lost. The jacket folded across his lap was covered in dust and had lost one of its silver buttons, but the embroidered wings on its chest and double bands at the wrist gleamed. He'd washed his hands and face in the small visitors' bathroom along the corridor, but still he looked a fright.

The nurse obviously guessed his thoughts. 'Don't worry, love. You look smashing. Last bed on the left. You can't miss her.'

He smoothed his hair, instinctively touching the scar tissue of his ear and cheek, suddenly nervous of seeing the woman who had hovered in his consciousness through the long, gruelling night as he wondered whether he would have the chance to learn her name, and why it felt so important that he did.

She was sleeping, a few tendrils of dark-blonde hair peeping from the bandage wrapped around her head to create a halo on the stiff pillow. He should leave now that he knew she was safe – she would not remember him, may even be alarmed by his presence – but he felt compelled to stay.

Suddenly her deep-set eyes opened slowly, long lashes revealing mossy-green eyes that fixed on him. '*Qui êtes vous?*' she said, a slight rasp in her voice. '*Je ne vous connais pas. Qu'est-ce que vous voulez?*'

'*Vous êtes Française?*' he said quietly, seeing her agitation, and she nodded curtly, wincing as she did so. 'Do you speak English?' Again, she nodded. 'Jolly good: my French is a little rusty. I'm Alec Scott. I helped you into the ambulance last night. You were caught in a raid, you see. I came to find out how you are.'

'A raid?' she said quietly, her soft, mellow voice lightly accented.

'Yes, a German bombing raid.'

'The Germans are bombing London?'

'I'm afraid so. You jumped out of a first-floor window. Scared me half to death.'

'I did? But tell me, why is Germany attacking London?'

'Goodness. You really don't remember, do you? We're at war.'

She paused, frowning as she fought to make connections. 'With Germany? Yes, I think I remember. And France is fighting too, *oui*?'

'Oh dear.' Alec pulled the chair close to the bed and sat beside her. France had been occupied by the Germans since June the previous year – she had clearly lost that much from her memory. Would he make it worse by shocking her with the truth? 'I'm afraid it's rather worse than that.'

'Worse than fighting a war?'

There was no point in shielding her from the truth. 'The thing is, your chap Pétain did a deal with the Germans. I'm sorry to say that most of France is under German control.'

Her hand flew to her mouth. 'How could I not remember such a terrible thing?'

He patted her hand gently. 'Chin up. The doctors have said it'll all come back to you soon. Some of the younger chaps in my squadron . . . well, they keep a stiff upper lip, but the war can play nasty games with you.'

'You are a pilot?' she said.

He nodded and brushed the dust from his peaked cap to show her the embroidered crown and wings badge. 'Flown a few sorties over your homeland in the last year. We'll beat them, you know, and your country will be free again.'

'And in the meantime you have rescued a lost Frenchwoman.' She took the cap from him and turned it around in her hands. 'Thank you . . .' she looked at his name on the label inside . . . 'Flight-Lieutenant Scott.'

'Alec, please. Call me Alec.'

She handed the cap back. 'Thank you . . . Alec.'

He saw her glance at the rippled burns scar stretching halfway across his cheek. 'War wound,' he explained, trying to turn his face away, but she surprised him, taking his chin in her hand and forcing him to look at her, before running her fingertips across the damaged flesh.

'You are a brave man, I think,' she said.

'War gives us no choice but to be brave.'

'I hope I am brave. That I have done things to be proud of.'

'I'm sure you have.' She looked so sad, her huge green eyes filling with tears, and he longed to help her. 'How about we find out who you are,' he said brightly, 'and then we can be properly introduced?'

For the first time, she smiled. 'Yes, I would like that.'

He turned around in the seat. 'Here, why don't you take a look in the pockets of your clothes? There might be something that will give us a clue. Your papers, maybe?' He took the red jacket, still bearing the patina of the bomb site, and passed it across to her. 'Looks like you caught a train to London from Hastings two days ago,' he said, examining a clipped train ticket she pulled from a pocket. 'It's on the south coast,' he explained when she looked confused. 'Although Lord knows how you'd have got there from France – the border is completely closed.'

'Nothing else here,' she said. 'No papers, no address, no name.'

'What about inside the jacket? Is there another pocket there?'

She reached inside the jacket and took a slim book from a pocket in the lining.

He smiled. 'Well, at least we know you can read! May I see? *La Vagabonde*,' he said, turning it over. 'Can't say I've read anything by Colette. Is she good?'

'You are asking the woman who cannot remember where she woke up yesterday?'

He was relieved to see her break into a smile again, her cheeks flushing slightly as the eye contact between them tipped suddenly from friendly to intimate. 'I should leave you in peace,' he said, longing to stay beside her. 'You don't want an old bore like me keeping you from resting.'

'Please, no. You are at present the only friend I have.'

He tried to imagine how she must feel: in a strange city, with no idea even of who she was. 'I'll come back later, if you like. Not much else to do, apart from ghastly, dull meetings while the squadron is being rested.'

'I would like that,' she said, and again there was a crackle of something intangible as their eyes met. 'And perhaps you can help me decide what I will do when I leave here.'

'I'd be delighted to.' He looked at her. 'You do have somewhere to go to?'

'I have no idea.'

'Well, perhaps we can find you a hotel?'

'When I have found my handbag and the means to pay for one, then I agree, that is an excellent idea.'

'Ah. Not so simple, is it?'

'*Je suis désolée.* I am sorry. This is my problem, not yours.'

He could see she was tiring. 'I'll let you rest, old thing, before Nurse kicks me out.' He stood, torn between shaking her hand and kissing her cheek. 'It was lovely to meet you while you're conscious,' he said.

'And you also. There is one more thing,' she said suddenly, then frowned.

'You remember something?'

'I keep hearing music.'

'A favourite song, perhaps? Something French?'

She shook her head. 'I am not sure.'

'It's something to go on, at least,' he said, trying to sound encouraging.

'I do not know why you would want to help a stranger, but thank you,' she said, reaching for his hand, her wide, green eyes searching his face.

He remembered holding the hand that he now wrapped within both of his, talking to her even though she hadn't been able to hear him. And how through the long hours digging and grubbing through the wreckage of Baker Street all he had been able to think about was her face, and how seeing it had changed something unalterably.

I would do anything for you, he wanted to tell her, running his thumb across her palm. I would walk on hot coals, march through deserts, cross oceans, just to hold this hand one more time. The realisation suddenly terrified him, and he pulled gently away from her.

'Alec, you promise you will return?' she said, sensing his hesitation.

For God's sake, man, what's the matter with you? he chided himself. You don't even know the woman, and this is hardly the time to be losing your heart. 'Of course I will.'

And when she smiled, it was like the first birdsong of spring, a cloud passing across the full moon, and he was lost.

6

Verity Cooper pushed through the steam-drenched glass door, the bell inaudible above the chatter of diners escaping the office for an hour. The restaurant was packed, so she hung her coat on a stand and waited politely whilst a young couple argued over their bill and eventually squeezed out from their table, allowing Verity to take their place.

She was already overheated in her tweed suit – perfect for a draughty Whitehall office but far too much for a packed Lyons Corner House at the height of the lunchtime rush. She took off her hat and pulled her compact from her handbag, dabbing powder on her now-shiny nose and flushed cheeks. She caught a glimpse of herself in the mirrored wall opposite, wondering what had possessed her to waste coupons on the flesh-coloured, snug sweater that merely emphasised her excess weight. Bill would have said she looked smashing, but then Bill would have said she looked smashing in a coal sack. She'd married a good egg, and heaven knew eggs were in short supply all round.

She looked around for a waitress, keen to order quickly. She didn't really have time for a break, but Alec had been insistent on buying her lunch, and she'd worried about him after he'd eventually turned up bruised and filthy from a night helping in the aftermath of the Baker Street bomb a few days ago. He was a grown man and she shouldn't fret, but that was the thing about being twins: one couldn't help it. And with Bill at sea and the children evacuated, she had the rare luxury of time with which to fret.

'Set lunch one and six – three courses and coffee,' a waitress said, coming across to clear the table. 'Just you, is it, madam?' she said as she piled up the previous diners' plates. She raised an eyebrow at Verity, straightening her starched, black-ribboned lace cap and fidgeting in the loose-fitting black uniform.

She couldn't have been more than sixteen, Verity thought: you knew you were getting old when the Nippies looked young. Although with this attitude, she may not be one for much longer, war or no war. 'No, I'm expecting my brother.'

'We're very busy. Would you like to order now for him?'

Verity picked up the folded menu on the table. 'Cheese on toast for me, and he'll have the hot pot. And a pot of tea for two, please.' A lesson in manners wouldn't go amiss either, she thought as the girl headed across the restaurant, stopping at a table of Canadian servicemen and flashing the smile that had been altogether missing from her encounter with Verity.

A slight hush spread through the establishment as the door opened and Alec stood looking for her. He'd always been a handsome chap, which often led to him being prey to the wrong sort, and in his uniform he was positively dashing. Ever since the Battle of Britain Alec and the rest of the RAF had been treated like demigods, and his scar from that final encounter with a Messerschmitt only added to his glamour. He hated attention, of course: he was shy beneath the handsome façade, so much so that she despaired of him ever plucking up the courage to find himself a nice wife.

'Well done for getting a spot, V,' he said as he joined her.

'I can't be too long, I'm afraid. They only let us out into the daylight for a short while.' She looked at him: was he a little paler than usual, his eyes a little brighter? She hoped he was taking care of himself but knew better than to nag him.

He laughed, placing his cap on the table. 'I refuse to believe anyone can tell Verity Cooper what to do. Not even Mr Cooper.'

'Especially Mr Cooper,' she said, smiling.

'Any word from Bill?' Alec asked.

She shook her head. 'I don't even know where he is. He could be anywhere from Norway to Spain, with those wretched German submarines stalking him. I tell you, I can't bear it, Alec.'

He took her hand. 'Bill runs a tight ship, and wherever he is, the safety of his men will be foremost. He won't take any risks. He wants to get back for you and the children, after all.'

She took a lace-trimmed handkerchief from her bag. 'Oh, I'm just being silly. Ignore me.'

'You're not being silly. Your husband's at sea and your children are in deepest Wales—'

'Shropshire. They're in Shropshire. With Bill's sister.'

'There you are, you see? Already an improvement.'

She smiled. 'I know you're trying to cheer me up, but you really don't have to.' She suspected it was Alec who needed cheering up: the past couple of years had been frightful, what with that awful business with Evelyn, and then dear Paddy, not that he ever spoke of it: so generous to everyone else, her brother was a closed book when it came to his own feelings.

Alec's recurrent childhood illness had in fact forced them both to stiffen their upper lips to match their parents'. Even after visiting her sick twin brother in hospital for what she had been told was the last time, her father had attempted to thrash the weakness from her: if their mother had managed not to cry, he'd said, then Verity could damned well pull herself together too. His training had clearly worked, as years later no one had cried at his funeral, including their mother, who had worn scarlet on her slightly smiling lips as she cast the first handful of soil into the old bastard's grave.

Verity quickly tucked her hankie into the sleeve of her sweater as the waitress returned, bearing their lunch on a tray and a broad smile for Alec.

'Let me know if you'd like a sweet after, sir,' she said, dropping Verity's plate on the table and carefully placing Alec's in front of him.

'The knife's facing the wrong way,' Verity muttered under her breath as she poked at the flabby toast covered in sweating cheese. 'So this is a pleasant surprise,' she said. 'What's it in honour of?'

'I just thought that we hardly see one another. You're at work all day, and when you're not off helping at the air-raid shelter I'm in late meetings or catching up with the chaps at the club.'

Verity had thought their revolving-door coexistence rather suited them both, but still it was sweet of him to think to take her out for lunch. 'Well, I shan't complain. It makes a change from eating a sandwich at my desk.'

'I still don't know why you didn't follow the children out to the sticks.'

'To be honest, I'm rather enjoying working again. That sounds dreadful, I know, and of course I miss the children, but

I feel useful for once. And it appears I'm rather good at my job. They're talking about moving me to a new department. All terribly cloak and dagger.'

'Well, that's marvellous. If Verity Cooper can't send Hitler packing, then there's no hope for us.'

'I suppose not,' she laughed and began pouring tea from the heavy china teapot. 'By the way, I wonder what happened to the woman you rescued the other night,' she said, dropping a sugar cube in each of their cups.

'She's in pretty good shape, considering.'

Verity paused, tongs in mid-air. 'You've visited her?'

He shuffled uncomfortably and Verity's heart sank as she recognised the signs. Of course she couldn't protect him, but after Evelyn had dumped him at the altar, she had rather hoped she would be able to find some nice, wholesome girl for him, someone she had vetted and would trust not to break her brother's heart. Someone who might do a little of the worrying for her. And now he seemed to have formed an attachment to a total stranger.

'A few times. She's rather lovely. French, you know?'

Verity raised an eyebrow. 'And what is a Frenchwoman doing in London in the middle of a war?'

'That's just it, you see. She doesn't know.'

Verity snorted. 'How can anyone not know why they're somewhere?'

'She's lost her memory since the bang on the head. The doctors say it will come back—'

'You've talked to her doctors?'

'Well, yes. She doesn't know a soul here, and she's terribly grateful for any help she can get.'

'And what is the name of this lovely Frenchwoman?'

'We have no idea!'

She leaned forward. 'Alec, this is no joke,' she whispered, aware of how close their neighbours were. 'She could be absolutely anyone. You know nothing about her.'

'I know she's alone in a strange country, she lost all her belongings in the raid, and that she has no one to help her.'

'She's not your responsibility.'

But he wasn't listening. 'She has no money, no papers, nowhere to stay . . .'

And as he trailed off, she understood. 'And you think she should stay with us. With me.' She sat back and folded her arms.

'I just think it's the decent thing to do. Until she can get to the Embassy or something. She could be a refugee.'

'She could be a spy. Or a fifth columnist. A Vichy agent. Have you thought about that? She could be plotting to blow up Bill's ship, for all we know.'

'Don't be so ridiculous.'

Verity felt herself flush. There was nothing ridiculous about being careful, especially when one's husband was floating on the cold, grey sea like a sitting duck. 'Then don't be so mean.'

'I'm sorry, but you're letting your imagination run away with you. She's just a girl in a bit of a tight spot, and we're in a position to help her.'

'But you could be redeployed at any time and I'd be left living with a stranger. I'm already looking after your wretched dog.' The chaps had enough to do, Alec had insisted when she questioned why Scout couldn't stay at the base, at which Verity had pointed out she also had plenty to do, thank you very much.

'Oh, you love Scout, I know you do. I've seen you pet him when you think I'm not looking.'

'What nonsense.'

'Besides, you won't be left with her. I have a few weeks' leave before I do my Mosquito training, and it would only be for a day or two. A week at most.'

Verity narrowed her eyes and stared at him. 'You've already invited her, haven't you?'

The silence between them was broken by the waitress arriving to take their dessert orders.

'Not for me, thank you,' Verity said, standing and shrugging her jacket back on. 'But do bring my brother a fool, if you have one.' She pinned her hat on and glared at him. 'And the bill.'

7

Verity finished tidying the breakfast things away, surprised at the sudden sound of footsteps in her daughter's bedroom upstairs. Even after all these months, it was easy to forget the children were away. And now the Frenchwoman was sleeping in Penny's bed, amongst Penny's things. She should have told Alec to park her at the French Embassy and let her get on with it, but with the Embassy attached firmly to the new Vichy government, how could he? And so ever since the woman had arrived with Alec in a taxi the previous evening, having apparently discharged herself from the hospital without a word to the staff there, Verity had tried to make her feel welcome. If she had come across as a little formal, well, that was just how she'd been brought up. No one liked a fuss, after all.

She looked at the kitchen clock as she took off her pinny and hung it on the back of the door. Alec had already left for a meeting at the Air Ministry and she herself needed to get a move on, having been called in early for an initial chat about the mysterious new posting.

The houseguest would have to entertain herself for the day, even if Verity felt uncomfortable about leaving her alone. If she were a spy, the woman was surely too exhausted to be of much use to Moseley and his acolytes. Verity had better say goodbye, all the same, and so she climbed the stairs and tapped on Penny's bedroom door before opening it.

She was standing at the lattice-taped window, staring out on to the street and clutching a rag doll. Verity tried to push back her irritation: it was just a silly doll, and not even one of Penny's favourites. 'I made that for Penny myself,' she said.

'I am sorry,' she said, replacing the doll on top of the bookcase. 'I hoped it might help me remember something of my own childhood.'

'You speak very good English.'

'Thank you. Although I do not know how I learned it.'

'I speak French,' Verity said. 'French nanny, then finishing school in Switzerland,' she explained. So well, in fact, that her language skills had helped smooth the path towards the imminent promotion. 'I know how tiring it can be talking in your second language, even without a bump on the head,' she said, gesturing to the small dressing on her houseguest's forehead. '*Alors, en Français?*'

The woman smiled, her relief at hearing her own language apparent. 'Thank you,' she went on in French. 'It may help my memory.'

'You still remember nothing?'

The woman shook her head. 'I know I am probably from Paris, but not much more.'

'Not even your name? Well, I suppose I shall have to call you Mademoiselle for now, or we shall get in a muddle.'

'I hope you do not mind me being here?' she said. 'I know it is an imposition.'

'Not at all.' Why should I mind giving my house over to a stranger from occupied Europe? Verity thought. A woman wearing the kind of Parisian clothes only Germans can still afford – that scarf alone had probably cost a week's food rations.

'And I hardly look like the perfect houseguest,' the woman said ruefully, following her hostess's eyes to the damaged red suit, the ivory silk pussybow blouse that looked like soiled bandages – all she'd been able to put on that morning after changing out of Verity's loaned winceyette nightie.

Verity's mouth twisted. 'Wait there a moment,' she said, leaving the woman hovering awkwardly in the middle of the room. 'They're probably not quite what you're used to,' she said a moment later, returning with an armful of folded clothes, 'and they might be a bit loose . . .' She saw the woman's horror at the dowdy, shapeless clothes, and her polite attempt to disguise it. 'I put in a couple of slips and some underwear, and there's a spare overcoat downstairs. London can be bitter at this time of year.'

'They're perfect, thank you,' she said, placing the scratchy sweaters and tweed on the satin eiderdown covering the bed.

'At least you'll be able to change for supper tonight. We can't have you walking around the place like some kind of refugee, can we?' Her face fell suddenly, and a flush suffused her cheeks. 'I'm sorry. That was thoughtless.'

'Not at all. And I will be out of your way as soon as the Embassy can help me.'

'You might try the Consulate too. It's less likely to . . .' To hand you over to the Nazis? 'Anyway, I have to go to work,' she added quickly. 'Alec will be home this afternoon, but try not to disturb him. He needs to rest. His health, you see . . .'

'I understand.'

Verity closed the door behind her and breathed deeply. The woman was too perfect, too beautiful, too charming, and Alec was already too smitten. She could not see his heart broken again. If the woman's identity did not become apparent soon, she would investigate it herself.

As the days went by, Alec was amused to observe the subtle game of cat and mouse as Verity attempted to keep the new houseguest at a safe distance from her brother. On the nights when the sirens were silent, Verity either encouraged Alec to spend time at his club or stayed up with them in the little sitting room whilst they all listened to the wireless news. It had been with obvious reluctance that she had sent them to the shelter together at the start of a particularly heavy night of bombing, whilst she left for WVS canteen duty. Deep underground, he and the Frenchwoman had held tightly to one another until the danger passed. A spark had been ignited and he had fallen for her – hard.

Alec had offered to take her to Baker Street that morning, hoping to jog her memory of the night of the bombing and her movements leading up to it, and as they approached the remains of the Claremont Hotel, her grip tightened on his arm.

'I cannot believe I survived this,' she said as they stood at the periphery of the bomb site.

The hotel and the two buildings on either side were no more now than a mountain of smashed brick, iron and timber. Smoke leaked from rubble, and for two hundred yards on either side, windows had been shattered, a carpet of lethal shards covering everything. Alec had worried that coming here would be traumatic for her, but seeing her face now, it was clear she remembered nothing of that night.

It was hard to hear themselves speak over the sound of screaming steel, as revving trucks attempted to pull the submerged bus from the vast crater blown into the road. The newly homeless picked over the ruins, cramming into prams and carts whatever they could find of their possessions amongst the tattered clothes and smashed furniture.

'Shall we see what we can find?' Alec asked gently. 'You must have had a handbag? Or a suitcase?' he said hopefully, whilst suspecting the impossibility of finding anything in the carnage in front of them.

A frown flickered across her forehead as she seemed to remember something, then shook her head. 'Every time I think I recall something, it fades so quickly.'

He took her hand. 'You mustn't give up, you know.'

'Thank you. But I do not think the answer is here.'

He knew she was right – what hadn't been destroyed in the blast would have been taken by scavengers by now – but he waved across to an ARP warden who ambled over, wiping sweat from his brow with a crumpled handkerchief.

'What is it, sir? We're pretty busy here.'

'Sorry to bother you, but do you know whether there is somewhere we can look for my friend's property she lost in the hotel?'

The man laughed. 'You'll be lucky, mate. If it's furniture or what not, you can try the depot out at Fulham. But everything else from the hotel was taken away by Special Branch. Strict instructions no one should touch it.'

'Is that usual?' Alec said.

The man shrugged. 'No such thing as usual, these days.'

'I'm sorry,' Alec said, as they turned into Wigmore Street. He looked at his watch. It was twelve thirty, and he didn't feel ready to break off their time together. 'Listen,' he said, 'you're probably exhausted, so do tell me to push off . . .' He stopped on the pavement, so that the man who had been walking behind them almost collided with them, glancing back briefly through thick tortoiseshell glasses before moving on. 'But do you have plans right now?'

She pushed a loose strand of hair beneath the scarf tied around her head. 'I may visit the French Embassy, but I imagine they take a long lunch hour.'

'Be careful,' he said. 'Marshal Pétain's government isn't necessarily the friend of the French it makes out to be. Perhaps I should come with you? Or you could approach De Gaulle's Free French office here?'

She shook her head. 'Thank you, but I am in London. There is nothing to be afraid of. What were you about to suggest?'

'How would you like to go to a lunchtime concert? It might help, since you mentioned the music you keep hearing.'

She was silent for a moment. 'What sort of concert?'

'A classical concert. You know, Beethoven, Brahms, that sort of thing. They hold them every day at the National Gallery. Myra Hess is playing today – she set them up.' She seemed uncertain, her focus elsewhere, and as his eyes glanced over the scratches on her exposed wrists, the bruising on her forehead, he worried he was asking too much of her. 'Of course, if it's too much . . .'

'Not at all. You are very thoughtful.'

'Then perhaps you don't want to go out wearing that dreadful thing?' he teased, looking down at the shapeless brown woollen shift beneath her red jacket.

She laughed. 'Verity lent it to me.'

'I'm surprised Bill lets her wear it,' Alec said. 'They really have been married too long. Although I'm glad to hear you're getting along. I know she can be a bit prickly at first, but she's a good sort.' Alec smiled at her. 'So: spot of lunchtime music?'

After a brief hesitation she threaded her hand beneath his elbow. 'Thank you. I would like that.'

As they walked, the warmth of her arm lent him a fresh lightness, and he had to force himself not to look at her, concentrating instead on the sound of her breath close to his, the scent of her hair and the sound of their matching, rhythmic footsteps.

Trafalgar Square was strangely quiet without its usual traffic, Londoners picking their way around the bomb-damaged pavements. Newspaper vendors called out the headlines from the early edition of the *Evening Standard*, which showed the King and Queen smiling in the aftermath of the Palace receiving a direct hit. More bombs on Berlin, by the looks of it, Alec thought, handing over a penny and folding the paper into his inside pocket.

The old girl had certainly taken a battering, he realised, as they joined the queue outside the National Gallery. At least half a dozen bombs had struck various parts of the building, and an unexploded one had gone off a few days ago during one of the concerts they were now waiting to see. The musicians had apparently not missed a beat as they played through a Mozart string quartet.

'I'm afraid it's rather bare,' he said, returning from the ticket office and seeing her looking around at the vast, empty space, the gaping holes where the glass roof had shattered, the marble floors still damp with last night's rain. 'Most of the works were taken out of London to storage when the Blitz began.'

'It is the same at the Louvre. They hid the paintings around the country.' She looked at him, eyes wide. 'I remember.'

'That's marvellous. You see, it will all start to come back.'

She shook her head quickly. 'I must be the most impossible company.' She looked around once more. 'Perhaps I will come back one day, when your artworks have returned,' she said.

'I very much hope you will.' He looked at her, trying to discover whether it would be him or the paintings that drew her back here.

'And perhaps you will come to France, if I ever return there.'

They paused and he took her hands, seeing his answer in her eyes. 'Once this war is over, I promise I shall.'

An usher waved them down a set of marble stairs to the crowded lower gallery, its seats all taken and people squeezed on to the stage behind the sleek black grand piano.

A hand suddenly grabbed at the Frenchwoman, and Alec watched her expression turn to terror as a young, dark-haired man held on to her arm. '*Sophie, c'est moi*,' he said, first in French, then accented English. 'It is me, Levi. You remember? We were in Vienna together. I managed to get out in '36.'

'I don't know . . .' she replied, trying to pull her sleeve from his grasp.

Alec stepped forward. 'She's had an accident recently. If you have a telephone number, perhaps she can contact you when she feels a little better?' he said, seeing the agitation on the Frenchwoman's face.

'Alec, please . . .' she said.

The man looked confused. 'We were friends. Sophie, I'm so happy you got out of France. And Hanne . . . how is she? And Max? Did they make it out too?'

'Please let me go.'

'I'm sorry,' Alec said. 'Perhaps another time . . .' He put his arm around her shoulder and led her away, finding them a space to sit on the floor in front of the stage, as she glanced back at the man still staring at her.

Dame Myra eventually took to the stage to warm applause, her matronly appearance and the Edwardian roll of her hair belying the lyricism that flowed from her fingers as she worked her way through a programme of Bach, Beethoven and Chopin. It was music to soothe the souls of those who had paid a shilling to be transported elsewhere for the duration of their lunch hour, many listening with closed eyes, some with tears dripping down winter-worn, sleep-deprived faces, oblivious to the icy draughts ripping through the ravaged building. And yet each note, each cadence, was witnessed by the unblinking Frenchwoman.

What was passing through her mind? What had the encounter with the young man unlocked in her? As she pressed against him, he felt her body absorb every note, respond to each change of direction, becoming tenser until suddenly she tore herself away from his side, fighting her way out through the scrum of office suits and twinsets.

*

She ran up the marble steps and stood gasping beneath the glassless skeleton of the ceiling light. Leaning against a tall marble column, she took in noisy lungfuls of smoggy air, trying to silence the music that still rang in her ears.

She closed her eyes, images flashing before her of a piano keyboard, her own hands playing it strongly, confidently; a shot of the indigo-blue silk sheathing her legs, lights along the ground to her right, so dazzling she could not see the audience beyond. She heard her name called: 'Sophie . . .' It was the name the man called Levi had used just now, and she knew that it fitted. Voices congratulating her, but something was wrong, the sickly scent of jasmine thrust into her arms making her gag; a man in grey uniform nearby, the light flashing across the eagle emblem on his chest, his red armband a wound on his sleeve. She couldn't breathe – she had to escape – and she forced her eyes open.

Everything was exactly as it had been moments before, other than the sleet now falling from the smog-yellow sky. Was the scene in her mind merely a construct of her imagination, triggered by the concert, by the sound of her name and the news reports of Paris she'd devoured? She held her hands up, turning them over as she stretched and flexed the long, supple fingers, wondering whether they held the secret of who Sophie truly was.

8

The first blush of spring bloomed across Saint James's Park, welcomed by Londoners desperate for an end to the long, cold winter and a shortening of the nights in which their city was battered and burned.

'Do you suppose there will be anything of London left at the end of all this?' Fred asked, idly tearing a crust from her sandwich and throwing it to the swans.

'You shouldn't waste that,' Verity scolded her friend. The Right Honourable Frederica St-John Davies, heiress to half of Monmouthshire, and Verity Cooper, naval wife, mother and secretary, had become unlikely but good friends and desk neighbours.

'Oh, don't be dreary, V. I want to enjoy my lunch hour, not have you banging on about rationing. It's all war, war, war these days.'

Verity looked at her friend. For all her bluster, she knew Fred was putting on a front and was as frightened as everyone else. There was something of the 'last days of decadence' about the way her friend spent every spare moment dancing or drinking when she wasn't scraping bodies out of bomb wreckage during her shifts as a volunteer ambulance driver. They all dealt with it in different ways, Verity supposed.

'So how's the mysterious houseguest?' Fred asked, lighting a cigarette.

'She's all right, I suppose. Except that Alec can't take his eyes off her. Do you know, he even came home with a dress from Harrods for her the other evening?'

'H. A. Rod's? Lucky girl. What did you get? That new scarf?'

Verity lifted her hand to her throat. 'This? No, she gave it to me.' Initially reluctant, she had been secretly delighted to accept the beautiful red and gold silk scarf she had only politely admired.

'Hermès,' Fred said, assessing the delicate astrological drawings printed across it. 'She's got class. I like the way you've tied it, with that natty little knot at the side. Looks rather French, I'd say.'

Verity felt herself redden. 'Anyway, she doesn't need dresses. I lent her all the clothes she could possibly need.' She looked at Fred. 'Oh, you're wondering what a Parisian would think of my frumpy old cast-offs?'

'Not at all. And although I rather wish she'd push off and leave your brother to me, she's at least a good influence on your wardrobe.'

'I don't want to sound unkind, but I wish she would too, Fred. I'm not sure it's good for Alec. He's like a besotted puppy around her. And after that ghastly business with the Woodward girl standing him up at the altar . . .'

'Yes, I heard about that. No wonder you're so protective.'

Verity sighed. 'He was such a sickly child, and I know I fuss over him, but Father was a Victorian bully, and Mother was too busy securing votes for women to bother with us. It was a tricky childhood.'

'Is there any other kind?'

'Probably not. I should just let him get on with things, but I'm really not sure about this woman. I haven't caught her radioing Berlin from her bedroom, but something's off.' She shook out her greaseproof sandwich paper and folded it, tucking it into her handbag. 'Alec took her to one of those Myra Hess concerts a couple of days ago, and apparently the girl ran out in the middle.'

'Can't say I blame her. Classical music is so dreary. I'd much rather a good swing band.' Fred dropped her cigarette, grinding it with the toe of her shoe. 'So how are you going to find out who she is? I assume you've contacted the police?'

Verity shook her head. 'Alec doesn't want to push her.'

'Maybe I could do a little digging for you? I've got a few contacts here and there.'

'So we can dispatch her and leave a vacancy for the Right Honourable Fred?' Verity stood, brushing crumbs from the wide lapels of her fitted winter coat. 'Now come along. You may be able to charm your way out of trouble for being late, but I have an interview in an hour.'

'The promotion?'

'Sort of.' Verity hesitated. Even though the job was unconfirmed until she passed her final vetting, she had already signed the Official Secrets Act and was unable to discuss the role. Not even with Bill, with whom there was a difficult conversation to be had when he realised the children would be staying in Shropshire as Verity took up her new position in Bedfordshire in the coming months.

So many secrets, she thought, as they walked back past lawns largely given over to allotments to feed the city. Would life ever return to normal? And if it did, could she be the housewife Bill had left behind?

Alec placed his hand on her back as the waiter showed them to their table, and she felt herself shiver at the light touch. He had brought her to the Hungaria, whose basement restaurant also acted as a bomb shelter, staff providing camp beds and hearty breakfasts in the event of an air raid – 'Bomb-proof, splinter-proof, blast-proof, gas-proof and boredom-proof!' she read on the menu she was handed.

The dining room was packed with Services uniforms, dinner jackets and party dresses that longed to forget the war for a few hours. She herself wore the floor-length evening dress Alec had bought for her, and although she was uncomfortable at the extravagant gift, she admired his taste. The bias-cut midnight-blue silk was pulled into gathers at the piped shoulder pads, and a bib of fine blue lace formed a modest décolletage from the high neck to the shaped bustline.

'It looks beautiful on you,' he said as the waiter left with their order. 'I hope I wasn't taking liberties in buying it.'

He was nervous, she realised, a hint of his occasional stammer punctuating his words. 'Not at all. A Parisienne without her wardrobe is easy to buy clothes for.'

Did he blush? She wasn't sure, but he quickly went on to explain that the sales assistant had searched Ladieswear for someone of a similar size, and he had been offered almost as good as a private fashion show.

She laughed. 'I expect you made their day: a handsome officer of the RAF!' And then it was her turn to blush as he looked down at the table, tapping his pipe and smiling. 'You have provided music too,' she said, watching the five members of a band, dressed immaculately in white tie and tails, make their way to a small stage.

'Fiddling while London burns, and all that. I say, are you all right?'

She watched one of the men flick the tails of his evening coat as he sat at the piano, and as she listened to the repeated A to which the other musicians tuned their instruments, for a brief moment she was transported elsewhere, catching the smile of a cellist seated across from her, drawing his bow across the instrument as he checked each string, and a dark-haired woman with deep-set eyes, adjusting the tuning pegs on her violin. She felt the expectant pause as the three watched one another, sound waiting to burst from their instruments.

'Sophie?'

She snapped back, almost surprised to see Alec before her. 'I'm sorry,' she said. 'For a moment . . .'

'Did you remember something?' he said.

'I don't know. Seeing the piano over there . . .'

'It was the piano that set you off the other day. Maybe if you sat at a piano, it would bring back more?'

'It might.' She looked at him. 'What if it brings back something I do not want to remember? What if something terrible brought me to London, and my mind has blocked it out?'

He took her hand. 'It's perfectly normal to block out things that distress us. I've done it myself.'

Again she saw pain in his eyes, a secret pain. British men were so intent on concealing their innermost feelings, but for the first time, there was a crack, and she sensed he might be willing to let her through. 'Alec, you can talk to me about anything . . .'

And then, just as quickly, it closed over and he smiled brightly at her. 'So, how did it go at the Embassy?'

That morning she had borrowed a map and found her way to Knightsbridge, taking in en route the large house in Carlton Gardens where the exiled General de Gaulle was busy rallying support for his Free French Forces, before arriving at the tall, white-stucco building opposite Hyde Park. It was a relief to speak her own tongue as she tried to explain her position to the receptionist at the Embassy and was invited to wait on a velvet-covered sofa in the lobby. She idly flicked through a journal whose publication had moved from Paris to Lyon, now in the Vichy-controlled sector of France, and whose editorial line was clearly on the side of German appeasement. She had put the magazine away, increasingly uncomfortable in the building that should have been a sanctuary but was feeling less like home by the minute.

She had watched the whispered discussion behind the desk and noted officials glancing across to her as the receptionist began talking quickly into a telephone. Something was wrong: she had made a mistake in coming here. She stood, straightening her skirt, and hurried across the hallway as the woman called her back. '*Madame, nous voulons vous aider, restez-vous* . . .'

It was with relief that she found herself back in the cold, sunny street. She was not convinced the woman did want to help her, and the experience had heightened the sense that she was being watched in London. She had become alert to every figure ostensibly reading a newspaper on a park bench, every glance from beneath a passing trilby, and only that morning had been certain a man was following her as she walked Scout across Primrose Hill.

'It went well,' she said now to Alec. 'They will see if anyone who fits my description has gone missing.'

The glasses on the table suddenly rattled, chandeliers tinkling overhead as muffled, low booms were heard outside.

He took her hand. 'We'll be fine down here,' he said. 'Safest place in London.' He frowned. 'I do hope Verity will be all right on her shift tonight.'

'She is working at the shelter?'

He nodded. 'Worries me sick, although I'm sure I'd know if something happened to her.'

'You are very close, I think?'

'We're twins. Always had a sort of sixth sense about one another. When I was terribly ill in hospital as a child, Verity developed the same symptoms, even though the doctors found nothing wrong with her at all.' He chuckled. 'Wanted a little piece of the attention, I expect. She didn't get a lot – even less than I did.' He looked around at the softly lit restaurant. 'At least she can't worry about us down here. I booked camp beds in case we get stranded. It's all very civilised – some guests even bring their nightwear,' he added, then turned around as the band began another number. 'One of my favourites,' he said, then hesitated. 'You wouldn't . . .' He screwed up his eyes slightly, as she sensed the words backing up inside him.

She placed her hand across the table, covering his. 'What is it, Alec?'

'You wouldn't . . . dance with me, would you?' He shook his head. 'It's just when a chap knows he's going to be flying again in a few weeks, he can't be blamed for asking a beautiful woman to dance.'

She smiled. 'I would love to dance with you.'

He took her hand and led her to the small dancefloor in front of the tuxedoed band, where couples swayed gently, eyes closed to the plucked double bass and singing clarinets, the pianist improvising as the red-gowned singer gently crooned the opening words. 'I'll be seeing you in all the old familiar places . . .'

She felt the rough twill of Alec's uniform on her cheek, the heat of his hand gently pressed on her back as they circled around the other couples, hands clasped and feet moving in perfect synchronicity. The fit of him against her took her breath away, the sheer miracle of his having survived the war so far, in order to be with her in this moment.

Another bang, closer by this time, but the band carried on and Alec held her tighter, their cheeks pressed together now, breathing as one, until another strike made a few of the women cry out. 'I'll find you in the morning sun and when the night is near,' the singer continued, as the band played on. 'I'll be looking at the moon, but I'll be seeing you.'

He stopped, pulling back and looking at her, their faces only inches apart. 'Sophie . . .' he said.

She frowned. 'What is it?'

'These days everything could be over in minutes, and I couldn't bear not to tell you.'

'Tell me what?'

'To tell you how I feel, of course. About you.'

She was aware that others were still moving around them as the song flowed into its final chorus.

'You'll think me ridiculous. We've barely met, and I don't even know your full name.' He hesitated. 'But I know I love you.' He looked down, bit his lip. 'You might have a husband, a family, even, but please don't blame a silly fool for taking a chance. This war – it makes one say things one might not dare in peacetime.'

She took his chin, lifting his face until their eyes met again and brushing her fingertips across his scarred, angry flesh. She had no idea whether she already belonged to another, whether someone was out there waiting for her, but in this moment, she knew how she felt, and he was right: wartime did not give one the luxury of waiting. Any of the bombs now falling over the city could ensure this was the last moment she ever spent with anyone. She kissed him gently on the lips. 'I love you too, Alec.'

Relief crinkled his eyes as he held her tight. 'Come away with me, my darling. I have a cottage in the country – it's cosy, but it has two bedrooms,' he added hurriedly. 'I could be called back any time now, and I don't want to lose a moment with you.' He frowned. 'What do you say?'

She smiled. 'I say I would pack my suitcase right away, but I have no idea where it is or what it looks like.'

It had been a ferocious night, one of the worst yet, wave after wave of strikes with barely a break between. No one had slept much on the little wooden camp beds, and all through the night Alec heard staff and guests alike comforting one another as solicitous staff brought extra blankets and cocoa and the pianist quietly played a string of melodies conducive to sleep. He looked at his watch: five a.m. and the bombers were surely almost back at their bases on the Continent by now.

Despite being used to napping in makeshift dormitories or an armchair in the mess as he awaited instructions to scramble at a moment's notice, Alec had only slept lightly. He laid his head back on his hands and looked up at the ceiling, wondering at the strangeness of having spent the night with Sophie, yet apart, everything between them suddenly changed. Was it the madness of war that had made her return his feelings? The understanding and warmth in her eyes was like nothing he had experienced before. If he'd recognised its lack in Evelyn, then he would never have allowed himself to be fooled into nearly marrying her.

As he lay there, three notes floated almost silently across the room, hanging there for a moment before more answered them. The pianist was gently luring the diners out of their slumber with music so sweet and mournful it might soften the shock of what they would discover above ground.

He sat up, seeing several of his neighbours propped up on their elbows as they listened to the exquisite playing. Noises from the kitchen ceased as staff came out to listen and the music grew and spiralled, rolling onward like a river in full spate. All were entranced by the performance by the tall, slim woman in blue silk, illuminated by the soft glow of the night-light above the stage.

As she reached the final bars, the glorious peal of birdsong hung poised in the air as she turned, searching for Alec. They walked towards one another until he took her hands in his, examining her slender fingers then kissing their tips.

'You play like an angel,' he said. 'What was that music? I've never heard it before.'

She shook her head. 'I do not know, but my hands do. This is who I am, Alec,' she said. 'This is what I am.'

9

London, 1997

'Something changed between them after that night,' Verity said. 'They were completely besotted, unless she was a better actress than I gave her credit for.'

'You were still uncertain of her?' Amy asked.

'There was so little about her to be certain of,' Verity said, shaking her head. 'She was polite, pleasant, likeable even, but they would choose someone like her, wouldn't they?'

'Wouldn't who?'

'The Germans, of course. Or Moseley and his blasted Blackshirts. She was a blank canvas, a woman so beautiful she could have persuaded Churchill to whisper secrets into her ear. "Keep mum, she's not so dumb . . ." You know that poster?'

Amy nodded, familiar with the famous illustration of an elegant blonde surrounded by attentive Forces officers.

'Well, that's what we were told. And then she turned up on the coat-tails of an active RAF pilot. It would have been unpatriotic of me not to be cautious. Especially when he informed me they were going away together to his cottage. I'm afraid we argued rather unpleasantly when I expressed my concerns to him. I should have tried the reverse psychology that always worked so well on Bill. On your husband too, I expect.'

Amy smiled. 'Nothing like telling some people not to do something, if you really want it done.'

'Exactly. Unfortunately, I told my dear brother not to go . . .'

'And he went?'

'He went. Alec had bought a cottage in Gloucestershire earlier in the war – he did his Hurricane training nearby and fell in love with the area. It was in a beautiful spot, tucked in a valley. Bill and I spent a weekend or two there when the children were away. You could stand on top of the common and see right across to Bristol, watch the bombs dropping and the fires raging. It really brought the war home to one, to see it like that, even though we were used to it in London.'

'Was Alec gone for long?'

'A few days, and I was quite happy to be left alone, to be honest. I had an interview coming up at work for a mysterious promotion, and I'd rather tired of the pair of them mooning around after one another. It was so hard, when I was missing Bill. I had the odd letter – mainly stripped out by the censor – but it didn't make up for his being away.' She paused. 'It wasn't that I didn't want Alec to be happy – I just had a bad feeling about the Frenchwoman.'

'What made you think something was wrong?'

'Everything – nothing. Just a feeling, you know? But enough to ask my friend Fred to see what she could find out. Fred knew people everywhere. The aristocracy are like that, don't you find?'

Amy had no idea, so she just nodded.

'Well, that's where it became rather complicated. You see, something happened while Alec was away, and it put me in a terrible fix.'

'Something to do with Sophie?'

'Fred turned up one evening. Right in the middle of the blackout, with nothing but a silly luminescent flower brooch to stop her being run over. She'd found something out about Sophie and wanted me to see it straight away.'

'What was it?'

'Photographs, mainly. She wanted me to telephone the police, but I couldn't do that to Alec. I had to find another way.' There was a pause as Verity began working at the threadbare arm of the chair once more. 'I am not proud of what I did next, but you understand what it is like to love someone so much that you would do anything for them?'

'Of course,' Amy said. 'And I've not lived through a war – at least only the Falklands War and the Gulf War, and I spent those safely tucked up thousands of miles away.'

'Exactly,' Verity said. 'And in 1941 the enemy was only across the Channel. We were vulnerable and frightened. I had to protect Alec. No one could have blamed me for what I did. Except myself, perhaps.'

Amy leaned forward. 'What did you do, Verity?' she asked quietly.

The old lady chewed on her lower lip, working through half a century of emotions as she eventually turned to Amy. 'I did something I have never told another soul, not even Bill, until this day.'

10

Gloucestershire, April 1941

Sophie sat back on her heels, halfway through cleaning the grate of the little fireplace as she looked around the cottage. One's home spoke volumes, she thought, taking in the bursting bookshelves, the photographs of family and of various Scouts-gone-by, the gramophone and haphazardly stacked long-playing records; the binoculars and guide to British birds kept by the window. He had been an estate manager in Devon before the war, she had learned, a man of the countryside who blended into this place. His cords and Arran sweater were of a piece with the tapestry cushion and paisley throws; his pipe smoke flavoured the air and his craggy complexion could have been hewn from the same quarry as the warm-gold stone of the cottage walls.

Alec had left a little while ago to collect eggs and milk from the neighbouring farm and a newspaper from the village. They had kissed at the doorway of the cottage, he holding her face in the palms of his hands, as she had teased that he would only be gone an hour, not a lifetime. She still felt the imprint of his lips on her own, the brush of his pencil-thin moustache. The lingering scent of his eau-de-cologne gave her a Pavlovian longing to lead him back up the tiny spiral staircase the minute he returned, flushed with the headiness of accepting his marriage proposal the previous evening.

He had told her of a broken engagement and then the horrors of the aerial battle that had left his ear and cheek scarred. She had sensed it was the first time he had ever spoken about parachuting from the burning aircraft, leaving his best friend dead as Alec floated to safety.

Which was why he had insisted they not wait, and that as soon as Sophie knew she was free to marry, they should do so. 'I need to know that when I come back from my next stint, Mrs Scott will be waiting for me,' he had said.

And she would love nothing more than to be here for him, if she could.

She wondered whether she had ever been so happy in her life, even though they both knew a future together was horribly uncertain.

Scout leapt up on to the window seat and began barking through the small, leaded window, and she damped down an instinctive fear of unexpected visitors, despite knowing it could only be Alec's return that had set the little dog off. '*Qu'est-ce que il y a*, Scout? What can you see? Is your master back already?'

Scout began barking more frantically at the sound of footsteps on the gravel path, and she stood quickly to open the door.

'Verity.' Sophie was shocked to find Alec's sister standing there, her smart London suit out of place in the rural setting. 'Alec has gone out, I am afraid.'

'I know.' Verity fiddled with the clasp of her handbag as she glanced around the cottage.

'Please, come in. I will make tea.'

'That won't be necessary,' Verity said, taking one of the armchairs beside the inglenook fireplace, her knees primly together. 'I think you'd better sit down too. We can have this conversation when Alec returns, but I rather think you'll prefer we do this alone.'

'Is something wrong?' Her ears began to ring as she took the other chair.

Verity looked out of the window. 'I really don't know how to do this, other than to show you what I have found.' She opened her handbag and pulled out an envelope. 'I want you to be assured that this gives me no pleasure,' she said. 'I haven't exactly been friendly to you, although I know that Alec loves you. I wanted to give you the benefit of the doubt, but I cannot bear to see him hurt. Especially by . . .' She sat up straight. 'Well, see for yourself,' she said, handing the envelope across.

Verity waited as Sophie pulled out half a dozen photographs. Silently, she looked at each one before looking up again. 'I do not understand.'

'Then let me help you,' Verity said, taking the photographs from her. She held up the first. 'This is you, performing at a recital at the German Institute in Paris. You used to play in a trio, but your violinist was Jewish and has apparently not been seen for quite a while. Oh, you don't remember? How about this one?' she said, picking up a photograph of a line-up of German officers and French artists. 'An artistic tour to Munich, to perform a series of concerts there. Apparently you speak rather good German. Oh, and it seems you have a special friend back in Paris.'

'Please, I do not want to look at it again.'

'But you must,' Verity said, forcing into her hand a black-and-white photograph of a German officer, Sophie's hand tucked beneath his arm as they smiled at the camera, a spray of long lilies and jasmine cradled in her other arm, her floor-length satin gown set off by the backdrop of chandeliers.

It was a man she had seen in her dreams, in the flashes of memory that sometimes caught her unawares, his wire-rimmed glasses and oiled blond hair suddenly familiar. 'This is a mistake.'

'I'm afraid not. Your friend here is Captain Bruno Becker. You often play for him and his fellow officers.'

This couldn't be. Everything she had learned about the Germans and the terrible war had horrified and sickened her. She looked up.

Verity held up her hand. 'Please, no excuses. Whatever you are doing here, you are not to do it around my brother, do you understand?'

'There must be an explanation.' She tried to force herself into the images Verity had shown her, found she began to fit them like a shoe that had at first seemed too tight. And with the discovery came more images: childhood games in the Tuileries, a spell at an English boarding school, a summer studying in Vienna.

Verity leaned closer. 'I think the best thing would be if you just left. Pack whatever you have with you – including my clothes, as frankly I never want to see them again – and go.'

'But Alec and I . . .' He had asked her to marry him, but to say this aloud to Verity now seemed ridiculous, and already the fantasy she had allowed to take shape in her imagination began to melt away.

Verity raised her eyebrows. 'Alec and you, nothing.' She pulled one more document from her handbag and handed it to Sophie. 'A copy of your marriage certificate.'

'I am married?' she said, staring at the words on the page before her, the name of the husband she couldn't even recall.

'If you have chosen not to wear a ring . . . well, that's your business. All I know is that this needs to be nipped in the bud. So,' she said, pulling her skirt down over her knees, 'it seems to me you have two choices. You either leave now and never contact my brother again, and I promise never to tell him what you really are. Or I call the police.'

Sophie hesitated. Would it break Alec's heart more to find her gone and hold on to the memory of his Sophie, or to see the woman he loved disgraced?

'So what is it to be?' Verity said.

She took a deep breath, letting it out slowly. 'Very well. I will leave. But I cannot accept what these photographs say. Once I have proved they are a lie, I will come back and explain everything. If I cannot, then Alec will never see me again.'

'I suppose I must admire your determination, however misplaced.' Verity looked at her watch. 'I shall be on the two o'clock to London. I suggest you wait until I have left and then catch the next train to wherever it is your people are waiting for you.' She stood, brushing her skirt straight, and stared at Sophie. 'I hope you are able to live with your choices. Goodbye.'

Alec strode across the common, his knapsack heavy with the morning's plunder. It was easier to procure supplies here than in the city, but still he had appreciated the farmer's wife putting in some precious cream she kept tucked away for airmen from the local base. The front page of his *Times* showed Saint Paul's Cathedral standing firm amidst the smoke and fire of another attack, although there was no mention of the appalling damage done to the East End. Anyone outside the capital would assume London was carrying on pluckily, rather than being slowly pummelled to death.

The chirruping of early skylarks was suddenly extinguished by the roar of a single Hawker Hurricane taking off from the airbase nearby. He stopped, holding a hand above his eyes as he watched it skim the valley nestled behind the common. A training sortie, he guessed, perhaps one of the Australian pilots who had been drafted in. Nothing could compare to the giddy sensation of soaring above the land, even though every sortie could be their last. Was that why they laughed so loud, clapped each other's backs so hard, joshing each other in the RAF slang that had become their second language?

Scout was barking at the door as he let himself into the cottage. 'What's up, fella?' he said, hanging his tweed jacket on the rack. 'I'm back, darling,' he called to Sophie. 'Managed to get us some bangers for supper tonight. I think old Mrs Walters in the butcher's has taken a shine to me. Didn't dare tell her half were for another lady, or I'd have been given tripe.'

He dropped the groceries on the kitchen table and put the kettle to boil on the old Rayburn, surprised Sophie hadn't appeared. Tucking his newspaper under his arm, he headed to the little sitting room. The small brush and pan sat on the hearth, ash from the fire scattered where she had obviously abandoned her task halfway through. 'Sophie?' If she were sleeping, she would surely have been woken by now. He took the tiny spiral stairs two at a time, holding on to the rope rail to steady himself, and burst open the door to the tiny bedroom.

The dressing table was clear of her few toiletries, and naked hangers rattled quietly in the wardrobe beside those bearing his shirts and uniform. He pulled out the drawers where she had kept her underclothes, but they were empty.

He began to panic: she would never have simply left without a word, but had someone taken her? He had often seen her looking around whenever they were in the street together, suddenly wanting to leave the little pub where he had introduced her to local ale and backgammon the other evening. He needed to contact the police straight away: surely one of the shops in the village would have a telephone he could use.

And then he spotted something on the bedside table. It was the book he had found with her. *La Vagabonde* – was that all she had been? he wondered as he thumbed through its yellowed pages. Passing through his life, leaving nothing but a dog-eared French paperback? He paused, seeing a note written on the inside cover. As he read the words in front of him, he heard once more the song they had danced to on the night he declared his love to her:

I'll find you in the morning sun and when the night is near.
I'll be looking at the moon, but I'll be seeing you.

She would be back. Whatever the reason for her sudden exit, with these words she had tried to tell him they would find one another again.

If someone had asked her, Sophie would not have been able to tell them how she had spent the last few hours, waiting until she imagined Alec would have given up looking for her at the station. She had sat in a small Stroud café, watching through the steamed-up window as she nursed a mug of tea and tried to force down a few mouthfuls of the inedible Spam sandwich she had ordered. At least she'd had the common sense to accept a few pounds from Verity: Alec's sister may have been paying for her to leave him, but to refuse the money would have been foolish. She had plenty for a train to wherever she chose, and enough for a bed and breakfast for a few days.

She tried to picture Alec alone in the cottage, wondering what he had done to frighten her away, or who it was he had allowed himself to fall in love with. Had he found her message to him? It was all she had dared say, but would it be enough to convince him to wait for her?

The café owner had begun to make closing-up noises, banging a mop and bucket around and ringing up the till. It was almost dark outside, shops putting up their blackout blinds. She picked up the small carpet bag and headed to the station, where she would buy a ticket for the first train and go wherever it took her. The streets were quiet, most people having hurried home by now. She looked around, the fears that had hounded her in London amplified without Alec's protection.

She stood at the edge of the dark, silent platform, wondering whether she was indeed the woman Verity thought her to be. Had survival forced her actions? Or had the Germans' ideology struck a chord within her?

The tracks hummed quietly as a distant goods train rumbled closer, maybe an army transport train bearing the means to fight Hitler, whilst she dined with his officers. She was as guilty by association as those monsters who had overrun her country and murdered her fellow French. She did not deserve to live.

The train was close now and she smelled the soot, her body picking up vibrations in the air and beneath her feet as the engine stormed towards her. She stood closer to the edge, the toes of one brown lace-up shoe reaching out, ready to take the step that would end all of this, that would give Alec the chance to move on with his life and allow her never to know what she had become.

The train was a hundred feet away now, fifty. She closed her eyes. 'I love you, Alec,' she said in French, taking her last breath before she jumped.

But as she moved forward, she felt herself dragged back by her arms and the long train thundered past, shaking the ground, its slipstream tugging at her hair and forcing her eyes shut. She staggered backwards, turning to find herself face to face with the round-faced man she had seen following her in London, and even in the little country pub along the valley, easily recognisable in his tortoiseshell glasses and long Crombie overcoat.

'Hello at last,' he said. Leading her by the arm, he guided her to the open rear door of a black car, its engine gently purring. He followed her inside, then signalled to the driver to move on before turning to her. 'You and the boss have got a lot to catch up on, wouldn't you say?'

'I sat by while she nearly took her own life, then I watched that man bundle her into a car and drive away with her,' Verity said. 'He could have been anyone. All I cared about was that she was no longer my problem. What sort of person does that?'

'Someone living in the middle of a war?' Amy replied.

'Maybe.'

'So who was he? This man?'

Verity shook her head. 'I don't know. It was too dark to make out his face. At the time I supposed he was something to do with Vichy France, or whoever I imagined was controlling her.'

'You were convinced she was an enemy agent?'

'Of course. I'd seen the evidence with my own eyes. What else could I think?'

'And this man who abducted her. He was English?'

'I only heard his voice from a distance, but yes. He was English. I imagined he was some sort of fifth columnist.'

'And you discovered where he took her?'

'Some months later, yes, but what happened when she arrived there is no clearer to me now than it is to you.'

As Verity closed her eyes, Amy could see that the old woman had given everything. Talking of the past had exhausted her, and if she had more to say, it would have to wait for another day. Amy took a tartan rug from the back of a chair and covered Verity's knees, slipping away quietly so as not to disturb her.

11

'This is incredible work,' Eleanor said, looking through Amy's notes. 'And you say Verity Cooper never told her family about any of this?'

Amy shook her head. 'Not even her husband. He believed she was a secretary at the War Office. And then after the war she just wanted to focus on her family. She has carried a lot of guilt about what happened that night.'

'So much so that you think she may not want to speak to you again?'

'I don't know. I can try. Although at the moment she is determined not even to tell me Colette's real name.'

'Maybe she can be persuaded, and maybe there is another way. This story feels to me as though it has significant historical importance. I'd like to think our department could be instrumental in bringing Colette's story to light.'

Amy looked at her. 'And you want me to be the one to do it?'

Eleanor gestured towards the papers littered across Amy's desk. 'Look how much you've done already. It would be pointless giving this to someone else now. And it is your area, after all. What do you say?'

'Well, obviously I'd say yes like a shot. This is a once-in-a-lifetime opportunity. But what about my other work? I can't just drop everything.'

'Some of it can wait, I'm sure, and some of it I can take off you. If you want?'

'Of course I want.' And she really did: she hadn't realised how invested she was. 'You know, I just started out wanting to pass on the letter, but then I met Verity and found myself drawn into the story. And of course then I had to find out what happened after the abduction at the station.'

'The abduction Verity Cooper witnessed?'

'Yes. She took a room at the station hotel that night and waited at the far end of the platform, to make sure the Frenchwoman left. She watched her almost throw herself under a train before being bundled into the back of a car.'

'She didn't see who by?'

'It was dark. She only knew it was a man in plainclothes.'

'That poor young woman. She must have been terrified.'

'Exactly what Verity Cooper said. And exactly, I believe, why she's not wanted to talk about this for all these years.'

'Not surprising. You did well to get her to open up at all. So what did happen after her abduction?'

Amy gestured for Eleanor to pull her chair closer to the desk and showed her a photocopy of some handwritten pages. 'I cross-checked all the training reports in Colette's file against dates in the diary of the head of Section VIII.'

Eleanor raised her eyebrows as she took the sheets from Amy. 'The MOD let you see this? I thought it was kept under heavy wraps.'

'It is. But I spoke with Stephen Owen at the MOD archive. You remember, he worked here for a while? He's the one who found Verity Cooper for me. He arranged clearance for me to see a redacted section relating to the date we know Colette was apprehended at the station. And look, this came from the Bletchley archive.' Amy reached down and pushed a floppy disk into the tower beneath her desk. After a few clicks of her mouse, a grainy film began to play on the screen, fleeting images of young men and women enjoying a brief, sunny respite from war.

'Ah yes,' Eleanor said. 'I saw this a few years ago. It's incredible. Lord knows how it was allowed to be filmed. Any one of these young people could have been recognised and compromised.'

'It was kept in a private collection for years, probably filmed by a staffer.' They watched the silent footage of bristly moustached Army officers alongside plainclothes agents relaxing in the grounds of Whaddon Hall, home to section VIII of the SIS, making the most of their freedom before being dropped behind enemy lines.

Amy paused the film suddenly, pointing at a kindly faced, middle-aged man in a pin-striped three-piece suit who was waving the camera away with an embarrassed smile, a pipe between his teeth. 'There he is.'

'Sir Richard Tremayne. The old devil himself. Never mentioned in anything other than fond tones. Never spoke of his war work. And you managed to get hold of his diary.'

'Well, about three heavily redacted pages, but yes.'

Eleanor clapped her hands together. 'This, Amy Novak, is why I recruited you. So,' she said, putting on her glasses, 'let's see what he had to say, shall we?'

12

Buckinghamshire, April 1941

They had travelled on dimmed headlamps for hours along dark country roads before reaching the fringes of a blackout-cloaked village. The car turned off the main road, idling at a red-brick castellated coach house whilst a sleepy army corporal opened a barrier and waved them through. The driver let Sophie out in front of the grand entrance to a square-set, stone country house, its harmonious façade boasting tall windows and slender columns. She stood for a moment, taking in the sounds of laughter and chatter as a group of men and women in a mix of civilian clothing and Services uniforms crossed the moonlit lawn behind her.

'Welcome to the madhouse!' one of the women said, smiling as they passed.

'Please don't take any notice. They all love it here really!' She turned to see a tall, greying man in a three-piece suit walk down the front steps towards her. He held out his hand. 'Richard Tremayne. Finally we meet.'

She hesitated, assessing his open, smiling face. If she was a collaborator, then why was this man, so clearly part of the British Establishment, welcoming her? Eventually she allowed him to squeeze her hand warmly. 'I am under arrest?' she said carefully, but he laughed, slapping her on the shoulder.

'Certainly not, my dear. Come along inside. The fire's lit in my office, and Cook's left a light supper for you. Jenkins will bring your bag won't you, old chap?' he said to her erstwhile abductor, who tipped his hat and nodded. 'Sorry if Jenkins seemed a bit off: strict instructions not to engage you in conversation. You're rather valuable, and we can't have you compromised.' He turned to take her indoors, then stopped suddenly, his expression serious. 'Really, I can't tell you what an honour it is finally to meet you.'

She followed him into a wide hallway with a winding staircase. Through an open door into what must once have been an elegant ballroom, secretaries and officials were hard at work at a jumble of desks despite the late hour, whilst a constant stream of papers was ferried back and forth across the hallway by young uniformed women and men in rolled-up shirtsleeves, cigarettes hanging from their lips.

'No rest here, I'm afraid,' Tremayne said, showing her into the larger part of a grand drawing room that had been partitioned to create further office space. 'Our people overseas work around the clock, as you know.' He gestured her towards the chair opposite his leather-covered desk, beside which a tray of tea and sandwiches awaited her. 'Spot of brandy to wash it down?' He reached for a cut-glass decanter and poured two glasses, smiling as she took one from him.

As she absorbed the fiery liquid, she felt herself begin to relax, although she stopped at one sip. It would be foolish to make herself vulnerable before she was certain where she was, and under whose instructions.

'I imagine you have many questions, particularly since your doctor at the hospital informed us of the concussion that has affected your memory.'

'You know about this?'

'Of course. It's why we've struggled to make contact with you. And it didn't help when you did a runner from the hospital. Any better yet?'

She shook her head. 'If you want to ask me difficult questions, you will be disappointed.'

'Not to worry. Our doctor here is marvellous. We'll have you back to normal in no time.'

'What is normal? And why am I here?'

'Good question.' He took a sip of his brandy and sat back. 'Let me explain. I work with Section VIII, part of the British Secret Intelligence Service. We place agents in occupied Europe and develop communications equipment for the field. My particular job is to recruit and train Allied spies.'

'You think I am a German spy? That is why I am here?'

He laughed. 'Hardly. Whatever makes you say that?'

'Someone showed me something,' she said, careful not to give too much away.

'The sooner we get your memory back, the better. Perhaps that will help,' he said, glancing down to a battered suitcase placed beside her chair. 'I'm afraid most of the contents are rather damaged, but it still might jog something.'

'But when I went back to look for my luggage, I was told everything had been taken away.'

'Ah yes, sorry about that. Afraid we got to it first. Surprised it survived. Couldn't find the book in there, but perhaps you had it on you.'

'Book? You mean the Colette novel?'

'You were meant to put it on the table at the café where you were to meet our contact, so we could be sure it was you.'

'So why did you take my belongings?'

'The material in that suitcase was far too sensitive to fall into the wrong hands. Here, look,' he said, taking a leather portfolio from a drawer in his desk as she went to stand beside him. 'This,' he said, pulling out a volume of sheet music, 'is the reason we asked you to travel all the way over here. It was inside the suitcase.'

'This is mine? So it is true I am a musician,' she said, looking at the scribbled fingerings in her own handwriting.

'You certainly are.'

'A woman who performs for the Nazis?'

'Ah, that. We'll come to that later, but yes, you are.'

'I have collaborated with the Germans?'

'Not so fast.' He pointed at the music. 'It's rather more complicated than that. As we're about to see.'

'But this is just music?'

'Indeed. Which is exactly what anyone was meant to think.' He laid the music on the table and reached for a slim, pocket-sized torch. 'However, we know better, don't we?' He turned his desk lamp off and shone the ultraviolet light closely over each page, leafing through the book until suddenly he stopped. 'Here we are.'

She leaned forward and looked. There, beneath the torchlight, her own handwriting appeared again, this time in luminous purple. 'What is it?' she said.

He sat up. 'Invisible ink,' he said, 'with which you have

given us a list of German submarine bases along the Normandy coast, and their exact coordinates.'

'But what if I am not what you think? What if I am working with the Germans?' she said.

'A collaborator?' he said. 'Certainly not. You are Agent Colette, one of our best. You speak excellent English, thanks to the British nanny your parents employed for many years, and you learned German at the Vienna conservatoire. You have the German command in Paris eating out of your hand. Incidentally,' he said suddenly, 'there are a couple of papers we were expecting. I don't suppose you were wearing that when you travelled, were you?'

She turned to look at the red jacket draped on the chair behind her. 'This? Yes, I was.'

'May I take a look?' He took the jacket from her and held it to his ear as he manipulated the fabric. 'Ah!' he said suddenly. 'I thought you might have.'

'I don't understand.'

He took a letter knife from his desk and she watched with horror as he carefully slit open the lining of one of the shoulders. 'Here we are,' he said, pulling out a tissue-thin folded piece of paper and opening it out on the desk.

'What is it?' she said, looking at the lightly pencilled series of letters and numbers.

'It's a list of active and captured operatives,' he explained. 'You risked your life to get this information to us, and I'm afraid we're going to ask you to risk it again, once you've recovered and finished the extra training we'll give you here.'

She rubbed a hand over her face, resting it across her mouth, and sighed deeply, weak with relief. Verity was wrong.

It had all been a mistake. 'I thought . . . that I had betrayed my country.'

'Well, you can jolly well unthink that. You are one of us, and we are indebted to you. So what do you say? Are you still game? . . . Willing to carry on?' he added as she frowned at the unfamiliar phrase.

'I will do whatever you need me to.' She had seen enough of the war even over the last few weeks to know she would do anything to help her country, and now she could tell Alec the truth, they could say goodbye before she returned to France. 'But I must tell this to a friend. He will be worried.'

Tremayne nodded slowly. 'Flight-Lieutenant Scott?'

'Yes. I left in rather a hurry and he doesn't know where I am. Or who I am, for that matter. If I can just see him once more . . .' But what was the point? She was married – at least that part of Verity's accusation had been beyond doubt.

'I'm sorry. If you reveal anything about yourself to anyone, we will have to remove you from active duty. I am the only person in this building who knows your identity beyond your code name, and it must stay that way. Unless you prefer to call it a day, of course? No one would blame you – you've more than done your bit already.'

She shook head. 'No, I will not stop. But please. I need to understand how this started.'

'Of course. But you might need the rest of that brandy.'

And so she sat silently, listening to the crackle of the fire as Tremayne explained how she had become involved in a spy network criss-crossing France.

*

Amy sat back, looking at Eleanor. 'And there it is – proof that Alec Scott's lover was the woman who headed up the Section VIII French network.'

'Tremayne was clearly very fond of her,' Eleanor said. 'Look at this line: "It was my utmost honour to stand on the steps of Whaddon Hall and welcome ████ after all those months. She was everything I had imagined and more: beautiful, sharp, even a little fragile. One could see immediately how the Germans had been beguiled by this incredible woman, whose fierce intellect and steely courage were masked by an exquisite femininity."'

'No wonder Verity's brother fell in love with her.'

'And do we know her real name yet?' Eleanor asked.

Amy shook her head. 'Only that her letter is signed off "S". Her name has been redacted everywhere I've looked.'

'How about her photograph?' Eleanor said, picking up the passport-sized headshot from the front of Colette's file. 'Looks like she could be a film star or something.'

'Even more so when you see this,' Amy said, going back to her computer screen. She let the film of Whaddon Hall play on a little longer, pausing it once more as the camera focused briefly on a tall blonde woman walking across the lawns in a slim skirt, papers clutched to her chest and a demure smile cast backwards towards the camera. 'Recognise her?'

'Agent Colette? Amy, this is extraordinary.'

'I know. I couldn't believe it when I saw her.'

'But we still don't know who she is?'

'No, and her file gives nothing away, other than that she seems to be some kind of society figure, judging by her photograph.'

'Can we run a check anywhere?'

'I guess I could look through some old newspapers.'

'How about Mrs Cooper? She was her handler, right?'

'Colette's identity was on a need-to-know basis, but I believe she knows, yes.'

'And she won't say?'

'Absolutely not.'

'She must know we'll find out somehow. A woman who looks like this can't be hard to track down. How about you give it a go?'

The library of the French Institute off Cromwell Road in leafy Kensington was one of Amy's favourite places. She always thought of this corner of London as 'Little France', with the Consulate, the Lycée and various restaurants and French-language bookshops creating a haven for Francophiles.

A former Art Deco ballroom, the library had tall windows that threw bright white light on the delicate iron balcony rails and racks of walnut bookcases, the warm-toned parquet floor that had seen decades' worth of dancers trip across the room to the strains of a tuxedo-clad band playing French jazz.

Amy had ordered a selection of publications to look through, in the hope of finding the woman whose photograph was clipped to the inside of Agent Colette's file. From the bull-ish battle cries of 1939 to the cessation of all French printing presses with the German invasion, Amy was able to trace the trajectory of France's demise. Right up to the middle of 1940, newspaper and magazine articles showed Allied victories, photographs of European royalty holding firm, smiling French soldiers heading off to what they hoped would be a second victory over Germany. But from August 1940, everything changed as editorial voices were muzzled and the French press fell into the hands of German censors.

Newspapers that had once been staples of the French reading diet found themselves banned, and where the vehemently anti-German *Les Temps* disappeared from newsstands, in its place collaborationist publications such as *Paris-Soir* flourished under German management. When Paris was liberated, it was to the offices of this newspaper that resistance forces made their way, seizing back control of the presses and ordering the arrest of the French editorial staff who had continued to publish under the aggressor. Its archive was rescued, and it was this that Amy was now able to call upon at the French Institute.

She flicked through several issues of the shamed, collaborationist rag, passing advertisements for Docteur Pierre toothpaste and *Soir de Paris* perfume. She read racing results, theatre reviews and stories of Allied failure, discovering a propagandised version of the war that bore little resemblance to reality.

And then she saw it. A small feature about a concert that had been given at the German Institute in Paris for Göring during his recent visit to the capital. A photograph showed a woman posing for the camera with two German officers, a bouquet of lilies cradled in her arms as she smiled at the camera.

She was beautiful, fragile, exquisite. She looked at ease, the complete collaborator, the men on either side of her gazing admiringly at her profile.

She was Agent Colette, and had clearly attended the concert.

Amy looked closely, trying to read the woman behind the thin smile, trying to see the war hero behind the coiffed hair and couture gown, the woman bundled into the back of a car at a Gloucestershire train station. The woman who had fought the Nazis from inside for nearly four years. And had then disappeared.

As Amy went on to read the article, her first shock was to discover that the woman in the photograph was the pianist who had performed the recital. Amy looked up briefly, stunned at the coincidence of the crossing of their paths, the final tie cementing this connection with a woman at the height of her career fifty years ago. Agent Colette had been a pianist. A woman Amy would have known instantly as one of her own tribe, a woman who had shared Amy's own experiences of the hours of work that went into one performance, who knew the thrill and the anguish of playing, the loneliness and the joy. And now, too, it seemed, the terror of operating under the Nazi gaze.

The second shock was the name of this woman, a name that had been all but eliminated from musical history.

13

'Sophie Clément?' Claire shook her head. 'Never heard of her.'

'You remember? The pianist collaborator? There was a massive row in the pub about her once, years ago,' Amy said. 'The night I met Michael.'

'Maybe,' Claire said. 'But you didn't recognise her photo when you first saw it in the file?'

'I'd never seen a photo of her. And never really wanted to. I mean, I'd heard her name, but she was pretty much off limits. None of her recordings survived, and no book ever mentioned her. She just melted away.'

'Until now.' Claire leafed through the photographs and old newspaper articles about Sophie Clément that Amy had photocopied and spread across Claire's kitchen table. Resistance magazines and leaflets showed vicious caricatures of Sophie as little more than Hitler's mistress in France. More sinister were cuttings from collaborationist propaganda publications, with more photographs of Sophie posing alongside high-ranking German officers. 'There's loads of this stuff.'

'Once I knew who she was, it was pretty easy to find more.'

'And you say Verity kept all of this quiet for fifty years? Even from her family?'

Amy nodded. 'She still feels guilty about the way she treated Sophie.'

'No wonder she's miserable. All those years of hanging on to guilt – it's not healthy.'

Amy couldn't help but notice Claire's brief but meaningful glance towards her. 'I didn't say she was miserable . . .'

'But you did say she was hanging on to her guilt. Know anyone else who does that, Amy . . . ?'

'I can feel bad that Michael and I rowed just before he died. Let me have that, please.'

'OK, but it's on very limited loan, and then you need to hand it over. I mean it. I'm not having you end up a sad old lady – Michael would never forgive me.' Claire beckoned through the kitchen window at Susie, who was preparing to pelt down the slide once more. 'Why don't you play outside too?' she said to Holly, pressed to Amy's side.

'I want to stay here.'

'Sorry,' Amy mouthed.

Susie ran into the kitchen, skidding as she approached the table. 'Do you want to go on the slide with me?' she said to Holly, chewing on one of her pigtails.

Claire reached into a drawer behind her and pulled out two tubes of Smarties. 'These are only to be eaten at the top of the slide. Now scram, kids.'

They watched Holly reluctantly follow Susie into the garden, passively going through the motions of playing on the slide, checking in with Amy with a brief glance every time she landed on the ground. Susie was so attentive and patient, occasionally coaxing a smile from Holly – Amy knew Claire had coached her into being gentle with her friend, but still, the child had a sweet nature. Holly was lucky.

'You're as bad as each other,' Claire said.

'What do you mean?'

'You and Holly. You were such a pair of livewires, and now look at you. As miserable as that old woman you've been telling me about.'

'Claire, we're grieving. Give us a break.'

Claire sighed. 'I'm sorry. It's horrible. I miss Michael too – I knew him first, after all.'

Amy smiled. 'It's not a competition.'

'Except that you stole my housemate away, so you owe it to me to make an effort.'

'That is so unfair.'

'You know what I mean – I just want to see you get out of this rut.'

'Maybe I like it in my rut.'

Claire raised an eyebrow. 'You, my friend, have never been a rut-dweller.' She nudged her. 'Come on, let's have some fun soon. A day's shopping and lunch. Like the old days. We can get you some new clothes. It's not the Victorian age – you are allowed to wear colours other than black,' she said, looking at Amy's black T-shirt and wide-legged black trousers. 'David can babysit the girls.'

'Maybe.' She picked up one of the photographs on the table.

'It is OK to have fun, you know? You are allowed to live your life, or what's the point in surviving?'

'I do wonder some days.'

'Oh, Amy. Please come back to us. We miss you.' Claire squeezed her friend's arm.

'I will. I'm just a bit stuck at the moment.'

'Well, at least you've got all this to take your mind off things,' Claire said, gesturing to the papers on the table.

'I know. And thanks for pushing me into it. I mean, look: Sophie Clément. I still can't believe she was Colette. She was considered as bad as Chanel during the war.'

'Oh yeah, didn't Coco shack up with a German officer?'

'At the Ritz, whilst the rest of France starved. And it's always been believed Sophie Clément was no better. Which is why no one cared when she disappeared at the end of the war, even though she was probably one of the greatest players of her generation – it was assumed she'd gone off to South America or been dealt with by the resistance.'

Claire picked up a photograph of Sophie Clément on the arm of a German officer and dangled it in front of Amy. 'She was a pianist, like you. That must feel weird. It's such a strong connection.'

'I guess so. We'd have understood each other, for sure. Not many people understand what you have to give up in order to play at that level.'

'I never did get how you were able to sit in those practice rooms while we drama students were off to the pub quicker than you could say Berkoff.'

'The sheer love of it, I guess.'

Claire looked at her. 'You don't miss it? Ever? You used to play literally *all* the time. You were so boring. Michael used to joke that he was only the second love of your life.'

'Well, he jumped to first position pretty quickly after the accident. Anyway, I don't want to talk about it. My life is different now. I have Holly, and my work . . . It's enough for now.'

'And you have Sophie. The collaborator who was actually a spy.'

Amy looked up. 'Who came up in conversation in that dodgy pub in Camden in 1985. The night you set me up with Michael. Isn't that a bit weird?'

'It is a bit. That was the night you and Michael left together and we didn't see either of you for a week after.'

Amy smiled. 'It was love at first sight. Or first pint, I don't know. Michael had been arguing with some beardy Politics student about whether it was OK to like Wagner's music, if you knew he was an antisemitic idol of Hitler.'

'And beardy guy didn't give a shit where the music came from, if it sounded good.'

'Exactly. Even when Michael pointed out that his own dad had been evacuated from Poland on one of the Kindertransport trains.'

'Michael could really give it what for when he was upset.'

'I think that's why I fell in love with him. His passion, you know? Well, and that black curly hair, and the crooked smile . . . Anyway, I remember saying I'd heard of Sophie Clément but would never listen to any of her recordings, because of what she did in the war. I never even wanted to see a picture of her. And now, here she is . . .'

Claire got up to put the kettle on. 'You're made for each other. Although I'd quite like it if you spent some time with alive people too.'

'I spend time with you. And I've seen Verity a couple of times.'

'I suppose geriatric people are a start.' Claire dropped a couple of teabags in a pot and turned to Amy. 'So tell me how a concert pianist became an international spy and I'll make you the best cuppa you've ever had.'

Amy smiled, glad to steer the conversation away from herself. She pointed to a photograph of Sophie with a dark-haired woman whom the newspaper caption named as her cousin Inès Arnaud, an employee at the Board of Trade. 'A lot of it was in her file, but I'm pretty sure it all started here.'

14

Paris, May 1940

It was impossible not to sense the change in the air by the end of May, even in the rarefied atmosphere of the exquisite Art Nouveau bar of the Hotel Lutetia, a stone's throw from Sophie's apartment. Where it was often difficult to find a table in this popular Left Bank haunt, tonight more tables were empty than full, their occupants hectic and overloud, ordering the finest champagne as though the world would end tomorrow.

Perhaps the world *was* ending, or at least the world as they knew it, Sophie thought. She recalled the concert they had just performed at the Salle Érard to an enthusiastic if reduced audience. She had sat at the mirror-polished piano, the folds of her ivory satin gown cascading to the ground as she looked around at the gilded columns and heavy chandeliers, the empty seats once occupied by bejewelled and bow-tied patrons, who had fled the city while they could. Those who remained listened with eyes closed as they tried to forget the terrible news that poured in daily of breaches to the Maginot Line, of British forces stranded on the Normandy coast. It was only a matter of time before the war reached Paris. Tonight's recital by the Phoenix Trio had been the last before the concert-hall doors closed indefinitely, and as the three musicians had accepted the standing ovation, tears had been shed on the stage as freely as in the auditorium.

It had been pointless trying to find a taxi in the empty Saturday-night streets, with fuel already a precious commodity and barely a car to be seen, and so the small party had walked to the Latin Quarter, the silent city their own. Sophie had been flanked by Fabien, his cello strapped to his back, and Hanne, clutching her violin case and fretting that she and her husband should go straight home, whilst their friends followed behind. They had watched artworks being loaded by darkness into waiting lorries outside the Louvre, to be dispersed to chateau cellars and attics across the country, workmen removing the precious stained-glass windows of the Sainte-Chapelle. Paris was holding its breath.

'I propose a toast to the Phoenix Trio and their next recital, wherever and whenever it may be,' Fabien's partner Jean-Paul announced, brushing his dark hair out of his eyes and refilling their champagne coupes from the bottles chilling in ice buckets beside the table.

Hanne shook her head. 'You're being optimistic.'

Sophie watched her friend. She had become increasingly worried about Hanne, whose habitual anxiety was ramping up to something more alarming, and who could blame her? The fresh influx of fellow Jews from across Europe told of a new status quo, far worse than that which had caused Hanne and Max to leave Vienna a decade ago. A rash of vile new French right-wing publications had fuelled disquiet that had already led to assaults in the street and the boycotting of Jewish businesses. And all this before the Germans had even arrived. Sophie had tried to persuade her friends to leave Paris weeks ago, but they had remained, determined to keep life as normal as possible for their little daughter.

'Well,' Sophie said now, brightly, 'we may not perform for a while, but no one can stop us playing together at my apartment. Where there is music, there is hope.'

'Speaking of which,' Max said, leaning down to pick up his briefcase. 'I have a gift for you, Sophie.'

She clapped her hands together. 'It is finished?'

He handed her a sheaf of manuscript paper tied with a red ribbon, his authorship unmistakable in the inky scrawl of notes scattered across each page and confirmed by his name written at the top, that day's date beneath it. 'Your new piano work, as promised.'

'Oh, Max. I don't know what to say.' She knew how much time he had taken away from his usual work as a film and theatre composer in order to write this piece for her, even though in recent months his regular employment had begun to fall away.

'Say you'll order more champagne,' Inès said, waving her empty coupe in the air.

Sophie leaned back to catch the passing waiter, holding an empty champagne bottle out towards him. '*Encore deux bouteilles, s'il vous plaît?*' The young man who had served her on many occasions blushed as he nodded at Sophie.

'He is so in love with you, Sophie. Give in to it: do not break his heart any longer,' Jean-Paul teased.

Inès gave a rasping laugh that reflected her strict diet of nicotine and champagne. 'My cousin will give in to no man. You should know that by now. Isn't that right, my darling ice maiden?'

Sophie shrugged her off, whilst Fabien watched his friend, knowing from experience what had caused Sophie to build the shell around herself. 'And single I shall remain,' she said, her joking tone lightening the mood around the table. 'Besides, all the men have gone, been conscripted or escaped, unless you hadn't noticed.'

Inès leaned across to Fabien and Jean-Paul. 'Apart from you two. And much as we adore you, neither is likely to keep a girl warm at night.'

Fabien smiled sadly, spreading his hands. 'If I could . . .'

'And Jean-Paul, you look positively like Clark Gable with that little moustache. Such a waste . . .'

'Besides, Inès, what would your Monsieur Lambert say?' Jean-Paul teased.

'He would simply take to the bed of one of his other lovers,' Inès shrugged. 'We have a very straightforward arrangement. He pays for his daughter's keep, and I keep a bed for him when he wants it.'

Sophie wasn't fooled by her cousin's nonchalance. Inès's long-standing affair with a wealthy industrialist often left her lonely, and frequently saw her deprived of the occasional handouts he gave her for the upkeep of little Geneviève, the daughter he refused to acknowledge. Sophie wondered whether Inès too had heard that Monsieur Lambert had taken his wife and three legitimate daughters out of the city and was reportedly already on a steamship to America.

Inès took a cigarette from her handbag and tapped it on the knee of her slim, plain black dress. She narrowed her deep-set eyes as she blew smoke towards the ceiling. 'All Paris will have soon is policemen and Germans.'

Hanne's face drained of colour. 'Please don't say that.'

Sophie patted her arm. 'Ignore my cousin. She loves to be gloomy,' she said, although she couldn't help but share Hanne's anxiety: things were not looking good for the Goldmann family.

Inès shrugged. 'Gloomy, maybe, but realistic. The phoney war is as good as over, and the real thing is coming our way. Half of my work at the Board of Trade now is about preparing to work with the Germans when they arrive.'

'If,' Sophie said.

Jean-Paul shook his head. 'I wish you were right.' He looked at Fabien beside him. 'In fact, we are thinking of going down to the coast to lay low for a while.'

'Abandoning the sinking ship?' The Germans had not even arrived, and already Sophie's world was disintegrating.

Fabien shrugged. 'It won't be safe for people like me and Jean-Paul here when . . . if the Germans arrive. Hanne, you and Max should come with us. This city will be no place for a child soon.'

Hanne looked up from where she had been turning the stem of her glass around between her fingers. Sophie noticed the slight tremor as she paused, heard the crack in her voice as she said, 'No. This is our home, and we won't move Miriam away from her friends.'

'And nor shall I be taking Geneviève anywhere,' Inès added. 'She would miss your little Miriam too much.'

Fabien slapped his hand on the table. 'Then we will stay too, won't we, Jean-Paul?'

Jean-Paul looked up from the book of matches he had been turning over in his hands, and Sophie saw his indecision.

Fabien might be of a delicate disposition, but he was also stubborn, and if he had decided they were to stay in Paris, Jean-Paul had no choice. 'Of course,' he said. 'We will stick together.'

There would be terrible times ahead, but they would deal with those as they came, and tonight Sophie wanted only joy. 'Jean-Paul was right,' she said. 'We must drink a toast, but not just to the Phoenix Trio: it should be to friendship, and to drinking champagne together at the Lutetia when this is all over.'

'Agreed,' said Inès, raising her glass.

Max and Hanne were slow to join in the toast, Hanne's eyes cast firmly down towards her lap, where her fingers fidgeted with the black velvet skirt of her dress. Sophie knew the Goldmanns had wanted to get home to their daughter, who was being watched over by a neighbour, but Max had obviously wanted to give Sophie the manuscript he had worked so hard on, and she picked it up once more, gently riffling through its pages.

Jean-Paul must have noticed Sophie's concern, for he stood, gesturing towards the grand piano across the salon. 'It may be a while before we can do this again, so why don't you play it for us? What is it called, Max?'

The composer shrugged. 'I haven't found a title for it yet.'

'Then let us choose one once we have heard it,' Inès said, standing too. She looked around the room of elegant diners, their curiosity piqued by the spectacle. 'Who would like to hear Sophie Clément perform the world premiere of Max Goldmann's new work?' she asked.

There followed a raucous call for Sophie to play, as the entire room stood and applauded, delighted at the opportunity of a private recital by Sophie Clément. As one of the waiters lifted the lid of the piano, pulling the stool out for her, her friends followed her towards the piano, standing beside it whilst she arranged the handwritten sheets of music before her.

The room fell silent as she began to play, unravelling from the score an opening melody so sweet it hung in the air like trailing perfume even as the music moved on to capture the instantly recognisable sounds of Paris: the bells of Notre Dame, the mournful songs squeezed from street-corner accordion players, the joyful games of children in the city's elegant parks, the raucous dance music of the Moulin Rouge, the chatter of old friends and cries of the vendors in the food market of Les Halles. And then, gradually, all that was left were the single notes of the opening melody, a nightingale singing its heart out in the still of the Paris night.

The final note faded, and the room held its breath until first one, then more of the impromptu audience burst into ecstatic applause, calling for Max and Sophie to take a bow. As they clasped hands and smiled at the beaming faces of friends and strangers, Inès came across to kiss them both on each cheek.

'I know what you must call this music,' she said. 'It is without doubt *The Song of Paris*.'

She continued to force studies and sonatas from the throw-covered grand piano in the apartment over the following days and weeks, committing to memory Max's *Song of Paris* despite the wanderings of her distracted mind. She left the apartment rarely, and only to buy what food was available as the break in supplies began to take hold and the German army hovered on the threshold of Paris.

The empty streets and shuttered windows of the grand boulevards lent the city a ghostly feel, and those who remained went about their business quickly and quietly, on foot or by bicycle. With the collapse of the French army and the retreat of the trapped Allies at Dunkirk, panic began to spread, and many rushed to railway stations, their belongings crammed into suitcases. Sophie had passed the Gare d'Orsay to see its concourse filled with teeming humanity, families desperately trying to squeeze on to already full trains. She had visited Hanne and Max in the emptying Marais district, begged them to leave too, but Hanne's state of mind was increasingly frail, and Max was uncertain she would manage a long journey anywhere.

And then on 10 June 1940 the exiled French government laid down arms and declared Paris an open city, sparing its destruction. That night, Sophie looked out of her top-floor window to see the horizon on fire, as all around the city fuel depots were set alight to keep these precious reserves from German hands. The air was thick with foul smoke, the trees empty of songbirds who had perished from the fumes.

Four days later, on 14 June, the German army marched into Paris.

Plenty walked the streets alongside Sophie for mile after mile, staring in silent shock at swastika flags already draped from the Arc de Triomphe, German guards in position in front of the Crillon and Le Meurice, grand hotels that had been requisitioned overnight as Nazi headquarters. Her feet aching and heart broken, she finally returned home past the Lutetia, its doors barred by German sentries.

The following weeks brought more troops, and far from the

barbarous murderers Paris had expected, these young men were under orders to treat Parisians with respect. They relinquished their seats on the Métro for Frenchwomen, politely asked for directions and dealt with the new necessary paperwork efficiently. Hitler planned to preserve Paris as an unspoiled tourist playground for his soldiers, it was said, the jewel in the crown of the Third Reich. As bars and shops gradually reopened, music halls and cabarets found themselves at capacity as German soldiers bought up every seat. Wives began to appear on the arms of their soldier husbands, frantically attempting to copy the fashions of the Parisiennes, who changed tack rapidly every time a German woman was seen wearing a hat that had been fashionable the day before, so that even millinery became a subtle game of cat and mouse.

Those with nothing to fear from the Germans found their way back to the city and the newly reopened Paris Opera, ordering costumes from Mainbocher and Lanvin as though the couturier salons had never closed.

For all the pleasantries floating on the surface of this new society, for those who did not fit the German model, life had taken a terrible turn. Sophie had been shocked to hear that a professor at the Paris Conservatoire had taken his life rather than discover what the Nazis held in store for an elderly Jewish émigré, and of a proposed directive denying her Jewish friends in the Orchestre Nationale the right to work. Already the systematic Aryanisation of Jewish businesses in the city had begun, so that when she tried to contact her lawyer Monsieur Lebrunon on some trivial business, she was told he had 'taken early retirement' and that the business was under new management. Priceless art was taken piece by piece to Berlin as Hitler's secret police moved into the abandoned townhouses on the wealthy avenue Foch.

'I don't think I can stand this much longer,' Sophie told Inès as they wandered the stripped galleries of the Louvre, looking away as passing German officers nodded politely. It was autumn, and the pressure of just four months of German occupation was already unbearable. Almost overnight, restaurant signs had been replaced with German ones advertising *Soldatenheime*, or 'Soldiers' Cafés', and the daily parade of German troops beneath the Arc de Triomphe and along the Champs-Élysées was so insulting to witness that many French chose to stay indoors. News creeping through of the bravery of British pilots fighting off the German Luftwaffe over the south coast of England raised spirits a little, but German-controlled French newspapers and magazines were full of photographs of the devastation of London as, night after night, bombs rained down on her.

'How do you think it feels working alongside them?' her cousin whispered back, glaring at a uniformed German woman staring openly at them. 'These "grey mice" are everywhere,' she said. 'They're like vermin. My office is overrun with them. I feel like laying rat poison for them – disguised in a pair of stockings, they'd gorge themselves on it.' She leaned towards Sophie. 'You have changed your perfume.'

'*Soir de Paris*. I couldn't bear to wear Chanel No. 5 after the way that woman has been carrying on with her German officer, living at the Ritz whilst Paris suffers.'

Inès shuddered. 'If only Coco Chanel were the only one. Some of the women at work are just as bad, flirting with the new German management.'

'Must you continue to work there?' Sophie asked.

Inès shrugged, her sharp, angular shoulders emphasised by the wide cut of her jacket and its nipped-in waist. 'It feels like the right thing to do for now, and Geneviève is safe with my parents in the country.'

'I'm sorry. You must miss her. I know I do.' Sophie's little goddaughter had been one of the joys of her life, but of course Inès wanted her as far away from Paris as possible. She only wished the Goldmanns would make similar provision for their little daughter.

Inès tilted her chin. 'More than anything. But how can I be a parent to her right now, with her father and his money gone and her home city crawling with Germans? At least where I am, I have some idea of where things are going.'

'And where are they going?'

'To hell,' Inès said.

Sophie looked at her cousin. A lifelong chain-smoker, Inès had never enjoyed a radiant complexion, but there was a new dullness to her skin that no amount of Helena Rubenstein could hide. 'Let's sit,' Sophie said. 'You have time before you return to the office?'

Inès nodded, and they found an empty bench.

Sophie looked across at the smooth, cold marble of the Venus de Milo standing across from them, her stance strong yet vulnerable. 'I know how she feels,' she said quietly.

'Who?' Inès asked.

'Venus. Unarmed, literally. Unable to defend herself, the embodiment of a Frenchwoman.'

'Of some Frenchwomen,' Inès replied.

'What do you mean?'

'Just that while you are practising your scales and arpeggios, some of us find it harder to sit by.'

'Inès, what are you talking about?'

She looked anxiously around. 'Ignore me. I'm tired.'

'If you're trying to tell me there is something I can do, then you must say it.'

'I just hear things in the office that could be useful in certain circles.'

'What sort of things?'

Inès looked at her. 'You know I can't tell you.'

'But what if I want to be useful too?' Sophie took her cousin's hand. 'Please, Inès. Tell me what I should do.'

'I don't know. You're a well-known figure here in Paris. It would be difficult for you to do anything.'

'And in some ways it would be easy – in plain sight, so to speak.'

'Maybe,' Inès said as she took a cigarette from her handbag. 'There's an Englishman I meet occasionally. They call him Kestrel. I'll talk to him – see if he can use you.'

As Inès rooted in the bag for a lighter, a German officer stopped in front of them, clicking his heels together and making Sophie jump. He bowed his head as he offered his own lighter. '*Mesdames*, may I help?' he asked in French.

Inès looked up, and he smiled in recognition. 'Mademoiselle Arnaud. How pleasant to see you.'

Sophie sensed a stiffening as Inès attempted to return his greeting. 'Good afternoon,' she replied, then turned to Sophie. 'Captain Becker is a cultural attaché to Paris and a regular visitor to the Board,' she explained. 'This is my cousin Mademoiselle

Clément,' she went on. 'She is a renowned musician here in Paris.'

He looked at Sophie, uncertainty turning to recognition and then pleasure. 'Sophie Clément? I have your recording of the Bach Preludes and Fugues,' he said, suddenly appearing even younger than she imagined him to be.

The thought of her recording being in the collection of a German officer stopped Sophie in her tracks, but Inès stepped in quickly. 'We have just been discussing how my cousin might introduce herself into German society here in Paris. Captain Becker, you have contacts at the German Institute, I believe?' she said.

'Indeed. We are very much hoping to make cultural ties with France.'

'Is that so,' Inès said quietly, frowning. 'I wonder . . .'

Two young Frenchwomen passed, wearing the newly fashionable cycling skirts all the rage now that bicycles were the main form of transport around the city. They stared at Sophie and Inès with open contempt.

The captain broke into the silence. 'Perhaps Mademoiselle Clément could be persuaded to play at the Institute one evening?'

'She'd be delighted, wouldn't you?' Inès said, eyes wide as she turned to face Sophie. 'You were just saying how you wish you could be useful.'

'Of course. Here,' Sophie said, pulling a notebook and pen from her handbag. 'My telephone number. Perhaps we can arrange a mutually convenient date.'

'Thank you,' he said.

'You're welcome,' she replied. '*Ich freue mich darauf*.'

'And I look forward to it also. You speak German?' he said delightedly.

'I studied in Vienna.'

'Of course. And now I am afraid I must take my leave of you. Good day to you, ladies.'

They waited while he walked slowly away, hands clasped behind his back.

'I think you just found your way to help,' Inès said, drawing on her cigarette. 'A beautiful woman who plays the piano and speaks German . . . they'll be eating out of your hand.'

15

Paris, November 1940

A sea of grey uniforms greeted Sophie as she walked on to the stage of what had until recently been the extravagantly Rococo concert salon of the Polish Embassy but was now the musical heart of the newly formed German Institute, established to cement cultural links between France and Germany. Few in her circle would have performed for such a crowd and in such a place, and the engagement guaranteed the loss of respect and friendship of many people.

She seated herself at the piano as though this were any other concert, rather than her first since the occupation five months earlier. Through the thick silence in the hall came the drone of Luftwaffe bombers as they passed over the city on their way to the English coast. She said a silent prayer for those preparing for another terrible night, before placing her hands on the keyboard.

She had put together a programme of German and Austrian music, designed to flatter her hosts, and whilst Sophie railed against the invader, she had no quarrel with his art. Drawing the sweetest tone from the piano, she played Mozart, Beethoven and Schumann, sickened to see these barbarians revel in her artistry with tears in their eyes as she eventually stood to accept their applause.

'They adore you,' Inès whispered as Sophie left the stage, a bouquet of pungent lilies and jasmine in her arms.

'Then I have done my job so far,' she said.

'You have only just started. Our friend Kestrel would like to meet you.'

'Kestrel?' Sophie looked at her, but Inès had turned away, nodding at an over-rouged, ostrich-feathered grande dame.

'Mademoiselle Clément, that was exquisite.' Captain Becker appeared at her side, the concert programme tucked beneath his arm. 'Your rendition of the slow movement of the Beethoven was like none other – far superior to the Schnabel recording of '33.' Sensing her surprise at his erudition, he looked away briefly. 'There are many people I would like you to meet. Please, do join me.'

Becker had arranged a post-concert drinks reception in a sumptuous salon whose mirrored walls reflected the emerald-green velvet of her backless, cowl-necked gown, conspicuous amongst the drab uniforms, and caused rainbows of light to bounce off her diamond brooch. Officers crowded around her, distinguishable from one another only by the slight variations of embellishment on their sleeves and shoulders, and she smiled at each one she was introduced to, politely conversing with them in their own language. They were proud to announce their military affiliations: Wehrmacht, Luftwaffe, Kriegsmarine, Abwehr, so that before long she had met a representative of every part of Hitler's army, from its air force to its navy and its secret service. She attempted to appear interested yet ignorant, attentive yet uncomprehending as they competed to impress her with their boasts of plans, campaigns, exercises. She saw them admire her corn-gold hair and green eyes, the occasional slips of the eye as they glanced at her tall, slim figure, and she knew she had them.

By the time she and Inès accepted the services of their chauffeurs to return them home, Sophie had secured invitations to several drinks parties and had promised to accompany Becker to dinner at Maxim's in order to smooth over any problems of translation during an informal meeting with a consortium of French industrialists.

It had begun.

The weeks went by, and as Sophie allowed Becker to take her to lunch or to walk in one of the many city parks, she learned to steel herself against the accusatory stares of those shocked to see a Parisienne socialising with a German officer. If she had met him in another time, she might have found Bruno Becker tolerable company. A keen amateur pianist, he was able to converse knowledgeably about music and had enjoyed a career as an illustrator of scientific books before the war. He was possibly a little younger than her thirty years, his blond hair neatly oiled and complexion that of a man brought up in the country. Although he clearly enjoyed her company, she had yet to decide whether his intentions exceeded friendly conversation, and so she remained guarded.

The snippets of information Becker naively let slip were voraciously absorbed by the man known as Kestrel, whom she met once a week in the back room of a barber's shop near the food market at Les Halles. It was from one of these 'letter boxes', as safe houses and resistance-supporting establishments used to move information around the city had become known, that she now cycled home with a note hidden beneath the inner sole of one of the men's brogues she had collected from a sympathetic cobbler.

Despite the blackout and the hat pulled low over his head, there was no mistaking Fabien as he left a café they had often frequented before the war. She braked sharply, pulling up alongside him. 'Fabien. I haven't seen you for weeks. Why don't you pick up your telephone? Or reply to my invitations?'

He turned to look at her, his eyes shadowed by the brim of his hat. 'Not now, Sophie. I have to get home.'

'Then let's go for lunch tomorrow.'

'You're not too busy?'

There was an edge to his tone, and instantly she knew he had heard about the concert at the German Institute, the ensuing invitations. 'I'm never too busy for you,' she said, skimming over his veiled accusation. 'Come to the apartment and we'll play – I miss you.'

'The invitation does not extend to Hanne, I presume?'

She hesitated. To openly welcome a Jew into her home would risk everything she was building with Kestrel.

'I thought not,' Fabien said.

'It's not like that.'

'Really? Hanne needs her friends right now, and I don't see you doing anything for her.'

It was true that things were increasingly difficult for Hanne and her family, and Sophie had not visited for some time. It was too dangerous to be seen in the Jewish district if she were to maintain the trust of the Germans, but until she could do more, she had been sending anonymous food parcels to the

Goldmanns. Hanne was struggling, she had heard, her playing completely abandoned and her fragile nerves at breaking point as the danger to the family became daily more apparent.

'It's difficult,' Sophie said, knowing how weak she sounded.

He sighed. 'It's difficult for all of us.' There was a new sadness about his already melancholic demeanour and she tried to take his arm, to make him look at her properly, but he shrugged her away. 'Don't let yourself be seen with the likes of me. Your new friends would not like it. There's talk that Jews will be wearing badges to distinguish them soon. It's only a matter of time before they invent one for the likes of me and Jean-Paul.'

'Fabien? Has something happened?'

He took off his hat, revealing the rough stitches across his eyebrow, the yellowing bruise. 'Just so you know who you're getting into bed with, this is what a German boot print looks like.'

'It's not like that. You know I wouldn't . . .' She longed to explain, but she had promised. One word and Kestrel would cut her off. She was close, she knew: Becker trusted her completely, and what she might discover at Maxim's could make a dramatic difference to the Allied efforts.

'The old Sophie wouldn't, but this one? I'm not so sure. Goodnight, and good luck with whatever it is you think you're doing.'

As she watched him walk away, she suddenly realised that the worst part of resistance was not fear; it was loneliness.

Sophie had arranged for Becker to collect her around the corner from her home. Having heard her neighbour mutter '*Pute*' under her breath as they passed in the communal hall, Sophie did not wish to give the old lady any more ammunition with which to brand her a 'whore'.

'The dress looks beautiful on you,' he said, jumping from the car to greet her. 'It was in the window of Schiaparelli, and I knew it had to be yours.'

Ever since she had pulled the tissue-wrapped navy crêpe gown from the box, it had torn at her conscience, but not to wear it this evening would have been a snub she could ill afford. The simplicity of its high slashed neck and the waist-deep plunging V that ran down its back was offset by the huge white-pearl lilies and silver-thread foliage sewn to its bodice. It was exquisite, its floor-length slim skirt falling from her hips, the short, puffed sleeves showing off her long, pale arms, and yet it was tainted, paid for with German money.

'It's perfect,' she said as she slipped into the back seat of the black Mercedes, to be driven through Paris to the Place de la Concorde and the restaurant now favoured by the German high command.

Across Paris belts were being tightened and buttons moved to accommodate shrinking waistlines, yet as Sophie followed Becker under the elegant pavement canopy of Maxim's, she saw that for some, their dinner jackets were as snug as ever. Whilst the BOFs – as Parisians called those who still ate well on *boeuf, oeufs et fromages* – flourished, families such as the Goldmanns could only dream of eating beef, eggs and cheese, struggling even to find shops that would still serve them.

The ubiquitous grey uniforms leeched the allure from this beloved Paris institution, and even the graceful Art Nouveau sweeps of gold and sylph-like female figures painted on its walls, the deep-rose glow from the stained-glass ceiling, could not soften the sight of German soldiers making themselves at home here. She glanced at the table that only a few months ago had been the favourite of the Duke of Windsor before he joined the exodus from Paris, and was shocked to see Hitler's closest ally seated there. It was common knowledge that Göring dined at Maxim's whilst expanding his art collection from the plundered collections of exiled Jewish dynasties, and now here he was, his small blue eyes never settling as he watched his fellow diners.

She wished she had Inès with her, to reassure her and to dissipate the attention of the men who stood as she and Becker arrived at the private booth where their party awaited them. Becker was proud to show her off, she realised, his comrades entranced by her fluency in German and her musical reputation, as one by one they kissed her hand.

She had done her homework with the help of Inès and Kestrel: the two men in dinner jackets were French industrialists plump on profits from Jewish businesses they had absorbed into their own. Their day of reckoning would come, she hoped, but for now she had to smile, to seem impressed as they reeled off their successes to her. Other than Becker, there to act as cultural liaison, the four uniformed officers were high-ranking representatives of the German army and navy, plus a Colonel Seelman of the SS, whose face betrayed nothing as he calculated the security of each word spoken, each gesture of the Frenchmen. To calm her racing heart, Sophie imagined this was just another performance: the men were her programme for the evening and their words the notes she would interpret. Kestrel had schooled her in how to create a mental list of key words of information: some agents created anacruses from the first letters of words, but Sophie's brain was trained to memorise notes, and so she would use the musical scale to translate key words into a melody she could later transcribe.

Introductions over, the Germans discussed in their own language how much information to share with the businessmen, and eventually negotiations commenced. They explained they were seeking partners for the mass production of a new submarine torpedo they planned to trial in the North Sea. Crippling critical imports to Great Britain was a vital part of the war effort, and the accuracy of this new weapon would have a serious impact on British military and merchant shipping. The Frenchmen sat up straighter, sensing the amount of noughts on a deal of this importance and allowing Sophie to translate into German their disingenuous claims that such a contract would be difficult to fulfil, that they would have to twist many arms.

The wine flowed fast as this dance of manners played out across the table and Seelman clicked his fingers, calling for service. Her heart caught as she saw the waiter cross the restaurant slowly towards them, his familiar lopsided gait the result of a shrapnel injury from the Great War. A one-time regular at Maxim's, Sophie had often given concert tickets to Valentin and his wife, a retired piano teacher now laid low with an illness requiring expensive medication. Regulars always tipped far above the norm for what was fondly known to be the slowest service in the city. Valentin looked at her now from beneath bushy snow-flecked eyebrows, his shock and disappointment quickly covered over.

'*Schnell*,' Seelman called to the elderly man, who advanced wearily towards their table, the habitual shake visible in his hands. 'Hurry up, man. Tell him we need more wine,' he said to Sophie. 'And to get rid of these dirty plates.'

As Valentin began collecting plates, one of the Germans laughed loudly, startling him, so that he knocked a glass of water into Seelman's lap.

There followed a silence as Seelman brushed himself down with a napkin, then stood and lifted his plate himself, tipping the leftover food on to the floor. 'Tell him to clear it up,' he said to Sophie. She relayed the order to the old waiter, longing to offer an assurance in French, but knowing Becker would understand her. Valentin slowly and painfully got to his knees and began scraping congealed lamb bones back on to the plate as the Germans joked at his expense. Seelman refilled the water glass, and the whole party watched in silence as he poured it slowly over the old man's thinning hair. He turned to Sophie. 'Now you may explain that he is no longer employed here.'

She knew she had the power to beg for clemency for the man whose wife depended on his income, but speaking out would end any further contact with these powerful figures. Already she had discovered a new torpedo was to be tested, and this was just the start. Through her diplomatic tweaks of language both parties felt represented, and agreements were being put in place. Throwing Valentin to the wolves would ensure her inclusion in future conversations.

Eyes across the room watched her, waiting for the denouement of this small spectacle as she spoke to the old man crouched on the ground, his face and shoulders soaked. 'You must leave,' she said, clearly enough for any French speakers to hear. 'You will not be returning here.'

She sat back down, and instead of allowing herself to see the hurt and desperation in his eyes, she focused on the information she would be passing on, the lives that could be saved. She would arrange regular anonymous payments to the elderly couple, in the hope that one day she would be able to explain herself.

As the meal came to its conclusion, the conversation fell into idle chitchat. With the bare bones of a deal struck, the Frenchmen excused themselves and Sophie seized upon her opportunity to leave, claiming a headache and insisting she would take a vélo taxi home, rather than inconvenience her hosts.

As she sat in the small open carriage of the rickshaw, her fur stole pulled tightly around her shoulders, she hummed to herself the musical prompt she had created for the planned testing of the new torpedo: 13 January '41 – 13141 – the first, third, then first, fourth and first notes of the scale, launched towards the British battleship beginning with the seventh note of the scale, from the coordinates that made up the first six notes of a Mozart sonata movement.

From Kestrel's point of view, the evening had gone well: she had done as he asked and was certain Becker would use her again. But as she was driven through the streets of Paris, it was the face of old Valentin that haunted her: his horror at Seelman's behaviour was nothing compared with the disappointment Sophie had seen in his eyes as he looked at her. It might as well have been Sophie who made him crawl on the floor like a dog, and she felt sick at having gone along with the cruel humiliation of a kind old man. She would have to steel herself: it would not be the last time she was forced to behave in this way, and the hatred of her countrymen was the price she would have to pay for fighting back.

16

Paris, February 1941

It was to the back room of a shabby bar in Montmartre that she was directed this time, via a note collected from one of the *bouquiniste* stalls lining the quays of the River Seine. The bookseller had barely acknowledged her as he handed her the pre-wrapped parcel in exchange for a few coins, just one more member of the wide network of vendors resisting beneath the German radar.

She was still shocked by her meeting with Jean-Paul and Fabien at their apartment, a space that had been second home to her over the years, where she knew every painting on the wall, many of which had been gifts to Jean-Paul, who as a set designer at the Palais Garnier had worked with some of the greatest names in theatre. Her own face smiled out from photographs of concerts and parties and villas on the Côte d'Azur.

Her dear friends had believed the layers of deceit she'd placed before the Germans, and it had been heartbreaking to see their disgust before she was able to explain her position within the resistance network leading back to London. She had hoped to persuade them to leave Paris, had pressed them both to accept the passage out of France she had arranged for them, but instead Jean-Paul had insisted he join her to fight for his country. Fabien, meanwhile, was in poor health and would not survive the occupation, especially with the German stance on homosexuality, and was finally persuaded to leave. Jean-Paul had promised to join him when he could, but as Fabien accepted this, they all knew there was no place for promises in this new world.

She pushed through the door and went straight to the copper-topped bar, where she explained she was here to take an inventory, following the agreed code. The barman silently waved her through to a tiny parlour where Kestrel waited for her, Radio Paris playing innocuous dance music loudly from a wireless. Many shunned the station that acted as soft propaganda for the German occupiers, preferring the illicit BBC Radio Londres, but it served well this evening to cover their conversation.

'You're late, Colette.'

'I was stopped at a roadblock,' Sophie replied, accustomed now to the code name the Englishman had given her. 'Don't worry – I talked my way through.'

'What have you got?' he said, holding out his hand. His French was impeccable, and the dark stubble he had allowed to grow on his chin made him appear as Parisian as any of her own friends. She supposed he could have been called handsome, if he were her type and if she were remotely interested.

She reached for her slim leather portfolio and pulled out a battered copy of a Beethoven sonata. 'Second but last page,' she said, leaning forward and watching as he flicked through.

He checked doors and curtains were closed then reached for a torch in his pocket and switched off the glass ceiling lamps.

In silence he sat again, holding the torch close to the page until faint purple lettering glowed. She had done well: with the help of the prompts she had memorised, almost everything useful of the conversation at Maxim's was now recorded here.

He switched the lights on once more. 'This is dynamite,' he said. 'Do you think they suspect you?'

She shook her head. 'Becker says they would like to use me again.'

'Good.' He sat back, legs crossed. 'I've got instructions for you. From the boss.'

'The boss?'

'They've been waiting to see whether you can be party to top-level stuff.' He tapped the sheet music in front of them. 'And this proves it pretty much conclusively. They want you to deliver it yourself.'

'To England?'

He nodded. 'You need to get an *Ausweis* pass from the Germans so you can cross the border into Vichy France. Tell them you have a sick relative or something. You'll take a train to the south, then across to Spain and down to Gibraltar. We'll pick you up there and fly you to England. You're leaving next week.'

'How long will I be gone?' she asked.

'A month or two. They'll want a full debrief in London and will offer you some proper training. Things are getting tight for me in Paris, and I need to get out for a while. We're all rather hoping you can take up the reins here.'

'But I'm a musician, not a professional spy.'

'And what do you think you were when you went to Maxim's?' he said. 'In war, everyone is a potential spy. Besides, you're a natural. You know how to keep your cool and you have high-level Germans eating out of your hand. So what do you say?'

Only weeks before, the Germans had opened fire on students who had naively marched along the Champs-Élysées to place a wreath at the grave of the unknown soldier buried beneath the Arc de Triomphe. If Paris had been unsure of how far it could push its luck, the execution of these young people had left no one in any doubt, and so Sophie had no hesitation in making her reply. 'I will do it.'

'Good girl. You'll need to take this with you too.' He handed her a list of code names of members of the network, those taken out of operation struck through, so that messages from these could be assumed to be compromised. She was to stitch the paper into her clothing, he explained: if this were found, the entire network would be in danger.

He smiled as they shook hands. 'It's been a pleasure knowing you, Colette. I hope we meet again when things have cooled down for me here.' But as the risks they took became ever clearer to her, she realised he believed it as little as she did.

Many of the crowd bustling through the Gare d'Austerlitz were Germans, either on the move or sporadically checking the papers of those hurrying to catch trains, so that Sophie remained on edge as she bought her ticket to Toulouse. The air was heavy with the steam of damp breath as Paris struggled through to the end of one of the coldest winters it had ever known. Restrictions on clothing were making their mark, but Parisiennes trotting past had not forsaken their reputation for stylishness, their heads adorned with all manner of creatively resourced turbans and repurposed scarves, the wooden soles of their shoes clacking on the marble floor.

Conspicuously well dressed, she was aware of the attention her red suit and matching tall felt fedora attracted as she walked purposefully across the concourse, her suitcase containing the music score clutched tightly in one hand and the ticket to Toulouse in the other.

As she climbed the steps to her carriage, a German officer placed his hand on her arm.

'Please, let me carry your suitcase, madame,' he said in broken French.

'Really, it's not heavy.'

He smiled. 'I insist.' He held out his hand, and realising that to argue would only arouse suspicion, she allowed him to place the suitcase on the luggage rack above her window seat. Eventually all the seats in the stuffy compartment were filled, and she found herself opposite a young woman clearly nervous of the German soldiers laughing loudly and making no attempt to disguise their interest in the two women. Sophie tried to distract her neighbour, speaking quickly in French about her fictitious aunt in Toulouse and asking her about her own family.

Sophie was long practised at controlling her nerves, and her hand did not shake once as she handed her ticket to the railway inspector. German guards glanced only briefly at the *Ausweis* Becker had arranged for her, asking cursorily the reason for her journey out of the occupied sector. Sophie watched the young woman display all the signs of someone with something to hide as she produced the identity card whose photograph bore a poor resemblance to its bearer. She intervened quickly, telling the guards in German that her friend was unwell, the woman's sweating, grey complexion testament to the sickness Sophie warned them was imminent, and so they retreated after only a brief glance at the woman's identity card, followed by the German passengers, who suddenly felt the need for new accommodation.

'Thank you,' the woman said quietly in the now empty compartment.

'You're Jewish, aren't you?' Sophie asked. 'Don't worry. I shan't say a word. But you must stay calm if they come back. You understand?'

The woman nodded, close to tears, and took the handkerchief Sophie offered her. 'My husband is in Montpelier. Our friends have arranged passage out for us.'

'Then you only have a few more days to be brave.'

They settled into silent contemplation of the countryside hurtling past the window, and with the next stop at Limoges at least a couple of hours away, Sophie had just allowed herself to doze off when she became aware that the train was braking. She opened her eyes to see they were pulling in to a small rural station. Along the carriage, German guards banged on compartment doors, ordering passengers out of the train and on to the platform with their luggage. She quickly explained to the young woman that they had arrived at the demarcation line and this was just a standard border check.

They stepped down from the train, surprised at the warmth of the early-spring air just a few hours south of the winter-bound capital, and formed a line along the platform, their luggage at their feet. The whimpers of a small child in his mother's arms broke through the silence as border guards and dog handlers worked their way along the line.

As they reached Sophie, one of the men poked at her suitcase with the barrel of his gun, gesturing for her to open it. She knelt, feeling the crackle of the paper stitched into her jacket shoulder as she popped open the clasps and stood back, the suitcase gaping open to reveal her carefully folded silk underwear. The man pushed a camisole aside to reveal the leather portfolio and bent to pick it up. He pulled out the music score and leafed through it, looking at her for a moment before dropping it back in the case and gesturing for her to get back on the train.

She hurriedly tidied away her belongings, aware that the guards had reached the young woman beside her.

'Papers,' one of the soldiers shouted in rough French, whilst the other fought to hold back the German Shepherd straining at its chain leash.

Sophie watched the woman hesitate before handing over her card with a shaking hand, and knew it was over. She had shown weakness, and there was nothing Sophie could do to help her as she listened to the men's muttered conversation and watched them examine the identity card.

'Date of birth,' the first guard shouted.

'Eighth of April 1917.'

'Address.'

'Rue Baraban, Lyon.'

'Building number.'

'Twenty-nine.'

'Apartment number.'

'Seven.'

'Address. Again.'

'Rue Baraban, Lyon.' Sophie watched helplessly as the woman began to fold in on herself, fear making her knees buckle and her head bow as the same questions were barked at her over and over.

'Apartment number.'

'Nine.'

It had only been a matter of time until they tripped her up and she made the mistake they had been waiting for. Even more chilling than seeing her taken away at gunpoint and loaded into the back of a truck, was the sight of the suitcase left on the platform. There was no need for luggage wherever they had taken her, and as Sophie resumed her seat and the train pulled away, the suitcase remained a horrible warning to others.

Having seen at first-hand how quickly events could turn, she was extra vigilant all through the change of train at Toulouse and the short walk to a car-parts warehouse in a small town close to the Pyrenees. Here she borrowed scruffy clothing and swapped her papers for the set Kestrel had made for her, stating that she was a secretary at the warehouse. Her suitcase was tucked beneath the driver's seat and the truck loaded with parts before setting out on the winding, bumpy journey across the mountains. Two days later she allowed herself only a short break at the safe house where the *passeur* dropped her before walking to the railway station that was the start of her journey down through Spain and across to Gibraltar.

By the time she was met by her British contact and taken to the airfield where her flight to England awaited her, she was ready for anything.

Over the next day or two, Amy spent hours poring over the articles she had found about Sophie, piecing the timeline together with the help of Colette's file until she had a clear picture of how the woman had found herself to be astray in London whilst on an important mission. The time she had gone missing fitted perfectly with Verity's account of the bombing and the subsequent relationship with Alec, whilst doctors' reports and logs of her training at Whaddon now only served to bring Sophie more clearly to life in Amy's imagination. But it was the fondness with which Tremayne referred to his anonymous asset in his diary that confirmed just how valuable and respected Agent Colette had been, both as an officer and a friend to those very few close to her in the security services.

Amy could only imagine how hard it must have been for Colette to forgo a reunion with Alec in order to carry on this extraordinarily dangerous, selfless work – if she herself had been given just one more chance to be with Michael, of course she would have snatched it. But increasingly Amy was beginning to see that Agent Colette could not be contained by everyday definitions of sacrifice and bravery, as Tremayne himself had clearly known.

17

Buckinghamshire, April 1941

'And that, madame, is how you found yourself in London,' Tremayne said. 'Of course, we hadn't banked on Jerry trying to bomb you out, and then on it being impossible to catch you on your own. The doctors at the hospital warned us not to alarm you, with the amnesia, but then you did a runner on us. Jenkins kept an eye on you, but we had a bit of a scare when you turned up at the French Embassy. Kestrel obviously did a good job teaching you the basics in Paris: you suspected something instantly, and like any good agent got yourself out of trouble.'

She was silent for a moment, listening to the popping of the fire whilst she absorbed the story Tremayne had told her, fragments of memory taking the place of horrible uncertainty and the half-truth Verity had given her.

'And what now? What about Alec?'

Tremayne leaned forward to top up her glass, but she held her hand over it. 'Flight-Lieutenant Scott has been a mixed blessing, from our point of view.'

'He rescued me,' Sophie said. 'We became . . . close.'

'Indeed. And that closeness is the problem. One of your advantages in the field is your lack of any emotional tie. As soon as an agent has a child, a wife, a lover, the Germans have a bargaining chip, and the agent a potential conflict of loyalty.'

'But apparently I have a husband, as of two days before I left Paris.'

'Ah yes . . . we heard about that.'

'So I am married?'

'Technically, I suppose. But I wouldn't worry too much about it.'

'I do not understand.'

He smiled. 'You will, but trust me when I say that if you both make it to the end of this war, you and your pilot can be together in all good conscience.' Tremayne's expression suddenly clouded over. 'My dear, you do know that if, as I hope will be the case, you agree to continue your work for us, it is very unlikely you will return to Britain until the war is over?'

'And equally unlikely I will survive the war?' she replied.

'I won't insult you by making a pretence of your chances of survival. That is down to your skill and your luck. We produce excellent agents here, but the Germans are getting better and better at tracking them down. At present, the average life expectancy of an agent in France is six months. We can teach you to be safe, but once you are in the field, our ability to look after you is limited.'

She nodded. 'I suppose I should be grateful Alec and I had even a little time together.'

'No one will force you to go back, you know. We will give you asylum for the duration of the war and I have a dozen jobs I could offer you, with your experience and language skills. You would be free to be with your pilot.'

'But you would lose your agent at the heart of German high command in Paris?'

He nodded. 'We would, but I don't expect you to rush into a decision. Apart from anything else, you suffered a nasty injury. You won't be going anywhere for a little while yet.'

She suddenly recalled a woman on a railway platform, remembered her horror at seeing her loaded into a German truck and taken to a future where there was no need for her belongings.

'I have already thought about it. I will return to Paris, but on one condition.'

'As long as I am at liberty to agree to your condition, then of course I will fulfil it. What would you like from me?'

'I want to write to Alec. Explaining why I left him. You may hold on to the letter until the war is over, or until . . . well, until I am no longer in a position to tell him in person.'

'You have my word your chap will get the letter, if it comes to it. Oh, and one more thing.'

'What is that?'

'With your unusually public position in Paris, your identity is top secret. No one over here other than myself is aware of your real name, and we need to keep it that way. All communications to, from and about you will refer only to your code name. I'm sure you understand?'

'Of course.'

Tremayne stood, holding out his hand to her. 'And now, Agent Colette, I insist you get some rest. We'll meet again tomorrow when the doctor has seen you.' He smiled, his expression displaying his respect and fondness for her, alongside the pain of nurturing his best people, only to send them to almost certain death.

She would survive, she told herself as she was led up the stairs towards her room. She would get through this war, and when she returned to England, it would be to marry Alec.

They had been gentle with her for the first week or so, and she fell into a routine of exercise, therapy and coaching fellow agents in French colloquialisms and the idiosyncrasies of life across the Channel. She enjoyed the camaraderie amongst these quick, intelligent people whose real names she would never know and who occasionally persuaded her to join them in the local pub after their evening meal in the village hall. Of course no one spoke of their old lives or their future missions, and even though the conversations mainly consisted of light ribbing and jokes about some of the training staff, they were a pleasant diversion.

Each day she met with the section psychiatrist given security clearance to work with her, as they examined photographs from her past, hoping to fit together the broken pieces of her timeline. He showed her hundreds of sheets of paper covered in ink blots, asking her to tell him what she saw in them, searching for clues in her answers. Sometimes she would lie on a chaise-longue whilst he took her back further to the pre-war years, shown in concert programmes and newspaper cuttings. Eventually he showed her a photograph of a goatee-bearded man old enough to be her father, and a wash of anger overcame her as she looked at the face of her one-time music professor.

Julien Renard had quickly spotted the vulnerability and need for affirmation in his anxious, seventeen-year-old protégée who was already scooping up prizes, and began a campaign of isolating her from her peers. By the time Fabien threatened to expose his abusive, controlling behaviour, Renard decided Sophie was more trouble than she was worth, and she went instead to Vienna, rebuilding her confidence with a gentle, grandmotherly teacher. She returned to Paris determined never to tolerate bullying again, and never to allow herself to enter into an intimate relationship.

Fragments were still missing, but these would return in time, the doctor told her. She did not know everything, but she knew enough.

During their final consultation, the doctor had closed her file and smiled at her. 'I have done everything I can, without the advantage that being in Paris will afford your recovery. Agent Colette, you are ready.'

The very next morning, she was woken at six a.m. and her training began in earnest.

The candy-pink magnolias gracing the grounds of the Hall were gradually superseded by bursts of fragrant roses as spring morphed into summer. Those who found themselves outside to enjoy a quiet moment's solitary contemplation could imagine they were here to enjoy a country-house weekend, rather than the imminent journey into a war zone.

After an intense six weeks of training, a last-night party for the outgoing agents was underway in the house, and Sophie had slipped outside for some fresh air. Distant thumps cut through the sounds of laughter and jive records as another night of ferocious bombing began across London, the glow of fires on the horizon to the south creating a strange sunset.

So much had happened in the months since that night in Baker Street, and even the weeks of training at the Hall seemed like years. She had spent hours at the dummy radio set up in the Hall, learning to assemble and operate the portable wireless transmitter that would accompany her. The simple rhythms of Morse code had been no challenge to a musician, so that she passed the module in record time and had quickly mastered the 'book code' used by agents overseas, a complicated double-transposition cipher system that was impossible for German operators to decode without the key.

She was shown the Nissen huts tucked behind the village church, where tall radio masts were the only visible clue to the activity that took place inside. Here radio operators sent and received messages from agents across the Continent and enabled Enigma-decrypted intelligence from nearby Bletchley Park to be shared with generals and naval commanders in the field. Sophie watched ranks of Wrens transcribe the dots and dashes that represented every perilous transmission by an agent on the ground. It was both comforting and chilling to see how her own messages would be taken down and sent across for decoding, any discrepancy in her style of transmission instantly alerting her assigned 'godmother' to the possibility she had been compromised.

Although she had detested the subsequent part of her training, it was possibly the most important part, Tremayne had stressed. Specialists had been brought in to teach the recruits how to use the revolvers they were to be issued, and simple combat skills were supplemented with silent-killing techniques. 'If it's a choice of your survival or a Nazi's,' the army sergeant had explained to them, 'there's no contest, so just get on with it.'

If she had been unsure whether she had the mettle to work undercover, the night she was taken in the early hours to a 'cell' in the basement of the Hall had persuaded her to do everything in her power to avoid arrest. She had been tied to a wooden chair in her nightdress, a sack over her head. The back story that had been drummed into her was tested to its extremes through the hours of Gestapo-style interrogation as she was forced to kneel on the ground in front of a steel bucket, her head held under ice-cold water every time she refused to talk, but still she did not crack.

Her thoughts were interrupted by the nightly drone of aircraft heading eastwards and she watched the familiar V-shaped formation of Lancasters loaded with the bombs that would be shed on German factories and homes. She wondered where Alec was right now, perhaps preparing as she was for a mission, or already airborne, thousands of feet above Europe.

If only they could have had one more night together. If only she could explain to him why she left and how much she longed for him. As if on cue, the strains of a slow dance made their way across the gardens, and as she closed her eyes and listened to the words she had written for Alec to find in her book, she remembered dancing in a London basement, so close that she could feel Alec's heart beating whilst the bombs fell around them.

I'll be looking at the moon, but I'll be seeing you.

'Well, here we are. We've taught you everything we can.' Tremayne stood backlit in front of the tall window. She had seen how much time he took to get to know each trainee agent who passed through his care, how he visited the families of those who didn't make it back, and she could only imagine how much he hated this part. 'Mrs Brooks has issued your clothing to you, and I'll take you through the rest of your equipment.'

She looked once more at the pile of folded clothes on the chair beside her. The Molyneux suit had been repaired, and with the rest of her own clothes ruined in the Baker Street bombing and Verity's screaming their Englishness, the wardrobe section had supplied everything she would need for the journey to Paris. Using silk donated by refugees from France, seamstresses had made underwear for her and a silk blouse with seams and buttons stitched in the particularly French style, its edges carefully frayed so it would not look too new. Even her toiletries were authentic, the labels copied from originals and made to appear mass produced. They had given her a bottle of *Soir de Paris*, and sniffing at the bottle, she realised the familiar smell must be her own perfume.

Tremayne opened a plain cardboard shoebox and pulled out two sets of forged identity cards and *Ausweis* passes. 'One of these is for Sophie Clément. The other,' he said, 'is for Madame Micheline Duchamp. You are completely happy with the details?'

Sophie nodded. 'Madame Duchamp, secretary for an automobile company, address in Limoges, two children, a widow. Parents live near Montpelier, father was an engineer . . .'

He nodded. 'Good, good. And here are the glasses and prosthetic teeth you will need in order to look like Madame Duchamp.' He placed four envelopes on the table. 'Three million francs in cash. This will cover rent for two safe houses and expenses for you and your team for a while. You may also need to pay for help getting stranded servicemen out from time to time. You won't meet them yourself, of course – can't blow your cover – but they can pass through your safe houses on their way out. This card of buttons may be helpful to them: each button has a compass hidden inside. And here are some silk maps – they fold up to practically nothing. No bigger than a scarf.' He took a box of playing cards and placed it on the desk. 'These might be useful too.' He took one of the cards out and eased the front from the back. 'See here? Peel the front off and you'll find a section of a map. Now,' he said, placing a small box on the table and removing the lid. 'We're very excited about these. Just come in. What do you reckon?'

'But I don't play golf.'

'Thought I might catch you out. These golf balls are luminescent. If for any reason the landing party out there can't light bonfires to guide our planes in for the parachute drops, these can be charged up during the day and used instead. Brilliant, eh?'

If it hadn't been for the deadly serious intentions of all these tricks, Sophie might almost have been entertained by Tremayne's display, but his next offering sobered her instantly.

'Now, your revolver,' he said, placing the small Colt .38 on the table. 'Keep it somewhere safe at home. You can't be caught with it on you. And this,' he said, handing her a long, slim blade topped with a large pearl, 'should cover you when you're on the streets, as long as you're wearing a hat.'

'A hat pin. How clever.'

'Now for the really important stuff,' he said, placing a battered, rolled-up tube of toothpaste on the table.

'What it is?' she asked, confused.

'Rolled inside is the list of codes for your new recruits. You'll need to get them each a copy of the book we've agreed for cipher keys. Your Colette volume will work well: if they leave it lying around, it won't look out of place in Paris. And of course every lady needs this . . .' He passed her a pot of Elizabeth Arden face powder. 'Look inside.'

She took the lid off the pot and pushed her finger through the powder until she found the tiny wax-paper-wrapped package. 'My radio crystal.'

'This,' he said, standing and fetching a small leather-covered suitcase, 'is your radio.'

She flipped open the two catches and found herself looking at a wireless transmitter identical to those she had been trained on, with its Morse pad, heavy battery pack, dials and headphones, long lengths of aerial and earth wire.

'There's a panel we'll pop on top, so you can place your clothing, music and whatnot inside and no one will know it's anything other than a suitcase. Try not to let anyone carry it for you – it weighs a ton. Once you're established, we'll arrange a parachute drop for the other radios and spare crystals.'

'You've thought of everything,' she said.

He nodded. 'We do our best. Want you chaps as safe as possible, you know? I'm rather hoping you'll be back to give us another of your recitals.'

They were nearly finished, she knew. A car would arrive within the hour to take her to the airfield in preparation for the flight that night, but there was one more thing she needed to do. She reached inside her jacket pocket and pulled out a letter. 'You will be sure to give this to Alec if . . .' She cleared her throat and looked Tremayne directly in the eye.

He tightened his lips and nodded. 'Of course,' he said, taking it from her, and she was grateful he did not patronise her with an empty promise that it wouldn't come to that. 'It will go in your file. I promise it will reach the right hands if necessary.'

'Thank you.' She stood to leave, but he stopped her.

'One more thing,' he said, and opened the drawer of his desk, handing her a packet of tablets.

'Aspirin?' she asked, taking them from him and reading the packaging.

'Afraid not.'

She looked at him, chilled by the realisation that she was holding the means to silence herself for ever if caught.

'Cyanide. Quick, possibly not painless, but preferable to some of the scenarios you might find yourself in. I pray it won't come to it, but . . .'

'I will make sure it does not.' She held out her hand. 'Thank you, Sir Richard, for everything.'

He pressed her hand warmly between his own. 'It's been an honour. Now come back safely, and for God's sake don't forget to bring some perfume for my wife, or she'll have my guts for garters.'

They seemed to have been airborne for hours, guided by the snaking moonlit ribbon of the River Loire, the sound of ack-ack fire on the Normandy coast far behind them. Her bones ached from the vibrations, she was shivering with cold and it was impossible to tell whether the ringing in her ears would ever end.

As they were given the thirty-minute warning, she reminded herself of the drill: 'Elbows in, legs together, ladies, like your mother taught you,' the sergeant had drummed into them. A heavy canvas holdall contained the suitcase plus her handbag and hat, and beneath her overalls she was dressed in the Molyneux suit, ready to be driven to the safe house overnight before the train journey back to Paris.

She closed her eyes as she felt a change in the reverberations of the engine, knowing they were close now. The dispatcher did a final check on each passenger, tightening straps and checking helmets were secure until finally the call came to open the doors and they were lined up.

The heavy door was slid open and she had her first view of her homeland in weeks. Moonlight sketched the outlines of fields and villages, the sparkling carpet of the Atlantic lying far to the west and the jagged outline of the Pyrenees to the south. Beneath them, she spotted the triangle of flaming bonfires that marked their landing zone.

'Good luck, miss,' the dispatcher shouted above the noise of the engine and the rush of wind as Sophie clutched the holdall, taking one last deep breath before stepping out of the plane, into the night and into the unknown.

Part Two

18

London, 1997

Saturday mornings were the hardest. Michael had always taken Holly swimming at the beginning of each weekend, giving Amy a couple of hours to herself. Often she used them no better than to scoop up washing from the floor or idly read the paper at the kitchen table, relishing the rare silence in their noisy home.

Michael had always been the 'fun' parent, and Amy hadn't minded. One of them had to make sure the fridge was stocked, the car had petrol, water was in the kettle and candles at hand in case of power cuts. She supposed it was partly the result of years of discipline as a young musician, but knew too that more recently life had taught her to protect herself and those she loved.

As the last year had raised her levels of caution, she found she didn't like this new version of herself, and nor had Holly that morning, when Amy cut their swimming session short. A non-swimmer herself, Amy already loathed the small pool full of over-excited toddlers, hated her face being splashed with heavily chlorinated bathwater, but Holly had been determined to break away from her and attempt to jump in on her own. 'But Daddy let me,' she had howled as Amy's patience broke and she dragged her daughter back to the changing rooms. A brittle truce had been called when Amy relented with a Happy Meal on the way home.

By lunchtime, Amy's anticipation of visiting Verity later that afternoon was tempered by the residual smell of chlorine and saturated fat as she and Holly settled on the sofa in front of a well-played video of *Mary Poppins*. At least, she supposed, she could lie down for ninety minutes and close her eyes. In truth, Amy missed the order and calm of her working life when trying to fill the Michael-less weekends. In her professional world everything was catalogued and organised, everything in its own place, whereas her home life was a mess. Her house was a mess, she was a mess, and she didn't know how to make it better.

Michael's parents had offered again to have Holly so that she could get away for a few days, but as much as she knew she needed a change of scenery, she also knew she wasn't ready to leave Holly. And Maria had a way of making Amy feel like she was getting it all wrong: feeding Holly wrong, sending her to the wrong school, living in the wrong part of London, being the wrong sort of working mother, punishing Holly's grandparents by not letting her see them. No wonder Michael had been so bad about keeping in touch: it was exhausting.

She must have slept, because she opened her eyes to see the credits of the film rolling, the space beside her empty. 'Holly? Where are you?'

She was aware of noise from along the hall, a little voice singing and the playing of random notes. She followed it to the open door of the room that Michael had used as a study before he filled it with the anniversary present that had caused their final row. Amy was sure she had kept it locked, but she was unsure of anything at the moment, other than that she never wanted to go in there and look at his final grand gesture.

Michael's desk, squashed into the corner of the room, was still covered in pages of scripts he had scribbled over, his chewed pencil lying on top of them, watched over by the plaster bust of Shakespeare on to which Holly had drawn purple glasses. On a side table stood an old record player, stacks of Michael's precious rare jazz albums on the floor beside it. He might have been about to walk straight through the door and start learning lines – except that it was now almost impossible to get past the shiny black grand piano.

'Holly, you know you're not allowed in here,' Amy said, seeing her daughter seated at the piano.

The little girl stopped playing, turning to stare at Amy. 'Why?'

'Because it's . . . it was Daddy's room, wasn't it?'

'But he said it would be your room when the piano came. And that you would let me play it. Daddy said you were the best pianist in the world. Were you?'

Amy's eyes stung with tears but she smiled at her daughter, this little freckle-cheeked version of herself. 'I think Daddy was exaggerating, sweetheart.'

'He wasn't. And he said playing the piano made you the happiest person in the world, until I came along.' She frowned. 'Why were you cross when the men brought the piano?'

Amy had a sudden flashback to the huge row that had flared up when Michael had led her blindfold into his study on the morning of their anniversary, his excitement at her seeing the piano quickly turning to frustration at her anger. He should have asked, he should have checked how she might feel. The whole subject was far too loaded for surprises, without even starting on his own unspoken guilt about the accident.

'I was surprised, I suppose,' she said now.

'Will you play a song for me?' Holly said, shifting across on the piano stool. 'Please?'

Amy shook her head, finding herself taking a step back, away from the instrument. Her eyes were fixed on the black and white keys, her fingers itching to reacquaint themselves with works lying dormant in her muscle memory, but then she took her left hand, rubbing at the scar at the base of her damaged fingers. 'I can't. Anyway, the piano is going back soon. We only have it for a year.' Unless she played it during that time, unless she cracked, in which case it was hers to keep. Well, that was not going to happen.

'Can I play for you? Look,' Holly said, pressing her little fingers hard on the keys. 'I made up a song.'

Amy watched Holly, tongue out to one side, play a simple tune whilst she hummed along to it. She was only five, but Amy knew this was young for a child to be playing with two hands. She should have known her own musical gene was strong enough to reach the next generation.

'Was I good?' Holly asked, eyes wide as she finished, a relaxed glow to her that Amy had not seen since Michael left them.

She reached over and hugged her daughter. 'You were good, my darling,' she said.

After dropping Holly at Claire's and promising she would stay for a glass of wine when she came back later, Amy paused at a flower stall to buy Verity a bunch of midnight-purple irises that caught her eye. She had a feeling the old lady would appreciate their uprightness and politeness in not hanging around longer than necessary. With time to spare, she walked past the station to the unfamiliar territory of the far end of Chiswick High Road, where she would catch a bus instead of her usual train.

A door opened suddenly and a blast of piano music floated briefly out on to the pavement. What was the world trying to do to her today? She stopped. The shop was either a recent addition to the High Road or her subconscious had blanked out its presence. 'Records of Note' boasted not only an extensive collection of classical and jazz recordings, but a small café. Michael would have loved this place. In fact Michael would barely have left it. She remembered the end of her conversation with Verity and on impulse pushed the door open, wondering if the impossible might in fact be possible.

Immediately she was hit by the comforting aromas of freshly ground coffee and leather sofas. The shop was spacious and light, a selection of books and sheet music for sale alongside CDs and second-hand records stacked neatly in racks, according to composer. The music she had heard came from a tiny raised stage at the back of the shop, where a man in jeans was playing an old Duke Ellington number on an upright piano.

'Hello?' she said, and then once again a little louder, making him stop suddenly and turn to look at her through thick-rimmed Jarvis Cocker glasses.

'Sorry,' he said, pushing them back up his nose. 'I didn't hear you. I get a bit carried away . . .' He looked at the irises clutched in her hand. 'Nice flowers.'

'Oh. Thanks. You work here?'

'If you call playing the piano and talking to fellow enthusiasts work, then yes, I do. Well, it's my shop actually. I'm Jay,' he said. 'Jay Martelli.'

'Amy. Amy Novak.'

His face suddenly fell. 'You're not related to Michael, are you?'

'Yes. Well, I was.'

'You're the wife? Gee, I'm sorry,' he said.

'You knew Michael?'

'He was in here a lot. We became buddies, I suppose. Fellow jazz nerds.' He was around her own age, she realised, and seeing the faded band T-shirt and scruffy 501s, she could see how he and Michael had been drawn to one another.

Amy smiled. 'That sounds about right.'

'You were a classical pianist, right?'

'Once upon a time.'

'You must have been chuffed when the piano arrived,' he said, smiling. 'Michael couldn't wait to see your face. At least you get to play again. That must be some small comfort, I guess?'

'It's a bit more complicated than that . . .'

Jay held his hands up. 'Hey, I'm sorry. None of my business. Listen, if there's anything I can do . . .'

Amy hesitated. 'Actually, there might be something.'

'Sure. Go ahead.'

'I'm hoping to get my hands on a rare recording.'

'You've come to the right place. What are you looking for?'

'I'm looking for a recording of Sophie Clément.'

He paused, frowning at her. 'You mean . . .'

She nodded. 'Yes, *the* Sophie Clément.'

Amy was surprised to see Verity open the door dressed in a smart lightweight coat, the now familiar red and gold scarf tied around her neck and her hand gripped around the handle of a walking stick. 'We're going out,' she said briskly. Amy had worried about the reception she might receive from Verity, having telephoned to tell her that she had discovered Agent Colette's identity herself. She had expected Verity to be angry, but instead the old lady had seemed almost relieved that the burden of the secret was no longer hers. She had even invited Amy to tell her what she had learned about Sophie. It seemed that both of them had gone too far along this road to turn back now, and Amy was getting to know Verity well enough to realise that her brusqueness was a default, rather than intentional.

Amy looked along the hallway, now almost bare of the boxes and bags that had cluttered it only a week or so earlier, wondering whether Penny had sanctioned the outing. 'I brought you these,' she said, producing the brown-paper-wrapped bunch of irises. 'Shall we put them in water first?'

Verity stared at the flowers, and Amy worried that she had made a mistake. 'You do like irises? They're a French variety, apparently.' The old lady seemed agitated, and Amy realised that bringing flowers to someone about to move house was a ridiculous idea. 'Sorry – you probably don't even have a vase to hand.'

'They just . . . they remind me of someone. It's a kind thought. Leave them in the kitchen sink in some water.'

They made their way slowly towards the brow of the hill, Verity's hand tucked beneath Amy's arm.

'I used to walk Alec's little dog up here,' Verity said, watching two Jack Russells tearing around after one another. 'He would bring it with him when he came to stay during the early years of the war. Always promised he would look after it himself. Never did. It was quite a sweet little thing really. Followed Sophie around like a shadow, of course.' She paused. 'So now you know who she is, how do you feel about her?'

'I found some old cuttings about her,' Amy said. 'They told me everything I thought I had known about Sophie Clément – everything I believed up until last week: that she was a collaborator, a Nazi supporter. But nothing I can find seems to suggest anyone ever found out she had worked for the Allies. She did an incredible job of covering her tracks.'

'I didn't know myself who she was until the fall of Paris. She was just Agent Colette to everyone but Tremayne.'

'It seems incredible.'

'Perhaps so, but she was at very high risk. Most of her own agents knew her only by her code name, and her intimate circle was very small. Most of those may not even have survived. She took her secret with her.'

'Until now. She was never heard of after the war?'

'Disappeared completely.' Verity sighed. 'All these years, her reputation could have been spared. I kept quiet to save my own reputation with my family. What sort of woman separates her brother from the woman he loved?'

'But you said it yourself: you'd signed away your right to talk about her.'

'I suppose so. Do you know, one of my greatest regrets is that I never heard her play.'

'I did. Once.'

'How so?'

'I heard a recording of her years ago, when I was a music student.'

'You are a musician?'

'I was. A pianist, like Sophie. I don't play any more.'

'But you were good?'

'I used to be.'

'No wonder you find her story so fascinating. Do you still play?'

Amy shook her head. 'I gave up years ago. But yes, it is probably partly why I've felt drawn to her story. Not everyone can understand what it's like to give up so much of your childhood to a vocation. Sport or dance are probably the only other careers where it's too late to take it up once you've hit about ten years old.'

'Goodness, I've never thought of it like that. She's even more remarkable than I realised at the time.' Verity sighed. 'It is heartbreaking to think that her own countrymen never knew what she did for them, that all her talent was consigned to the past. I suppose I was ashamed at my own part in sending her away, at breaking my own brother's heart. We bury these things, don't we?'

Amy squeezed Verity's hand. 'We do, but then we have to find our own way to live with them.'

They had reached the brow of the hill, with its picture-book view of the London skyline, the dome of Saint Paul's and the Post Office Tower shimmering on the horizon.

As they sat, Verity looked up to the wide, clear sky above them, where a blue kite tugged against the string held by a small girl and her father. 'Early in the war I used to come up here on nights when the bombing let up. You could see the British planes heading south towards the Continent, and I often wondered whether it was Alec up there. If anything had happened to him, I would have been devastated.'

'You were twins – it's understandable.'

'After Sophie left, Alec flew every fighter mission he was offered. He was on borrowed time, outliving the life expectancy of a pilot, but he had this mad obsession with ending the war so that he and Sophie could be together.'

'How long did this go on for?'

'Until early '43, when he got himself transferred to another squadron.'

'And where were you by this stage?'

'I'd been given a nominal rank in the WAAF and put into uniform in the summer of 1941, shortly after Sophie left. I was Flight Officer Cooper, SIS French Division, receiving intelligence and passing it on to the relevant armed force. Sophie and her network provided the intelligence, and Alec acted upon it. Somewhere in the middle, there was I. And not one of us had any idea how close we all were to one another.'

19

April 1943

Ten thousand feet above the vast expanse of night-black northern Europe, tiny crystals of ice had formed inside the glass cockpit canopy and Alec was glad of the fur-lined jacket he wore over his flying suit. The dimmed UV dials told him they were cruising at a steady 200 mph and two of the three fuel tanks were still full, but they could have been anywhere.

'Sure you're not taking us to the North Pole, Jock?' he joked into the radio to the navigator sitting beside him in the cramped cockpit.

'Not unless they're heading there too, sir,' he replied, pointing at the radar showing three Lancasters and the two other Mosquitoes from their squadron, protecting the heavy bombers from stray German fighter planes.

Only twenty-two years old and already the best navigator in the squadron, the only thing that ruffled Jock Cameron was the fiancée who broke off and reinstated their engagement with more regularity than the scramble sirens that screamed across the station most days. Alec had happily agreed to be his best man at the wedding planned during their next chunk of leave. 'No point hanging about,' Jock had said. 'She might change her mind again!' Although they had laughed, they both knew the life expectancy of an airman did not allow for procrastination.

'Fox 24 to Cricket 39, do you read me?'

The voice cutting through the crackle of the radio jolted him back into the moment. 'Reading you, Fox 24.'

'Heading for target. See you on the home run.'

Alec glanced above to the huge bombers they were escorting on a night-intruder mission to a Munich munitions factory the intelligence services had caught wind of through an agent in Paris. Ahead, the horizon glowed gold where the advance party had shed their incendiary bombs, lighting up the targets for the Lancasters that now began to peel away from their escort. Alec executed a steep turn away from the plumes of acrid smoke, but there was no escaping the horrific smell of those caught at the tail end of the chain, the innocents ordered to do a night shift at the factory, or hurrying home to put the children to bed, in the wrong place at the wrong time. Collateral, they would no doubt be described as in Whitehall.

'Scoutmaster to scouts,' Alec called into the radio to the Mosquito pilots flying in formation behind him, as they approached the nearby airbase where Messerschmitts were already scrambling. 'You two chaps stay low, and I'll pick off anything that tries to slice in from above.'

Flashes of anti-aircraft fire crackled and fizzed as guns were trained on the incoming predators. The Mosquitoes came in low, strafing the runway with bullets and scattering figures rushing to embark the fleet of fighter planes lined up on the ground. One of Alec's men let loose a bomb that instantly laid waste to two aircraft and an armoured personnel carrier.

'Bandit at three o'clock, sir,' Jock called out, as a Focke-Wulf approached from behind and let rip a volley of gunfire.

'Hold on to your sporran, Jock,' Alec said, pulling their

plane into a steep climb then corkscrewing away from the threat.

A burst of bullets came from almost directly ahead as another appeared, and Alec pressed his thumb on the machine-gun trigger. He struck instantly, fire streaming from the nose of the German aircraft. It spun towards the ground, one wing ripped from its fuselage as it skidded towards a hangar before bursting into flames.

The radio crackled into life and Alec pulled himself back into operation-leader mode. 'Mission accomplished,' the Lancaster pilot said. 'Scouts at ease.' The horizon was now blanketed in flames, the work of the heavy bombers done as they turned their empty bellies towards home.

Alec quickly ordered the retreat, urging his squadron comrades to stay close by on the home run. 'Over to you, Jock. Let's get this old girl back to base, shall we?'

'Aye, sir.'

He switched channels, checking in with the control tower back in the East Anglian fens. 'Heading home. All scouts in good order.'

'Excellent news. Make contact again when you're drying your feet, and we'll get the kettle on,' replied the WAAF on duty that night.

'Roger and out.' He looked at the clock – they should cross the British coast in time for an early breakfast.

One more mission down, one more mission nearer the end of this damned war.

The Hall was as quiet as any twenty-four-hour operation could ever be as the dawn chorus burst from the ancient trees in the surrounding grounds. Verity had slept poorly in her attic room. As soon as she had heard which squadron would be escorting the raid on the Munich factory, she had known it would be Alec up there: he never missed a sortie. And this particular one was entirely due to intelligence received from Agent Colette, for whom Verity had assumed responsibility when she took up her role as assistant to Chief Staff Officer Tremayne twelve months ago. She was doubly invested in the success of this mission.

Verity was astounded at how easily she had slipped into life at Whaddon Hall, and how little she missed her old life. Not Bill and the children, of course – she thought of them daily – but the grinding dullness of her pre-war routine was something she was glad to leave behind.

She glanced at the letter on her bedside table, only a few words from husband to wife blacked out by the censors – probably just little details such as the weather or sightings of porpoises, knowing Bill, but ones that could be dangerous in the wrong hands. Verity had read, however, that Bill would be back in London briefly in a few weeks, and that he very much looked forward to the four of them spending time together as a family. Verity was torn: it would be lovely, of course, but could she trail around Primrose Hill with bored children, knowing her girls in the field relied on her? Take herself off shopping with Fred? Dust off her pinny and set to in the kitchen while Bill read his paper? She couldn't help a ridiculous fear that if she took off the uniform Bill did not even know she wore, she would never put it back on again.

A figure trotted through the early-morning mist hovering above the lawns, bearing a file that could only mean fresh communications had been received. Verity quickly dressed, patting her hair into shape and straightening her tie before applying a slash of red lipstick. She was already downstairs by the time Tremayne appeared at his office door.

'Just beat me to it,' he said. 'Come inside.' By the embers in the hearth and the mess of paperwork on his desk, Verity guessed he too had suffered a wakeful night. 'First news first,' he said, waving her towards a chair. 'This is in from the Wing Commander of 614 Squadron.' He glanced at her, knowing the familial connection.

She scanned the report, seeing that the Mosquito squadron's support of a Lancaster mission had been successful. All aircraft were on their way back to base and the factory rendered inoperable. 'Thank you, sir. Good to see the tail end of the intel from Colette.'

'Indeed. This should put a stop to the Jerries' production of those latest submarine torpedoes for a while. Dare say your old man will be rather relieved too. Perhaps you'd like to let Colette know she didn't put herself at risk for nothing.'

'Of course.'

'Now, let's get some breakfast and you can brief me on the new intake. I have to get off back to Berkshire this evening, or Felicity will tear a strip off me.' He looked at her. 'And you could do with a few days off, Cooper. Any chance that husband of yours will get shore leave?'

'Well, as it happens, he will be back in London soon, but . . .'

'That's settled, then. As soon as he's back, have a break. You've earned it.'

The subject closed, Verity followed him out of the office and across to the dining room where early risers were tucking into bacon and eggs from a nearby farm. Verity had a flashback to family breakfasts where the children squabbled and Bill refused to put down his newspaper and back her up. She had a little time to prepare herself for home life, but was it enough?

The return trip was uneventful, the mass of land broken only by the occasional smoke and fire of other Allied raids until eventually the silvery-grey surface of the North Sea appeared. The cover of night dissipated into milky dawn as they crossed the shipping lanes that had become the backdrop to a long and gruelling war of attrition, the seabed swarming with deadly submarines. Alec caught the shadows of a fleet of Navy warships and thought of Bill. No wonder Verity was so touchy these days.

His concentration momentarily lost, he was surprised by the flash of sunlight bouncing off the cockpit of a small plane approaching from the north. The German Stuka must have been returning from a night sortie over the North Sea and had the trio of British Mosquitoes in its sights, spraying an opportunistic line of bullets across the wooden fuselage of Alec's aircraft before banking steeply and making a tight turn away.

'Damn.' Alec watched the fuel gauge drop as the damaged drop tank began shedding its load. 'As the crow flies, Jock. No hanging about now. The last tank's pretty low.'

'Nearly there, sir,' Jock said. 'Shift her eleven degrees east.'

Alec suddenly ducked at the sound of an explosion to the right, shielding his face to avoid the shattered glass that burst into the cockpit. 'Bastard must have hit the engine,' he shouted to Jock, activating the right-side fire extinguisher and switching to single-engine mode as he looked out towards the fire engulfing the massive Merlin, its propellers now flaming Catherine wheels.

They were only a few miles from base, roads and houses visible as he eased back on the throttle and lowered the landing gear in preparation. 'Cricket 39 to control. Preparing to land. Fire crew at the ready – one engine hit, fuel status critical.' He searched for the strips of lights that would guide them safely into the airfield in the half light. 'Hold on, Jocky boy, might be a bumpy landing.'

Finally the runway came into view and he slammed on the brakes, pushing the engine into reverse and leaning hard into the back of his seat as the wheels hit the ground, bouncing once before he forced the damaged craft into an ungraceful, lopsided halt and fire engines raced towards them. He quickly undid the safety harness and unstrapped his oxygen mask, turning to Jock. The blood had drained from the young Scot's face, his boyish freckles a vivid rash on his pale complexion. 'Come on, man. Let's get you out,' Alec said, shaking Jock by the shoulder as ladders were pulled up on either side of the cockpit.

'Head down, sir,' came a voice to his left. 'We're coming in.'

An axe began breaking the glass on Alec's side of the cockpit, and as the ground crew pulled him from his seat, he shouted to the rescue team across the other side. 'What are you waiting for?' he yelled. 'This man needs a doctor.' As one of the men shook his head, Alec followed his gaze to the long shard of glass penetrating the navigator's neck.

'He's already dead, sir. We need to get you out before something blows.'

Rough hands grabbed him by the shoulders and pulled him out of the plane, away from Jock's lifeless body. He would not be best man at his navigator's wedding, he now realised; instead of giving a speech, he would be reading yet another eulogy.

He couldn't do it any longer. There had to be a better way to fight this war.

20

October 1943

Sophie reached up to unhook the aerial wire draped across the fly-dusted light fitting and around empty hooks on the bare walls. The storeroom above an old ironmongery in the unfashionable twentieth arrondissement had so far found itself outside the range of the black detector vans that prowled around the city. Only a fortnight ago, two of Sophie's own agents had been arrested mid transmission, and she was taking no chances, transmitting only to the schedule agreed with her godmother.

She needed Kestrel back from London, with the promise of more radios, more agents and more cash. A lot more cash. She was now paying rent to three landlords around the city: one apartment was used to house downed airmen, one as a safe house for Jews and resistance members and another to store equipment. Yet still she needed more apartments, more 'letter boxes' and more couriers.

She wound the aerial neatly into its casing and collected the earth wire from where she had attached it to the radiator, then took the crystal out of the radio set and hid it in her hat lining. She lifted the radio into its suitcase and placed it in a wooden tea chest covered with an old sheet, a box of tap washers on top.

With curfew only an hour away, Sophie locked the door behind her and checked the dark stairwell before making her way to the alley where she had parked her bicycle behind the overfull dustbins. Her music case tucked inside the bicycle's wicker basket, if stopped she would say she was returning from a rehearsal.

Her route took her through the Marais, the Jewish quarter that now was almost devoid of all life. Many shops had been boarded up, yellow Stars of David painted across them, anti-semitic posters hanging in flayed shreds from lampposts and broken-down doors. The empty homes and businesses here were of interest only to passing vagrants, now the looters had done their work.

Sophie braked, dropping her feet to the ground as she found herself at the end of rue Ferdinand Duval, where Hanne had been gunned down in cold blood outside the family apartment. Was it better that the Goldmanns never saw the buses arrive in the Marais that awful day in July last year, to take away the Jewish mothers and children left behind in the last round-up? The stories of the Vélodrome d'Hiver where they had been kept without food, water or sanitation for days on end before deportation, were beyond comprehension. Those few left in Paris were forced to work in the former department store that was now a sorting depot for the property of Jewish families who would never return.

Sophie hadn't been able to save Hanne, even if she had given money to help the 'Cherry Road', the network that rescued orphaned Jewish children from Paris. She found some small comfort in knowing that the little Goldmann girl had made it safely to England, thanks to the schoolteacher and her husband at the heart of the network. She had received word from Lisbon that Fabien had arrived safely, and although she wished she had persuaded Jean-Paul to leave with him, Sophie was glad to have this great bear of a man at her side – solid, reliable and angry enough to keep fighting.

For a moment she imagined she heard the sweet, honeyed tone of the Italian violin that had been an extension of Hanne. Where was that instrument now? Was it being played by German hands, or burned for firewood to keep a family warm for a few minutes?

If Sophie ever had doubts about her courage and her determination to keep working, she only had to see the empty, ghostly windows that had rained tears of shattered glass on to the street below, and she knew she wouldn't stop until she was dragged into an interrogation cell.

Besides, London was sending more agents on the next Lysander flight, the new night-time agent-pick-up shuttle service. There was no room for amateurs, she had warned Tremayne. The young woman in Lyon who had been tortured by Klaus Barbie should never have been sent out. Sophie had taken just one look at her shaking hands, heard the heedless slide into an English curse as she dropped her cup of coffee, and had known there would be trouble.

As she made her way south across the bridge spanning the inky-black Seine, its lamps cold and dark in the blackout, she paused on the isle suspended between the two banks. She looked up, past the darkened windows of the Sainte-Chapelle, its famous stained glass long since removed and hidden away, as high above Paris a flock of heavy British bombers flew overhead. She wondered if their mission was the result of the hurriedly typed Morse messages she'd sent to London, another link in the chain that began with a loose tongue at a cocktail party and ended in a fireball dropped by a British pilot.

As ever when a British plane flew overhead, her thoughts were drawn to Alec, and she smiled as she remembered those precious few days together, buried in the English countryside. Their honeymoon, they had called it, until they could be together properly. And they would: she knew it. She had to believe they would find one another again, or she could not carry on this life.

'Sorry we kept you waiting, old chap. All the team were out on ops last night, so it's a bit of a late start this morning.' Wing Commander Carlisle waved Alec towards a stiff-backed chair next to a table littered with maps and unfiled paperwork. The man himself looked as though he had slept in his uniform, his shirt unbuttoned and grey stubble peppering his chin. 'Battle of Britain?' he said, flicking through Alec's file. 'Good man.'

'I flew Hurricanes in '40 and moved on to Mosquitoes after that.'

'Got yourself a couple of gongs already, I see. Distinguished Flying Cross – impressive. They don't hand those out to any old airman. So what brings you here? Surely flying a Mozzie takes some beating?'

'She's a fine aircraft, sir, but I'm looking to do something different.'

The senior officer looked at him. 'Slaughter fatigue, eh?'

Alec nodded. 'Something like that.'

'Can't blame a fellow for that. Was a Spitfire pilot myself in '39 and '40. Shooting young fellows out of the sky and seeing my muckers blown to pieces. Dreadful work.' He shook his head. 'So you're interested in Special Duties. Think you'd like to have a go at what we do here?'

'To be perfectly honest, sir, I'm not entirely certain what you do here.'

Carlisle narrowed his eyes, taking in Alec's burns. 'Not looking for something less dangerous, I hope? There's nothing easy about the work 161 Squadron does.'

'I'm no coward, sir.'

'Of course not. But I have to warn you our pilots can get into some nasty scrapes.' He put the file down and lifted his feet on to the desk. 'I can see you are very well qualified for this role: you've got far more than the five hundred hours of night flying we need, and your strike record speaks volumes about your skill. As does your CO, by the way, who will be jolly sorry to lose you. Tell me,' he said, 'have you ever flown a Lysander?'

Alec was surprised: the small workhorse aircraft was used to photograph shipping in the Channel and drop Navy supplies, its pilots often teased for having an easy life. 'No, sir.'

Carlisle gestured for Alec to join him at the ops table, where a map of France and the English Channel lay open. 'It's our job,' he explained, 'to get agents in and out of France by night.' He pointed to a spot on the Sussex coast. 'For two weeks a month, either side of the full moon, we are based here at RAF Tangmere. We are put up in civilian accommodation nearby, and the Lysanders kept at the far end of the airfield, out of sight.'

'What sort of agents?' Alec asked.

'SIS – Secret Intelligence Service spies, and SOE, naturally. You know of them?'

'Of course,' said Alec. The Special Operations Executive had been set up by Churchill to play havoc with German military activity, bombing railways and ambushing patrols.

'We drop them into France then pick up any incoming Joes, as we call them, and intelligence for the return trip.'

'And all by night.'

'Correct. Our pilots are guided in by a series of flares and have less than ten minutes on the ground before taking off. Assuming the ground is not waterlogged and there are no Germans waiting to ambush you. They fly without lights or navigator, risk being shot down the minute they hit the French coast.' He looked at Alec. 'How's your French, by the way?'

'Pretty good.'

'Good enough to make your way back through France if you have to?'

'I'd say so. I had a French nanny as a child and spent a year travelling around France a while back. And my . . . well, my fiancée, I suppose, is French.' It sounded so real when he said it, that he could imagine she was waiting back at the cottage for him.

'We'd best look after you for her, in that case.'

'So I'm in?'

'I haven't put you off joining us?'

'Wild horses wouldn't stop me, sir.'

'How about wild Germans?'

'Let them try.'

Carlisle clapped him on the back. 'Good fellow. Better get you trained up, then, hadn't we?'

*

Amy watched a passenger airliner scud across London, skimming the dome of Saint Paul's and the ever-encroaching peaks of the high-rise office buildings overtaking the City, aware that she was sitting close to where the Primrose Hill anti-aircraft battery had been positioned to counter-attack from German bombers only fifty years earlier.

'It's strange how the wheels turn sometimes,' Verity said suddenly, the breeze tugging at her silk scarf. 'I thought I'd done my best in keeping them apart, but if you believe in such a thing, fate had a way of holding those two together, even if they didn't know it. Of course I had no idea Alec had left his squadron – he could no more talk to me about his work than I about mine.'

'You were Sophie's assigned case officer by then?'

'"Case officer" sounds so cold, so businesslike, but my agents and I built up relationships across enemy lines. They used to call me their "godmother". Even though I'd been instrumental in the recruitment and training of many of them, there were some I never met, but still there was a closeness between us.'

'And were they mostly successful?'

Verity sighed. 'To some extent. You must understand that things were pretty desperate in France. The Germans had picked off most of our operators in '43 – some were turned in by Vichy-supported French, some by their own colleagues. Life expectancy for an agent was down to six weeks and the recruitment criteria were relaxed to the point where we were sending out inexperienced, unsuitable operatives. Pressure was on to provide Sophie with the back-up she needed, as she took more and more risks, and so we had no choice but to send whoever we could, especially if they spoke French. There was one girl in particular, a radio operator. She failed almost everything in her training – it was like sending a child out there.'

'It must have been incredibly hard to send them off on active duty,' Amy said, recalling agents such as Violette Szabo and Noor Inayat Khan, the desperate communications from their families trying to discover what had happened to these young women who never returned.

'It was the hardest thing I have ever done. I knew exactly where they were and what they were doing, whilst their own mothers and husbands thought they were working in a nice safe office somewhere. So many Allied successes originated from the bravery of those young men and women, so many lives were saved. And so many lost.'

They sat in silence for a moment, distant sirens cutting through the whisper of wind among the trees scattered on the lower flanks of the hill.

Eventually Verity turned to Amy. 'I think I'd like to go home now.'

Amy was sure that as Verity stood unsteadily, she appeared smaller, frailer, and that her hand gripped Amy's arm a little tighter than before as they made their way slowly back to Chalcot Crescent.

'The joys of buying meals for one.'

Amy turned around, surprised to see Jay standing beside her at the ready-meals aisle.

'Although I have to say that if you are going to go all-out wallowing, nothing can beat the roast dinner for one.'

Amy held out the chicken curry she'd been staring at for five minutes. 'I can't face another plate of fish fingers. Sometimes you just need something grown-up, you know?'

Jay nodded. 'And nothing says "grown-up" more than an orange chicken curry with ready-cooked rice. That looks disgusting, by the way. I'd stick with fish fingers. I've kind of come to like them now.'

'You've got a youngster too?'

'Yeah. I mean, Sam would probably prefer the curry – he has very sophisticated tastes for a six-year-old – but I insist on fish fingers.'

'It's Jay, right? From the shop?'

'Amy? Yeah, I'm digging out recordings by dodgy Nazi pianists for you.'

'Of course. Any luck?'

He pushed his glasses back up his nose. 'Well, yeah, actually. Managed to track a couple of things down. I should have them in the shop in a few days.' He looked around. 'No daughter today?'

'She's at my friend's. They've gone for a pizza and then to the cinema. I've been working.'

'On a Saturday?'

'I was interviewing someone.'

'To do with the Nazi pianist thing?'

'Well, yes, actually.'

'That is so cool.' He hesitated. 'I don't suppose you fancy a coffee sometime?'

'Oh.'

He screwed up his eyes. 'Not a date coffee. Just a coffee. A cup of coffee. In a café. Sorry – say no if you can't or if you think I'm pushy. I'm just really interested in hearing more about this Sophie Clément stuff. I mean, if you're allowed to talk about it?'

'I guess I am.'

'Or we could just take the kids to the park and drink shit coffee in the playground?'

Amy hesitated. What was there to lose? 'OK, you're on. Playground it is. After school next week sometime? Wednesday, if that's any good?'

'Wednesday works for us. And Amy, I hope you don't think it's . . .' He frowned. 'What I mean to say is, I really liked Michael and I'd like to get to know you too. As a friend. I love meeting new people, but the last six months . . . well, I'm not looking for a girlfriend. Sorry, now I sound like an arse.'

Amy laughed. 'It's fine. I'm not either. I mean, a boyfriend. But a new friend would be great. And actually it's good for Holly to meet new children.'

'Cool.' He took the ready meal from her. 'And please don't buy that. Not if you still want to be here next Wednesday.'

21

October 1943

Verity laid her glasses on the desk and rubbed her eyes, which ached from the hour she had just spent decoding the morning's messages. She looked down at the matrix she had formed from the most recent cipher from the port of Brest, transmitted by a young French seamstress employed by the German navy. Whilst she quietly mended their life jackets, German submariners chatted amongst themselves about upcoming raids, oblivious to the woman within earshot. Once she had identified the cipher key, five transpositions of the message had returned it to its original form, which Verity now typed up for Tremayne to call through to the Admiralty: '3 U-boats leave Brest 2200 hours 19 November, target merchant convoy 49° 10' N, 20° 05' W.'

It could be Bill's ship shot out of the sea, she thought, looking out across the grounds of the Hall, where staff shared cigarette breaks in the pale sunshine. She wondered whether his third year at sea would cure him of his dream of retiring to the coast and spare her tramping up and down shingly beaches, obsessing about the weather and other people's dogs. As she thought about it, however, she realised she would retire anywhere with Bill, as long as he came home safely.

Meanwhile it would be back to the bank for him, and back to the kitchen for Verity. Bill was awfully old fashioned, but times had changed and so had she. During his last visit home, instead of making the most of one another's company, they had squabbled as he accused her of enjoying the war. He just wanted to sit down to a home-cooked meal with his wife and children. Was that too much to ask? She had looked at his face, drawn and tired. She couldn't know what he had seen, although the reports she read spoke of men perishing in burning oil slicks, whole ships going down with not a single survivor. No, it probably wasn't too much to ask, and she vowed to be nicer during his upcoming shore leave.

As she stamped 'TOP SECRET' in red across the envelope to Tremayne, she looked up suddenly as a Wren tapped on the door and poked her head through at Verity's invitation to come in. The young woman could barely conceal her smile. 'You're wanted in Sir Richard's office, ma'am,' she said. 'Straight away.'

'What is it, Dixon?'

'It's Kestrel, ma'am. He's back.'

The heightened buzz as Verity crossed the hall was palpable, the thrill of an agent's safe return bringing a bounce to the step of even the most serious staffers.

'Bit early, I know, but care to join us?' Tremayne said, waving the whisky decanter as she closed his office door behind her.

'I think I can be persuaded.' She turned towards the man sprawling in the wing-backed chair beside the fireplace. 'Welcome back, Kestrel,' she said, shaking his hand.

'We're only borrowing him,' Tremayne said, handing the man a glass of amber liquid. 'Sorry, old chap. As soon as you've debriefed fully, you're back over there.'

'Just glad to be back long enough to get a few nights' sleep without worrying about the Hun breaking down my bedroom door.' He laughed, seeing the shock on their faces. 'No, seriously, it's good to be home.'

He yawned and rubbed a hand over his stubbled face, still filthy from the long and dangerous journey to the landing strip. 'Suppose you want a summary before you'll let a chap have a bath and a kip?'

'Afraid so,' said Tremayne. 'Then I'll see if we can't get Cook to rustle you up some eggs and bacon.'

'Throw in another glass of that single malt and you've got a deal.' Kestrel heaved himself up from the armchair, and as he lifted the suitcase on to Tremayne's desk Verity saw dried blood on the back of his hand, the silhouette of the agency-issued Colt .45 inside his jacket pocket.

'Tricky journey?' she asked.

He shrugged. 'Bit of a scuffle on the ground. Nothing we couldn't handle.'

'Still, we need to think about changing the landing site. Cooper, borrow someone from the RAF to help find a suitable strip. Within thirty miles of the city,' Tremayne went on as Verity pulled a notebook from her pocket and began scribbling. 'Nowhere too claggy, preferably with a friendly farmer and an active unit nearby, and no more than two hours' walk from a railway station. You've got that?'

'Sir.' She nodded.

'And while you're at it,' Kestrel said, 'we need more agents, more flights, more supplies. Any chance those chaps running the Lysander pick-ups can send more planes? Things are getting hot on the ground, and we need to rotate personnel. Besides, the amount of intel we're receiving is more than we can send at present. I'd hate Colette to have to decide what simply won't fit in the plane.'

Tremayne nodded. 'I agree. We've already persuaded the Air Ministry to allocate more crew.'

'Anyway,' Kestrel said, unclipping the locks on the case, 'first things first. These are for you, ma'am. Special delivery from Colette.' He pulled out a tissue-paper parcel, tied with a ribbon.

She opened it carefully, smiling at the bottle of *Soir de Paris*, knowing it was Colette's own preferred scent. A note had been attached:

My dearest godmother

Wear this and think of me – I cannot bear to think of you smelling of violet water and wet tweed, like most Englishwomen.

Send coffee and whisky – your British pilots are drinking me dry.

Félicitations,

Your goddaughter

'Oh, and mustn't forget you, old chap. Trust they taught you to catch in the First Eleven,' Kestrel said, tossing a small bottle of Armagnac towards Tremayne. 'And here's some perfume for your old lady. Colette seemed to think this was her favourite,' he said, and pulled out a bottle of Nina Ricci.

'Sorry to say I haven't a clue, but I'm sure Felicity will be delighted.'

Tremayne waved Verity towards one of the seats facing the chair where Kestrel stretched his long legs out in front of him, the soles of his shoes still showing traces of French mud. She'd heard that the family who housed agents in their home near to the Lysander base would scrape the shoes of incoming agents and spread it on their vegetable garden, so that French agents could quite literally enjoy a meal grown on French soil.

'Sorry to throw you straight in, Kestrel,' he said, 'but you know we didn't get you back here just to deliver presents?'

Kestrel laughed, taking a cigarette from his jacket pocket and allowing Tremayne to light it for him. 'Hardly. Although I think you'll be rather pleased with what Colette has sent you. That woman,' he said, taking a long drag on the cigarette, 'has balls of steel. Sorry, ma'am.'

'No offence taken,' Verity said, smiling.

'So what's the overall personnel picture like over there?' Tremayne asked.

'We've got one of our men employed as a dockhand in Bordeaux. Trustworthy, French, brother a POW in Germany. There's another down in Marseille, again reporting back on German maritime movement. He supplied the report that allowed the Navy to bomb that arms shipment to North Africa.'

Tremayne nodded. 'Jolly good job too. We've our work cut out down there.'

'Then there's the garage mechanic near the Spanish border. He's part of the Comet escape line, finds shelter for the airmen we help on their way down to Gibraltar, looks out for our people crossing to Spain. Oh, and we've recently recruited a policeman in Pau who supplies false papers. It's all a darn sight harder since the Hun overran the whole country.'

'And Paris?'

Kestrel rubbed his hand across his eyes. 'Paris is difficult now they've taken out most of our radio operators there.'

Tremayne nodded, Verity reading in his face the anguish of the night they had stayed up waiting in vain for contact from the two young female operatives sent out weeks earlier, who had barely lasted a full month before they were arrested. To say things were difficult in Paris was a desperate understatement. The Germans had taken to cutting the electricity supply in parts of the city where they believed operators were transmitting. If radio activity was picked up once the supply was cut off, a detector van would be dispatched to the area, where it could pinpoint the source of the signal almost to the apartment. The young women had been sitting ducks, their lines open as they tried to reach London. One of the women had held firm, despite days of torture at the SS headquarters in avenue Foch. The other, barely twenty-one years old, had capitulated, giving the Germans all operator codes and transmission schedules. Since then, it had been assumed that every transmission was filtered through German channels, engineered to mislead the Allies.

'She desperately needs more radios over there. More operators. New codes. Couriers. Anything you can give her.'

'We're doing what we can. In fact, we're sending more personnel as soon as they've finished their training.'

'Sir—' Verity began, anxious to stop him making promises about the new intake, at least one of whom concerned her greatly.

'As I say, leave it with us,' Tremayne interrupted, and Verity caught a rare hint of irritation in his voice.

'Right you are, old boy,' Kestrel went on. 'But she's extremely vulnerable.'

'You don't think they're on to her?' Sir Richard stopped pacing, his arms folded and the fingers of one hand tapping the sleeve of his jacket.

Kestrel shook his head. 'Not yet. The Germans love her more than ever, even though that visit they arranged for her at the prisoner-of-war camp backfired on them completely.'

'How so?' Verity asked, seizing a slim opportunity to find out more about the woman she knew so well, yet not at all. There were rumours at the Hall that Colette was a dancer or an actress, a high-profile member of Parisian society.

Kestrel glanced at Tremayne, who subtly shook his head, so that Verity knew she could expect to hear nothing she didn't already know about her agent. 'Our man on the inside snapped her posing with a bunch of smiling POWS, giving us photographs of them all to use for fake ID. Sources on the ground managed to get four British airmen out and seven Frenchmen. I tell you, she's quite brilliant. Speaking of which,' he said, 'this is what you're really after.' He leaned down and pulled from the case a sheaf of completed questionnaires.

Tremayne leafed through them and passed them on to Verity, who glanced at the scrawled answers after each of the questions SIS had compiled for their agents: troop movements, aircraft spotted, maritime schedules, small details that would be relayed to the War Office and integrated into Churchill and Roosevelt's strategy for an invasion of occupied France.

'And, of course, this.' Kestrel handed Tremayne a tatty French newspaper.

'*Je Suis Partout*?' Tremayne said. 'Isn't this the collaborationist rag?'

Kestrel nodded. 'Awful antisemitic stuff in there. *I Am Everywhere* is a pretty appropriate name, given that Paris is crawling with German filth.' He nodded towards the paper. 'Page seventeen.'

'Close the shutters, would you, Cooper?' Tremayne said. Verity pulled the heavy wooden shutters across the tall windows and he reached for a torch. As Tremayne held the ultraviolet light over the paper, a faint lilac scrawl appeared, the typically French copperplate distorted by having been written down blind. He looked up at Kestrel. 'It's in English. You know what this is?'

He shook his head. 'Less I'm told, less I can be questioned about.'

'Good man. Let's keep it that way. Listen, why don't you scrounge that breakfast off Cook, and we'll catch up later.'

'Shan't argue with that.' Kestrel heaved himself up out of the chair, wincing with pain. 'Oh, just one more thing, sir. She asked if you've sent the letter yet. She said you'd know what she meant.'

'The letter?' Verity said, looking at Tremayne.

'A letter she wanted me to hand on to some fellow.'

Verity felt her stomach drop. So Colette had a love. It was always so much better if the agents had no romantic entanglement. 'And have you?'

He shook his head. 'Not while they're both . . .' He hesitated. 'Well, no point yet.'

Kestrel hoisted his canvas bag over his shoulder. 'I'll pass that on when I get back. But right now all I can think about is a hot bath and clean sheets.'

Verity and Tremayne waited whilst an ATS sergeant arrived to take the agent to his quarters, and Verity couldn't help but smile at his attempt to persuade the young woman to join him for a pint at the local pub that evening, as she led him up the wide marble staircase.

Tremayne headed back to his desk, motioning for Verity to pull up a chair beside him. 'Let's take a proper look at this, shall we?'

The message covered a few square inches of the paper, carefully avoiding overwriting the photographs of what looked like German soldiers on a tourists' tour of Paris. As Tremayne read out the English text, Verity wrote down each word, until a chilling picture emerged of the next phase of the Germans' campaign.

Tremayne turned to Verity. 'I need to put in calls to the War Office and the Air Chief Marshal's office immediately. Make sure Colette is safe when you make contact later, would you?'

'Of course, sir,' Verity answered, understanding his concern. With each piece of classified information she shared with London, Colette put herself in an ever more dangerous position.

They were little more than boys in uniforms, trying to impress the remaining stalwarts of the Marquise de Chabot's soirée. A few writers and playwrights who early on had placed their bets on a long German occupation now found themselves part of a strange new social circle. At its heart were German officers who had read Rimbaud and Hugo and possibly even admired the Poussins in the Louvre in a former life. They were intellectuals, conversationalists, popular with their new French friends. There was not a ballet, opera nor private view that did not issue invitations to the German military command, the likes of the powder-faced old dragon Chabot flitting around them like moths to the flame. Or rats around sewers, Sophie preferred to think.

It was past one in the morning, and Sophie longed to slip out of the Maggy Rouff black satin gown and unclip the diamond serpent brooch Becker had given her. The young German seemed content merely to enjoy her company and to show her off, and had never made her feel physically threatened, for which she was grateful. Becker also served as a useful barrier between herself and some of the more predatory officers she had encountered.

Most, however, were as foolish as Becker when it came to a beautiful woman: the wider her eyes and the more incredulous she seemed at what they had been discussing that evening, the more they felt compelled to impress her. 'A new weapon? Surely not. It can destroy a city at what range? You're teasing me. I know I'm just a silly woman, but even I can tell you're exaggerating . . . Oh really, as if you could build an underground base on the Normandy coast without the British finding out. And in such a pretty town . . .'

And then Seelman had arrived unexpectedly at the party and the little group had quickly dissolved, like children caught misbehaving. Sophie had made her excuses and gone to the bathroom, leaning her hands on the marble sink as she looked at her reflection, repeating to herself everything she needed to remember for the morning transmission. She made a note to contact the seamstress in Brest and commission a report into industrial traffic into the port, changes of routine, new personnel. In that way, Sophie could put together enough intelligence to force an attack similar to that which would be taking place any day now.

Becker was in animated conversation with Seelman as she returned to the drawing room, and looked distinctly uncomfortable in the other man's company. He puzzled her, this Nazi who had audibly gasped when they were out walking together and had seen the first of the yellow stars Jewish Parisians were suddenly forced to wear; who had disappeared for a week after the atrocities at the Vél d'Hiver. And yet where so many Frenchmen had avoided German statutory work orders and gone underground to work for their country, this man had chosen to follow orders. And now she needed him to take her home.

'Ah, Mademoiselle Clément,' Seelman said, kissing her gloved fingers as she joined them. 'When may I expect you to play the Steinway piano in my new apartment?'

'Soon. Nothing would give me greater pleasure.'

Becker attempted a light laugh. 'I hope you're not attempting to steal her from me, sir?'

Before Seelman could respond, a young sergeant appeared at his side. 'Sir,' he said breathlessly. 'I must speak with you. Urgently.'

Sophie strained to hear what was said as the man whispered into Seelman's ear, catching just enough to tell her that the newspaper had found its way to London with Kestrel.

'Darling Bruno,' she said, placing her hand on Becker's arm. 'I'm so tired. Please take me home.' She tipped her head on one side and smiled at him, her lips a soft moue.

'I'm afraid I have to go. There's been some rather bad news.'

'Worse than a woman having to make her way home alone?' She knew she sounded ridiculous but had to keep up the little-girl act, especially in front of Seelman.

'There's been a raid—'

'That's enough, Becker,' the older man said, putting his hand heavily on the captain's shoulder. 'We don't want to trouble Mademoiselle Clément with the dirty business of war. Besides, tongues have been loosened enough already, don't you think?' He stared at her for a moment, before clicking his fingers, calling over the butler. 'Fetch a taxi for the lady. It is time she went home.'

Had he discovered the source of the leak? She had not been the only one at the table at La Tour d'Argent last week, taking in the view of Paris through its sixth-floor panoramic windows as they dined on pressed duck and dusty bottles of Château Margaux: any of the French businessmen there were fool enough to boast about their lucrative new contract, and Becker's obvious anxiety reflected his potential role in this. In the meantime she would need to exercise discretion around Seelman.

'Good evening to you both,' she said. 'And Colonel Seelman, do let me know when I may visit.'

'Don't worry, Mademoiselle Clément,' he replied, his grey eyes fixed on hers. 'You may be sure to receive an invitation from me.'

22

'Here's the report you requested, ma'am.'

Verity waited until the young woman had closed the door quietly behind her, then opened the sealed manila folder.

'Physical training: Fail,' she read. 'Wireless training: Adequate. Psychiatric report: Subject presented high levels of anxiety at odds with temperament required of operational agent. Firearms training: Recommend repeat course. Simulated interrogation: Disclosed classified information after twenty minutes. Conclusion: Unsuitable for field work.'

Early recruits had been very much of a type, Tremayne preferring graduates headhunted from government and the military, who would understand discipline and dedication. That they were fluent in the language of the country they were to be deployed in was a given, but he especially sought out those with dual nationality. He had been easily persuaded of the value of women in the field, and Verity's stable of female agents had steadily grown.

Now, however, it seemed that anyone with a French second cousin thrice removed was eligible for active duty behind enemy lines. She closed the file and tapped it on her desk, straightening the papers inside. She needed to speak with this young candidate sooner rather than later, and there was no time like the present.

Verity eventually found the young woman on a stone bench outside, almost hidden by an overgrown laurel hedge, fallen leaves pooled around its base. 'Nine three seven?' Verity said.

The woman jumped at hearing her candidate number, then looked away, dabbing at her eyes with a handkerchief. She was barely twenty. Were they really sending children out there now? No wonder the girl had cracked under interrogation: in her Peter-Pan-collared blue dress, she looked more suited to the nursery than to the theatre of war.

Verity joined her on the cold bench. 'Aren't you frozen out here?'

The girl shook her head.

Verity hesitated. 'I've just had your results in,' she said eventually. She was fond of the young woman, and knew she'd take this news badly.

'I'll get it right next time, I promise.' The girl's East London vowels tripped over themselves in their hurry to come out. 'I just wasn't expecting the interrogation.'

Verity looked at her wide blue eyes, the long lashes that still bore a sprinkling of tears. She knew how utterly horrible the surprise night-time interrogations were – who wouldn't struggle with being dragged from their bed and waterboarded in a cellar? – but the simulation was child's play in comparison to the treatment an agent could expect. And Daphne Wilson had capitulated in minutes.

'That's rather the point, though, don't you see?' Verity said, swallowing her exasperation. 'The Germans will not warn you they're coming. We have to think of your safety,' she said gently, 'and that of the agents whose lives would be at risk if intelligence is leaked.'

Fresh tears sprang from the young woman's eyes, and she angrily scrubbed them away with the heel of her hand. 'Our dad always said I talk too much. "Daphne Wilson," he'd say, "you 'ave a mouth like a runaway racehorse."'

Verity held up one hand. 'Please, whilst you are here you cannot use your real name. We need to know you can keep yourself safe.'

She closed her eyes. 'I've done it again, haven't I?'

Verity nodded. 'I hope you can see why I have concerns recommending you for service.'

'But I want to go.'

'You can do your bit here.' She tapped the file sitting on her knee. 'You passed the radio operator's module. With a bit more work on your Morse, we can easily find a place for you.'

'There's only one number I keep forgetting.'

'I know, but it's one of the numbers in your candidate name, so if you can't remember the code for seven, how are we ever to know it's you? And what if you were to transmit coordinates for a drop, and they included the number seven?'

'But I know it, honestly. Dash dot dot dot.'

Verity raised her eyes heavenwards. 'It's dash dash dot dot dot.'

'But you need me. I'm half French: my mum was born in Paris and I spent most of my school holidays there.'

In theory Daphne was textbook spy material: young and attractive enough not to be taken seriously by the Germans, and with a native command of the French language. Her family had perished in the Blitz in the East End, and so her emotional ties were limited. If her results in physical training were less than stellar, that might not have mattered in Paris, where she would not be required to execute manoeuvres on rough terrain, but there was nothing one could do about her lack of steel.

'Please 'ave a word for me, ma'am?' the young woman said.

'I can't make any promises.'

Daphne looked out across the jigsaw of fields and coppice beyond the boundary of the Hall. 'I lost everything. I can't bear to do nothing.'

Verity thought of her own family: Alec airborne somewhere over German soil, Bill at sea, her children becoming more and more accustomed to their new life in the countryside. Was there a single family in Europe that hadn't been torn apart by this dreadful war?

The Parc de Vincennes beyond the imposing fortress was as beautiful as ever, its naked trees charcoal sketches against the milky sky. Winter had arrived early, but despite the bitter cold, the park was littered with office workers seeking a quiet space in which to eat their meagre lunches, and hollow-cheeked mothers avoiding the polite nods of German officers taking their daily constitutional.

A cheap scarf tied under her chin and round, white-framed sunglasses covering her eyes, Sophie made her way along the wide paths, avoiding the frozen puddles and tightening her thin coat around her. Eventually she reached the Lac Daumesnil, the boats tethered at its fringe trapped within a thin layer of ice and lined with the frozen mulch of the previous autumn. He was already there, a newspaper held open in front of him, so that had she not recognised his build and his clothing, she might have missed him.

'So how was the seaside?' she asked as she sat on the bench overlooking the water and pulled a paperback book from her handbag, her breath a soft cloud of steam hanging in the cold air.

Jean-Paul turned the page of his newspaper, his face partially hidden by the deep brim of his trilby. 'They took the bait,' he replied without turning to look at her.

'Good. I'll let London know.' The Germans had obviously discovered the fake hideout near Le Touquet, with its badly hidden maps of a potential Allied incursion into occupied France, several hundred miles north of where plans were already being laid.

'And how is Fabien?' he asked, his voice level, even though she knew the pain hidden within the simple words.

'I heard he is well in Lisbon. The climate suits him.'

Jean-Paul's determination to become involved in Sophie's network had effectively cut him off from his lover until the war was over, and where Sophie's instinct had been to refuse, she knew she had no right to deny him the opportunity to play his part.

'I'm glad,' he said eventually.

She looked out at the geese scudding across the surface of the lake. 'I'd understand if you wanted to join him. I could arrange passage for you.'

'I can't leave now. Not when you've lost so many people.'

'I never expect anyone to carry on for longer than their heart is in it.'

'My heart is in this, trust me. Besides, something big is brewing.'

'What do you mean?'

They paused as an elderly couple walked past, hunched over in their threadbare overcoats, their hands clasped.

'They're preparing a new depot, about a mile in from the coast near Boulogne. Whatever it is, access to intelligence is restricted. I need you to keep your ear to the ground here in Paris.' He hesitated. 'Seelman's name has been mentioned.'

Sophie felt herself shiver. 'You want me to get close to him?'

'Don't take any risks – he's a nasty piece of work. But he might be our only way of discovering what's going on.'

'I'll see what I can do.'

They stopped again at the sound of raised voices, and both looked along the path to the source of the fracas.

'Isn't that your tame German?' Jean-Paul said, as they watched the officer brushing away a young man who had him by the arm.

Sophie watched as Becker walked briskly on, cheeks flushed. 'Do you think he saw us?' she asked.

Jean-Paul turned another page of the newspaper and glanced up at the angry Frenchman stalking past them as he shot backward glances at the departing German officer, then caught Jean-Paul's stare briefly.

'You know him?' Sophie asked, as the man walked away.

'I've seen him around.'

'What do you think is going on there?'

Jean-Paul shrugged. 'You're the spy.'

'Speaking of which,' she said, 'my godmother in London has promised a new operator with the next full moon. Can you make arrangements to meet whoever it is?'

'Of course.'

'Thank you. And I'll see what I can glean from Seelman.'

'Be careful, Sophie.'

She snapped her book closed and stood, placing it inside her handbag and catching his eye briefly. 'I will.'

'And give my love to . . .' He trailed off, his voice breaking.

'I don't need to. He already knows he has it. *Au revoir, mon cher ami.*'

'*Au revoir, ma patronne*,' he replied. '*Vive la France et vive l'amour.*'

'Long live love indeed.'

'You will find him again,' he said softly. 'I know it.'

She closed her eyes for a second, then looked out across the frozen lake. 'I know it too.'

Verity tapped lightly on Tremayne's door. 'I just wondered whether you'd had time to look at 937's report?' she asked as she entered. 'You agree we can't possibly let her go out there?'

He was standing at the tall window, his arms folded and back to her. 'It's not that simple,' he said, turning to face her.

She gently closed the door behind her. 'Sir, she's no more than a child. I know she wants to do her bit, but she failed almost every part of the training.'

'She got a decent score for wireless operation.'

'On the third attempt.'

He sighed, picking up an opened letter from his desk. 'War Office got wind of the intel from Colette that something big is brewing. They want more bodies on the ground – native French speakers. Too many slip-ups recently.'

'Then we keep looking.'

'There's no time, Cooper. Another cell in Paris was arrested last night and Colette will soon be stranded. She's too high profile to take risks transmitting, so the new girl can just concentrate on that. She's going out on the next moon period. That's all there is to it.'

It was always terrible sending young women agents over, especially for the first time, but never had she been party to sending one over as ill qualified as this young woman. 'I can't agree that it's the right thing, sir, but I will do everything I can to prepare her.'

'She has two weeks, Cooper. Do your best for her.'

'I will.'

'And Cooper . . .'

'Yes, sir?'

'I don't like this any more than you do. My hands are tied. I'm sorry.'

She closed the door behind her and leaned against it, thinking of the woman just about young enough to be her own daughter. It was wrong and cruel to send her out there, and for the very first time, Verity found herself missing the blissful ignorance of her pre-war life.

23

November 1943

Alec and Peter Tempest-Jones had spent the morning testing the aircraft they would be flying out on a double mission that evening. Lunch over, they had holed themselves up in the ops room of the cottage, planning their routes and cutting maps into long, folded strips they could keep on their knees. They had examined repeatedly the reconnaissance photographs and read the hourly reports from meteorological forecasters and Fighter Command. Poor weather, and there would be no mission.

As evening crept closer, all eyes were on the scramble telephone that provided a direct link to the Air Ministry, and from the window of the bedroom he shared with two other pilots, Alec watched the intelligence services arrive from London in black cars, bearing the paperwork and codes the Joes would need to pass on in France. A little later the agents were brought by car from their nearby accommodation, their escorting officers close by their sides, where they would remain right until the cockpit hatch was closed.

Tradition at the cottage demanded that pilots and agents dined together directly before a mission, and so Alec changed into battle dress, a plain roll-necked sweater beneath the blouson jacket he could shed quickly to pass as a civilian if he got into trouble. He had long ago packed an emergency bag of French-style civilian clothing, alongside playing cards with maps printed on the inside, fake ID, food capsules and some French currency. He had even been issued a fountain pen that released tear gas instead of ink. It was his first Lysander mission, and he was taking no chances.

The sitting room was already abuzz with lively chatter, Tempest-Jones deep in conversation with two Frenchmen, one of whom Alec recognised as a former colonel now operating on behalf of De Gaulle and the Allies. He had come across the second man in London: François Mitterrand was a well-known figure working to consolidate resistance movements. Amongst the suits and uniforms, Alec spotted Wing Commander Carlisle chatting with a pretty young woman who looked utterly terrified, a dark-suited escort officer glued to her side.

'Scotty, over here,' Carlisle called across.

She could not have been much older than twenty, Alec realised, her wide eyes flitting around the room and cheeks flushed. Her escort might as well have been there to prevent her bolting, rather than to assist her. Alec caught the eyes behind thick tortoiseshell glasses before the plainclothes officer looked away.

'Flight-Lieutenant Scott, meet one of your passengers,' Wing Commander Carlisle said, turning to the girl. 'It's her first time out, so give her a gentle ride, would you, old chap?'

He saw she was staring at his scar and smiled reassuringly at her. 'Don't worry – I'm a perfectly safe driver.'

'Of course. I'm sorry . . .' She held her hand out to shake his. 'Pleased to meet you. I'm D—'

Her escort coughed loudly, and she blushed, biting her lower lip.

He took her hand, shaking it warmly. 'I'll do my best to get you there safely, miss.'

'Scotty here will look after you. He's a Battle of Britain hero,' Carlisle added.

Alec sighed. 'No more heroic than you people doing your bit over there.'

She stood a little taller and raised her chin. 'I am half French,' she said. 'How can I not do my bit?'

'But we're not letting you do anything until you've had a good feed,' Carlisle said, slapping her on the back and making her jump. 'No drink for you, Scotty, but I reckon a glass of brandy and a good dinner will do this young lady a world of good.'

The atmosphere around the table was one of forced jollity, and other than the French colonel, the agents were mainly subdued, Alec's passenger pushing food around her plate as though she might run to the bathroom at any moment.

Eventually the agents were taken to the ops room for last-minute briefings with the intelligence services and a WAAF officer was despatched to listen to the BBC for the coded message that would tell them Operation Sarabande was confirmed at the French end.

Peter came to sit beside Alec at the almost empty table. 'So how are you feeling, old boy? Ready for your first mission?' he said, as one of the pilots not flying that night settled himself at the old upright piano at the far end of the dining room and began playing quietly.

'As ready as I'll ever be.' Alec pressed some tobacco into his pipe and tamped it down, accepting the match TJ offered him.

'Looks like we're set fair for tonight. Clear skies and a

gentle north-westerly – makes it a darn sight easier when the full moon does the work for us.'

'I think I'll need an easy one tonight – bit worried about one of my passengers, to be honest.'

'Yes, she's young all right. Looks pretty skittish. But I suppose the desk-pilots know what they're doing. She'll be all right when she gets there. Colette will look after her.'

'Colette?'

Peter nodded. 'Only met her once myself, but she's pretty formidable. Runs the network in Paris.'

'You've flown her?'

'Year or so back. Had dinner with her and a couple of other Joes in this very room.'

'She obviously made an impression?'

Peter laughed. 'Once seen, never forgotten. We all hope she'll make another trip back here, so we can fight over who flies her, but she's too high profile to risk travelling. When the war is over, I'll be first in the queue to invite her out for dinner, I tell you.'

They were interrupted by Carlisle's second-in-command appearing at the door. 'Car's ready to take you across to your kites, chaps,' he said. 'Grab your things – you're off.'

Ground crew scurried across the secluded dispersal point as Alec performed the final checks in the juddering aircraft. A hundred feet away, the single propellor of TJ's black Lysander was a mere blur, his friend dimly lit by the orange glow of the cockpit nightlights. The rear cockpits had already been loaded with luggage and boxes of supplies, along with a Thermos of hot coffee and flask of brandy for passengers on the return flight.

Alec was handed up his maps and pistol, and as the ground crew stepped back, a car arrived with the outgoing agents, who were fitted with their life jackets and parachutes before being helped up the fixed ladders to the rear cockpits. He glanced back in time to see his young passenger's pale features lit up by blue moonlight as she scrambled into her seat and was strapped in, followed by the French colonel, their radio headsets fitted so that pilot and passengers could communicate. Finally they were given the all-clear to take off and he followed Tempest-Jones to the short runway where the two aircraft took off smoothly, the pilots switching off their lights as they reached the broad, shimmering stretch of Channel broken occasionally by the long shadows of patrolling warships.

Flitting beams of searchlights and familiar patterns of flashing beacons eventually identified the French port of Cherbourg ahead. Vulnerable to attack from anti-aircraft fire, the two Lysanders climbed several hundred feet to conceal themselves within a layer of cloud, but not before they had been spotted and flashes of fire shot into the air towards them. The cloud thickened as they penetrated deeper into France, and for an hour they flew by instruments alone, until finally they broke free and saw the silver thread of the River Loire far beneath them, a wide fork in its path guiding them to the remote field where a crew of local resistants waited to guide them in.

Alec spotted the square, tree-fringed reservoir shown in the reconnaissance photographs, which bordered the landing site. In Morse code he flashed the agreed letter 'M', finally receiving the 'F' he had been told to expect in reply. He took a wide turn and suddenly there were the three bonfires in the shape of an upturned L, figures scattered cross the wide field. He landed exactly to the left of the first bonfire and taxied towards the second, at which he turned sharply right and returned diagonally from the third, slowing as much as possible without stopping, as men from the reception committee climbed up to help his passengers out.

'Good luck,' he shouted as the young woman and the colonel made their way down the little ladder and were hurried away.

Luggage was quickly unloaded and swapped, and two men in heavy overcoats and wide-brimmed hats climbed the ladder to take their seats behind him. Within three minutes the cockpit lid had been fastened back on and Alec had returned to the first lamp, where he pushed the little plane into full throttle and heaved her back into the air, TJ coming in directly behind him to repeat the exercise.

'Well done, old man,' TJ called across the radio. 'Got yourself your first star. See you back at base.'

24

London, 1997

Amy was about to leave for work when the telephone rang. She put a hand over one ear in order to hear the voice at the other end above the shouting of Holly, who had taken against the new shoes Amy had caved in to buying after half an hour's debate in the shop the previous week.

'Penny. How lovely to hear from you. How's Verity?'

'Not too bad, but she's caught a bit of a cold.' Penny laughed as Holly squealed from the kitchen. 'Sounds like you've got your hands full there.'

'You could say that. It's the shoe tantrum this morning. Makes a change from the coat one. Or the breakfast one, I suppose.'

'I remember it well. You should try Mum's trick and evacuate her to Shropshire.'

'I fear she'd be sent straight back.'

'Change the locks. She'll soon get the message. Listen, Amy, I just wanted to say sorry if I've been a little brusque with you. I have to think of Mum's health, you know?'

'Of course. And I'm sorry if I've seemed pushy.'

'I must admit I was worried at first, but you seem to be good for her. She probably hasn't had a new friend since 1953.'

'I like her too,' Amy replied, realising how fond she had become of Verity.

'Just don't let her overdo it.' Penny hesitated. 'You can't tell me what you talk about, can you? She's so secretive about it.'

Amy was torn. Of course Penny had a right to know, but Verity remained adamant that her family not be told about her war activities. It was not Amy's secret to tell. 'It's nothing in particular. I think she just enjoys talking about the war with someone eager to hear how it was first-hand.'

'Right.' Penny did not sound convinced. 'Anyway, the reason I called is that Mum asked me to tell you the name of a girl she told you about the other day. Someone who went to France. Hold on, I've got it written down here . . . Daphne Wilson. Her family owned a pie shop in the East End. Why would Mum know someone from an East End pie shop?'

Amy thought on her feet. 'I think they were secretaries together at the War Office.'

'Hm. Anyway, I'll let you know when Mum's better. I know she'd love to see you – it seems to have given her a purpose.'

'Me too,' Amy said.

And it was true: the story of the spy and the pilot had begun to attach itself to her unconscious, so that some mornings, instead of her day starting with the agonising absence of Michael, she awoke to find herself thinking about Sophie. She kept a photocopy of Sophie's letter folded in her handbag – a reminder that loss was not Amy's private preserve, and that hope truly was one of the greatest gifts. Of course she could not hope that Michael would come back, but she could begin to hope for an easier, happier way forward, surrounded by old friends and new. She'd even let Claire persuade her to come to a string quartet recital at the Wigmore Hall – no pianos, no pressure, but it had reminded her of the pleasure music had always given her, and that she'd denied herself for so long. She had no intention of playing again, but listening might just be possible. Music had been a weapon for Sophie – maybe for Amy it could be a balm.

And as her own mood gradually improved, she'd been surprised to hear Holly's Reception class teacher tell her the little girl had begun to join in a little at playtime. It was all just tiny steps, but the slow unfolding of Sophie's story was clearly having benefits on all of them.

Wilson's Pie and Eel Emporium had stood on Bethnal Green Road since 1902, according to the hand-painted green and gold sign above its façade of mirror-polished plate glass and hand-fired tiles, an architectural antique in an area of post-war high-rises built to accommodate the displaced community.

As Amy pushed the door open, she found herself in a London that had not changed in decades. It was not impossible to imagine the taxi drivers huddled on benches were dockworkers filling up after a long shift, or to see why the photographs stuck to the tiled walls included celebrity customers ranging from the Kray twins to soap stars. Above the melee of accents from Cockney to Bangladeshi to yuppie, a small wall-hung television gave a rolling account of the latest alleged romance of Princess Diana as the man behind the counter asked for Amy's order.

'I don't want that,' Holly said, gripping her hand and pointing to a picture of chunks of eel in sticky jelly.

''Ow about a nice pie, darlin'?' the man said. 'Make you big and strong.'

Holly shook her head, leaning against Amy's leg.

'Sorry,' Amy said. 'Fussy eater. I'll have pie and mash, and she can have some of mine. Oh, and some tea, please.'

The man winked, rubbing his hands on his white apron. 'I'll chuck 'er in a fruit pie and ice cream. You sit yourselves down and I'll bring your food over.'

They settled at one of the Formica-topped tables, and Amy pulled a colouring book and crayons out for Holly, buying herself a little time to look around the shop where a young SIS agent had spent much of her childhood, presumably helping keep the place afloat when a whole generation of Wilsons was wiped out overnight. The café prided itself on being a family business, and framed photographs included a handlebar-moustached Mr Wilson in 1902, eel deliveries being made by horse and cart and the recent presentation of a food award to the rosy-cheeked man behind the counter.

''Ere you go, love.' Two plates were placed in front of them, Amy's bearing a generous dollop of mash and a beef pie slathered in green parsley sauce.

'Is this the same recipe you've always used at Wilson's?' Amy asked.

'As devised by my great-great-grandfather,' the man replied proudly.

'So you're a Wilson?'

'Billy Wilson. Took over from my old ma a few years back. And she took over from 'er gran before that. Not that she's ever let go, mind, even of 'er maiden name! The only reason she's not sitting on that stool behind the counter watching me like an 'awk is because she's popped out for fags.'

'Was it your great-gran who ran the shop during the war, then?' Amy asked, taking a paper napkin and mopping ice cream from Holly's chin.

'Old Elsie never shut for a single day, not even when 'er own son and daughter got killed in a bombing raid. They don't make 'em like that these days. Anyway, don't let me stop you eating. I can talk the 'ind leg off a donkey, just like Ma.'

'Please, don't worry. In fact, I'm rather hoping your mum will talk to me too.'

He frowned. 'Really?'

Amy hesitated. She had met enough war veterans, both military and civilian, to know that it was not an easy topic to broach. 'I'm a researcher,' she said, hedging her bets. 'Talking to people who lived through the war in this area. Maybe your mum has some memories of that time?'

He shrugged. 'You can ask. She's never told me much about it. Just 'elped out in the shop, I think.' He looked up as the bell rang and a woman with sensible slacks and a bottle-blonde colour and set pushed the door open with her shoulder. 'Speak of the devil – you can ask 'er yourself. 'Ere, Mum, someone wants to talk to you.'

The woman leaned heavily on her two walking sticks, staring at Amy with piercing blue eyes. 'What can I do for you?'

'I'm Amy Novak,' she replied, deciding to be up front. 'I'm an archivist and I'm researching a connection between your family and the intelligence services in France during the war.' She watched as a wash of shock passed over the woman's face.

'Wasn't your mum French?' Billy asked.

'Get behind that counter, Billy Wilson,' the woman snapped, 'and stop your gossip.'

Amy tried again. 'I'm sorry to ask,' she said, 'but are you Daphne Wilson?'

'What if I am?'

'Does the number 937 mean anything to you?'

The woman took a moment before she replied. 'I've nothing to say to you. And once you've finished your lunch, I suggest you don't come back.'

'You should've said,' Billy whispered, as she disappeared through the door to the back room. 'I'd have had a word with her first, smoothed the waters, like. She can be tricky when she wants to be.'

'I'm sorry,' Amy said. 'But I think she might want to hear what I have to tell her.'

'Listen, leave your number with me. I'll see if I can't talk her round.' He watched as Amy scribbled down her mobile telephone number. 'You sayin' there was a spy in our family?'

'I'm just dotting the "i"s on something I've been looking into.'

He didn't look convinced, glancing across at their table as he left them and went back to the counter.

'Why was the lady cross?' Holly asked.

'I think something happened to her when she was young. She's probably still sad about it.'

'Will I still be sad when I'm old? Because Daddy died?'

Amy squeezed her tightly. 'You'll always miss him, but you'll fill your life with people you love and things that make you happy.'

'So why don't you?'

'Why don't I what?'

'Why don't you do what makes you happy?'

'But I do. I love my job, and I love you.'

'Daddy said you loved playing the piano. Why won't you play it?'

'It's not that simple.'

'Why?'

Amy sighed. 'I'm not a pianist any more. And that's fine.'

'Then I'll be a pianist instead.' Holly frowned, looking at the door behind the counter. 'Do you know what made that lady sad?' she said, stabbing at the pie with her fork, so that sweet, purply juices ran into the melted ice cream.

'Not yet,' Amy replied. 'But I hope to find out.'

25

France, November 1943

Daphne felt her eyes closing, the rhythmic swaying of the train tempting her towards sleep. The few wakeful hours on a mattress in a farmhouse attic had been spent in a state of high alert for the knock at the door that would end in her arrest before she'd even arrived in Paris.

The farmer and his wife had taken her in but wished to know nothing of her, other than that she would be gone by the time they rose to tend to the cattle. The ticket master at the station four kilometres away did not care about her aching feet, or the muscles that burned from the weight of the heavy suitcase with its secret cargo. Her fellow passengers on the stop-start journey to Paris were aloof and self-contained, avoiding eye contact with the German soldiers who shared their carriage. Daphne had never felt more alone.

She spotted splatters of mud on her city shoes and bent to brush away the tell-tale reminder of the night-time landing. As she did so, she saw the folded ticket a previous passenger had dropped on the floor near her feet. She had been told by a returning agent about these little symbols of resistance folded into the shape of the V for victory, and she suddenly felt comforted, knowing that beneath the smooth veneer ran a passionate seam of resistance.

As the train left behind the suburbs scarred with blackened craters and pulled in beneath the glass canopy of the Gare du Nord, Daphne stood to retrieve her luggage. A German soldier intervened, lifting the hefty suitcase from the rack and joking in rough French that she must be hiding gold in there. Another train had just arrived at the neighbouring platform, a giant swastika painted on its front, and dozens of German soldiers disembarked, heading towards the military exit signposted in German. Her mouth was dry by the time she showed her fake papers to the guard at the ticket barrier, trying not to stare at the machine gun strapped across his chest.

Already she could see how completely life had changed here, and after a few seconds' confusion, she realised that the big station clock had been set an hour ahead, to German time, so that even the daily rhythm of life was forced into step with the occupiers. Soldiers patrolled the wide concourse with heavy-set bulldogs, and yet French passengers took no notice of them: had three years of occupation made them so indifferent? Her tall trilby had seemed ostentatious in London but fitted in perfectly with the elaborate millinery Parisian ladies sported around her: a striking turban fashioned from a blanket, a cap-like felt hat piled with net and silk flowers, each woman expressing her defiance through the refusal to give up her stylishness.

She had been told only that she would be given instructions on arrival at the station, and so Daphne began to walk slowly towards the exit, past newspaper vendors selling German publications and diluted, propagandised versions of the titles she remembered her grandfather reading. Unsure of whether she should leave the busy concourse, she stopped outside a grubby café, placing the case on the ground as she pretended to read the menu.

She jumped as a man in a flapping raincoat, cigarette hanging from his mouth, brushed past her, making her drop her gloves. '*Pardon, mademoiselle*,' he said, bending to pick them up.

'Thank you.' She screwed up her face, angry at having slipped automatically into English already, just at the sight of a handsome face – he did look rather like a film star with that thin moustache – but if the man had noticed, he pretended not to have done so.

'*Suivez-moi*,' he went on quietly in French. 'Follow me but stay well back. Take the Métro carriage behind mine to Denfert-Rochereau. When we leave the station, if I stop to tie my shoe-lace, I've spotted trouble. Make your way to the florist's on rue Daguerre. Tell her you want roses for your aunt in Picardie.' He looked down at the suitcase. 'And for God's sake do not let that out of your sight or out of your hand again.'

There was so much she wanted to ask, but already she sensed she had failed, and as he moved away towards the entrance to the underground train, she grabbed the suitcase and walked quickly behind him, the weight of the radio banging painfully against her leg.

Don't cry, Daphne, she told herself angrily, feeling tears of shame pricking at her eyes. She heard her dad's voice telling her that she could be anything she wanted, if she just pulled herself together. Well, she jolly well would. She was Agent Bluebird now and she'd do him proud.

Sophie let herself into the building on rue Boulard where she had rented a small furnished apartment. The heavy clang of a bucket at the end of the hallway alerted her to the presence of Monsieur Chabot, the caretaker who watched comings and goings with studied indifference. It was the old man who had shown Sophie the scruffy apartment, who had nodded sagely and winked as she explained she needed somewhere to meet friends whilst her husband was in town. He had told her his son had died in the early days of the war and his grandson was interned in a prisoner-of-war camp in Germany. Monsieur Chabot was no friend of the Germans. Did he suspect the goings-on in the attic apartment were more than lovers' trysts? Maybe, but the clandestine resistance newspaper she had once caught him reading suggested he would not betray her.

'*Bonjour, monsieur*,' she said. 'Did you enjoy the brandy I gave you?'

He laughed. 'Oh yes. You are too kind, madame.'

'Not at all. We all have to look after one another, don't we?' She searched for complicity in his hooded eyes and was reassured to see an answering spark. 'I have a new maid arriving today,' she said. 'She will stay here, but she won't bother you.'

He chuckled. 'She can bother me whenever she likes.'

Sophie smiled. 'You are an old devil.'

He frowned suddenly. 'I will make sure to let her know if you have any unexpected visitors.'

She hesitated. 'Thank you. But as I say, she is just a maid, and I am just a woman hoping not to be caught by her husband.'

'Of course.'

The tiny two-bedroomed attic apartment had worked out perfectly: off the busy rue Daguerre, where even now Parisians still flocked to buy what groceries were available, it was easy for members of Sophie's network to merge into the bustle of daily life and slip into the little side street unnoticed. Here she had set up a temporary headquarters where agents could bring papers and collect cash and supplies, and downed Allied airmen could spend a night or two. No doubt she would have to find somewhere else before long, but in the meantime she was careful to hide incriminating papers behind a ceiling-height ventilation grille screwed securely shut.

She had brought with her enough provisions for a few days: the new recruit would need to acclimatise whilst Sophie showed her the ropes and she made her first transmissions. Once she had found her feet there was plenty for her to do, especially since the spider's web of 'letter boxes' criss-crossing the city had lost so many couriers over the last months.

She heard footsteps on the narrow marble stairs outside and fetched three tumblers and what little was left of the brandy she had unwisely entrusted to the two British pilots who had moved on the day before. She couldn't be angry: anywhere around Europe someone might be helping Alec in similar circumstances.

'I brought your new maid,' Jean-Paul said, ushering a young woman inside before locking the door behind him.

Her blue eyes wide as dinner plates, Sophie's latest recruit stepped cautiously across the threshold. 'I'm delighted to meet you, madame,' Agent Bluebird said in a tinkling voice more suited to a shopgirl than a spy.

Good God, Sophie thought, looking at her smooth, shaking hands, the bottom lip pulled between white teeth. They've sent me a child. 'How old are you?' she asked, taking a cigarette from a gold case and offering it to her. 'Old enough to smoke?' She knew her tone was harsh, but if this girl wasn't up to the job, they needed to get her out, for her own good as well as that of the network.

'Yes, I'm old enough. I just don't like cigarettes.' She tilted her chin and stared back at the older woman before glancing at the brandy bottle. 'But I'd like a drink, please. I've had a hell of a day.'

So she had balls. Sophie smiled at the girl. 'Every day is a hell of a day over here, trust me.'

Daphne lay under a mountain of blankets, listening to the scrabbling of pigeons on the roof above. The curfew-shrouded city was silent apart from the occasional rumble of aeroplanes high overhead, and every minute or so the rotating beam of an anti-aircraft searchlight pushed through the gap in the thin curtains and crawled across the walls and ceiling.

She knew she should sleep, but she could not stop replaying the evening spent with La Patronne and the man who had brought her to this cold, damp attic that would be her home until it was time to move on. She would have to become accustomed to this new uncertainty, where life was no longer measured by shop hours and Saturday cinema trips, but by the ever-present risk of arrest and the need to be quicker and nimbler than the enemy.

Daphne was not sure what she had expected of the legendary Colette, but it was not this delicate, porcelain-featured creature whose chic blonde hair and willowy figure were straight from the pages of a fashion magazine. The woman's character was clear the moment she had spoken, however, displaying the cool confidence of someone either in complete control or well-practised in making a show of it.

Daphne may call her Sophie in private, she had gone on to say, since she would come to know her identity soon enough, but to anyone else she was Madame Laurent, in whose name the apartment was leased, one of several aliases Sophie used around the city.

She went on to examine the contents of Daphne's suitcase, and putting aside the questionnaires from Tremayne, she had checked the banknotes and peeled several off for Daphne, smiling at the wrapped gifts sent from England for her.

Sophie had spent some time testing Daphne on the use of the radio, pleased with the groundwork laid down back at the Hall, but insistent, to the point of almost making Daphne cry, that the young woman repeat the golden rules back to her over and over. She must never leave the radio or her codes lying around; never stay on air too long, trying to rouse London; never resume a communication after a power cut; she must stick doggedly to her invented identity and back story if questioned.

Daphne had known all this, of course, but it was not until she had seen for herself the shrapnel-pocked streets, the few remaining Jews wearing yellow stars, and the entitlement with which the German soldiers dominated the city, that it had truly hit her what she had agreed to become part of.

This was no longer theoretical, she now knew; this was war.

Sophie wrapped her silk kimono around her nightdress and wandered through her silent apartment, unable to sleep. She smoked one of the cigarettes her godmother had sent along with coffee and whisky and some precious chocolate – 'To help you achieve a perfect English figure', her case officer had joked in the little note attached, which had been drenched in violet water so that Sophie had not known whether to laugh or to choke when she opened it. She often wondered what the woman looked like, even how old she was. It was so strange that her closest day-to-day connection in SIS was someone she would not recognise in the street.

She lit another cigarette directly from the first, trying to calm her nerves. She was performing at the German Institute and at a private salon over the next few days and had agreed to an interview with a glossy women's magazine, in which she would chirpily enthuse about how wonderful cultural life was in Paris under German rule. Added to this stress were rumours that one of her agents had been betrayed by a mole: reports of the Gestapo arresting a man matching the description of the agent had come alongside sightings of the other in a Monaco casino, gambling several thousand francs of the money that had arrived with a Lysander drop four weeks earlier.

Despite all this, an Allied invasion the following year was looking possible, and her efforts to undermine German defences were proving consistently effective. Becker was becoming sloppy and Seelman's secrets were almost in her grasp. She had to keep going.

26

Monday, 10 January 1944

Seated in the window of Prunier, the fashionable sixteenth-arrondissement caviar house, Sophie could not avoid the hostile stares of passing Parisians whose eyes were caught not only by the joyful mermaid-scale mosaics and classic Art Deco exterior of the establishment, but by its new clientele of red-faced German peasants and their doughy wives.

Becker was talking, she realised, a fast-flowing, animated monologue about a peacetime visit to Monet's garden at Giverny with a French artist friend of whom he had obviously been fond. A lover, perhaps, or a fiancée? Sophie was not paying a great deal of attention, and nor did she particularly care. 'I tried for years to capture what Monet had managed so easily,' Becker was saying, 'until I wept with the frustration of it.'

'You are an artist?' she said, coming out of her reverie and looking at him in surprise. Although she found his company agreeable, she had never thought of Becker as much more than her entrée to senior Nazis.

'I had hopes of being, once,' he said. 'I even studied for a while in Paris.'

Of course. Why else would he speak the language so well? Know his way around the city without one of the tourist maps produced for German soldiers? She saw now that Becker was indeed of a nature that understood her artistic temperament. Throughout the hours walking in the parks together, or whilst he accompanied her to fashion shows at the great couture houses where Nazi wives managed to make a Lelong gown look like a cheap department-store garment, she had reluctantly wondered whether they might have become friends in different circumstances.

'How does an artist become a Nazi?' she asked, instantly regretting her bluntness.

'To understand that, you would need to live in Germany right now.' He frowned, his thin, light eyebrows puckering as he lowered his gaze to their unfinished platter of oysters.

'Tell me something,' she said, the impulse to ask a question that had nagged at her suddenly too strong to ignore.

'As long as it does not relate to military installations,' he said, his pale blue eyes catching hers then flicking quickly away.

Had he guessed it was she who was passing on the information she purported not to understand whilst acting as interpreter for meetings, or that was given willingly by senior officers desperate to impress her? And if so, why did he continue to include her in such meetings? Was it infatuation, the desire for her company?

'We have known each other many months now, and yet . . .' She hesitated, pulling at the petals of one of the roses in the exquisite table arrangement and letting it fall on the starched white tablecloth. 'In all this time you have always behaved like a complete gentleman towards me.'

He smiled. 'To take advantage of you would be to insult your talent.'

There it was again: the pedestal setting her apart from others. It had protected her for many years, but suddenly she craved the freedom she had felt with Alec, who had found her in that moment she had stepped down from it. Tomorrow, however, she would need its protection more than ever.

She looked across the flickering lamplight towards Becker. 'I have received an invitation from Seelman,' she said, her anxiety mirrored in the brief clouding of his expression. 'He has asked me to join him for dinner in his rooms tomorrow.' Seelman who had ordered the execution of six schoolboys caught singing the Marseillaise at the Tomb of the Unknown Soldier; whose foot soldiers had arrested two of Sophie's best agents in the last cull of her network; who had helped coordinate the Vél d'Hiv round-ups.

It was also Seelman, however, who attended meetings at the highest level, who had access to the kind of information that made sense of the hand-drawn map arriving in Paris tomorrow from the Atlantic coast, outlining the latest German defences.

'You are going alone?'

She nodded. 'Is there anything I need to know? Anything that will . . .'

'That will ensure your evening is, shall we say, without its complications?'

'Exactly.'

'I only know the man professionally. He has a reputation for being . . . firm, a good supporter of our leader.' Was that a nervous flicker that crossed his face? Sophie wondered, before he went on. 'He is a cultured man with a passion for Bach, I believe.'

'Then I must play Bach for him.'

'Be careful,' he suddenly said. 'I wouldn't like to think I had introduced you to the man, only for him to . . .'

'He does not frighten me. But thank you.'

A waiter appeared at Becker's left shoulder, leaving a silver dish bearing the bill for lunch. As Becker peeled a wad of notes from his wallet, Sophie's eye was drawn to a young Frenchman loitering on the corner outside the restaurant, his gaze fixed on her. He didn't look like one of the many beggars who had appeared around the city and was certainly not dressed for Prunier prices. He was not one of her people, and she wondered briefly if he were about to throw a missile through the window of the German-favoured restaurant or draw a pistol, his target the collaborator whose lunch had been paid for by the Third Reich.

She looked back towards Becker, anxious to distract him from the potential trouble simmering outside, but her companion was already staring in the direction of the man, the hinges of his smooth jaw working rhythmically as their eyes locked. It was Becker the man was watching, she realised, as a feverish flush crawled across the German's pale features.

Verity walked between the great Doric pillars of the Euston arch, wondering how on earth the station had survived the worst of the Blitz. To one side, destroyed office buildings remained uncleared, and the remains of a block of flats destroyed by a landmine provided an eerie memorial to the hundred who had died there. She thought back to the day she had brought Robert and Penny here, one weeping mother amongst many. She had imagined she would be nothing without her children, and yet now it was her agents who caused her to lie awake, wondering whether they were safe, comfortable, alive even. It was motherhood on a different level.

Only a day ago she had arrived at Euston herself in time for Bill's week of shore leave. In her neat uniform, cap pinned to her hair and stripes on her sleeves, she was 'Ma'am', not 'Madam', soldier not housewife. Men doffed their caps to her not out of gentlemanliness but deference. And yet as soon as she had opened the door of number 72 and changed into her 'mufti', she was Mrs Cooper once more. She'd looked at herself in the tall bedroom mirror and seen just another slightly plump, slightly unfashionable middle-aged housewife.

As she made her way across to the platform where the Shrewsbury train was due, she spotted the headline on the lunchtime edition of the newspaper. Another Japanese warship sunk – pray to God Bill was not sent to the Far East. She couldn't bear it. She so hoped she and Bill didn't squabble this time. These precious few days should be happy ones, full of the children's chatter about country life and with good home-cooked food on the table. Perhaps she and Bill might even go out to dinner: she had saved up enough clothes coupons to go to Fenwick's and treat herself to a new frock from the government-approved CC41 range.

The train was on time, and through the clouds of smutty steam she saw Robert and Penny lifted down by their chaperone, an apple-cheeked matron plucked straight from a Shropshire dairy. Was there a hanging back as the children looked around at the vast station and its platforms teeming with soldiers? How strange this must all seem to these small people who had left the city before the worst of the bombing, and who with four country Christmases under their belts now thought of the fields and farmyard as their home. Would they even want to be here, with parents who didn't know the names of their teachers, or what they ate for breakfast?

And then Penny spotted her, breaking free and running along the platform on legs that seemed to have grown another six inches. Verity threw her arms around her daughter, surprised at the smell of unfamiliar washing powder on the clothes another woman had bought for her.

'Give your mom a cuddle, then, young man,' the chaperone said in a soft accent halfway between Welsh and Midlands.

'Robert, sweetheart.' Verity crouched down, trying to smile through the hurt of his uncertainty. 'Look who I brought with me.' She unclipped her handbag and pulled out the tatty, one-eared teddy that kept vigil on the little boy's bed. 'And even better than that, Daddy is coming home tonight. Won't that be just lovely?'

Finally, his frown relaxed and he took the toy from Verity, allowing himself to be wrapped in her arms, his back gradually unstiffening.

They would have a perfect few days. She would put Whaddon Hall and Colette and all the other agents out of her mind and try to be a wife and mother Bill would be glad to come home to.

Daphne was relieved to see only a handful of soldiers in the queue outside the shabby cinema with its hand-painted German signage. The poster for *Pierre et Jean*, the latest production by the German-run company that now managed the French film industry, showed a smiling Renée Saint-Cyr in full Belle Époque finery. The men were probably simply seeking somewhere dark in which to entertain the French girls who hung on their arms, stamping their wooden-soled shoes on the icy pavement, who in turn were looking for somewhere warmer than home. Winter continued to bite in the city as fuel rationing hit hard, and the Paris skyline was devoid of chimney smoke. Unlike the improvised blanket coat of the girl in front of her, Daphne's, made by government seamstresses in London, was of a thin fabric that had been rubbed and frayed until it was as useful against the northerly winds and freezing fogs as a paper bag. At least she did not have to worry about fitting in.

Eventually she bought her ticket and found a seat close to the back of the auditorium, one space away from the aisle, according to the instructions she had collected inside a magazine from a news kiosk the previous day, and placed her coat and handbag on the seat to her right. This was her first important assignment, aside from moving cash and messages across the city, and of course the daily transmissions to London. She knew she was probably bottom of the list, but Inès was in Dieppe with members of the Trade Board, Jean-Paul had travelled south for a few days and many of the remaining agents in the network were in hiding.

Daphne struggled to concentrate on the story of family secrets, anticipating the latecomer who pushed through the auditorium doors and leaned towards her. 'I'm sorry,' he whispered in French with a light accent that could have been anything from Dutch to Swedish. 'My bicycle was stolen outside the bank.' At the agreed code, Daphne moved her belongings so that he could sit beside her. She dared not turn to look, but her skin prickled with the proximity of a fellow agent and she caught the scent of cold air clinging to his clothing.

As the film eventually ended and newsreels charting supposed German victories began, the lights came on to discourage protest, although the sight of tanks and weapons caused some women in the theatre to scream in terror. A young man suddenly stood, unfurling a French flag and shouting, 'Victory to the Allies, the Allies are coming.' German guards rushed down the aisle, and the first to reach the student felled him with a blow to the head from a rifle butt. As people clamoured to leave their seats, Daphne turned to her neighbour, but the seat beside her was empty, her coat laid across it once more.

A small, bulky envelope had been hidden beneath the coat, and she quickly pushed it into her handbag before rising from her seat and slipping into the empty foyer. With shaking hands, she put her coat back on and hurried outside, where late afternoon had already become dusk and a filthy fog shrouded the unlit streets. She zigzagged through narrow, shadowy alleys until she reached a restaurant kitchen where one of a network of bicycles was always kept for agents to pick up and drop as needed.

She placed her handbag in the basket and gently lifted the corner of the envelope to see what was so important that it had caused the execution of two agents in Brest. The delicate line drawing on fine tissue paper seemed to be some kind of map, and she immediately wished she had not seen it.

As one of the kitchen porters began to shoo her away, Daphne realised she would not be the only one in trouble if she were found here. She squeezed the envelope through a slit in the waistband lining at the back of her coat and felt the small package drop to the hem, then wheeled the bike across the cobbles of the tiny backstreet.

It would be a half-hour ride to the café where two Canadian airmen waited in the basement to take the map back to London. With every corner turned, every revolution of the pedals, the weight of the package reminded her that she was one random spot check from danger.

27

Tuesday, 11 January 1944

Sophie cradled the delicate champagne coupe, pops of chilled vintage Krug splashing her hand. There was little to see through the tiny slit in the tall, floor-length shutters as Paris lay within its nightly blackout. Beyond the jagged roofline a full moon had risen. The Lysander flight would make it across that night to collect the Canadian airmen and the map that had cost the lives of two of her agents. Recent fortifications shown on the map proved that inaccurate information drip-fed to German listening services over the last weeks had made its mark.

'One can see the Bois de Boulogne from the balcony during daylight,' Seelman said, coming alongside her to close the shutters. 'But I'd prefer the Allies not to use my lights to guide their bombers into the city.'

She stepped back, the hem of her Shiraz-purple velvet gown brushing the deep pile of the silk rug stretching across the elegant drawing room. She had chosen to dress demurely in the short-sleeved, high-necked gown, the slimness of its skirt emphasised by its wide shoulders and gathered yoke. She wore no other adornment than the matching velvet hair net that held her dark-blonde waves, and she ran her hand across it as she waited for Seelman to direct her, now they had eaten.

The dinner had been delivered from the kitchens of the Ritz and served by Seelman's butler at the long table set for two in the candlelit dining room. Seelman had barely touched the foie gras or duck breasts laid before them, instead watching Sophie, so that the overly rich food became even harder to swallow, and she had to claim a sparrow's appetite.

'Please. Take a seat.' He gestured towards one of two gilt Louis XIV sofas on either side of the marble fireplace and sat opposite her, his legs stretched before him. The grey uniform blended into the dove-coloured silk upholstery, the polished leather of his boots reflecting the chandeliers dripping from the ceiling.

'It is a beautiful apartment,' she said, as she looked around at the ornate panelling and the mottled wall mirrors that caught the flickering glow of the fire, the throw-covered grand piano at the far end of the room. Her eye alighted on a silver-framed photograph of an elderly couple posing with their grandchildren. 'Is this your family?'

He laughed, a dry, humourless rattle. 'Hardly.' He stood, taking the photograph from the mantelpiece and handing it to her. 'These are the people who lived here before we . . . cleansed your beautiful city of their types. Imagine,' he said, pointing at the old man's face, 'someone like that owning a house like this.'

She looked at the smiling faces for whom this elegant Haussmann gem had been a family home. Had they been doctors, bankers, industrialists, publishers? Had those small children run laughing around this very room? 'You kept the photograph?' she asked, trying to mask her horror.

'I kept everything. So much simpler than starting from scratch, and for Jews they had exceptional taste.' He gestured towards the open doors leading to a book-lined study. 'There is even a fine library.'

'It doesn't feel strange? To live amongst their belongings?'

He frowned. 'Why should it? These are just things, material objects, some old enough to have belonged to many people. I am merely the next custodian in line. As will someone be after me. But let us not waste the evening talking about such things. Now we have dined, I hope you will play the old Jew's piano for me. It's a rather fine instrument.'

'You have played it?'

He shook his head. 'I merely dabble. You are the artist, the caster of spells and teller of stories.'

Feeling her nerve falter, she reminded herself that she was here because Seelman was a powerful man with powerful secrets, the man into whose Gestapo headquarters in avenue Foch so many of her agents had disappeared. She was here because the British fleet was vulnerable to attack from the new bases along the Belgian coast, and her godmother at Whaddon had a husband on one of those ships. She was here to help end this terrible war, but how far would she have to go to secure this man's confidence in her? Would a recital of Bach satisfy him, or were his sights set on a sexual conquest?

'But first I have a gift for you,' he said suddenly, and took a small box from a marble-topped side table, coming to sit beside her, his knee so close to hers that if she had believed him to be anything other than cold blooded, she might have felt his warmth. 'Open it.'

She untied the velvet ribbon and lifted the lid.

'Here, let me,' he said. He shook the slim, rectangular bottle gently then removed the stopper, taking her wrist and brushing the perfume-drenched glass tip against the feathering of blue veins and below her ears. She tried not to flinch as he took her wrist, inhaling deeply and closing his eyes.

'What perfume is this?' she said, not recognising the sickly-sweet scent, which was strong enough to overpower the violet overtones of the *Soir de Paris* she already wore.

'Something you will not find here in Paris,' he said, looking up at her. 'On each woman, it will smell slightly different, revealing something of her.'

'And what does it reveal of me?' she asked.

He pressed her wrist to his nose once more. 'You, Mademoiselle Clément, are an enigma. I cannot quite place you, although there is something . . .' He moved closer, lifting her chin as he leaned into her neck, taking short, sharp breaths, like an animal sniffing at its prey. 'Here, just beneath the ear, is where you keep your secrets.'

She leaned away from him. 'I have no secrets.'

'We all have secrets, perhaps even from ourselves. But as a performer you have learned to present only what you want to be seen.'

'You are an expert on scent?' she asked, moving the conversation away from dangerous ground.

'I developed this perfume myself. Back in Germany I cultivate roses for their scent. I have even written a book about it. Each variety is like a different woman, with her own temperament and sensitivities. I plan to create a hybrid of one of your ancient French varieties with one of my own.'

'Plant eugenics?' she said, feeling herself grow cold, despite the heat of the fire.

‘Exactly. There is no shame in creating the best of anything, breeding out imperfections and impurities. Don’t you agree?’

She finally allowed herself to meet his grey eyes, trying to see in them some humanity but finding only a blank coldness. She had no choice but to nod her agreement.

‘I’m glad to see that we are of one accord.’ He turned her hand over, examining her fingers, the network of veins running along the back of her hand. ‘To think that you have the entire pianistic canon quite literally at the tips of these fingers. How terrible it would be for all of us,’ he went on, tightening his grip so that she instinctively flinched, ‘if anything were ever to happen to them.’

She pulled her hand away. ‘Then I had better be careful it doesn’t.’

He stood, straightening his jacket. ‘I think it is time you played for your supper, don’t you?’

She had never felt less like playing in her life, but she followed him across the room to the piano. She sat, adjusting the position of the seat beneath her and finding the pedals with her feet, stretching her toes to accommodate the high kitten heels.

‘What would you like me to play?’ she said, brushing her fingertips across the keys.

‘How about the piece that is already on the piano?’

A dog-eared copy of Beethoven’s *Moonlight Sonata* was covered in pencil markings instructing the pianist to beware habitual wrong notes and highlighting passages for extra practice. ‘Is this yours?’ she asked.

He laughed, clasping his hands behind his back. ‘No, it was

there when I arrived. One of the Jews must have been trying to play it.'

She looked closer, reading the child-like scribble: 'Esther Bloch, aged 12.' It was just as well that he stood behind her as she began to play the haunting, yearning opening bars of the sonata, tipping her head upwards, eyes wide as she tried to prevent tears from falling on to the keys. On the street below she heard the shouts of German soldiers, gunfire in the distance. She glanced at the photographs arranged on the piano lid, looking for the girl Esther who had played this very music on this instrument, and knowing it was probably Kaspar Seelman who had ensured she would never play it again.

She had almost reached the final bars when a sharp rap was heard at the drawing-room door and Seelman snapped at her to stop.

A young officer entered and saluted. 'Sir,' he said, 'you are needed on the telephone.'

Seelman cursed under his breath and turned to Sophie. 'You must excuse me. Please, amuse yourself and I will return shortly.'

She waited for the sound of boots on the marble stairs to disappear and made her way to the old library where she had seen Seelman's desk. This was a private study rather than official office, but she flicked through the correspondence spread across the leather-topped desk – letters from an accountant, a housekeeper in Germany, bills from horticulturalists. If Seelman kept sensitive material here, it would be well hidden.

She glanced at the spines of the few books piled on the desk and was about to give up when she spotted the title of the small, slim hardback at the bottom of the pile: *Cultivating Floral Scent: A Guide* by Kaspar Seelman.

She flicked hurriedly through its pages, stopping as she spotted a folded letter inside the back cover, addressed to Seelman at 84 avenue Foch and marked as highly confidential. As she slipped it from the envelope and scanned its contents, she realised she had hit gold.

She'd just managed to memorise the important details when she heard voices in the stairwell. Quickly replacing the letter in the book, she rearranged the desk and hurried back to the drawing room to seat herself on the fireside sofa once more. By the time Seelman returned, she appeared to be in a post-prandial doze from which he had awoken her.

'I'm afraid something has come up, Mademoiselle Clément. Perhaps we can continue this another time?'

'Of course,' she replied, gathering her belongings as she focused on the coded pattern of notes playing over and over in her head.

She followed his valet to the black car waiting on the street, heavy flecks of wet snow illuminated in its headlamps. As she was driven across the quiet city, the silence was broken only by the rhythmic sweep of the wipers pushing aside fat snowflakes that slapped against the windscreen and the shush of tyres through sleet.

Sophie looked at her watch as they crossed the river towards the Rive Gauche: there were still a couple of hours until curfew, and this intelligence absolutely had to go out with Daphne's evening transmission.

She leaned forward towards the driver. 'I think I would like to walk the last part,' she said, as the Art Deco frontage of the Hotel Lutetia came into view.

'But it is snowing.'

'I have had a little too much champagne and need to clear my head. You can drop me here. I promise I will not tell anyone,' she added, holding out a precious hundred-franc note, which, to her relief, after a few seconds' hesitation he tucked in his breast pocket. She could not risk a confrontation with her neighbour if she were seen being delivered home in a German car. She needed to keep her head clear, the memorised intelligence as fresh as possible.

Conspicuous in her evening gown and furs, she let herself into her apartment and changed quickly into flat brogues, wide-legged trousers and a belted coat, a dark trilby covering her hair. Certain the driver had gone by now, she ducked into a side street, zigzagging for half an hour until she reached rue Boulard.

She opened the front door to the apartment block, hesitating at the sound of voices from Monsieur Chabon's apartment. The old caretaker lived alone, and not wanting any surprises whilst her radio operator was mid-transmission, Sophie crossed the tiled hallway towards his apartment. If there were a German visitor in the building, she needed to know.

The door was open slightly, and Sophie opened it to see Monsieur Chabon coming out of his tiny kitchen, jumping at the sight of her. 'Madame,' he said. 'Can I help you?'

'I thought I heard voices,' she replied. 'I just wanted to make sure you are all right.' He was a good man, thoughtful towards Daphne, and she hated putting him at risk.

'It must have been the radio,' he said, glancing towards the silent set in the tiny sitting room. 'I was listening to a play.'

'Of course. I'm sorry I disturbed you.' She backed away, and he hurriedly shut the door behind her.

She made her way through the gloom towards the narrow, winding staircase, avoiding the cage lift. Something had shifted in the old gentleman. Perhaps it was time to move Daphne on.

Condensation had frozen on the inside of the attic windows, and although her instinct was to stay warm under the piled-up blankets as she heard loud banging and shouts downstairs, Daphne knew this was not an option.

She had slept fitfully after Sophie's visit earlier that evening, picking up on her anxiety as Sophie wrote down the message to be sent urgently to London later that night, checking Daphne's transpositions of the sequence of letters and adjusting them a couple of times. She would get better at it, Sophie told her patiently as she corrected Daphne's consistently wrong translation of the number seven, but Daphne could tell the woman was frustrated at her slowness.

Daphne had waited until two and a half hours after curfew, when the operators at Whaddon would be tuned in ready for her prearranged transmission, and then carefully set up the radio, standing on a chair to throw the aerial out of the window and hook it over the guttering, then attaching the earth wire to the ice-cold radiator. She tapped away at the Morse key, one ear to the door in case Monsieur Chabon let himself in to leave her a few lumps of coal.

She had kept the transmission as short as possible before

packing the radio away and hiding the suitcase in a basket of dirty laundry under her bed. With every moment that passed she felt a little safer, but the sound of vehicles drawing up on the street below suddenly affirmed her fears. She slipped out of bed quickly and checked she had left nothing out, before taking the small revolver from beneath her pillow, gripping it out of sight in her cardigan pocket.

She heard German voices on the stairs, terrified cries as soldiers made their way up through the building. There was nowhere for her to go, the bars over the tiny roof window too narrow to escape through. She had no choice but to brave it out, to seem unconcerned, annoyed at the intrusion. This was her opportunity to show Sophie she was up to the job.

She looked once more towards the table that had served as a desk only recently and saw she had dropped the slip of paper Sophie had given her, the pre-encrypted message written on it. She picked it up quickly and tore it into small pieces, cramming them into her mouth, the rough creases scraping her throat as she forced them down with a glass of water.

When the banging eventually reached her door, she faced down the two soldiers with a mask of irritability, asking how they dare disturb a young woman at this time of night. Still they pushed past her, taking in the still-warm rumple of blankets on the bed and lifting the pillow, unaware of the pistol-shaped dent in the mattress beneath it. They poked their rifles through clothing draped on the chair and checked the almost-empty chest of drawers.

One of them pointed at the basket under the bed. '*Montrez*,' he said in rough French. 'Show me.'

She had to remind herself to keep breathing as she pulled out the wide basket of clothing, trying to disguise the weight of the hidden radio. 'Here,' she said, channelling her nerves into a display of anger as she held up a pair of silk pants. 'You want to look through my underwear?' she yelled. 'You would like this done to your sisters?'

They might not have understood what she screamed at them, but they were young enough to be embarrassed, and one of them signalled for her to put the basket back, before they made their way out of the apartment.

She locked the door behind them and let out a long breath, waiting a few moments before she risked opening the shutters a crack to look out on to the street. Four floors above ground level and with no lighting on the street, it was impossible to make out the faces of the two figures being bundled into the back of a van. Somewhere in the building, there would be empty beds that night.

It was risky visiting too often, but Sophie felt compelled to check Daphne had successfully sent the message the previous evening. If the information she had found at Seelman's apartment was true, London could expect worse than the Blitz of the early years of the war.

She let herself into the narrow lobby and shook the snow from her clothes. Hearing the radio, she called out a greeting to Monsieur Chabon but was surprised he did not reply. She tapped lightly on the open door. 'Monsieur?' His usual armchair was empty, the apartment meticulously tidy, the collaborationist Radio Paris churning out a lunchtime concert of anodyne music-hall numbers.

'*Qui est là?*' said a voice from within the apartment, and Sophie was taken aback by the sight of the old woman who shuffled to the door.

'I am Madame Laurent,' Sophie said, using the false name with which she had signed the tenancy agreement. 'I rent an apartment here.'

The woman puckered her unevenly painted black eyebrows. 'Ah yes,' she said. 'The tenant who uses the apartment by the hour.'

Sophie bit back the temptation to defend herself but knew the cover story had to remain watertight. 'Where is Monsieur Chabon?' she went on.

The elderly woman folded her arms over the apron hanging loosely on her tiny frame. 'He has . . . been replaced. I am the new concierge.'

'Why?'

'He was hiding a Jewess in the cellar. His wife, they say. He kept her down there for eighteen months. Not that I care: if people are stupid enough to put themselves and others at risk, they only have themselves to blame.'

Sophie thought back to the hastily hidden underground newspaper she had spotted the old man reading, his obvious concern the night before. His replacement had already installed a portrait of Marshal Pétain, whose puppet Vichy government had supported Hitler so completely. It was time to find somewhere new.

'I suppose you're right,' she said, anxious to end the conversation. 'I had better check on my maid. Girls are so lazy these days, don't you agree?'

She saw the conflict in the woman's face as she longed to pick an argument but could find no fault in Sophie's assertion.

Instead she narrowed her eyes. 'If I catch her up to no good, she'll be out. I'm watching, madame.'

'I have no doubt you are,' Sophie muttered under her breath as she turned away.

28

London, 1997

'Don't look so worried.' Verity was sitting up, the table beside her bed crammed with books and copies of *The Times* folded open to reveal completed cryptic crosswords.

'Sorry. I'm not good with hospitals. You look much better than I expected.'

'I'm fine. It's a fuss about nothing.' She lifted her hand, the canula taped to it attached to a drip. 'I'll be out in a day or so.'

Amy had been grateful to hear from Penny, even if it was to tell her that Verity's cold had developed into a nasty chest infection and she had been admitted to hospital for observation. She was feeling much better and was accepting visitors, if Amy would like to see her.

She had been torn, still traumatised by the morning she had followed Michael's ambulance from the scene of the accident, the faded Monet print on the wall of the relatives' room where they had put her while he was in surgery seared on her memory.

And so, glad as she was to see Verity, the sounds of beeping machines, nurse-station chatter and bumping trolleys, the smell of antiseptic and illness made her want to run outside into the warm spring air, to block out the memories clamouring to escape the dark room where she had hidden them.

'You look terribly peaky. I thought I was meant to be the invalid.'

Amy looked up. 'It's the first time I've been in a hospital since . . .' She hesitated. 'It's where I said goodbye to Michael, even though I'll never know whether he could hear me.'

'How terrible. I never had the chance to say goodbye to Alec. I've never really felt able to lay him to rest.'

'It was pretty horrific this way, but yes, at least I had that. I just wish . . .'

'Wish what?'

'That we hadn't parted on such bad terms. We had a terrible row, when he was only trying to be kind.'

'Oh, you poor girl.'

'He'd bought me an anniversary present, and I rather threw it back in his face.' She shook her head. 'Not literally – it was a piano.'

'But surely you'd have been delighted? You told me yourself you'd been a pianist.'

'*Had* been. That was the problem.'

'I don't understand.'

Amy held out her left hand, the third and fourth fingers curling in towards the palm. 'An accident.'

'Oh my goodness.'

'Grim, isn't it?'

'You poor woman. Can you tell me what happened? After all, I've had to open up to you – fair's fair.'

Amy returned Verity's smile. 'I suppose it is.' She rubbed at the scar on her palm. 'Michael and I were walking back from the Tube after a concert. We took a short cut through a park, and . . . Well, we were jumped. A guy in a hoodie wanted my handbag.

Michael stood up to him, a knife appeared, and my hand somehow got caught in the middle. Two tendons were slashed. The surgeons did what they could, but the damage was pretty bad.'

'How awful,' Verity said. 'And you never played again?'

Amy shook her head. 'That's why Michael and I argued. He thought leasing the piano would help, but if I can't play like I used to, I don't want to play at all.'

'I'm sorry. You must miss it.'

'I have my work . . .'

'Which you're obviously passionate about.'

'And my daughter . . .'

'Whom you adore, but nothing has ever quite taken the place of your music, and your husband probably knew that.'

'Ouch.' Amy smiled.

'Have you played the piano?'

Amy shook her head. 'No. I felt steamrollered into something painful, and I told him so. Just before he died. I was horrible.'

'We can't live our lives as though every goodbye is the final one. Instead we bicker, we blame, we take for granted the most precious thing we have. We are human, with all the pain that brings with it. I expect you were exhausted, trying to run a home, a career, a young family. Perhaps he wasn't always as perfect as you choose to remember; perhaps there was a reason of his own for wanting you to play again.'

Amy looked at Verity, considering for the first time that maybe Michael's gesture had been as much about assuaging his guilt at not being the one whose hand was damaged. And she had denied him that resolution. 'You are a wise woman, Mrs Cooper.'

'Often, I am. But not always. Especially when it came to my own marriage.'

'It can't have been easy balancing the sort of war work you were doing with running a home. Especially if you couldn't talk to your husband about it.'

'And especially as things hotted up in France. I was insufferable to poor Bill. It was impossible to switch off when my girls were in danger.'

'Sophie was in trouble?'

Verity nodded. 'She'd got hold of the sort of information that alters the course of a war, and from a thoroughly nasty character. Seelman, he was called. Colonel Kaspar Seelman of the SS. One of his own men even made an assassination attempt on his life towards the end of the war.'

'And Sophie was close to him?'

'Terrifyingly so. It reached a head in January 1944, just as I was home on leave, unfortunately for Bill. The Allies were acting upon the intelligence she had stolen from Seelman, and I had to pretend there was nothing more on my mind than what film we might watch at the flicks. All I wanted to do was get back to Whaddon and arrange extrication for her. As soon as the Allied strike against the Germans took place, she was in extreme danger.'

'Had she gone into hiding?'

Verity shook her head. 'She had refused to, insisting it would make the Germans suspicious if she disappeared. So many times I have imagined what that night was like for her, as all hell prepared to rain down on her.'

'If only we could change history. All we can do is live with what has happened, I suppose.'

'Like you are?' Verity asked.

'Like I'm trying to.'

'They seem to get on OK, don't they?' Amy watched Holly chase after Jay's little boy, who thankfully didn't seem too embarrassed to have her tagging along. She suspected Jay had done a Claire and told Sam to be nice, but it seemed to be working, and Sam no doubt understood the confusion of upheavals. Holly had been fascinated by Jay at first, refusing to leave the bench where he and Amy sat surrounded by snack detritus and pestering him to push her on the swings, but Sam had eventually coaxed her on to the roundabout, where she now lay back, her pale hair blowing in the wind as they spun around, watching Amy with each revolution.

'Sam's a good boy. He's actually always preferred playing with girls.'

'Well, I appreciate it. Believe it or not, given the glum face, but Holly seems to be having more fun than she has for a long time.'

'I'm glad. Me too, even if a damp West London playground on a Wednesday afternoon is rather the definition of despair.'

'Cup of shit coffee always helps,' Amy said, raising her polystyrene cup so that the grey-brown contents sloshed over the new cut-off jeans Claire had claimed made her look ten years younger.

Jay nodded. 'It does. But yes, this is undrinkable.'

Amy looked at the other parents dotted around the playground, some engaging with the play equipment more than their kids, and others staring despondently into space. 'Someone once told me we're meant to enjoy this.'

'Well, they were probably comparing it to a trip to a municipal swimming pool during toddler time.'

Amy laughed. 'So you hate that too? I feel so much better.' He was easy to talk to, and to her relief it didn't feel like a date at all.

'It's not always easy, is it? Especially on your own. Not that I mind being on my own, but people just assume that because you're a single parent, you're desperate to hook up, right? If one more mum in Sam's class tries to set me up, I'll leave town.'

'You don't get that when you're a widow. People are petrified of you.'

'Yeah, well, you are quite scary.' He smiled as she cuffed him.

'It's like they don't know what to say, and so they say nothing. It's the same with Holly: they don't know what to do with her. She's forgotten how to have fun.'

'She always seemed really outgoing when Michael brought her to the shop.'

'She used to be. Not now.'

'Give her time. It's tough.'

'I know. And to be fair, she has asked to have her friend Susie over for tea at the weekend, so that's something.' She took a sip of the coffee, before remembering how awful it was and tipping it on the ground beside the bench. 'I sometimes wonder . . .'

'Wonder what?'

'Well, Holly heard us arguing, the day Michael died.'

'Parents argue. People argue. She sees it in the playground every day.'

'I know, but maybe it's made it harder for her.' She watched Holly trail round after Sam, joining him as he examined something he had found on the ground.

'What did you argue about?' He shook his head. 'Sorry – tell me to mind my own business.'

'That stupid piano.'

Jay's eyes widened behind his heavy glasses. 'The one he leased?'

She nodded. 'Holly had had us up all night with a vomiting bug – I guess it wasn't the moment for him to make a grand gesture. And especially one involving a piano.'

'Oh yeah, he said you used to play.'

'He got angry, said it would do me good to play again. Do Holly good to hear me. He said I was making them all miserable by not letting go of what happened with the accident.'

'Ouch. If it helps, you don't strike me as miserable. Hey, you should see me on a bad day.' He whistled.

'Well, this conversation has turned pretty miserable! I'm sorry. I think it was being in the hospital today brought it all back.' She hesitated. 'I keep seeing him lying on the road. His Discman had fallen off and Charlie Parker was still playing through the headphones. Silly the things you remember, isn't it?'

'I know what you mean. When Mel told me she was leaving me for some guy at work, all I could think about was the Cheerios that had fallen underneath the kitchen counter. I can still see them now. Four in a row.'

'Perhaps it's our way of coping: focus on the little things until we can deal with the big ones.'

'Makes sense. And how are the big things?'

She smiled. 'Still big, but maybe they always will be. It's what we do with them that counts.'

'If only you could prick them with a needle and shrink them . . . or her. Or him. Sorry.'

Amy looked at him, the flash of hurt that disappeared as quickly as it had appeared. 'You miss her?'

'It's obvious?'

'Takes one to know one.'

'It's been six months. I need to get over it, but yes, I do miss Mel. So does Sam when he's at mine.'

'You're allowed to miss her, you know.'

'You miss Michael?'

'Every day.' And she did, but she had noticed that gradually the missing wasn't like a stab in the heart. It was still a pretty powerful punch, but it was softening, becoming manageable.

'Jeez, what a cheerful pair we are. Anyway, you said you were at the hospital today? Everything OK?'

'Yes. I was visiting a friend. Someone who knew the Nazi pianist, actually.'

'You're kidding? Did you tell her you're looking for recordings of Sophie Clément?'

'I did.'

'Oh, that reminds me. I tracked down a cassette, taken from a live broadcast of a concert she gave during the war – a dealer in France found the tape in a job lot he bought a few years back. It's a recording of a recording of a radio programme, so not great quality apparently, but it's got historical worth, I guess. I should have it in a few days.'

'That's amazing. Thank you so much.'

They paused as Holly and Sam came running across and pulled at Jay's hands. 'You've got to push us on the swings,' Sam said. 'Really high.'

Holly joined in as Jay groaned. 'You have to! Sam says.'

'Sorry – she gets a bit hyper around men. It's because she misses having one around, I suppose.'

Jay turned to Amy. 'It's fine. But looks like you'll have to tell me about Sophie another time.'

She watched as Jay scooped Holly on to his shoulders and galloped her across to the swings, Sam chasing behind. And as Holly squealed, she realised it was the first time she had heard her daughter laugh – a proper chuckling, carefree laugh – for a year.

29

Saturday, 15 January 1944

As she stamped her feet on the cold pavement, Verity wished they had decided to stay at home and throw some precious coal on the fire. Instead they had joined the queue snaking around Leicester Square for the matinee of *Casablanca* at the Ritz cinema, icy drizzle glistening on Bill's trilby and the shoulders of their coats.

Bill squeezed her hand and she instinctively leaned against him. If only they could leave their bodies to speak for them in these simple, familiar gestures, things would be fine. At least, she supposed, in the cinema they could pretend the squabble over the supper table hadn't happened, and that Verity hadn't snapped at the children. When she had eventually tucked them in, Robert cried that he wanted his other mother. 'But I'm your mother,' she'd insisted, distraught at being displaced by Bill's sister. What had she expected would happen if she sent them away for over three years, though?

Which, unfortunately, was exactly what Bill said when she told him.

And so they squabbled again.

She would never have imagined that the return of her dear husband would be so difficult. Why could Bill not iron his own shirt? What was the point of tidying away the children's books if they were only to pick them up again five minutes later? And maybe she had forgotten how to cook one of the revolting Woolton pies that were meant to stretch rations, but was that so awful? Had Bill wanted a drudge when he married her? He'd wanted someone who didn't put a silly secretarial job before her own family, he'd replied.

It was unfortunate that the telephone happened to ring at that moment, and that Bill answered it to someone who claimed to be from Verity's office. And when she was unable to tell him that the call was to inform her that highly sensitive intelligence from one of her agents about a convoy of deadly rockets had been forwarded to the Air Ministry, Bill had exploded. Why the devil was she being disturbed at home? In fact, why the devil was she working at all?

He was under stress, she knew: Bill's fleet would be headed to the North Sea soon, and she was all too aware of the dangers from German U-boats. And so she had changed into her smart new frock and poured them both a sherry, knowing he would disapprove of the whisky she had become rather partial to at Whaddon Hall. She didn't want to fight: there was enough conflict in the world already.

The queue moved forward a little and Bill wrapped his arm around her as they shuffled along. 'I'm sorry if I was beastly, darling.'

'And I'm sorry if I was a harpy.'

'I was thinking,' he said. 'How about we have a night away somewhere, even a hotel in London. We could get an overnight babysitter.' He smiled. 'We never had a proper wedding night, did we? Your mother did rather put a spanner in the works.'

Verity laughed. 'Dear old Mother. I can't believe I let her arrange for the entire family to come on honeymoon with us.'

'So what do you say? Monday? It's my last night of leave. We mustn't waste this time together. It might—'

He stopped, and as Verity watched him looking around at the fellow servicemen queuing to spend one and six for ninety minutes of distraction with their girls, she understood that he had almost said the thing no one was allowed to say these days.

She was torn: the strike was due to take place on Monday and although she was officially on leave, Tremayne had made it clear he would prefer her to return after the weekend. And yet she really ought to put Bill first. She leaned up and kissed her husband on the cheek. 'I'd love to go away with you,' she said. After all, Monday was days away: anything could happen in the meantime.

Verity stood back as he paid for the tickets, her mind wandering to the telephone conversation with Tremayne. Colette's intelligence had been forwarded immediately to Bomber Command, Tremayne had explained on the telephone, and if Harris decided in his regular nine a.m. briefing the next morning that it was a priority, the attack on the train convoy would be scheduled for two nights' time. Should they try to get Colette out while it was still possible?

She settled into the seat beside Bill, but as hard as she tried to lose herself in the drama of Rick's Bar, it was impossible to concentrate. 'We'll always have Paris,' Bogart told Bacall, and Verity felt sick at the thought of her young women trapped in what had once been the city of love but was now a snake's pit of arrests and deportations.

Of course she wanted a night away with Bill, but more and

more she felt her place was at Whaddon Hall. Her children's lives weren't under threat, but those of her 'girls' most definitely were.

Sophie and Inès were just two cousins strolling alongside the Seine, enjoying the last of the afternoon sunshine, the architectural jewels of the Île de la Cité mere phantoms through the thick swirling mist across the surface of the river. Even the gargoyles of Notre-Dame, those solid sentinels that for seven hundred years had watched Paris revolt, repair and now resist, were hidden from view.

Antiquarian booksellers stood by their *bouquiniste* stalls on the Quai Voltaire, hoping to pick up some trade from the German customers who collected anything from rare art volumes to racy fiction. Today, however, the Germans' focus was on patrolling the streets rather than book shopping.

'Is it me, or are there more around than usual?' Sophie asked as another truckload of soldiers drove past.

'No, you are right,' Inès replied. 'They're everywhere.'

They paused at a stall selling beautiful engravings and Sophie flicked through antique maps of Paris. 'I think I know why they're rattled,' she said quietly as the stallholder wandered away to chat with his neighbour.

'What do you know?'

'They're transporting the first consignment of a new rocket by train from Germany to a base near Boulogne next week. They're far more deadly than the bombs they've been dropping on London and don't even need pilots to launch them.'

Inès let out a long breath, which condensed and dispersed instantly into the mist. 'This is terrible. How do you know?'

'Our contact in Boulogne reported a new warehouse facility, and there is talk from soldiers in the local bars that something big is on its way. Seelman was kind enough to confirm it.'

'Seelman?' Inès pulled at Sophie's arm, turning her around. 'He never gives anything away, not like some of those other idiots. How did you find out?'

'He invited me to his apartment.'

'No. Please tell me you didn't accept. He's dangerous. You've heard the stories of what happens to those taken to the avenue Foch? Don't you know what he might do to you?'

Sophie looked around, making sure they were not overheard. 'What choice did I have? If this is all true, it could put back an Allied invasion by months and cause tens of thousands more deaths. So yes, I had dinner at Seelman's apartment.'

'And he just told you all about these new weapons?'

'Of course not. I looked through his desk while he left the apartment. I found a letter confirming the date, time and route of a railway convoy transporting the first delivery of weapons. I don't think it's information that's even been shared amongst the military.'

They paused while an old gentleman joined them, browsing briefly before shuffling away.

'If the Allies act on this, you realise it might point straight to you?' Inès said.

'It could just be a lucky strike. The British and Americans are always taking out moving trains. Or the Maquis could be responsible.'

'The Maquis don't have the means for an air strike. When is this all happening?'

'Monday night. I have a recital at the German Institute that evening.'

'Then cancel it.'

'Seelman will be even more suspicious if I do. Besides, the concert is being broadcast on Radio Paris. I can't afford not to be there.'

'Sophie, enough.'

'It won't be enough until these bastards are beaten. Inès, come to the concert and make sure Jean-Paul is there too. The attack on the train is due shortly after the second half begins – if it happens, I need you to give me a sign so I can slip away after the concert. And if there is a change to the Germans' plan, Jean-Paul must get word to Daphne – she will need to contact London.'

'I don't know . . .'

Sophie took her cousin's hands, sheathed in soft calfskin. 'Please do this. And then I promise I will get away for a while,' she said, knowing her chances of getting away at all were frighteningly slim.

The muffled call of a distant foghorn sounded from far upriver, and the two women looked out towards the milky mist hiding the far bank from view.

'Tell me,' Inès said. 'Seelman . . . did he . . . ? I couldn't bear to think of it. After everything you went through when you were younger.'

Sophie shook her head. 'No. And he doesn't frighten me. Somehow, meeting Alec changed all of that.'

'I'm glad. You deserve happiness, my darling.'

'As do you and that adorable daughter of yours. I'm sorry you have been away from Geneviève for so long.'

'We will be together again once this is all over. I'm just happy she is safe.' Inès slipped her hand through Sophie's arm. 'And I hope you and your pilot find each other again.'

'We will,' Sophie said, as they made their way slowly along the quay. 'I know it.'

'I got you a sherry,' Alec said, waking Scout, who had been sleeping at his feet. Verity had never been a great one for a pub, and she seemed distinctly unhappy with this one, screwing her face up against the pall of cigarette smoke and flinching at the robust language of some of the regulars. With an hour to kill after meetings in London before heading back to Tangmere, Alec had wanted to catch up with his sister. Things had been strained between them ever since Sophie had left, and Alec hated unresolved conflict. Especially these days.

'I can't stay long. Bill is picking the children up from the babysitter. We've just been to the cinema. Are they feeding you properly at that base of yours?' she said, looking him up and down.

'Don't fuss, V,' he replied, the old sibling irritation rising to the surface.

'I'm allowed to worry about my twin brother, aren't I?'

Alec had imagined Bill's shore leave would improve his sister's demeanour, but seeing she was agitated, he decided to stick to safe ground and ask her about her work, knowing she had moved on from the War Office to something out of town.

'I can't talk about it, Alec.' She sipped at the sherry he had bought her and quickly put it down again. 'Where the devil do they get this stuff?' she said. 'I know there's a war on, but really. This is fit only for aviation fuel.'

'Can I get you something else?'

She sighed. 'No. Thank you, but I don't have long. Bill has arranged a night away for us on Monday, and I've lots to do.'

'You don't seem too excited. Everything all right?'

She sighed. 'Just something at work worrying me.'

'So much that you don't want to go away?'

She nodded. 'It is rather. But Bill is already fussing about my having a job at all.'

'Bill would prefer you in a pinny to a uniform?'

'Bill's a good husband.'

'But he has expectations of how a wife should behave? It's a miracle you've managed to keep a lid on that brain of yours for so long.'

'Father always used to say a good brain was wasted on a woman. Do you remember?'

Alec laughed. 'Do I? He never got over his disappointment at me being the dunce and you being the clever one. Lord knows how he coped with Mother discovering she had a brain and sharing it with the Suffragettes. Anyway, Bill should be proud of you for doing your bit.'

'There's a war going on. I don't have a choice.'

'I hope you manage to find a way to keep something like this in your life when it's over. You're wasted as a housewife. And besides, your cooking is frightful.'

She cuffed him on the arm, smiling reluctantly. 'So, apart from flying, what have you been up to? Have you been to the cottage lately?'

He looked up at her. 'Yes, but it doesn't seem the same since Sophie left.'

'Don't be silly. You love it there. So does Scout. He'll be missing chasing squirrels, won't you, little chap?' she said, leaning under the table and rubbing the ears of the old terrier. 'You're not still stuck on that ridiculous theory about her being abducted, are you? I tell you, Alec, she was no good. You're well rid of her.'

'You don't know that,' he said.

'You only knew her for a few weeks.'

'I knew her better than anyone I have ever known in my life.'

Verity laughed. 'Don't be ridiculous. She was a complete stranger.'

He stiffened. 'She was a frightened woman, a long way from home.'

'Please get over this. Why don't we meet up with Fred when we're next in London? She simply adores you—'

Alec slammed his glass down on the table. 'I do not want to be set up with one of your silly friends, Verity. I will find Sophie when this is over, and I will marry her. It's the only thing keeping me going.' He saw the roll of Verity's eyes, but chose to look away, not trusting his temper now it was on one of its rare outings from its box.

'So how about you tell me what you are flying these days?' Verity said.

Scout stirred slightly as Alec reached into his pocket for his pipe and tobacco. He knew she was trying to change the subject, to repair the atmosphere between them, but he was no longer in the mood for chitchat. 'I couldn't say.'

'There's no need to be childish, just because I didn't like your five-minute fancy.'

'You see? You can't stop yourself, can you?' He shook his head. 'I can't tell you, because I'm on Special Duties ops.'

'Oh. Well, I hope it's safer than flying those Mosquitoes.'

He sensed she wanted to offer him a little comfort, but that was not Verity's way, and still bristling from her attack on Sophie, he felt disinclined to put her mind at ease.

He looked at his watch. 'This has been lovely, but I have to get back to the base.'

'And I have to get back to . . .'

'Your pinny?' he asked, feeling a ridiculous urge to make her cross.

Instead, she just stared at him. 'Grow up, Alec,' she said, pulling on her badly knitted beret.

He watched her leave, the bell on the door ringing as she briefly let in the sounds of the street outside. Why had they got themselves into a silly argument? Life was too short, and even shorter in these days of war.

30

Monday, 17 January 1944

Daphne looked around the dusty attic that had been home for the last two nights. The flight from the apartment on the rue Boulard had been swift, and Sophie had paid the concierge an extra three months' rent as Jean-Paul cleared out all traces of their belongings and carried Daphne's heavy suitcase down the stairs.

For now, Daphne found herself in the attic of Sophie's own apartment, where she came down for food and ablutions when the coast was clear. There were often visitors: sometimes the cousin, who spoke quietly with her; sometimes people paying unexpected calls or delivering flowers; and sometimes it was male voices she heard downstairs, the chatter of polite conversation as Sophie spoke in fluent German with her guests.

But there had been no visitors that afternoon and as soon as dusk had turned to dark, Daphne was to leave the apartment via a window to the roof, making her way down the metal service ladder and across the city to a derelict print shop where Jean-Paul had earlier moved the wireless set. From what Daphne had worked out from the messages she had sent, the Allies were planning an air strike that night whilst Sophie was due to perform a recital. If the strike went ahead, they were all in danger and Daphne needed to be away from the apartment.

For hours Sophie had practised in preparation for the concert – scales, studies, fiendishly difficult passages from the programme – until suddenly Daphne heard her play a song her own parents used to dance to in the family kitchen in Stepney. 'I'll be seeing you in all the old familiar places . . .' Daphne found herself humming along, remembering how she and her younger sisters had laughed at their parents behaving like newlyweds, and how Dad had told them they'd understand one of these days, if they ever met anyone half as good as their mum. At least they'd had that, she thought now. If Daphne ever needed to remember why she was here in Paris, scared out of her wits, she just had to recall arriving in Tredegar Road to find a pile of smoking rubble where her home had once stood.

Downstairs the wistful song trailed away, as though Sophie too were caught in some reverie. 'I'll be looking at the moon, but I'll be seeing you . . .' Who was it she saw? Daphne wondered.

'Darling, are you ready?' Bill called from the bottom of the stairs.

'Nearly.' Verity stood at the end of the bed, hands on hips as she looked at the underwear spread on the eiderdown. There was nothing fit for a romantic night away, unless overwashed grey liberty bodices were the thing these days. Oh dear, would Bill be disappointed? This was the least of her concerns, however, as her favourite agent would be walking slowly into dangerous territory later that evening. Verity couldn't bear to think of it. There was nothing she could do for now, other than carry on as normal.

'At last. I was beginning to think you didn't want to come,' Bill said, planting a kiss on the top of her head as she reached the bottom of the stairs, case in hand. 'Best hurry. The train to Maidenhead leaves in under an hour.'

She was just checking her make-up in the hall mirror when the telephone rang.

'I'm not answering it,' he said, shrugging on his overcoat. 'The Admiralty know I'm to be left alone tonight.'

Verity glanced at the Bakelite telephone, the receiver rattling in its cradle. What if it were Whaddon? She couldn't simply ignore it. 'They might be about to tell you to take an extra day's leave,' she said.

Bill laughed. 'It doesn't work like that, you know. Whoever it is, they're persistent, I'll give them that,' he said, as the telephone continued to ring.

'But I really do think . . .'

He looked at her. 'You think it might be for you?'

'I don't know . . .' Almost to her relief, it finally stopped ringing.

Bill took her case from her. 'There we go. Decision made,' he said, opening the front door.

'I suppose so.' She took her hat from beside his peaked naval cap and breathed deeply. If the call had been important, they would have rung back by now.

'Damned thing,' Bill said, as the telephone rang once more. He must have seen her hesitate, for he threw her a warning look. 'Don't answer it, Verity. I mean it.'

She was torn, halfway across the hallway. 'I'm sorry, Bill,' she said, turning towards the little table and picking up the receiver.

'Cooper? Tremayne here. Bomber Command have approved the raid tonight. I need you back here. A car will be with you shortly. Cooper? Are you there?'

She looked at Bill, who put down the suitcases and shook his head at her. 'Yes, I am.'

'You'll be ready to leave in thirty minutes?'

'Yes, sir. I'll see you in a little while.'

She put the receiver carefully back in the cradle. 'I'm sorry,' she said.

'One night, Verity. I just asked you to put us first for one night. All this week you've been distracted. You don't want to be here. You want to be doing whatever that blasted job of yours is.'

'Bill, it's not like that. My work . . . it's important.'

'More important than your family? For God's sake, woman. You're a secretary, not Field-Marshal Montgomery.'

Stung, she longed to tell him that she was case officer to one of the most valuable assets in occupied France, but she couldn't. Aside from the security risk, she had signed the Official Secrets Act, and breathing a word even to her own husband could end in a prison sentence.

'Suit yourself, Verity. You go back to your little job, and I'll get the children to Shropshire before I go back to mine. At least one of us cares about them.'

'Bill, please . . .' she said, but he had already turned his broad back on her, closing the door behind him and leaving her alone in the hallway with the two abandoned suitcases. She seemed to have hurt everyone she loved, but she would make it up to them. Once Colette was safe.

*

Sophie closed the piano lid. It was nearly five o'clock and there was no more she could do to prepare for the evening's recital. Her gown was secured in a long dress carrier, her shoes, jewellery and make-up packed in the small holdall, and stitched into her coat lining were a roll of banknotes, a spare radio crystal and operating schedule, along with the fake ID, glasses and prosthetic teeth that would help her travel incognito.

She had tuned in to BBC Londres and heard the agreed signal that the air strike was confirmed for that evening: 'The elephant wears a red hat,' the announcer had said through the crackle of German interference, and it had felt as though he were issuing Sophie's death sentence with those simple words. There was still time for her to get out of Paris, but if she did not make an appearance that evening, Seelman would know something was up.

She looked across the room to the box containing the corsage of strangely odourless orchids Seelman had sent that afternoon. Although they sickened her, she would wear them while she played to Seelman and his vile comrades.

Would she ever again see this apartment that had been home for ten years, witnessing everything from joyous parties to hours of serious rehearsal? She could still hear the beautiful strains of Hanne's violin echoing around the filigree-plastered walls, the vibration of Fabien's cello through the bare floorboards, see Max taking *The Song of Paris* from the music desk on the piano, making alteration after alteration until he was happy. She glanced at the portrait of herself in the ivory gown she would wear that evening, the gown she had worn in the Lutetia on the last night she and her friends had all been together.

In the street below, a black Mercedes sedan pulled up and Becker emerged from the back seat. She had almost begun to feel a fondness for the man, sensing Becker had a secret of his own and that the value he placed on their friendship was higher than she had at first thought.

And there was no doubt: if the mission to take out the train convoy that night was successful, she would need all the friends she could get.

31

'You should start making your way to the stage,' Inès said. 'The live broadcast will begin soon.'

Sophie finished dabbing powder on her brow, then pursed her crimson lips once more and clipped shut her make-up bag. Her blonde shoulder-length hair had been pulled away from her face and set into wide, shiny rolls piled high on her head, a dazzling diamond clip to one side, twin drop earrings shivering at her jawline. She looked away from the mirror towards Inès, dressed in elegant black, face paler than usual and cheeks pinched with worry. 'You look as though you could do with a little of this rouge,' she said.

'I don't think anyone will notice me this evening.' Inès took Sophie's hands as she stood. 'You are a goddess,' she said, looking her cousin up and down. The creamy-white satin gown matched Sophie's skin tone almost perfectly, its figure-hugging silhouette that of a screen siren of the previous decade, almost more bedroom than concert hall. Delicate spaghetti straps suspended the triangular cups of the bodice, criss-crossing her long bare back, from where the bias-cut skirt fell into a short train.

Inès suddenly threw her arms around Sophie, holding her tight.

Sophie laughed. 'What's this all about? Since when did my frosty cousin start hugging people?' She leaned back. 'Inès, are you all right?'

'I'm fine.' Her cousin pulled away, reaching for the corsage on the dressing table. 'Here, let me.' Inès pressed a few pins between her closed lips and secured the orchids to the left breast of Sophie's dress.

Sophie touched the pale, waxy petals, feeling their weight drag at the gown. 'I hope Seelman does not think I'm wearing these to please him.'

Inès squeezed her hand. 'I will stay close, I promise. And Becker will look out for you. He seems to have a soft spot for you.' She sighed. 'I wish I had never involved you in all of this.'

'If you hadn't, I would have found another way.' Sophie had no regrets, but in truth she knew that if the RAF strike was successful, she would be lucky to leave this building a free woman.

'I'm sorry,' Inès said, turning away.

Sophie took her arm. 'There is nothing to be sorry about. I made my own decision. And besides, the Lysander is on standby for tomorrow night.'

Inès nodded. 'Of course. Jean-Paul is in the auditorium right now, and Daphne ready to confirm your extrication if you need it.'

'It feels wrong to be concerned for myself,' Sophie said. 'If the train is bombed, I am in danger. If not, then many lives will be lost, but I remain safe. How can I live with that?'

'Because of all the lives you have already saved.'

In the corridor outside the dressing room a bell rang out. 'Five minutes,' the stage manager shouted through her closed door.

She looked across to where her packed bag waited, her coat draped across it. 'Inès, keep my coat with you until the interval. It has my false papers and crystal and some other essentials hidden inside. The strike is not due to happen until the second half, but I can't take any chances. I may not have time to return for it.'

The two-minute bell rang and Sophie made her way to the dimly lit corridor, to find Becker waiting for her. He kissed her cheek, pressing her hands in his. 'I wish you all the luck in the world,' he said so solemnly that she almost laughed.

'I don't need luck,' she said. 'Just the hours of practice I've already done.'

She paused as the stage door was held open for her. Bright lights dazzled her briefly as she left Becker and walked on stage. Across the sea of grey uniforms, she saw the tall, broad figure of Jean-Paul slip into a seat on the back row, waiting for a sign from her that he should seek Inès. A microphone leaned in towards the piano, and another was suspended from the ceiling, the radio engineers watching from the box where she saw the live-recording light switch from green to red. France was listening.

She ran her fingers lightly across the keys then dropped her arms to her sides, shaking her hands to loosen any tension. She looked up, seeing the gilt frame and grid of wire-bound strings reflected in the gleaming underside of the raised piano lid. Beyond, Seelman watched with folded arms from the wings.

At this very moment, a train was hurtling across Europe, bearing the means to destroy cities and lives, ships and factories, whilst on an airfield in south-east England, final checks would be made to the bombers about to take off across the Channel on a mission prompted by her own actions. And yet she had to perform as though there were nothing on her mind but the notes poised at the tips of her fingers.

She played in her mind the opening bar of Chopin's explosive Revolutionary Study with which she had chosen to begin the programme, a bold, angry work that left no room for nerves. She closed her eyes, losing the room around her and falling into the trance-like space she needed to occupy. She placed her strong, slender fingers on the keys. Let the fireworks begin, she said quietly to herself.

It was dark as the black Packard stopped at the twin castellated gatehouses of the Hall, its headlamp dimmers throwing shadows across the gravelled drive as a young corporal waved them through. The car had barely stopped before Verity let herself out, hurrying through the porticoed entrance, where she was intercepted by a WAAF section officer.

Verity followed the young woman to the ballroom, its parquet floors and mirrored walls now barely visible behind the scrum of desks and wall maps with red threads pinned across them. It was impossible to imagine dance music above the cacophony of Oxbridge voices shouting to one another across the room, the staccato drill of typewriters and teleprinters and clicking of heels as Wrens brought wireless messages back and forth from the huts on Windy Ridge.

'Ah, Cooper,' Tremayne said from across the smoke-filled room, waving her to join him at a quiet corner desk with the Brigadier who ran Section VIII and one of what Alec called the desk pilots from the Air Ministry. Both men had removed their service jackets and sat in shirtsleeves and tie. 'You know the

Brigadier, of course, and this is Air Commodore Ogilvie from Bomber Command.'

'So it's your girl out there who found out about this?' said the RAF officer.

'Yes, sir,' Verity replied, glad she had changed into her uniform, its stripes affording her professional respect from these men.

'Fine work.' The Brigadier unwrapped his wire-framed glasses from around his ears and wiped the round lenses with a handkerchief. 'No one even at Bletchley had caught wind of this. Without Colette, those rockets would have been headed towards London by the end of the month.'

'When will the attack take place?' Verity asked.

Ogilvie looked at his watch. 'In about an hour. Bomber Command plan to intercept the convoy somewhere near Maastricht at around 1945 hours GMT. There's a good five-mile stretch with no topographical obstacles or tunnels and good visibility if the cloud cover stays away. Very little urban development in the area.'

'Should we have insisted on extricating her, do you think?' Verity asked Tremayne.

'Good question. As soon as that train is taken out, she will be extremely vulnerable, but disappearing before now might have alerted the Germans.'

'What can we do to help her?'

'Ogilvie here will feed us updates on the attack, and we're keeping comms open all evening so that Colette's wireless operator can contact us at any time. Bluebird has been told to let us know by midnight whether Colette has checked in.

I need you ready to decrypt anything that comes in from either of them.'

'And if she doesn't check in? If neither of them does?'

Tremayne and the Brigadier looked at one another, and the soldier folded his arms across his green shirt and red braces. 'As you know, Ogilvie here has asked for a Lysander to be on standby for extrication tomorrow night. Let's hope Colette can get to the pick-up.'

'And Agent Bluebird?' Verity asked. 'Will she be extricated?'

Tremayne hesitated, tapping the end of his pencil on the desk. 'We can't afford to take out any wireless operators right now. Other agents rely on her too.'

Verity knew he was right, but she could hardly bear to think of the lone young woman stranded in Nazi-occupied France. If this war ran on for another ten years, she realised, it could be Penny out there.

Alec had been in the middle of a game of chess with Tempest-Jones, Scout stretched out at his feet, when the duty officer appeared in the cottage sitting room. 'Bad news, Scotty, I'm afraid,' he said, looking down at the board and moving one of TJ's pieces, Alec quickly following with a check mate.

'It'll be bad news all right if you do that again,' TJ said, replacing the pieces.

Alec looked up. 'What's the news, then?'

'You're not off duty tomorrow after all.'

'I thought all the missions had been allocated? Anyway, the moon period's almost over.'

'I know. But another one's come up. Might need someone lifted out tomorrow night, apparently, and you're top of the list, old chap. You're happy for me to tell the CO you're on standby?'

'Of course. Gives me time to bag a few more games off TJ, apart from anything else.'

The duty officer bent down and scratched Scout's head. 'And us all a bit more time to spoil this fella, eh?' he said before taking his leave.

Alec was happy staying on – the chaps were good company, and he had only planned on spending a few days at the cottage in Gloucestershire. One more trip to France made no difference, even if conditions wouldn't be as good as for the full moon a week ago: he had only one thing to lose, and every mission brought him closer to finding it once again.

'Can I get you anything?'

'Thank you, Inès, but no.'

'Not even a glass of water? You must be wrung out after that first half.'

Sophie sat in the armchair in the dressing room, eyes closed and every muscle buzzing from the exertion of the Chopin followed by a showy set of Liszt variations. 'Maybe just a cigarette and some fresh air.'

Inès looked at the clock above the door. 'I don't think you should. You only have ten minutes.'

'Do please stop pacing around, Inès. You're making me quite nervous.' Sophie pushed herself up from the seat, checking her hair and make-up in the mirror. 'The convoy should be intercepted within the hour,' she said. 'Do you think we'll know when it happens?'

'Seelman has been close to the telephone offstage all evening so far. I suspect he will be informed immediately. Does Becker know about the train?' Inès said. 'He's incredibly jumpy.'

'He's not the only one. You're a bag of nerves yourself.'

'Do you blame me?'

'Of course not. Inès, I have a bad feeling about this. I think I should try to get away. Perhaps if I can get to the bathroom, I can escape through the window.'

'No,' Inès said.

Sophie was surprised at her cousin's sudden sharp tone. 'Why not? If I stay, I'm a dead woman.'

'And if you go . . .'

Sophie looked at her. 'Then so are you.'

Angry red pinpoints had appeared on her cousin's cheeks. 'I just want this all over.'

'I'm frightened,' Sophie said, feeling her carapace crumble, her hands shaking as she picked up a cigarette. 'For the first time, I am truly frightened.' She threw a fur wrap around her shoulders. 'I can't bear it. I'm going to smoke this outside.'

'Don't go,' Inès called after her. 'Please.'

Sophie turned around. 'I will be back. I promise.'

It was easy to sweet-talk the guards into letting her slip out of the stage door, where she found a dark corner and leaned against the wall of the building, taking in long, deep lungfuls of smoke. Frost hung in the air, winter extending its grip on the already exhausted, shivering city. She may have reached the end of the line, but she would not give up without a fight.

She dropped the cigarette, hesitating at the sound of voices just inside the door. Seelman was talking with another German, and she pressed herself further back into the shadows.

'What makes you so certain there has been a leak?' the gruff-voiced older man said.

'I'm not. But I'm also not taking any chances – I have my suspicions about a certain individual. If the convoy is intercepted tonight, it will be because she leaked information. Not even the driver of the train knows what it is carrying.'

'And if there has been a leak? You're not concerned about our losing a whole consignment of weapons?'

'No, I am not.'

'Well, I wish I shared your confidence.'

'We cannot lose, trust me,' Seelman said. 'Either there is no leak and the weapons arrive safely at their new base, or there is a leak and Churchill sends the RAF in.'

'And how the hell does that make a win from our point of view?'

'Simple. There are two trains.'

'Two consignments?'

'No, sir. Just one. Four kilometres east of Liège is a tunnel half a mile long. Our convoy will slow down as it approaches, then wait inside as we switch it for another.'

'You're moving the cargo to another train?'

'No, this will be a dummy train carrying prisoners. Mainly Jewish women and children, but also a few Allied servicemen who have found themselves on the wrong side of the track. If Churchill attacks this train, he will be responsible for the death of innocent people being transported to safety by our good Führer, and for the deaths of his own men. Once we know whether the train has been attacked, we either continue to Boulogne or reroute if the line is damaged. By the time the concert is finished, I will know for certain whether my hunch about an informer is right.'

'I must congratulate you, Seelman. This is excellent work. I will be commending you to our Chancellor.'

'Thank you, sir. But now we must hurry, or we will miss the second half.'

The other man let out a rasping laugh. 'I wouldn't want to miss a second of Fräulein Clément's performance. You say she will be our guest afterwards?'

'One way or the other, I guarantee it.'

She listened to the men walk away and glanced around the scruffy yard. The two guards who had been watching over the entrance to the street had wandered off, presumably for a change of shift. With no street lighting, if she ran, she could make it to one of her safe houses nearby within fifteen minutes. A Lysander on standby for the next night, she could be in England within thirty-six hours. But that would leave the trainload of women, children and servicemen exposed to attack by the RAF. Not only would it be devastating for the families of those involved, but it would be a serious blow to morale, just when occupied Europe and the Allies needed the confidence of the world.

She had no choice: she would not be running anywhere. She had to get this new intelligence to Daphne straight away. There was just time to tell Inès to find Jean-Paul and pass on what she had learned, and then she must play.

'Mademoiselle,' said the stage manager, spotting her reappear through the door. 'I have looked everywhere for you. The second half is due to start.'

'I have to visit my dressing room first,' she said.

'There is no time. Please. Follow me.'

Sophie stood firm. 'I must insist. It's a personal matter—'

'Ah, here she is.'

She turned quickly, in time to see Seelman approach. He looked down at the corsage of orchids, and she instinctively held her hand over the bare flesh of her chest. 'There is something so fragile about them, don't you think?' he said, taking one of the delicate white blooms between his fingers and twisting it, so that it came away in his hand. 'Mademoiselle Clément is ready, I believe,' Seelman said to the stage manager. 'Unless there is anything more urgent you need to attend to?' he asked her.

She rolled her shoulders back, returning his stare. 'Only my rather urgent need to use my bathroom.' She turned to the stage manager. 'I will be quick, I promise.'

She felt Seelman's eyes on her as she hurried to her dressing room, closing the door behind her. 'Inès, you must find Jean-Paul straight away.' She quickly told the other woman about the change of the Germans' plans, the information Daphne would need to transmit as soon as possible.

'But what about you?' Inès said.

'I can look after myself. Please, do this, and then go.'

'Sophie, I can't leave you here.'

'You must. If the British act on this in time, you are in danger too. Please, don't let me have your life on my conscience. Think of little Geneviève.' She kissed her cousin on both cheeks. 'Now I must go.'

Inès held her tight, and both women stood back to look at one another for what might be the last time. '*Bon courage, ma cousine*,' Inès said, wiping tears from her eyes. 'Remember that I love you.'

'I love you too, Inès. We will meet at the Lutetia when this is all over, no?'

There was a loud knocking, and Sophie opened her eyes wide, willing tears away as she opened the door, not looking back as she was ushered on to the stage to receive a standing ovation from the still-dazzled audience.

This would have to be the performance of her life.

32

London, 1997

'You got them!'

'They're a bit scratched, I'm afraid,' Jay said, watching Amy examine the record sleeves he had laid out on the shop counter for her.

'I'm just amazed they still exist.' Jay had located two recordings of Sophie Clément, one a selection of Romanic music played with the Phoenix Trio, the cover of which showed Sophie posing at the piano, a cellist and violinist leaning against it. The other was part of a collection of Beethoven sonatas she had recorded in the early thirties.

'These are incredible. What do I owe you?'

Jay held his hands up. 'Nothing. Honestly.'

'I can't just take them.'

'You can if I tell you to.'

Amy turned to Holly, who was happily playing the piano at the back of the shop. 'Holly, that's not yours,' she said. 'Sorry – she's a bit obsessed at the moment.'

'Takes after her mother?'

'Sort of.'

'Looks like her too, with that amazing hair. It's the colour of . . . I don't know. Mango sorbet.'

She laughed. 'Mango sorbet? Thanks a bunch!'

'In a good way. Goes with that green dress you're wearing.' He shook his head. 'Tell the man who lives in ancient band T-shirts to shut up. Oh,' he said, reaching beneath the counter, 'and here's the cassette I told you about, taken from a live broadcast of a concert she gave during the war – a dealer in France found the tape in a job lot he bought a few years back.'

Amy took the cassette box from him. Written carefully on the white cardboard insert were the following words: 'Radio Paris Recital by Sophie Clément at the German Institute, Monday, 17 January 1944.'

'Mean anything to you?' Jay asked.

'Radio Paris was a collaborationist radio station.'

'That makes sense, with her being a Nazi sympathiser,' Jay snorted.

'It's not quite that straightforward.'

'How do you mean?'

Amy hesitated. 'I guess this is all public domain now anyway, with her file being declassified.'

'What file?'

'Sophie Clément's SIS file.'

'Oh, OK. You're an archivist, right? So the government were keeping an eye on her?'

'More than that. They were employing her.'

A bus rattled past the window, so that it was impossible to speak for a moment. Jay rubbed his hand across his close-cropped hair. 'Wow. They kept that quiet.'

'So much so that no one in Paris knew, apart from a handful of agents. And possibly her cousin. She even had a secret husband.'

'No way?' Jay's brown eyes opened wide.

'Seems so, even though she was in love with an RAF pilot.'

'Incredible.'

Amy breathed out. 'You would not believe how brave that woman was.'

Jay looked at his watch. 'Listen, I don't know if you've got plans, but I'm about to shut the shop. We could grab a takeaway and bring it back here, listen to the tape, if you like.'

Amy looked at Holly, who had tired of playing the piano and was lying on the floor, thrashing about with boredom. She turned to Jay. 'Sorry. She's tired. I should take her home. And I've got a friend coming over later. Claire,' she added. 'Fellow mum. Helps with childcare. Feeds me wine. That kind of friend.'

'The best kind.' He shook his head. 'No worries. Take the tape and tell me about it another time.'

'You could come too,' Amy added. 'I mean, the house is a tip but I've got a cassette player somewhere. Claire and I were only going to get drunk and whinge about other mums. You'd be saving us from ourselves.'

'Really?'

'Of course,' she said. 'A takeaway can go towards thanking you for this lot. But you might have to read Holly a story.'

'That's cool with me,' Jay said.

'I want five stories,' Holly shouted, running across and bashing into Jay's legs.

Jay laughed. 'Five it is. But only if I get to choose them.'

'Looks like we've got a deal, then,' Amy said.

33

Monday, 17 January 1944

Daphne sat up straight at the sound of movement in the empty printmaker's shop downstairs. The wireless transmitter was set up in front of her ready for use, and it would take a few moments to retrieve the aerial through the attic rooflight and pack everything away if she were disturbed. She crouched down, peering through a gap in the floorboards where an overhead light hung below, and let out a long sigh of relief.

She stood back as Jean-Paul balanced on a chair to push open the hatch door to the attic and waited for her to drop the ladder down. 'You are ready to transmit?' he said.

'Yes, of course,' she replied, her pulse racing as she sensed the urgency in his voice. She sat at the small table at the far end of the narrow attic, where various leads attached the heavy portable battery, Bakelite headphones and Morse key to the wireless set. She took a pencil and paper, ready to encrypt the message whilst he held a torch over her.

'Target switched for train carrying prisoners, tunnel 4k E Liège,' Jean-Paul read from Inès' scribbled note. 'Attack tunnel once decoy clear.'

Daphne wrote the message out clearly in capital letters, then found the paperback she worked from, randomly choosing page 162, paragraph five, then the fourth word as the cipher code: 16254. She wrote this word down, UNMENTIONABLE forming the first line of a grid underneath which she placed the message in rows of thirteen letters before numbering the cipher-key letters alphabetically:

13	8	7	3	9	12	5	11	10	1	2	6	4
U	N	M	E	N	T	I	O	N	A	B	L	E
T	A	R	G	E	T	S	W	I	T	C	H	E
D	F	O	R	T	R	A	I	N	C	A	R	R
Y	I	N	G	P	R	I	S	O	N	E	R	S
T	U	N	N	E	L	F	O	U	R	K	E	L
I	E	G	E	A	T	T	A	C	K	W	H	E
N	D	E	C	O	Y	C	L	E	A	R	X	X

She then rewrote each column in alphabetical order, starting with TCNRKA from beneath the letter A, and forming a new grid beneath the cipher word, which she then transposed once more, using the same method.

'Can't you go any faster?' Jean-Paul said.

Daphne was already going as fast as she could, without thinking of the train full of innocent people about to be blown to pieces. 'I have to do this twice more. It won't take too long now.' Finally she was ready to transmit, and tapped out her agreed code for the day, followed by the five-number cipher key. 'Come on,' she said quietly, waiting for a response from London.

'What's the hold-up?' Jean-Paul was pacing up and down the attic, rubbing his chin with his hand.

'I can't transmit until I know they're there.'

He held up a hand. 'Did you hear that?'

She took the headphones off and listened carefully. 'Sounds like a truck or something.'

'It's a detector van,' he said. 'They're everywhere tonight.'

She put the headphones back on then turned and smiled at him. 'Got them.'

'Good. Now hurry.'

'You could go without me. I'll finish this then follow on.'

He shook his head. 'I promised Sophie I would get you out of here if anything happened.'

She began tapping in the coded message, leaving enough space between each set of dots and dashes that her communication could not be misinterpreted.

'*Merde*,' Jean-Paul said, as the light downstairs buzzed then fell dark. 'The power is off in the building. They must have caught your signal. They're trying to work out where a battery could be operating a radio. How much longer will you be?'

'Two, three minutes?'

'They're outside,' he went on. 'They know you're here. Stop now, or they'll find us.'

'But what about the train? Innocent people will be killed.'

Jean-Paul put his palms on his head. 'And we will be if you don't put that away now.'

Already she could hear the front door being smashed down, three floors beneath them, dogs barking in the stairwell. She hesitated: there was almost time to hide the machine away, perhaps to make an exit through the rooflight, but suddenly she saw her parents dancing, the smouldering ruins of her family home. She could never knowingly allow another family to go through what she had. Daphne began tapping once more.

'Jesus Christ. Put that fucking thing away now. That's an order.' He pulled his revolver out from the holster hidden beneath his jacket and pointed it towards her.

There were only a dozen letters remaining, and so she carried on, her hand shaking as she pressed the pad of her middle finger firmly on the Morse key, tapping out the arhythmic beat even as the shouts in the storeroom beneath them reached a crescendo. As she finished, Jean-Paul snatched the paper from her, demanding she give him the transmission schedule and list of codes and taking a packet of matches from his pocket. One by one the matches failed to strike as he attempted to set light to the papers. 'Shit. They must be damp,' he said, his own hand now shaking as he dropped match after match to the ground.

Daphne held her breath as she waited for the confirmation code from London, the headphones pressed to her ears as Jean-Paul aimed his revolver at the soldier who had reached the top of the ladder.

'Has it gone?' he called across to her, barely audible above the screamed orders as a Gestapo officer pulled a revolver from beneath his black leather trenchcoat and ordered Daphne to stop.

And then there it was: the three figures that meant her message had been received and the raid would be diverted. 'QS5, QS5,' she shouted triumphantly across to Jean-Paul, seeing his relief just before a bullet ripped into his arm and the officer snatched the papers from him.

Verity looked up as a Wren jogged across the ballroom waving a red Wireless Transmission form. 'Ma'am, this has just come in,' she said breathlessly.

Verity examined the time of transmission, 937's identifying code and the cipher key above the grid of letters. The girl had managed to get the number seven wrong again, but it had almost become part of her style now and helped identify her.

'Let's see what she has to say.' Tremayne handed Verity a pencil and clean sheet of paper and the paperback book in which she quickly identified 937's chosen word. 'Cooper's a lightning cryptographer,' he told Ogilvie and the Brigadier as they watched Verity form a second grid from the letters sent from Paris. 'If you ever need your crossword finished, she's your woman.'

'Do you mind?' she said, glancing up. 'I'm trying to concentrate.'

The men fell silent as she moved the pencil lightly across the paper to create first one then two more grids, until the decrypted message sat before them. She pushed it over to Ogilvie. 'Looks like this one's for you.'

He took it from her then showed it to Tremayne. 'Just in the nick of time,' he said. 'We need to send this to Bomber Command ops room immediately.'

'Follow me,' Verity said, leading them to a bank of teleprinter operators. 'This is a secure line. Dictate your message to Miss Lawrence here and we'll have it over in a jiffy.'

It was a tense few moments as they waited for the response

from High Wycombe, but finally a message appeared on the neighbouring machine: instead of bombing the original target, the Mosquitoes would now destroy the tunnel whilst the convoy of rockets remained undercover there.

'Don't know about you, but I could do with a brandy while we wait for confirmation that the operation was successful. Ogilvie, Cooper, Brigadier? Let's go to my office.'

Verity had underestimated Bluebird, she realised as she sat beside Tremayne's fire in an armchair: it took real courage to create a cipher under pressure. But was the girl safe? Had she been caught whilst transmitting? And what about Colette? To have obtained such last-minute intelligence, she must have been dangerously close to her source. Had she managed to slip away to a safe house somewhere? Both women had agreed to radio in their safe status at midnight, and until then Verity could not rest.

Eventually the telephone on Tremayne's desk rang and he handed it across to Ogilvie, who nodded and said, 'Very good.' He replaced the receiver and looked at them all. 'It's done. The tunnel has been destroyed, and the intensity of the explosion confirms the presence of the rockets. The decoy train was intercepted by a Maquis group on the ground, just inside the French border. They have released the prisoners, including four of our own airmen, and are arranging safe passage for them.' He stood, putting on his jacket, its gold braid gleaming in the firelight. 'Good work, chaps,' he said. 'That'll show Jerry.'

As Tremayne showed the Air Commodore out, Verity couldn't get out of her mind the image of the young wireless operator tearfully begging Verity to recommend her for service.

'Worried about your girls, Cooper?' Tremayne asked. 'We'll

do our best to get Colette out, I promise. The Lysander is on standby for tomorrow – let Tangmere know as soon as we have confirmation she's on the move, would you?'

'Of course.' She would not sit here waiting for news to be brought to her: she would take a bicycle and head through the blackout-dark village and past the church towards the huts, so that she would be the first to know when her girls radioed in their status at midnight.

'I would like to make a change to this evening's programme,' Sophie said in perfect German, looking out over the heads of the audience, her voice breaking slightly.

She had spotted Jean-Paul slip away from the auditorium and knew that whilst her team would do their best to prevent the attack on the decoy train, it was most likely all over for her now. She suddenly felt sick of the whole thing: sick of having to flatter these murdering monsters who would sacrifice women and children without a care, sick of being called a collaborationist whore behind her back, sick of worrying about the safety of the frightened Englishwoman young enough almost to be her daughter. She was sick of eating the Germans' food and drinking their champagne, and now sick of playing their music.

'I know you were expecting to hear Beethoven,' she said, 'but instead I would like to play something composed for me by Max Goldmann, a dear friend who is no longer with us.' She hesitated, glancing at the radio microphones that would broadcast what she was about to say and do. 'Before Max was murdered by your soldiers, he wrote this work – *The Song of Paris* – for me and for his beloved home city. You may recognise some of the sounds of Paris, but you will also hear the dignity of our soul and assimilation of the cultures that have made this city what it is. Ladies and gentlemen, I give you the first concert performance of *The Song of Paris* by Max Goldmann.'

As a murmur of disquiet spread across the auditorium and Sophie sat at the piano, she saw the radio producer had already terminated the broadcast. There were more soldiers alongside Seelman in the wings now, and armed soldiers had appeared at the back of the auditorium. She was grateful to see that Inès had gone, a pale-faced Becker taking her place in the wings.

She played the haunting opening bars of *The Song of Paris*, their melody bringing back her dear friends as clearly as a perfume returns one instantly to a forgotten time. Max had put his soul into this one-movement love poem to the city that had adopted his family and she almost imagined him standing over her, asking her to make tweaks, to bring out certain passages. As the music morphed into a passing reference to the music of the Goldmanns' Jewish heritage, she became aware of more pockets of disturbance around the concert hall. Still she played, nauseous with fear yet never missing a beat, every note exactly as its creator had intended, even though the trilling songs of the Bois de Boulogne were now almost inaudible above the low boos and loud heckles. She had gone too far, but she didn't care.

Off stage, figures rushed back and forth with telegrams, and Seelman stared at her as the piece of paper he had held in his hand floated slowly down to the ground.

Her hands paused, poised above the keys. It had happened. Daphne had sent the message. The convoy had been destroyed and the prisoners saved.

If she managed to make it out of the building, in twenty-four hours a plane would arrive to get her out of France until the heat had died down. A few moments ago, that might have been possible, but the rapidly changing atmosphere of the concert hall suggested that escape was no longer an option.

She had risked her life but saved her reputation. All of Paris would soon know that she had made fools of the Germans.

She stood slowly, ignoring the cries of 'Jewish bitch' and 'Allied whore', the programmes waved in disgust at her. All she saw was Seelman as she headed towards the wings, trench-coated officers of the Gestapo on either side of him. Let them do their worst, she said quietly as she tilted her chin. She was Sophie Clément, head of the most successful resistance network in France. They could not defeat her – she had already defeated them.

Only a couple of operators remained in the corrugated-tin-roofed radio hut for the night shift, Verity having taken over from the woman manning the radio kept available for receiving and transmitting to agents overseas. The small paraffin heaters were no match for the icy draught after which Windy Ridge was aptly named, and so Verity had shrugged on an unclaimed overcoat from the rack near the door.

As midnight came and went, Verity knew she should give up, but what if Colette or Bluebird were to radio in just after she had tucked herself up in her bunk for the night? It was unthinkable.

Minutes ticked by as she watched the idle machine in front of her, willing it to bear news, until suddenly a red light flickered into life and she grabbed the headphones just in time to hear the faint but unmistakable rhythm of Morse code carried across the airwaves.

'BLUEBIRD937. Safe. Further intel 1700 tomorrow,' she read from her scribbled transcription.

Her initial relief morphing into cautious scrutiny, she looked again at the message. It was not unheard of for operators to send uncoded messages when they were under pressure, and so she could forgive Bluebird for doing so. And yet something else nagged at her.

BLUEBIRD937. 1700.

For the first time ever, the young woman had entered the correct code for the number seven. Twice.

Whoever had sent this message was not her agent.

Bluebird was in trouble and Colette had failed to check in.

One or both women had been arrested.

34

London, 1997

Amy and Jay sat on the floor, leaning against the sofa where Claire lay prone, dropping Maltesers into her mouth. Amy had worried about Jay gatecrashing their evening, but Claire was delighted to have a new adult to talk to, and something of a competition had developed between Claire and Holly for Jay's attention. Maybe she should start having people around again: Holly had clearly missed the buzz of their revolving-door social lives.

With Holly finally in bed, Claire's interrogation of Jay's domestic arrangements and ensuing sympathy about the barely-begun divorce led via an affectionate character assassination of her husband David, to her inviting Jay for dinner sometime with Amy.

Amy had eventually sent Claire to the kitchen for another bottle. 'I'm sorry,' she said to Jay. 'She doesn't get out much.'

'It's fine. Neither do I. Talking to two new people? It's like being a student again.'

Amy had laughed. 'Freshers' week relived – all those new faces you can't wait to dump after the first term.' She hesitated. 'I hope you don't think she's trying to . . . well, you know.'

He frowned. 'Oh, yeah, right. Maybe she is, but don't worry. I'm on the rebound – don't touch me with a bargepole.'

'And I've got more baggage than the belly of a Boeing 747.'

He laughed. 'You're funny, you know?'

'Me?' Amy had always thought of Michael as the funny one.

Claire reappeared, sloshing wine into their glasses and collapsing on the sofa. 'So are we going to listen to this pianist woman, then?' she said.

Amy gave them both a summary of what she knew about Sophie so far, the circumstances surrounding the recording of this January 1944 recital, and pushed the cassette into the machine.

It was the first time in years, Amy realised, that she had properly listened to piano music. As Sophie played to them across half a century she felt the old tingle in her hands, found her fingers involuntarily following the familiar scores, despite the poor quality of the recording. She closed her eyes, trying to catch the nuances of phrasing, hearing new voices in music she thought she knew inside out. It was a beautiful, exceptional performance that left Amy breathless.

The recording broke off briefly for the interval, and the second half of the recital was about to begin when Sophie's own voice followed that of the radio announcer. What sounded like a faint murmur grew louder as Sophie's voice was raised.

'*Ich möchte das Programm des heutigen Abends ändern*,' Sophie was heard to say.

'What's that?' Claire asked, reaching across to press the pause button on the machine.

'"I will make a change to the programme," I think,' Jay replied. He shrugged. 'I speak a bit of German. She's going to play something by a friend of hers called Max Goldmann.'

They listened to the tinny crackle of Sophie's voice as she continued: '*Bevor er und seine Frau von Ihren Soldaten ermordet wurden, schrieb er dieses Werk – Das Lied von Paris – für mich und—*'

And then silence.

'Did they just cut her off mid-speech?' Claire asked.

'Sounds like it,' Amy replied. 'Jay, what did she say?'

'Rewind it a bit,' he replied, leaning closer to the machine.

They listened once more to Sophie's mellow voice, the hairs on Amy's arms standing up at the intimacy of hearing her speak.

Eventually Jay looked up at them both. 'The music was called *The Song of Paris*?'

'What else did she say?' Amy asked.

'"Before Max was murdered by your soldiers . . ."'

'Wow.' Amy looked at Jay in disbelief.

'No wonder they cut the mics,' Claire said.

Amy looked at Jay. 'Do you think Max was Sophie's mystery husband?'

'More likely a relative of Hanne Goldmann, the violinist on that record,' he replied, gesturing towards the album on the coffee table.

'Of course.' Amy picked the record up, pulling out the sleeve notes and scanning them quickly. '"Cellist Fabien Dupont was a fellow student of Mademoiselle Clément at the Paris Conservatoire . . ." et cetera, et cetera. Ah – here.' She pointed at a paragraph. '"Hanne Goldmann is the wife of composer Max,"' she read. '"The three musicians met whilst they were students in Vienna." Sophie was making a stand. Publicly. About her friends.'

'And that was the night she was arrested?' Jay said. 'Kind of explains it.'

'She knew she'd been uncovered as a spy, and I guess she'd had enough of being seen as a collaborator.'

Claire rubbed her hands vigorously along her upper arms. 'Gives you the creeps, listening to that. It's one thing seeing films about the war, but hearing a woman on the point of actual arrest . . .'

Amy nodded. 'I know. And she was never seen in public again.'

'Well, this has been jolly,' Claire said, standing unsteadily. 'I think I might head home and have myself some nightmares about Nazis. Hey, Jay, about that dinner. Amy's coming over to ours next week. Why don't you come too?'

Amy glared at Claire, while Jay stared at his shoes, unsure what to say. 'Yes, come,' she said. 'David's a great cook, and Claire pours a great glass of wine.'

'Really?'

'Sure. We'd love to have you. David will want to bore you with his seventies LP collection though, I warn you . . .'

'If it comes to a bore-off, I can stand my ground.'

'Cool. See you next week – Amy can show you how to find us.' Claire wandered into the kitchen to fetch her coat, and Jay turned to Amy.

'It's late,' he said. 'I should go too. Thanks for a great evening.'

'Despite the pissed friend and the Nazis? Being doorstepped into a dinner party? Oh, and the manic five-year-old.'

He laughed. 'Despite even her. I'm available for bedtime

stories whenever.' He shook his head. 'For Holly. Sorry, I'm rambling . . .'

They said goodbye, and Amy found Claire searching for her handbag in the sitting room. 'He's nice,' Claire said. 'I hope you didn't mind me asking him to dinner?'

'He is, and no. It's fine. As long as you're not trying to throw us together?'

Claire hugged her. 'I'm just glad to see you've made a friend. And your own age!' She stood back and looked at Amy. 'He wouldn't mind, you know?'

'Who?'

'Michael. He'd have wanted you to meet new people, do new things. Maybe not replace him quite yet, but you know what I mean.'

'I do. It just still feels wrong to be carrying on with my life.'

'I know. But you have to. You have no choice. Besides, I heard Jay's ex-wife is a piece of work. Sounds like he needs a bit of cheering up too. You could be good for each other.'

'You're right. Thanks, Claire.'

It had been an emotional evening, she thought as she cleared up glasses and bowls of nibbles once Claire had finally left, but it had felt good to have people in the house.

The phone in the hallway suddenly rang, and her stomach fell with the unconscious fear of late-night telephone calls. 'Hello?' she said cautiously into the receiver.

'Sorry to call late,' Billy Wilson said. 'It's Mum. She wants to talk.'

35

Monday, 17 January 1944

Daphne wondered whether the noise ever ceased in this god-forsaken building as she sat in the corner of the dark attic cell, hugging her knees. She would not let them know how frightened she was, how the noises from the interrogation rooms below, the constant barking of orders and banging of doors, made her sick with terror. What was even worse was the pacing of her anonymous fellow prisoners across their own tiny cells, their muffled sobs and angry shouts.

Through the barred rooflight of her cell, she could still see pinpricks of stars. It seemed hours since the black car had cruised into the courtyard of 84 avenue Foch. Daphne had often taken long detours between 'letter boxes' in order to stay away from the Gestapo headquarters in which so many of her predecessors had disappeared, and now she found herself locked in an attic garret there.

As soon as she had arrived through the rear entrance of the building, she had been manhandled into a room on the second floor where German operators played their 'radio game' around the clock, sending bogus messages to London with the compromised codes and radio schedules of captured agents. They had sat her at one of their machines, yelling at her to contact London. She had refused, even at gunpoint, but using the codes taken from Jean-Paul, they transmitted a bogus message to London in her name. She had not cared: Flight Officer Cooper would know instantly it was not her.

Things would undoubtedly become worse for her, but she would not crumble as she had at Whaddon Hall under night-time interrogation; she would not betray Sophie. There was a plan, she knew, for her *patronne* to be extricated the next night, and she willed herself to forget the few details she knew.

She listened to voices along the landing as her fellow agents and operators quietly sang the Marseillaise. Was Sophie amongst them? Or was she already on her way to the Lysander pick-up?

She heard German voices and the rattle of keys as another prisoner was brought up the stairs and locked into the room beside hers. As he shouted his defiance at his departing captors, she recognised the deep voice rhythmically chanting '*Vive la France!*', echoed by other prisoners.

It was Jean-Paul. He was alive, and she was not alone.

For a few ridiculous moments, Sophie had imagined the Gestapo truck was driving her home as they made their way past the locked *bouquiniste* stalls and the unusually quiet cafés of the rue Saint-Germain before turning towards the ancient military Prison du Cherche-Midi, only a few minutes' walk from her apartment. She had been bundled into a tiny cell on the ground floor, with barely room to move around the narrow bunk and its festering mattress. In the cell beside her, a woman sobbed for help from the unmoved guard patrolling the corridor: she had been mistakenly arrested, her baby left alone in a freezing-cold apartment for three days.

She too would freeze in her flimsy gown, Sophie realised. If she were not to die of hypothermia before they collected her for interrogation, she would have to wrap herself in the filthy, thin blanket folded on the narrow wooden bunk. She ripped the corsage of orchids from her bodice and pulled the blanket around her, taking in her surroundings.

The cell was more coffin than room, a jug of water and slops pail in one corner and a chair in the other, a bitter wind blowing through the glassless barred window. She could not stay here. In twenty-four hours a plane would be waiting to take her back to London. She had evaded capture under her false identity in Marseille only months ago, by bribing the driver of the police van to release her, and under another pseudonym had given the slip to members of the Milice, who had raided a bar where she awaited a contact. Somewhere between the Prison du Cherche-Midi and avenue Foch she would escape. She just had to work out how and where.

She jumped at the sound of keys in the lock and turned to see the guard opening the door. 'Visitor,' he said in German to her, standing back to let an officer through into the tiny space.

'You can leave us. I'll call you to let me out again,' Becker said, waiting for the man to grunt his assent and close the door behind them.

'Why are you here?' she said. 'I thought Seelman was keeping me all for himself.'

'He doesn't know I'm here. No one is allowed to speak to you. You're a VIP prisoner.'

'I should be honoured, I suppose. Although I don't care for the accommodation.'

He tried to laugh but struggled to raise anything more than a desperate mutter. Becker was frightened, she realised, as vulnerable to punishment as she was if Seelman found out he had been here.

'I don't have long,' he said. 'As soon as he knows I've visited you – and they are probably telephoning him as we speak – they will remove me.'

'Have you come to say goodbye?' she asked, as the prospect of a summary execution in the prison yard flashed across her mind.

'I hope not.' He had brought a large leather attaché case with him, embossed with the Nazi eagle and swastika. He took out a folded item of clothing. 'Your coat,' he said. 'I retrieved it from your dressing room.'

'Thank you.' She took the coat from him, watching to see if she was being tricked. 'Do you know if Inès is safe?'

He looked uncomfortable. 'She is. Please don't concern yourself with her.'

There was an edge to his voice, but she sensed he would not say more. 'You know what is in my coat?' she said.

He nodded.

'And yet you are helping me. Why, Becker? Why put yourself at risk for me?'

He sighed. 'Sometimes we are not always what we seem.'

'I don't understand.'

'Maybe not. But your husband does.'

'My husband?'

'Forgive me, but I needed to understand why a husband would stay away from a woman as beautiful as you.'

'My husband is away on business . . .' she said, beginning the familiar lie, then faltering.

'He is in Paris. It was he who left your concert early . . .'

'You're wrong.'

'. . . he I saw you with in the Bois de Vincennes.'

Sophie remembered the meeting on a park bench, seeing Becker involved in an altercation nearby.

'Your husband knows what I am, and I know why you married him. You are a good and generous person, but there is nowhere safe for men like us in this world. Maybe there never will be, but I can't do this any longer. A friend was arrested last night. An old friend I had known in this city before the war.'

'The artist you spoke of?' Sophie said, confused. 'She is in custody?'

He nodded. 'Not she, but he. You saw him yourself, outside the restaurant where we lunched that day.'

She thought back, recalling the young man she had assumed to be a lone-wolf resistant, remembering Jean-Paul's reaction to seeing Becker in the park. She took Becker's pale, cold hand. 'I am sorry. Truly sorry.'

He smiled. 'Sometimes it is enough to know there are people like you in the world.'

'And sometimes it is enough to meet people who inspire us. I am glad I have known you, Becker.'

'Bruno,' he said. 'Always remember me as Bruno, who found and lost the love of his life in this city of yours. And who had the honour of knowing you for a short while.'

'Perhaps we will meet again when this is all over?'

'Perhaps.' He looked across at the window. 'I met a stonemason once, who had worked on many prisons. He told me that when the bars have been set in wet concrete and the gap measured by prison officials, it is common for the mason to push one of the bars an inch or two across, to widen the gap. They call it the "bar of freedom". A silly story, but interesting nonetheless. Here, there is one more thing I wanted you to have.' He reached into the case and pulled out a small bottle of olive oil. 'I'm told it is good for softening the skin, although it can be a little slippery.'

She took it from him, glancing across to the window and then back again. 'Thank you . . . Bruno.'

'There is a change of guards at five a.m. Apparently the morning shift always arrives late,' he said. 'And now I must take my leave. *Vive la France*,' he added, to her surprise, before turning his back on her and banging his fist on the door for the guard to let him out.

36

Tuesday, 18 January 1944

Sophie waited through the night, listening to the hours and half-hours ringing in harmony from church bells across the city. Every so often she walked across to the window where at first glance the gaps between bars appeared the same, but stretching her hand between each pair of bars, she could see by her span usually measured in piano keys that one of the gaps was indeed wider. She experimented, placing the chair on the bunk and reaching her head a little through the space left by a generous stonemason. It was incredibly tight, but possible at the right angle, and if her pelvis would fit through, she would be free. At her lowest weight since childhood, she knew she had a chance.

Across the yard a small metal gate led to the street, and she watched a couple of guards come and go through this, seemingly without any need to lock and unlock it. It must have been assumed that escape was impossible, or the consequences feared more than incarceration itself.

The hours ticked by, and as she heard the fifteen minutes to five peal across the still-dark, sleepy city, she began to prepare. She stripped off the white gown, ripping fifty centimetres off its hem so that it would not show below the coat's hemline, then covered her face and naked body with the oil Becker had brought.

As five o'clock chimed she took her coat and shoes, and checking the coast was clear dropped them to the ground outside and tied the dress around her neck. The pain as she forced her head through the bars was excruciating, and at the sound of dogs in the distance she panicked, wondering whether she would be able to retract it if guards appeared. The patrol changed direction and she twisted, pushing first her right then her left shoulder through the ice-cold bars, the oil allowing her bones to ease inch by inch towards safety. Bruise after bruise burst on her pale flesh and she tasted blood. With one final, screaming twist of her hips, her second leg was through and she was free.

She jumped the few feet to the ground below, wincing as the landing jarred her hip, and took the dress from around her neck, slipping it on quickly and covering it with the coat. She waited in the shadows as she heard voices, then crossed the yard on all fours, grateful for the blackout. It was only a moment before she had passed through the gate and on to the street beyond, wearing the thick, round-framed glasses ripped from the lining of her coat pocket, the discarded hem of the dress tied into an innocuous turban to disguise her blonde hair.

With daylight two hours away, she hoped to make her way undetected to a nearby safe house where she would contact London on the radio hidden in the pharmacy basement and apply the bottle of dark hair dye she would find there. Public transport would be impossible once her disappearance had been discovered, but the network owned a vegetable warehouse near the Place de la Bastille, along with a truck converted from an old car in order to gain the commercial status required for obtaining fuel.

This time tomorrow she could be back at Whaddon, working out how she might continue her resistance work now she was exposed, and how she might help Daphne and Jean-Paul. Once she had done that, she would beg Tremayne to tell Alec she was safe.

Verity sat at her desk, working through jobs that had piled up in her absence. The morning shift was by now ensconced in the signals hut, under instructions to send any communications from the Paris network straight across to her.

It was that day of the month in which Verity posted pre-written, deliberately uninformative letters from each of her agents to their families, reporting on the fictitious cover roles their loved ones believed them to be performing: Mrs and Mrs Hardwick would be relieved to hear their daughter was enjoying her work with the FANYs at a hospital in Guildford, while in actual fact young Gloria was on covert operations, posing as a barmaid in a grotty Lyon suburb. Agent Skylark's elderly refugee mother would much rather not have heard that her war-widowed daughter had returned to France and was working undercover in a laundry processing German uniforms.

She had just begun writing to one of the military dentists they used, requesting he exchange a new agent's existing fillings for the type commonly used in France, when she heard a tap at the door.

'Come,' she said, taking off her glasses and placing them on the desk.

'This is just in, ma'am.'

Verity took the red form from the young woman. 'You acknowledged receipt to the sender immediately, as I asked?'

'Yes, ma'am.'

She waited until the woman had left, then took a clean sheet of paper and began working through the matrix of jumbled letters, the paperback on her desk giving her the chosen cipher key. The message was brief:

My dearest godmother,
The cow jumps over the moon.

It was Colette. Verity's agent was alive and would listen for these few words on the BBC that night as confirmation that her extrication was going ahead.

She picked up the telephone. 'Operation Minuet is on,' she said to the duty officer at 161 Squadron.

Alec whistled to Scout, calling the dog back across the dew-sprinkled meadow. The sun had just risen on a crisp, clear day, and as the pilots of last night's successful double mission slept off their cooked breakfasts back at the cottage, Alec wondered whether he would be tucked up in bed with a double brandy and a plate of eggs and bacon inside him the next morning.

He opened the back door of the cottage, Scout rushing through as Alec hung up his Air Force-issued greatcoat and made his way to the dining room. He helped himself to tea from the large pot keeping warm alongside racks of toast and scrambled eggs straight from the cottage henhouse.

'Scotty, there you are,' the duty officer said. 'Bring your breakfast to the ops room. You're flying tonight. The squadron leader's waiting for you, along with some chap from SIS.'

'Any news on who the Joe is?'

The duty officer shrugged. 'All I know is she's French and very high profile. The top brass are pretty rattled.'

It made no difference to Alec: every trip was as important to him as the last, no life less valuable than another. His focus was only on doing the best job he could, and this mission would be no exception. He would do everything in his power to bring this woman back safely, whoever she was.

37

London, 1997

'You didn't tell us Jay was a pianist too,' Claire said, as they listened to him play the little upright David had bought years ago in order to teach himself jazz piano, but which had sat neglected in the corner of the huge kitchen ever since, resting place only to bills, school letters and stray socks.

Amy smiled. After a lovely meal, it was nice not to be the one people turned to for entertainment, just to be able to listen to someone else play, even if it did make her wistful for the days when playing brought her as much pleasure as it obviously did Jay. And actually he was good. Really good. He didn't read music, like Amy did, but his playing was instinctive, learned by ear, full of fun and joy. Holly and Susie stood on either side of him in their pyjamas, telling him to play Spice Girls songs, which he churned out as though they were the finest Oscar Peterson numbers, but when they began to shout for the *Teletubbies* theme tune, David clapped his hands loudly.

'Enough. Go to bed, horrible children, and leave the adults to drink and swear in peace.' He scooped a small girl under each arm. 'Say goodnight and promise you won't come down again until morning,' he said, turning them to face the others around the table, then carrying them shrieking out of the kitchen and upstairs.

It was the first time in a long while that Amy had enjoyed an evening of such simple, happy pleasure. She sat at her friends' familiar kitchen table wearing a brick-orange, full-skirted vintage number she'd picked up in Camden Passage on the way back from taking Holly to visit Michael's parents, glad to ring the changes but also to feel so comfortable in these surroundings, even if it was Jay not Michael sitting beside her. And for once Holly had not clung to her legs or refused to play with Susie – after some initial hesitation she had thrown herself into the occasion, perhaps seeing her mother relax a little and allowing herself to do so as well.

'We have a breakthrough. I'd say she's happy sleeping over,' Claire said, noticing Amy's stare towards the doorway.

'I'd say she's going to be a nightmare, after all that chocolate you gave them,' Amy laughed.

Claire sloshed more red wine in her glass and leaned back in her chair. 'Ah, they'll be fine. Chocolate is God's gift to parents, wouldn't you say, Jay?'

'That and Valium. Yup. Works in my house.'

'And why did you let them back down again?' Amy said. 'Jay had read them a million stories.'

'That would be the allure of my piano playing,' he shrugged modestly.

'I blame David for forcing you to play,' Amy said.

Claire wagged a finger at Jay. 'I warned you not to get my husband on to the subject of music.'

Jay spread his hands. 'What can I say? It's my thing. I'm as bad.'

'No wonder you and Michael got on. Jeez, Amy, do you remember the nights David and Michael would play record after record, arguing about which was the best version of some obscure song? We could have left them at it for a fortnight and they'd only have noticed when they got hungry.'

'Music's like that,' Amy said.

'You should know. And so should this one here,' Claire said, holding out a hand to her husband, who had just reappeared in the kitchen.

David kissed her hand then refilled his wine glass and sat beside her, an arm draped around his wife's shoulder. 'What should I know?' he said.

'About how music can be an obsession, what with you being a sound engineer.' Claire held up a finger. 'And no, do not start boring Jay about it.' She clearly saw the disappointment on Jay's face, and went on, 'Well, maybe another time. God, you two boys are made for each other.' She laughed. 'Look, you've virtually got the same clothes on.'

Amy smiled as the two men indignantly explained the difference between their vintage Stones and vintage Velvet Underground T-shirts, pointing out that Jay wore a jacket over his, while David had gone for the open-shirt look.

Claire rolled her eyes. 'See? Music nerds.'

'Hey, David,' Jay said, 'maybe Amy should get you to clean up that cassette I found?'

Claire sat up, her long earrings quivering as she lit a cigarette. 'Yes! Remember, I told you about the dead pianist woman, David?'

'Oh, yeah,' he said, taking a chocolate from the box open on the table. 'I'd love to. Her story sounds amazing.'

'It is,' Amy said.

Claire waved her cigarette towards Amy. 'You should so write a book about her.'

'A book?'

Jay bounced in his seat. 'That would be amazing.'

'I don't know. I haven't got time, apart from anything else.'

'So ask your boss. It would be kind of work, wouldn't it?' Claire said.

'Well, yes, but we still don't know what happened to Sophie, where she ended up.'

'Then,' David said, 'you must find out. Go to Paris, if that's what it takes.'

'Paris?'

'Isn't that where she disappeared?' Claire said.

'Well, yes, but I can't just go to Paris.'

'Sure you can,' David said. 'We'll look after Holly.'

'Or,' Claire said, 'Michael's parents could come and look after her?'

'Really? You know what Maria's like.'

'Sure, she thinks you're a goyishe stain on her family, but she adores Holly. It would be good for all of them.'

'True.'

'And if you write the book, you could publish David's remastering of the cassette at the same time,' Jay said.

'Guys!' Amy held up her hands. 'You're jumping way ahead of yourselves. I haven't even met with this Daphne woman who was her radio operator. She might know where Sophie ended up, and there'd be no point in going to Paris.'

'Maybe,' Claire said, then narrowed her eyes. 'But you know you want to, don't you?'

38

'I hope you don't mind meeting out of doors. I'm not keen on unfamiliar indoor spaces, and I don't want to have this conversation in front of Billy.'

'Of course not, Mrs Wilson.' Amy sat beside her on the bench, pushing aside a discarded *Evening Standard*, its front page splashed with images of Princess Diana frolicking on a Mediterranean yacht.

'There are worse places than Vicky Park to pass the time of day, I suppose,' Daphne said. 'You should have seen it before the war. Dad used to bring us boating on this lake. There was a beautiful Chinese pagoda across the water there – just a bit more of our history Hitler stole.'

She closed her eyes as the sun peeked through the clouds, and even in repose her features spoke of the pain of secrets held for too long.

'What made you change your mind about meeting me?' Amy said, watching a mother and toddler throw bread to some tatty-looking mallards.

'Justice, I suppose. Knowing that for all these years people have thought bad of her. And now you come along and stir it all up.' Daphne shifted on the bench, wincing as she turned on her hip. 'Don't get old,' she said to Amy. 'It's a bloody pain. That's the only thing that makes it better – knowing she'll never have to get old. That wouldn't have been her style. There was something about her . . .' she hesitated . . . 'like she was too beautiful for this world. No wonder men fell over themselves for her.'

'She seems to have been an incredible woman. And so brave. Do you think she was ever frightened?'

'You'd never have known it, to watch her, but some of the situations she got herself into must have been terrifying.'

'What sort of situations?'

'Oh, you know, high-level parties and such. Mixing with some nasty, dangerous men. Never stopped her, though. She just kept coming up with the goods.' Daphne chuckled. 'I must have driven her mad, even though she really looked after me. Our training officer – the Sodmother, we called her – thought I wasn't up to the job when they sent me out, and I daresay I wasn't. The only thing I had going for me was that I spoke French – learned it off my mum.'

'The Sodmother?' Amy asked, smiling.

'She was our "godmother", our handler, made sure we were all right. She could be a bit strict if anyone messed around on their training – some of the girls called her the Sodmother for a joke, and I suppose it stuck.' She shook head. 'Not that we'd ever dare say it to her face! No, she was a good sort. Don't suppose her job was easy either. What was her name now?' Daphne drummed her heavily ringed fingers on her Crimplene trouser leg.

'Verity Cooper, maybe?'

'Blow me down. How do you know that?'

Amy smiled. 'I've been speaking to her recently about Sophie.'

'She's still alive? Well, bugger me. I haven't thought about her in years.'

'She remembers you.'

The old lady chortled. 'I bet she does. I can hear her now, drumming my Morse code into me.'

'You were a radio operator in Paris?'

'That's right. Sophie would bring me the information she'd got off the Germans, and I'd send it off to London. It was risky. She had to move me loads of times. I ended up sleeping in her attic, right at the end.'

'And were there any more of you?'

'More agents? Yes, but I never got to meet them, apart from Jean-Paul.'

'Jean-Paul?'

'Old friend of hers, I think. They were close.'

'A couple?'

Daphne laughed. 'I should say not.'

'It's just that Verity thought she might have been married.'

'Not to Jean-Paul, that's for sure. Nor anyone else I knew of, although I got the feeling she had someone in England.'

'She did. A pilot. He was Verity Cooper's brother. He flew you out to Paris.'

'On the Lysander?' Daphne stared at her. 'Yes, I remember him now. I can see why Sophie fell in love with him. He was a gent, looked after me even though he must have known I was petrified. Good-looking, you could tell, despite the burns. Someone told me he'd been shot down in the Battle of Britain.'

'Daphne, I really hate to ask you to talk about this stuff, but I'm trying to find out for Verity what happened to Sophie. I think she still feels guilty about a lot of things.'

Daphne sighed. 'She's not the only one. If I could have done anything differently, I don't know whether I would, looking back, but if I'd been more careful transmitting that night, she might never have been arrested. I'd rather have died than let her down again. Or Jean-Paul, for that matter.'

'And many more lives would have been lost, from what I gather. It sounds like Sophie would have been proud of you.'

'But I got her arrested. How was I meant to live with that? All I could do was try to stay strong when they found me.'

'Was that the night of the concert?'

'You know about that?'

'I came across a tape recording of it.'

'You listened to it?' Daphne shuddered. 'I can't even bear to hear the piano played now.' She turned to Amy. 'You want to know why I agreed to talk to you?'

'Of course.'

'Because of what Seelman did. To me, to her, to so many of us. To the Jewish families he cleared from Paris.'

'It was Seelman who interrogated you?'

Daphne pressed a hand against her mouth, holding back her sobs as she nodded slowly.

'Daphne, you don't have to tell me. I don't want to distress you.'

She turned to Amy, her blue eyes bright with anger. 'I do have to tell you. I want you to know exactly what sort of animal he was.'

39

Tuesday, 18 January 1944

At least three times during the night they had dragged her down to the bowels of the building. Three times Daphne had been made to stand barefoot in the middle of the cold cellar, the bare lightbulb illuminating the typist taking down every word of her interrogation. Sometimes they threatened violence, but most terrifying were the treacly questions designed to lure her into handing over even the most innocuous facts. How had she met Jean-Paul? Had he coerced her into working for him? They could protect her. Besides, the pianist had already told them everything.

Daphne knew they were lying. Nothing on earth would persuade Sophie to talk, and nothing would persuade Daphne to betray her. Even when they knocked her to the ground, or when she received stinging lashes from a leather strap across the back of her knees. Even when they plunged her hooded head into a bucket of freezing water and she heard her own underwater screams, slipping into unconsciousness only to be pulled from the water long enough to take a single breath, so that she thought her lungs might burst.

They had left her soaking wet in her freezing cell for a few hours now, long enough to hear Jean-Paul and other prisoners come and go to the lower floors. She had almost fallen into a light sleep when her door was opened once more and she braced herself for what was to come.

This time it was a new face she saw before her. 'Good afternoon,' he said. 'I am Colonel Seelman. Perhaps you would care to join me for lunch?'

She shrank back against the wall, never taking her eyes off his almost hairless brow, the blond hair plastered to his head. His quietly spoken French and good manners frightened her more than the feral inhumanity of her night-time inquisitors.

'You,' he said to the guard at her door. 'Fetch her some dry clothing then bring her down.' He turned back to Daphne. 'The fire is lit in my office, Agent Bluebird. I think you will find it more comfortable there.' Seelman nodded his head briefly, then turned and left.

She told herself not to fall for these tricks: she would sit beside his fire but she would not eat with him, even if he produced the finest chateaubriand in Paris. She would not partake of so much as a sip of his coffee.

Daphne heard a light tapping on the thin partition wall separating her from Jean-Paul's. He was trying to tell her something. She listened carefully, translating each letter until the Morse code spelled out the events that had prompted the change of tactic: Sophie had escaped and the Germans had no idea where to find her.

She closed her eyes, imagining Sophie already on her way to the pick-up zone. Only she and Jean-Paul knew the location of the Lysander pick-up – they would give Seelman nothing.

*

Alec looked out of the ops room window as yet another black car pulled into the cottage drive. 'How many secret service officers does it take to greet one spy off a plane?'

Tempest-Jones joined him. 'That's Tremayne – don't often see him down here. Shows how valuable this one is.'

Alec watched an avuncular-looking man in well-cut civvies walk across and shake hands with Wing Commander Carlisle. 'Better make a good show of it, then,' Alec said, turning back to the maps spread across the table. 'Read those coordinates out to me again, would you, TJ? There's a good chap.' Alec worked silently with the angled ruler, marking with a pin the small field north of Paris, near the town of Compiègne, where he would collect his passenger.

'Not too far to that one – done it myself,' TJ said. 'Two and a half hours each way. What time's the pick-up?'

'0100 hours.'

'Marvellous. You'll be back in time for a nightcap.'

Alec looked up as the door was opened.

'Flight-Lieutenant Scott,' said Carlisle, 'this is Sir Richard Tremayne. He's here to confirm the details with you.'

'So you're the fellow bringing our agent back this evening?' Tremayne said, joining Alec at the table.

'Yes, sir.'

'Scott, you say?'

'Alec Scott.'

'Flight-Lieutenant Scott.' The older man narrowed his eyes. 'Been a pilot long?'

'Signed up right at the beginning of the war. 614 Squadron, trained at Aston Down in Gloucestershire.'

'You live down there?'

'I have a cottage there, yes.'

'Where exactly?'

'I'm sorry, I don't understand . . .'

'I said where?'

Alec sighed. The man was Secret Services: it was easier just to answer. 'A little place called Burleigh, near Stroud. You wouldn't know it.'

Tremayne suddenly turned to Carlisle. 'This is the only chap you've got free tonight?'

The man looked puzzled. 'Yes. The others have gone back to our sister base at Tempsford, and last night's pilots flew almost to the south of France and back. Why?'

'I don't think he is suitable.'

'Scotty here is one of our best. Spitfires and Mosquitoes before he came here, and not a failed op to his name. If he doesn't fly tonight, the mission is off.'

'Is there a problem?' Alec said.

'It seems we have no other option, so I hope not.' Tremayne sat back, his arms folded across his chest. 'Nothing must go wrong with this mission,' he said, staring at Alec. 'I must insist you do not speak to your passenger. At all. On arrival back here at Tangmere, my second-in-command will escort the passenger straight off the airbase. There will be no interaction between you. Am I clear?'

'Sir, we have a very strict policy about not sharing personal details with passengers. Scotty knows this perfectly well.'

'Am I clear?' he said again, slowly.

As he and Tremayne looked at one another, Alec sensed

there was something more to this strange conversation, something it was pointless trying to discover. 'You are clear,' he replied eventually.

'Sorry to be heavy handed, but my agent's safety is my priority.'

Alec nodded. 'It is my priority too.'

'Good chap. Now here are the agreed Morse code signals: you will send out the letter H and receive a P in return. It is imperative that this agent is extricated – our entire network in northern France will be under attack if not.'

'Please trust me, sir,' he said to Tremayne. 'I want to get your agent home safely as much as you do.'

Tremayne nodded then smiled. 'Thank you, Scott. I know you do.'

She cycled through the Latin Quarter, past the silent Sorbonne university and towards the River Seine, careful not to slip on the sleet-washed cobbles as light began to leach from the fading day. The river, once sparkling with the reflections of the tall lamps festooned along its banks, was a treacly ribbon of unbroken black velvet in the gloomy dusk. As she left behind familiar landmarks, she imagined the strains of *The Song of Paris*, but Max's music now spoke of a city haunted by the ghosts of those who would never return.

It seemed impossible that she would ever want to leave this city, but in England she could recover from the years of leading a double life, which had taken their toll on her sleep, her weight, her peace of mind. She could find Alec and start a new life with him. She would repair bridges with Verity –

perhaps even ask her 'godmother' at Whaddon to vouch for her integrity. But that would mean abandoning her country, which she could never do. And besides, how could she leave Daphne, Jean-Paul, all the people who depended on her? And so she knew that once it was safe, she would be back to fight on.

She checked the length of the metal-veined Pont Sully that leapfrogged the Île Saint-Louis to the far bank of the Seine. There were German roadblocks all across the city, and even with her hair now dyed dark, thick, black-rimmed glasses and prosthetic teeth helping disguise her, she was by no means safe. She pressed her blue-cold fingers around the handlebars and set off along quiet streets towards the backstreet vegetable warehouse where Kestrel awaited her, avoiding the wide boulevard leading towards the Place de la Bastille. Once a place of celebration for Parisians, it was now a hotspot for trouble, and so Sophie slipped into the unlit matrix of streets to the east.

'Good God, woman, what happened to your hair?' Kestrel said as she dragged the bicycle through the service door at the back of the warehouse. 'And what are you wearing? Did you just get married?'

'Strangely, they did not supply me with a travelling costume at the Prison du Cherche-Midi,' she said, looking down at the white gown.

'Gorgeous as ever, *chérie*, even if you look like you've been in a bar brawl.'

She rolled her eyes. 'You never give up.'

'Could be my last chance for a while. Can't blame a chap for trying.'

'And you can't blame a woman for saying no.'

'Still that bloody pilot, eh?'

'Still that bloody pilot, *oui*.'

He threw an arm around her shoulders. 'I shall miss you, old thing. Paris won't be the same without you.'

'I shall be back.'

'I hope not. It won't be safe for you for a long while.'

'And Inès?'

A light frown creased his forehead. 'Let's just say your cousin is lying low for a while.'

'Has something happened to her? Or Geneviève?'

'They are both safe.'

'What about Daphne? Jean-Paul?'

He hesitated. 'I'm sorry. They were taken to avenue Foch last night.'

'They are still alive?'

He nodded. 'But now there's even more urgency to extricating you. We're to listen to the BBC in . . .' he glanced at his watch . . . 'well, about now. They'll broadcast confirmation the Lysander's on for tonight.'

'I can't leave them here.'

'You have no choice. If one of them talks and you're not on that plane, you're dead.'

'They wouldn't,' she snapped back, certain of their loyalty, but knowing how far some of her previous agents had been pushed: the toughest had gone to their deaths with their toenails removed but their lips sealed, but never had she blamed any of the others for cracking.

Kestrel was right: she needed to get out.

He took her to a small room at the back of the warehouse and began fiddling with the dials of a large radio. 'Here we go,' he said, as the clipped-voiced BBC announcer said through the crackle of German signal jamming, 'And now for this evening's messages.'

They listened to the stream of coded sentences until finally they heard the one they were waiting for: 'The cow jumps over the moon.' Sophie's rescue flight was being prepared, her pilot planning his route and making final checks to the aircraft.

'Come on, then. Let's get you loaded up,' Kestrel said.

It took him a little time to help squeeze her slim frame into an old sack before tucking her into the far corner of the flatbed truck, hidden behind sacks of potatoes and turnips. Two hours before curfew, the old truck sputtered out of the yard and headed north-east out of the city, passing easily through two roadblocks before reaching the cover of dark country lanes.

Verity settled into the deep leather seat of the Packard, checking once again that she had packed the gift she had bought for Colette. This far out of season and with floristry an unnecessary wartime luxury, instead of flowers she had sent to Harrods for a pretty scarf.

She thought of the scarf Alec's Frenchwoman had given her. She often wondered what had happened to Sophie Clément, the few photographs that crept through merely confirming she was as embedded with the Nazis now as she had been back then. When she thought of the bravery of her 'goddaughters' compared with the vile collaborationist behaviour of women like Clément, she could only hope time would deal them justice.

Should she have told Alec what she'd found out? It had seemed kinder at the time to let him think the woman had just disappeared, but even after nearly three years he still mooned over her. Perhaps the time had come to tell him the truth so that he could lay her ghost to rest.

'How long before we reach Tangmere?' she called to the driver.

'Two hours, ma'am.'

She would not be in time to meet the pilot assigned to the mission but would be able to watch his progress on the huge maps in the ops room.

And by the morning she would be returning to Whaddon, SIS's prize agent at her side.

40

'Good luck, sir,' the dispersal sergeant shouted above the roar of the engine before closing the cockpit hatch and making his way back down the ladder.

Alec checked once more that the folded maps were safely secured on his knee and his revolver and escape bag stashed within easy reach. 'Chocks away,' he radioed to the ground crew, then turned the aircraft towards the runway. He accelerated hard before easing the Lysander into the air. Ahead the moon shimmered low in the sky, its reflection sprayed across the rough surface of the English Channel. He forced the plane up to six thousand feet and switched off the navigation lights, relaxing as the airspeed levelled out.

It would be little over an hour before he reached the town of Cabourg on the Normandy coast, where he would make his first turn towards the landing strip. He checked his instruments once more, stiffening slightly as the plane made its way out of the safety of Allied airspace.

Daphne lay facing the wall, waiting for the rattle of the key in her door. After an entire night and day of hour-on, hour-off interrogations, alternating with Jean-Paul, it was not a case of if, but when they came.

She shifted on the dirty mattress, wincing as the blood-soaked bandages on her bare feet and hands caught on the blanket. The next time they took her down she would have to be carried, the doctor had warned the guards. He had taken such care over her, gently cleaning the wounds their cane had dug into her tender flesh and apologising as she cried out. What had brought a man of medicine to this terrible place of death and torture? Had he a family, maybe a daughter of Daphne's own age, who would suffer if he didn't play his part?

There had been nothing of his humanity about Seelman, who had failed to win her over with food she desperately craved but refused to touch. He had failed to intimidate her with first veiled then increasingly explicit threats of violence when she refused to tell him where Sophie's safe houses were, or how her *patronne* was to be spirited out of France. He claimed to abhor violence, told her he had never hurt a woman in his life, but it had not stopped him delegating this work to his two thugs. But as long as she and Jean-Paul held out until the Lysander was safely on its way back to England, she didn't care what they did to her. They had threatened to shoot her if she gave them nothing next time. Well, let them. If Jean-Paul could stand their threats, then so could she.

She heard voices on the stairs once more, the dragging of feet as one prisoner was brought back to make room for another's suffering. It was Jean-Paul, she realised as she heard them open his door. She was relieved he was to be spared temporarily but terrified at what might follow for her. She waited, bracing herself for the rough hands that would drag her upright, but instead the voices made their way to the far end of the corridor, and it was an unfamiliar British woman's voice she heard screaming for mercy as she was manhandled out of the attic and down the stairs.

A lone voice began singing the '*Chant des Partisans*', the song taken up by the Free French and the resistance as their anthem: 'The wind is blowing through the graves, and freedom soon will come.'

She tapped on Jean-Paul's wall, using Morse to ask what had happened during this last bout of questioning. Hearing nothing in return, she tried to sit up, but was felled by the pain in her feet. Again she tried to rouse him, banging her fists on the wall.

Eventually a series of dots and dashes was tapped from the neighbouring cell. 'They threatened to hurt Fabien.'

She thought of Jean-Paul's lover, whose health was frail and who would never survive the brutality of the SS. He had left Paris, supposedly safe in Lisbon for the time being, but nowhere was out of reach of Hitler's Gestapo. They had found Jean-Paul's Achilles heel and Sophie was in danger.

'You didn't tell them where she is being picked up?' she quickly tapped, waiting an eternity for his response.

'Tell her I am sorry,' she heard eventually.

'What have you done?' she replied, but already knowing the answer.

There was a long pause until he responded. 'May God forgive me.'

41

London, 1997

'You can have no idea how it felt, beaten and broken in that horrible place and knowing it might all have been for nothing.'

No wonder the woman could not bear confined spaces, Amy thought, noticing the shake in Daphne's hands. She saw Amy looking and turned them over, resting her hands palms upwards on her thighs. Amy covered her mouth as she tried to swallow back her shock. The deep scarring forced Daphne's fingers to curl claw-like towards one another. 'I suppose I should be glad I wasn't a pianist too.'

'I'm so sorry.'

'Don't be sorry. I'm alive, aren't I?'

Amy rubbed at the scar on her own hand. How minor her ordeal seemed now, even if it had changed everything. Had it though? What if she had chosen a new path at some point anyway? What if the pressure had been too much? Hadn't she found a career she loved, made a good life for herself, even if she had lost Michael? The attacker had taken a career from her, but Michael had been right: the only one who had taken music from her was herself.

'I was one of the lucky ones, so they told me,' Daphne went on. 'They wanted to give me a medal after the war. A medal?

For being arrested?' She shook her head. 'Told them to stuff it. What I really wanted was someone to take away the memories, but no one could do that, and so I just asked to be left alone. Let my gran look after me until I was strong enough to work in the shop again. Then I met my Sidney, and I was happy for a bit. But I still get nightmares, you know? Loud noises frighten me, knocking at the door sends me hiding in the bathroom. I can't sleep without a light on.'

'And then I turned up.'

'It was a bit of a shock, I must say.' She sighed. 'You must think I'm daft.'

'Not at all. These days it would be called post-traumatic stress disorder. You'd be given counselling, medication,' Amy said, remembering the flood of offers of help she had received after Michael's death, from the police, her GP, her friends. And yet she'd refused it too. She'd wanted to deal with things her own way.

'I keep thinking that if I found a bit of peace of mind, it would help. You understand? I felt it was all my fault, but maybe it wasn't. Feeling guilty won't bring her back, although I've always liked to think she found that man of hers again.'

'I do understand. Daphne, I want to find out exactly what happened to Sophie. There's nothing else you can remember that might help?'

'I know they sent a Lysander for her, but once I'd been deported, all I heard were rumours. And then everything was such a mess at the end of the war . . . missing persons, possible sightings. No one knew where anyone was. I heard Kestrel made it back, though—'

'Kestrel? You mean Bruce Tomlinson?'

'I never knew his real name. They interviewed him for days, apparently. He'd come across all sorts in prison after his own arrest: agents, servicemen, resistance members. He was the one who got her out of Paris that night.' She sighed. 'I should be getting going. Billy will be here to fetch me.' She stood slowly on what Amy could see now were specially made orthopaedic shoes.

They strolled slowly across the grass, weaving through groups of picnicking young mums and toddlers, posturing teenagers and sad souls poking through the litter spilling from bins.

'Give her my regards,' Daphne said as they parted. 'The old Sodmother. She was good to me.'

Amy watched Billy drive her away then made her way towards Mile End station, along the canal leading to the docks that had taken such a battering during the Blitz. She stopped as her phone rang, and smiled when she saw the name of the caller. 'Hi, Jay.'

'Hey. How did it go?'

'Pretty harrowing.'

'So you were right about the concert?'

'Yes. Daphne was being arrested as it took place. She must already have been in custody by the time Sophie was taken away. I'm going to Verity's on Sunday to talk to her about it.'

'Let me know if you fancy a drink when you get back – I'll be Samless, and Sunday evenings are usually pretty dull.'

'Sure. That'd be great. Oh, and Jay?'

'Yeah?'

'Don't tell Claire. We all had such a great time at dinner there last week, and she and David have got it into their heads that – well, you know.'

'Nothing to tell. Honest,' he said, and she could hear the smile in his voice.

Amy was enjoying having a no-strings male friend happy to share the minutiae of each other's day. It was a comfort and a pleasure, and she didn't want it spoiled by the misguided expectations of well-meaning friends.

For now, however, she had to get back to work: there was a particular file she wanted to call up and check over before she left the office for the weekend. She was certain she had stumbled on something that had slipped through the net. Kestrel still had secrets to divulge, even after all these years. If Amy was nervous about what she might find, she was even more nervous about how she might break it to Verity.

Despite the warm sunshine flooding through the conservatory windows, a tartan rug was spread across Verity's knees, her cashmere twinset a contrast to Amy's muslin summer dress and strappy silver sandals. A portable oxygen machine stood beside the rattan chair and the glass side table was littered with packets of pills. 'Straighten my cushions, would you?' she said to Amy.

'What's that perfume you're wearing?' Amy said, catching hints of bergamot and violet as she leaned across to help.

'*Soir de Paris*. I've worn it for years, although they stopped making it for a while. Colette used to send it over from Paris for me. It was her own favourite, apparently. There was a real fondness, you know? I cared as much for her – for all my agents – as I did my own children. Does that sound terrible?'

Amy shook her head. 'Not at all. You were responsible for them. And I'm sure they all knew how much you cared. Certainly Daphne Wilson does.'

Verity looked at her. 'So you found her?'

'Yes. Still living above the shop on Bethnal Green Road.'

'And you told her you had spoken with me?'

Amy nodded. 'She sent her love to you.'

'There's a turn-up for the books!' Verity looked serious suddenly. 'And how is she? How are her hands? And her feet?'

'Pretty bad. She walks with sticks. I imagine the damage to her feet was irreparable.'

'Some of those Nazis were sociopaths, and Seelman was one of the worst. One of his own men tried to assassinate him, you know?'

'Well, at least there were some who had a conscience. Daphne told me about the night of the concert, and that you'd arranged a rescue flight for Sophie.'

'But not what happened on the night of the rescue?'

'No. What did happen?'

Verity hesitated. 'The events of that night have sat with me for too long. I never even told Bill about them.'

Amy worried that she might be expecting too much of an elderly lady fresh out of hospital. 'If it's too distressing, we don't have to talk about it.'

'And then the next part of the story will die with me and you will never forgive me.'

'That is actually true,' Amy said, smiling. 'I really wouldn't.'

Verity frowned at her. 'You seem a little distracted. Is everything all right?'

So it was obvious. The papers Amy had tucked in her handbag seemed to burn against her side, but she smiled, knowing this was not the moment to share their contents. 'I'm fine. Just a little tired.'

'In that case, I had better tell you about the night when all our hopes were pinned on a little black plane making its way through German defences. The night I was to meet Agent Colette at last.'

42

Wednesday, 19 January 1944

'It is past midnight. We must go, madame.'

She jumped at the man's voice, an intrusion into the shuttered, candlelit farmhouse kitchen where Kestrel had left her. She had sat in anxious but companionable silence with the old farmer and his wife, who watched, smiling, as she forced down their homemade brandy.

'*Sois prudent, Roland*,' the old woman said, taking her son's hand as he came to stand at the table.

'I'll be careful, I promise.' A decade older than Sophie, Roland had been born and bred in this part of the country, his local knowledge and loyalty to the resistance making him an obvious choice to find and prepare suitable landing sites. He was dressed in dark clothing, his British-issued Sten gun slung across his shoulder. 'We need to go,' he said, beckoning to her. 'It's a twenty-minute walk to the field. The others are waiting there.'

She thanked the old couple then shrugged on her coat, checking her pockets once more for her pistol. Everything else was packed inside a small leather poacher's bag that she strapped across her shoulder.

'Ready?'

'As I will ever be,' she replied, following Roland out to the farmyard and on to the rutted lane.

The Normandy coast was partially hidden by a sea fog that blurred the edges between land and water. Avoiding the heavily fortified port of Le Havre, he searched instead for the long channel of water that led inland alongside Caen. Once safely past the seaboard defences, he searched for the matrix of poplar-lined main roads that would help him set course for the landing zone.

Bright flashes of orange light exploded below him, and he spiralled away from weaving searchlight beams into the cover of a blanket of light cloud. With no navigation lights, the black aeroplane was hard to spot against the night sky, but he could not afford to take any chances.

Once out of range of this latest line of defence, he dropped below the cloud and took a compass bearing, watching for the serpentine turns of the River Seine looping a course from Paris to Rouen. A series of lakes within a flat, wooded basin of the river would mark the halfway point of the French leg of the flight.

He shivered, pulling the long white silk scarf a little tighter around his neck and shrugging his shoulders deeper into the sheepskin lining of his flying jacket. The fading moonlight brought into clear relief the sprinkling of snow across low-lying hills, shard-like frozen ditches punctuating farmland. In other circumstances, it would have been beautiful, but tonight he would be glad for all this to be behind him, the English chalk downs leading him and his passenger safely back to base.

*

Roland pointed ahead as they paused to rest. 'There's an old hunting track that takes us across the near field and down to a small wood where we can stay out of sight for most of the way. No one ever comes up this road, now the farm at the far end is empty. We should be safe.'

And so they set out, Sophie struggling in the ill-fitting boots she had been given. All was silent, apart from their rhythmic steps and the jangle of the fittings on Roland's rifle strap, as they entered the wood, Sophie jumping at the nocturnal rustlings of boar in the undergrowth.

Roland grabbed her arm suddenly. 'Wait.'

'What is it?'

'Do you see lights?'

'Where?'

'Out on the road, behind us.'

They stood still, looking around at the moving shadows made by the intermittent moonlight pushing through the tree canopy. 'I don't see anything. Didn't you say no one uses the road?'

He sighed. 'Probably just poachers.'

Finally they climbed through a section of broken fencing and stepped over the bicycles hidden in the brambles at the periphery of the field. Half a dozen men dressed in shabby overcoats and shapeless jackets, black berets pulled over their heads, hurried across to greet them before moving to their positions. Roland produced a long torch, pointing it downwards into his pocket to check it worked before tucking it under his arm. It would be he who flashed the agreed Morse letter to the pilot before his men lit the bonfires. All that was required of

Sophie was that she be ready to run to the fixed ladder attached to the moving Lysander.

With only a little while to go, all eyes were fixed on the sky, willing the shadowy-black form of the Lysander to appear and flash the agreed letter that would tell them the aircraft had found its destination.

'I'm early. I know they're not expected back for a few hours. I hope it's not inconvenient?' Verity asked as the batman let her into the cottage.

'Not at all, ma'am. They're all in the ops room. We don't know the difference between night and day here. I can offer you a nightcap or a morning cuppa, whichever you prefer.'

'Tea would be marvellous, thank you,' she said, allowing him to take her mackintosh as he led her through to what must once have been a cosy reception room. A handful of uniformed chaps sat around in wooden chairs, within close reach of the green telephone Verity recognised as one of the scrambled lines used to communicate confidential information between Whitehall and the Services.

'Ah, you must be Flight Officer Cooper,' said one, rising from the desk to shake her hand.

'Yes, I'm here to meet my agent.'

'Wing Commander Carlisle. This is Group Captain Stewart from the Air Ministry, and of course you know Major General Menzies from SIS?'

'Good to see you again, sir,' she said as the tall, grey-suited chief of the intelligence services rose to shake her hand. She had come across 'C', as he was known, frequently at briefing sessions in which she and Tremayne kept him updated on their agents' activities and statuses.

'You too, Cooper,' he said. 'Hope you won't mind me borrowing Colette before you take her away? One or two things we need to debrief her on as soon as she lands.'

'Not at all.' Verity sat in an empty chair and glanced at the maps spread out on the table in the middle of the room. 'Any word of your pilot yet?'

'Fighter Command at Bentley Priory are keeping us updated. He's safely over the Channel and a little over sixty miles from the landing zone. Should be there within the hour. Met reports are positive, so he shouldn't encounter any trouble from the weather. Just have to hope everything's tickety-boo on the ground. Reliable, this agent of yours?'

Verity nodded. 'Absolutely. Although her wireless operator has been taken prisoner, hence the urgency of the extrication.'

'We must be prepared for the worst,' Menzies said, sitting back and rubbing his greying moustache. 'The Frenchman they've arrested is a solid chap, but I hear the girl did appallingly in her training. Do you think she'll hold out long enough for Colette to get out?'

Verity felt herself bristle. Bluebird had proved herself far superior to the statistics her tests had suggested. 'I have every faith in her, sir.'

'Well, if she can keep quiet for a couple more hours, I suppose it doesn't matter what she does after that,' he said, his Eton vowels increasingly irritating Verity.

'I'd prefer to believe we might extricate her too at some point. This is a vulnerable young woman, not just a machine sending messages.' Menzies had done marvellous work overseeing the operations at Bletchley, but she did wonder sometimes whether some of these men leading the war from their desks gave any thought to the real people behind enemy lines.

'Don't worry,' said Carlisle, sensing friction in the already highly charged atmosphere. 'The pilot's one of our best. Not a failed mission to his name.'

As the batman appeared with a tray of tea for Verity, a dog began barking from somewhere inside the cottage, setting her nerves on edge. She called back the batman as he was about to leave with the empty tea tray. 'I say,' she said, 'I couldn't swap this tea for a brandy, could I?'

43

Through the fug of the morphine the doctor had given her, Daphne was aware that the residents of the attic had now enjoyed a few hours' reprieve, and that an unusual number of cars were coming and going from the courtyard below. The incessant, pointless banging on the door by a young Englishwoman further along was now the only soundtrack to the night. Something was happening, and the Germans were on high alert.

Jean-Paul's message to her played over in her mind. Had he told the Germans where to find Sophie? He had known where she was to be picked up by plane, and where a few hours ago Daphne would never have believed Jean-Paul capable of talking, now she was not so sure.

She had wanted to tell Jean-Paul that she had tried to be strong enough for both of them, that when they took her down and she saw they had covered the Chinoiserie carpet with tarpaulins, when they pinned her face down on a table, still she did not speak. But all that was wasted now, and her strength would only offend him.

It must be late, and although she couldn't think of food, she was relieved to hear the clanking of metal bowls and jugs that meant she might find out how Jean-Paul was faring. As the two guards worked their way along the attic corridor, Daphne crawled towards the door on one hip, dragging the bloody mess of her feet behind her, hoping she might catch a glimpse as their cells were opened briefly.

As Jean-Paul's door was unlocked, so she heard the key in her own. The guard had been about to deposit the plate on the floor of her cell when the other shouted to him.

'*Schnell*,' the man said. 'Quickly.'

Daphne knew only a little German, but she knew enough to recognise trouble. The door to her cell still slightly ajar, she dragged herself to the threshold, and seeing both guards push their way into Jean-Paul's cell, she climbed to her knees, desperate to know what had happened.

Slowly, painfully, she made her way out to the landing towards the open door of Jean-Paul's cell. The two guards knelt on the ground, trying to rouse the Frenchman lying on his back, his grey face staring unseeingly at the ceiling, a trail of foamy spittle spilled from his open mouth. There was no point, she could have told them. The cuff of his jacket was ripped, the empty casing of the hidden suicide pill on the ground beside him.

The cyanide would have worked quickly and efficiently, she consoled herself. No longer would he have to torment himself with the betrayal that was beaten out of him.

'Did you hear that?' Sophie said. 'Did that sound like an aircraft to you?'

Roland looked beyond the fringe of trees lining the field, and to the track that ended at the woodland they had crossed. He suddenly squeezed her arm as the thrum of an engine overhead became louder. 'I think your fellow is here.'

'*Ici*,' called one of the men. '*L'avion est ici*,' as the men began heading to their positions.

They both looked upwards, in time to see the shadow of a small aircraft come into focus, flashing his navigation lights to create the letter H before passing low across the field.

'That's him,' said Roland. 'I'll send the return signal so he knows he's in the right place.' He ran out to the field, raising his torch and flashing five dots in return. 'Get the flares lit,' he shouted to the men posted by the small bonfires. 'We've got five minutes to turn this around.'

Sophie grabbed the poacher's bag, running across so she could be ready as the small plane landed. She looked up at the sky just as the Lysander passed in front of the low moon, dropping in height as it prepared to land.

Verity didn't know how they could sit so calmly, chatting about country-house parties and cricket scores. She supposed they were used to this and had learned to cover up the tension with inane conversation. She knew the men in 161 Squadron were a tight bunch, a small and secret band of heroes unable to discuss their work outside of the team. These evenings when they sat up in the cottage waiting for news of one of their own must be terrible. They lived, worked, joshed together, and the banter merely disguised the fear of an empty bunk upstairs come morning.

With no desire to join the gentlemen's-club chitchat, she quietly scanned the wall maps and meteorological reports. A black-and-white surveillance photograph showed the landing field, its flare path marked in red pen.

Verity suddenly caught herself biting her nails, a childhood habit knocked out of her by her housemistress years ago. She was frightened for Colette, frightened for Bluebird, indeed for all those she loved: her darling Bill, preparing to go to the torpedo-infested sea once more; Alec, flying his own war somewhere over Europe. She had left both her husband and her brother on a sour note, just when there was no place for discord.

From somewhere in the house, the dog began barking again, the noise piercing her ears like knitting needles.

'Can't someone keep that animal quiet?' she said, and the three men turned to her, almost surprised to find her still there.

'Not until his master's back,' Carlisle said.

'Well, perhaps his master would care to hurry up?'

Carlisle smiled. 'He's doing his best. Right now he should be touching down in Compiègne. That's the squadron mascot barking its little head off out the back.'

The green telephone suddenly rang and the Wing Commander picked it up. He made a few affirmative noises into the receiver before putting it down. 'Fighter Command. He's been picked up on radar on target. Looks like our fellow has found your agent, Cooper. All being well, they should be heading home in a few minutes.'

Verity let out a long sigh. A few minutes might as well have been a few days.

The field looked exactly as it had done in the reconnaissance photographs, at the far end of a strip of woodland with a small, rectangular raised reservoir one field to its left.

Suddenly the letter P was flashed faintly from the centre of the field, and flaming torches were lit on the ground, forming the inverted L shape he knew so well. A flash of light to his right confused him slightly as he turned the small aircraft and made one final lap of the surrounding field, dropping to two hundred feet, one hundred feet, then twenty as he reached the first flare, the stubbly ground coming into clear view. His wheels struck and he pulled back the throttle just enough to maintain the power needed for take-off again.

The incoming agent ran across to the pick-up point, a flash of white clothing beneath her coat and her head covered with a dark beret, as armed resistance fighters surrounded her. And then suddenly her face was illuminated, a bright white light startling her as it settled on her, and then another.

Even though it took all his concentration to turn the aircraft, he could not take his eyes off the woman caught in the glare. The Frenchmen surrounding her hoisted their rifles, dazzled, spinning around but unable to find anything in their sights as they attempted to protect her from an invisible enemy. Terrified as she must have been, she stood tall, her eyes focused on the Lysander.

It was Sophie. After three long years without her, it was as though they had only parted yesterday. Of course that was why Tremayne had been so reluctant to use him – the older man must have somehow known about the connection between the two of them. And now it was up to him to make good on his promise to Tremayne and get her out to safety.

Alec kept his eye on the final burning torch, seconds away from where Sophie stood. He just needed one man to open the cockpit for her and help her inside. The plane juddered, complaining against the terrain, and he gripped the wheel hard, sweat breaking out on his forehead as he made the first turn, then headed back along the diagonal.

All-terrain vehicles had appeared from the edges of the field, eating up the distance between him and Sophie and disgorging grey-uniformed soldiers who quickly outnumbered the Frenchmen. One man had managed to hold his ground, keeping the Germans at bay with gunfire as he grabbed Sophie by the arm and pulled her towards where the aircraft would collect her.

All they needed was thirty seconds.

Daphne banged on the door. 'Tell Seelman I'll talk,' she shouted, her throat raw from trying to rouse them.

She had heard the doctor pronounce Jean-Paul dead; heard the porters take away the body. There was still time, perhaps, to undo whatever he had been forced to tell them. She would make something up, use the information she had in order to send their men elsewhere and buy some time for Sophie. When they found out she had been lying they would shoot her, or worse, but she didn't care.

Eventually a guard appeared through the small, high window cut in the door. 'What?' he said in rough French.

'I want to talk to Seelman. I know where he can find her.'

The man sighed. 'He has no need of you.'

'You don't understand. I've changed my mind. I want to help him.'

'The only person you want to help is that bitch boss of yours. Well, you're too late. Seelman has already found her.'

'I don't believe you.'

'If you had a bag, I'd tell you to pack it,' he said. 'You're out of here tomorrow.'

'I'm being released?'

He laughed. 'Released? No, you're being deported first thing in the morning.'

It was all over. She was being sent to one of the camps she had heard about, where if she was lucky she would starve to death. There would be no chance of escape, no chance to carry on her work, no chance to see Sophie again. Suddenly, she envied Jean-Paul the release the cyanide capsule had given him – her release, if it ever came, would be a slow and brutal one. She had fought her hardest, but it was over.

Sophie spun on the spot, dazzled by the searchlights trained on her and unsure of the direction of the gunfire audible above the roar of the Lysander's engine.

'Run to the plane,' Roland shouted. 'I'll hold them off.'

As she ducked out of the light, a young Frenchman fell to his knees in front of her, his rifle still in his hands. Germans had appeared from everywhere, breaking through the hedgerows in bursts of machine-gun fire and attempting to surround the Lysander as it approached her.

One of Roland's men had climbed to the top of the ladder, raising the hatch for her. '*Viens, viens*,' he shouted, holding out a hand to her as she ran parallel to the plane.

She risked a look backwards, just in time to see Roland take a bullet in his shoulder and crash to the ground. She took her pistol from her pocket and fired a few shots at the Germans rushing towards the plane. She was close enough to see the pilot now, his head silhouetted within the glass canopy, his face obscured by his leather flying helmet.

She caught the hand of the Frenchman who pulled her up to grab hold of the first rung of the ladder. More shots, and she felt his weight slump above her before he tumbled to the ground. With only five more rungs to climb, she dragged herself higher as the little plane prepared to take off again, its engine crescendoing as it accelerated into the last leg of the turnaround.

Shots embedded themselves into the fuselage of the Lysander, and she cried out as a bullet grazed her calf. The plane was gathering speed, seconds away from losing contact with French soil, and she used every muscle in her exhausted, battered body to lift herself the last few feet to safety. But something was dragging at her leg, the pain of the fresh wound searingly bright, and she looked down to see a motorcycle driving alongside the plane, its pillion passenger clasping her ankle. She kicked furiously but was unable to unclamp his grip, and it was with horror that she found her hold on the ladder weakening. She fired off a final shot from her pistol, taking out the driver but bringing his passenger and herself crashing to the ground.

Grey figures clambered up the ladder, throwing open the pilot's cockpit, and her arms were pinned behind her back as she was forced to watch flashes of gunfire as the pilot defended himself in the still-moving aircraft.

And finally she saw him as the grounded aircraft lost its course, the Germans bailing out just as it careered towards a large tree on the periphery of the field and exploded into flames.

'Alec!' she screamed as she watched fire engulf the aircraft.

A figure stood in front of her, blocking her view as his hand took her chin roughly, forcing her to look up at him. 'I think it's time we continued our conversation, don't you?' Seelman said.

Verity stood outside, her cigarette smoke hovering in the still, cold air. She looked up into the clear sky, at the waning moon that shone over a war no one had wanted.

'Ma'am? You're wanted inside.'

She turned, surprised to see the batman at the back door. 'Is there news?' she said.

'Couldn't say, ma'am. They just asked me to fetch you.'

'Thank you,' she said, grinding out her cigarette on the gravel.

The men were standing as she returned to the ops room, and she could tell instantly that the atmosphere had changed.

'Has something happened?' she asked.

'Bad news, I'm afraid,' said the Group Captain, his curt tone barely disguising his obvious distress.

His face told her everything she needed to know, yet still she couldn't help hoping that the situation, whatever it was, was not hopeless.

'A German ambush was waiting at the pick-up,' Carlisle explained. 'Our pilot put up a good fight on the ground, but his plane lost control and caught fire. Afraid he didn't make it.'

'And my agent?'

He shook his head. 'Arrested. One of the locals involved in the operation managed to get away and radio the news to us.

I'm afraid it's not looking good. Chap called Seelman has her in custody.'

Menzies called to one of the plainclothes officers waiting in the sitting room beyond. 'Get my car straight away, would you? I need to get back to London.' He turned to Verity as he collected his coat and briefcase. 'I'm sorry, Cooper. Never a good night when we lose one of our own. We'll debrief tomorrow, when we know more?'

'Of course, sir.' Verity sat down, her legs suddenly weakened, the ringing in her ears only compounded by the barking of the dog, which suddenly sounded closer.

'For God's sake, man. We really don't need this right now,' Carlisle said to the batman, who was trying to grab hold of a small white dog running frantically around outside the door.

'I couldn't keep him in the kitchen, sir. Something's got his goat.'

Verity looked up just as the dog slipped through the man's hands and ran across the room to her, scratching at her skirt and whining for her attention.

'Sorry, ma'am,' the batman said. 'He's not usually like this. Only ever wants his master.'

'This is the pilot's dog, you say?'

'Yes, ma'am. Scout's his name.'

'Scout,' she said quietly, looking at the familiar brown ear, the embossed leather collar she herself had bought, as she bent down and picked up the little dog.

No wonder Alec had not been able to talk about his work, collecting and delivering her own agents. He was performing one of the most dangerous missions of the war, and they had not spoken since their argument. Why had she allowed herself to fall out with him, and over a silly woman? Would it have hurt to have pretended to go along with it? And what of the little voice in the back of her head, that asked whether Verity had been wrong about her? Nothing was as it seemed in these times of war, as she knew more than most.

And now they were trying to tell her he was dead.

'Let me take the dog,' Carlisle said.

'No!' she snapped back, then seeing the confusion on the men's faces, she shook her head. 'This is my brother's dog. It's Alec's dog.'

'Alec?' Carlisle said. 'Alec Scott? You're his sister? Good God, I'm so sorry.'

She nodded, accepting the quiet condolences of the men, looking at the dog's familiar face, stroking his soft ears. 'I won't believe he's dead,' she said.

'I'm afraid it's impossible he would have survived. We must accept facts.'

She had always believed she would know if Alec died somewhere across this vast theatre of war, but maybe the emptiness she now felt was her sign that he really was gone. She buried her face in the little terrier's fur. 'What are we going to do, Scout?' she sobbed.

She had been prepared for the mission to be difficult, knew there were no guarantees, but she had never imagined driving back to Whaddon Hall with an empty seat beside her, her best agent in Gestapo hands and her brother's body in a remote French field across enemy lines.

44

London, 1997

The light had begun to fade in the garden beyond the window, a blackbird singing at the end of the day as Amy watched Verity turn away. 'I never saw him again.'

Amy hesitated. 'And Colette . . . Sophie?'

There was a pause, the ticking of the old grandfather clock in the hallway cutting into the silence. 'It was months before I was given access to her file. As the Germans retreated from France in late 1944 and the concentration camps were liberated the following year, reports started coming through from returning prisoners and I needed to know who she was, in order to trace her. The shock when I opened it to find that photograph of her clipped inside – my nemesis and my hero.' She sighed. 'She arrived in London in 1941 having survived the Nazis, a terrifying journey from France and the Baker Street bombing, all to help her country. And I sent her away, like a common tramp. I will never forgive myself.'

'But she was married. You said so yourself.'

Verity shook her head. 'Tremayne told me it had been a marriage in name only. Sophie and Alec could have been together, and she would have made him happy. They came so close to meeting again that night near Compiègne and never even knew it.'

'You're certain of that?' Amy asked.

She nodded. 'Alec's plane exploded. There was no chance he could have escaped the blaze.'

'And what about Sophie?'

'What was left of her network survived only because of her refusal to talk. In the end he would not even allow her the dignity of her fellow Frenchmen knowing what she had done, encouraging the belief that she was a collaborator even as she was deported.'

'You had evidence she was sent to a camp?'

'Tremayne sent me to Paris to look for my girls amongst those freed from the camps. It was heartbreaking to find so few still alive. And those who did survive struggled to adjust to normal life. Some volunteered for duties in the Far East.'

'Like Kestrel?'

'You know about him?'

'I saw his file. I know he joined SOE in 1945.'

'Then you probably know more than I do. He was arrested shortly after Sophie. I never saw him again. His information was still classified when I worked with Tremayne.'

The image of the craggy-featured agent pinned to the front of his file was still fresh in Amy's mind, as was the shock of what she had discovered within it. There were wrong moments to share difficult news, but Amy realised there was nothing to be gained by waiting for the right one. 'Verity, I found something in Kestrel's file. I don't know how to say this to you, but you have a right to hear it.'

The old lady looked up. 'To hear what?'

Amy had read over and over Kestrel's deposition after his

release from a prisoner-of-war camp weeks after the liberation of Paris. He had been interviewed extensively about every prisoner he had encountered, the details recorded carefully so that cross-referencing might help track down the missing. 'Kestrel – Bruce Tomlinson – was incarcerated at Fresnes prison in Paris from March to July 1944.'

'God, that awful place.' Verity shuddered. 'I heard so many terrible stories about it.'

'While he was there he encountered several captured servicemen. Canadians, Poles, some Americans, and a British pilot.' Amy stopped, her throat tightening as she tried to find the words.

'Just spit it out,' Verity said. 'Please.'

'He recognised the British airman as the Lysander pilot who had flown him from Tangmere a few months earlier. He didn't know the man's name, but he was able to describe him. There was some confusion because the man he described had already died in a German ambush whilst on a mission in France in January that year, and so it was not followed up.'

'Why are you telling me this?'

'Bruce Tomlinson's description of the pilot and his facial injuries fits your brother perfectly.'

'But Alec was dead.'

Amy shook her head. 'Alec survived. At least until that point where he was seen at Fresnes.'

The old woman's shoulders suddenly shook. 'Oh, that poor man. I can't bear it. Fresnes was a living hell. But he got out?'

Amy felt tears burn in her own eyes. 'I wish I could say something to make this better. I'm so sorry. Alec was kept at Fresnes until the Germans realised the Allied forces were making significant gains after the success of the Normandy landings. They began a systematic emptying of Fresnes prison over the weeks leading up to the liberation of Paris.'

'They moved him elsewhere?'

'They relocated many prisoners, but there were some who would never leave Fresnes. Bruce's statement describes Seelman entering the male block at five a.m. the day he himself was deported.'

'And Alec left with him?'

'I'm afraid not. Seelman rounded up twenty-three prisoners that morning and took them out to the exercise yard. The sun was only just rising, but the yard was floodlit and Bruce managed to watch from his cell window.' Amy paused. 'He recognised your brother amongst the men forced to kneel on the ground. Seelman shot them one by one himself.' Amy took Verity's hand. 'I'm so sorry.'

Verity closed her eyes. 'All these years, I imagined him in that corner of rural France. It gave me some peace, in a way, to know he'd died somewhere beautiful. I went to visit the place, but even as I stood in that field, I think I knew he wasn't there. Does that sound strange to you?'

'Not at all.' Amy hesitated. There was something else she had wanted to talk with Verity about, something that had been planted in her head at Claire and David's and that had grown roots. She had spoken to Eleanor, who was happy to give her a six-month sabbatical, and now she needed permission to do justice to the project. 'Verity, I want to tell you something.'

'What is it?'

'I'm thinking about writing a book about Sophie.'

'A book?'

She nodded. 'An account of her life. It may not happen, and I'd need time off work for it, but I'd like to use what we've talked about. I'd like to tell the story of Sophie's war.'

'Even after what I did to her?'

'Please, you have to stop thinking like that. You were a lifeline to those young women. To Sophie. That's what counts.'

'But you don't know the end of the story. Nothing was ever confirmed about her whereabouts at the end of the war. And Alec? You'd write about him?'

'I'd like to. But not without your permission.'

'I can't stop you writing anything. And Sophie's story is public property now. I'd rather it were you telling it than a stranger. Even if there is no proper ending.'

'Verity, I really want to tell your story too. You are an integral part of all this. I would struggle to write the book if you do not feature in it.'

'Me?' She frowned. 'I don't know. You ask a great deal. You've seen how hard it has been for me.'

'Of course, and I've also seen what an incredible contribution you made to the war effort. It deserves to be recognised.'

'But my own family know nothing of this.'

'Don't you think they deserve to? I know if my mother had done what you did, I would have wanted to know.'

'I need to think about it.'

'I understand.' Amy was torn: she did not want to write about Verity without her agreement, but the book would suffer without her contribution. 'And of course I can't write it until

I know what happened to her. I want to go to Paris,' she said. 'There may be surviving members of the network who were never traced. There might just be something that leads somewhere else . . . I don't know. It seems like madness, now I've said it out loud.'

'You'll find nothing in Paris,' Verity said. 'I looked for her there too. As the Germans left, we moved swiftly in to connect with those agents still operating and uncover the whereabouts of any still missing.'

'And did you find Sophie?'

'I didn't. But I found out exactly what I had sent those young women into. Had I known sooner, I may not have had the stomach for the job.'

Amy listened as Verity described the strange post-occupation atmosphere in France, the desperate search for missing agents. 'Thank you, Verity,' she said as the older woman finished.

'I'm not sure what for. I haven't been able to tell you what happened to Sophie, but maybe that was always for you to discover.'

'What do you mean?'

'There's something of her about you. The dedication, the quiet strength. The music.'

She was tired, Amy could see. 'I should go,' she said. 'But please think about what I've asked, about the book.'

'I will.' Verity took her hand. 'And in the meantime, go to Paris, retrace my steps and hers. Go for me, and for Alec and Sophie. For Daphne Wilson. And for yourself.' Her hand suddenly went to the silk scarf she always wore, and she handed it to Amy. 'Take this with you. It was hers.'

‘It belonged to Sophie Clément?’ Amy looked at the red and gold silk square illustrated with delicate drawings of night-time constellations.

‘She gave it to me, here in this very house. I have a feeling she would want you to have it.’

Part Three

45

Paris, 1997

It had been hard waving Holly goodbye, as Amy left her with her grandparents, but Jay had come to Waterloo with her, insisting on being her personal bag-carrier.

'You just want to be sure I go!' she'd joked as they hugged before she headed through the barriers towards her train.

'I also want to be sure you get back,' he said. 'I'll be here to meet you – if you want, that is.'

She had wanted, and it had felt reassuring as the train sped across the English countryside before plunging beneath the Channel. She hadn't been able to help recalling Verity's description of her own trip to Paris in late 1944 to establish an office in a hotel near Châtelet in order to locate her 'girls', as news of missing agents began to filter through the aid agencies and government organisations trawling camps and prisons in the aftermath of the German retreat from France. Tremayne, meanwhile, would travel further east to meet with the anonymous German asset who had been working from the inside and was now assisting the search for war criminals.

Instead of Amy's smooth train journey, Verity had made the choppy Channel crossing in a Navy gunboat before being allocated a space in an army truck following the trail of the invading Allied forces across Normandy. Her description of children shouting 'Yankee' as they held their hands out for sweets and cigarettes, and of the shaven-headed young women who had consorted with German soldiers being paraded around the streets with swastikas painted on their foreheads, would remain with Amy for a long time. Verity had seen at first-hand the atrocities committed by the retreating Germans who had strung young men from lampposts and locked resistance fighters into burning farmhouses; even within the sanctuary of a church, women and children had been shot dead. By the time Verity arrived in Paris, she thought she had discovered the depths of human depravity.

And now, here Amy was in Paris, so different to the starving, war-worn city Verity had discovered at the end of her long journey. Paris may have been restored to her former glory, yet she still held on to some of her secrets, and Amy could only hope to uncover just one of those.

She watched the passing lights of the Seine evening pleasure cruises stroke the peeling wallpaper of her hotel room, wondering why she had allowed what now seemed an insane whim to lead her to this shabby hotel room with its chipped 'Welcome to Paris' ashtray and stained bedcover. Eleanor had been delighted at her suggestion of writing a book and had been only too happy to allow her a week's paid leave for this trip, and despite her anxieties, one glance at the Hermès scarf draped across a chair told Amy that she had had no choice but to find the end of Sophie's story.

Through the background laughter on the telephone line to Chiswick, Amy had ascertained Holly was having a ball with Michael's parents. Hearing the lightness in Maria's voice as she recounted their day, Amy regretted pushing them away over the last year. Yes, she'd wanted to manage things her own way, but she'd denied her parents-in-law the chance to feel useful, and for Holly to spend time with them.

Over-exhaustion and a fretful mind would not allow her to sleep yet, and so she made her way to the window, where she pushed open the shutters to a view across the Seine broken only by the poplars lining the quay, the sky to her right a spectacle of light beams bursting from the Tour Eiffel.

Her thoughts ranged over what she had discovered so far. Having asked in a couple of shops for recordings of Sophie's playing and received either total ignorance or disdainful disgust, it was clear she had her work cut out if she were to restore Sophie's reputation. Her only lead had not responded to her letter and was unlikely to want to break silence after all these years. All she could do for now was retrace Verity's steps around post-occupation Paris during those strange, harrowing months searching for her missing agents.

Later that night, Amy dreamed she was sitting at the grand piano on which she used to have lessons as a student, the wide, tall windows of the large teaching room looking out across a patchwork of London roofs. A light breeze rattled the venetian blinds, dusty sunbeams squeezing through to backlight the teacher smoking in front of them.

Amy began to play the music on the stand in front of her, a relatively uncomplicated Chopin waltz she had learned as a teenager. Even in her sleep, Amy felt her fingers twitch as they worked their way to the end.

'Good,' her professor said, walking across the room on clicking heels to join her, one hand resting on the piano, her cigarette smoke winding across Amy's line of vision. 'I told you not to give up, didn't I?'

Amy turned, blessed that the beautiful, enigmatic smile was cast on her, and that she had pleased the woman dressed in a fitted red suit, her blonde hair smoothed into a chignon. 'You did. Thank you, Sophie,' she said.

She sat up suddenly, disorientated in the unfamiliar room, her senses still alert to every nuance of her dream, and the complex violet notes of *Soir de Paris* lingering in her nostrils.

Dazzled by the bright sunlight and heavy traffic circumnavigating the Arc de Triomphe as she emerged from the Métro, Amy took a moment to orientate herself within the satellite of wide, leafy boulevards. How must the battle-worn American and British heroes of the Normandy landings and the hungry, shabby Parisians have appeared to each other as De Gaulle led the triumphant French First Army through the famous arch after four years of occupation?

As Amy walked south-west along the avenue Foch, she tried to imagine how it had felt for a young woman from Stepney to be driven here in a German patrol car months before those celebratory scenes. One never knew one's strength until it was tested, Amy supposed, but if her reaction to Michael's death was anything to go by, her own capacity for stoicism was far from heroic.

Number 84 sat shorter than its neighbours, its wide row of attic dormers echoed by four floors of tall, shuttered windows with views towards the Bois de Boulogne. A grand private residence once more, number 84 had shed its macabre past. Amy watched the automatic gates open to the private road leading to a leafy courtyard at the rear of the building, and a black limousine glide through, its passenger invisible through the darkened windows.

She wished she knew far less than she did about this terrible place, but Verity's account of her visit here in late 1944 sat heavily in Amy's heart.

The French capital in October 1944 was a barely navigable storm of confusion, lies and wishful thinking as records were discovered to have been destroyed by the fleeing Germans and collaborator files were seized by the new French government. As word began to trickle through of returning agents and freed prisoners, Verity distributed photographs and details of her own agents, in the hope that the Chinese whispers of refugee identification might lead to a sighting or report of their whereabouts. All around the city, families posted photographs of their missing loved ones on billboards as through that winter and spring refugees from the camps began to arrive in the city by train, a terrible reminder of the outward journeys from which many would not return.

Verity walked around 84 avenue Foch, recently the headquarters of the Gestapo, accompanied by a British Army brigadier and a representative from the Red Cross. She couldn't decide what chilled her the most. Was it Seelman's office, his fine brandy and vintage French horticultural books still on the desk? Or perhaps the interrogation room on the second floor, the report of the last interview still wound inside a typewriter?

Far worse was the attic, its cell walls covered in graffiti scratched with whatever had been at hand. Resistance fighters and captured agents had written their names and dates of incarceration as a crumb trail towards rescue while they awaited torture in the rooms below or deportment to the east. Verity recognised many of the names, including the signature of SOE agent Noor Inayat Khan, who had attempted a rooftop escape from here with SIS's own Léon Faye before deportation to Pforzheim prison in Germany. An involuntary cry burst from her as she found Daphne Wilson's name daubed in what looked like blood.

'We believe the head of your network was also brought to avenue Foch,' the Brigadier said as they entered the basement, once a punishment chamber and now the scene of a forensic inspection. 'Here,' he said, leading her to the far end and holding a torch to a section of dark-stained wall littered with bullet holes. 'Your agent's name is scratched here,' he said, 'but we cannot be certain if she was one of the prisoners executed before the Germans left the building.'

'Is there any evidence of further whereabouts for her?' she asked.

'Not yet,' the woman from the Red Cross told her, 'although any remaining prisoners were deported to internment camps. We may yet find her name on a passenger list.'

'And she would have been kept prisoner under the Geneva Convention in these camps?'

'Not necessarily.' The Brigadier hesitated briefly. 'Passenger manifest forms for deportation convoys were found in Seelman's office. We believe several agents and resistance activists were removed to concentration camps.'

'Concentration camps? But our people are entitled to the same protocol as any captured armed forces personnel. They should have been kept in military camps,' Verity protested.

'I'm afraid protocols do not come into it with these people,' the Brigadier said. 'Perhaps you would like to see the lists we found in Seelman's office?'

A few typed sheets of paper had been retrieved from the ashes of the last fire Seelman enjoyed in his office, and seeing nowhere else she might work, Verity laid out the singed papers on Seelman's own desk. Amongst the surviving paperwork was a signed memo from Berlin ordering the deportation of the British wireless transmitter operator known as Bluebird, whom Seelman had described as stubborn and unresponsive. She had failed to provide any information on the escape of Sophie Clément from the Prison du Cherche-Midi, and following the divulgence by another prisoner of the location of Clément's extrication, Bluebird had been transferred by armed guard to a holding prison at Karlsruhe before transportation to Ravensbrück camp. Verity cross-checked passenger lists for prison convoy trains and there indeed was Daphne's name. At least now she could forward the information to the American unit handling the processing of internees and write to Daphne's grandmother with news of her latest-known whereabouts.

But what of Sophie after the ambush at Compiègne? The date scratched next to her name in the basement suggested she had been brought here to avenue Foch immediately afterwards, but no documentation appeared to have survived. 'Was there anything else here mentioning her name?' Verity asked the Red Cross official.

'Sorry, ma'am. This is all we have. Anything that wasn't destroyed was taken away by the Germans. We've had teams checking everywhere, from dustbins to drains.'

'Have you found any record of a Colette?'

The woman checked through the sheets of paper cross-referencing names of missing persons. 'The only Colette we've found mentioned is in the interrogation report of a French agent who committed suicide whilst in custody. I'll fetch it for you.'

The transcript of an interview with Jean-Paul Joubert was an uncensored record of a brutal interrogation in which he had been questioned over the whereabouts of his wife. The timings on the document suggested the man had held out for some time, until threats were made towards a Fabien Dupont if the location of Madame Joubert was not revealed. Eventually Joubert had given details of a Lysander pick-up near Compiègne on 18 January 1944. Verity knew no other flights had been scheduled that night: the wife the man was interrogated about had to be Sophie, and Seelman had deliberately avoided recording her identity by using her married name.

So she had been married to a resistance agent: it made sense. But why had they married so quickly before her trip to London? Were they just another couple trying to seal their relationship whilst there was still a chance, or was there more to the timing? Whatever the case, Verity was sad. Yes, the woman had been married, but she had also lost a man broken down into betraying her. In the worst of circumstances, Sophie would have been free to marry Alec after all.

Verity checked the passenger lists once more, and there she was, listed as Madame Sophie Joubert, on a convoy that left Drancy station, on the outskirts of Paris, on 10 March 1944 for the interim internment camp at Karlsruhe. Her name was marked 'N + N': *Nacht und Nebel*, Night and Fog, the classification allocated to prisoners who were to remain untraceable in a final act of cruelty to their families, and her final destination after Karlsruhe scrubbed out in black pen. Even if Verity could confirm which camp she eventually arrived at, no record would be found of her there, and no other prisoner would have been allowed to see her long enough to identify her. In the unlikely event of her avoiding execution, Sophie Clément had disappeared, as was confirmed by her next of kin.

Verity eventually returned to London with both good and bad news. Four of her 'girls' had been positively identified in camps to the east, and after being debriefed and checked over by Red Cross doctors on arrival in Paris would return to London on the first available passage. For other families, the best she could offer was the knowledge that their daughters, wives and sisters had acted with bravery and determination. The George Cross for which they would be recommended would not even begin to make up for these terrible losses, Verity thought bitterly.

The following April she received word that Daphne Wilson had been freed from Ravensbrück camp by the Swedish Red Cross in a prisoner-exchange and taken to a hospital in Gothenburg, from where she would be flown to Scotland and catch a train to London Euston.

It had been a ghostly version of Daphne Wilson who walked slowly along the platform of Euston station on crutches carrying a brown paper parcel containing everything she owned, her hair cropped and her once-rosy cheeks grey and sunken as Verity ran to meet her.

Verity had been prepared for the rage and anger she had witnessed in some of the girls who had returned from similarly harrowing experiences, but Daphne never resented the work she had been asked to do, and would have done it all over again. Verity had tried to reassure her she had acted admirably: many lives were saved, and there was still hope Sophie might be traced amongst the survivors emerging from incarceration.

But whatever they had done to her in avenue Foch and in the freezing-cold camp, Daphne had wept that it was not enough to make up for what had happened to Sophie after she last saw her *patronne* chained to a group of female prisoners at Karlsruhe railway station in March 1944. The two women watched one another, and as Sophie was pushed into a windowless wagon at rifle point, she turned to smile briefly at Daphne.

As the network of camps across Europe was gradually liberated, the lists of survivors were checked over and over, but Sophie Clément's name never appeared. She had become one of the tens of thousands never to be seen again.

The focus of the war shifted to the Russian Front and the Far East, and Verity's work was complete. She would be returned to civilian life, and her relief was overwhelming. Never again would she begrudge the security Bill had given her.

Amy took one last look at number 84, standing back to let an elderly lady and her miniature dog pass by on the wide grassy verge. Was this Frenchwoman one of the lucky ones who had returned to reclaim her place in the city? Amy could not look at anyone of her parents' age or above and not try to imagine what they had seen in this beautiful city, what secrets they held on to.

At that moment, her telephone rang, and seeing it was a Paris number, Amy answered quickly, her heart racing as the caller gave his name. Finally she had an opportunity to extend her search for Sophie.

46

It had been Jay's suggestion to research the two other members of the Phoenix Trio. Whilst all signs indicated Hanne Goldmann had not survived the war and her husband Max had died at Auschwitz, Fabien Dupont had been active on the Paris orchestral circuit in the years following the war, and had continued working with a select cohort of students at the Paris Conservatoire.

Using headed paper from the Archives, Amy had written to Monsieur Dupont at the conservatoire, explaining only slightly disingenuously that she was visiting Paris to research a book about cultural life during the occupation and was seeking interviews with eminent artists of the period. Perhaps it was a result of her enthusiasm about recordings she had heard of his playing, but he had finally responded to her enquiry, calling her on the number she had included in her letter. After initial pleasantries, however, Fabien Dupont had been shocked at her admission that the book was to be about Sophie Clément, and it had taken some persuasion and the mention of Verity Cooper before he agreed to meet Amy for lunch.

The clientele enjoying the summer sunshine at pavement tables on the rue Spontini were far from the chattering, wide-eyed tourists inhabiting Paris's honeypots. Here expressions were disguised by dark sunglasses, the hands waving cigarettes weighed down with diamonds and Swiss watches, casually expensive hair offset by tiny lapdogs. These were not people on a lunch break from work – they were on a lunch break from leisure.

Amy was shown across the thick-carpeted room past red-velvet booths highlighted by gleaming brass rails, soft light bouncing off the etched, tarnished wall mirrors. It was easy to spot Fabien, sitting alone at a table, his chin-length grey hair swept back off his face, a thin cashmere scarf thrown over one shoulder and his shabby corduroy jacket well-cut enough to shriek of its original cost. He looked up from a book of sheet music as the maître d' pulled out a heavy, deeply cushioned chair for Amy.

'You are not what I expected,' he said in English to her.

'You expected a mousy English historian?' she replied, glad she had chosen to wear the black fitted Agnès B. dress that had caught her eye the day before, and had tucked her long, strawberry-blonde hair into a chignon. She nodded towards the book. 'Shostakovich cello sonata? The second movement is fiendish.'

He looked surprised. 'You know the work?'

'I've played it.'

'You are a cellist?'

She shook her head. 'A pianist.'

'This is not the sort of work an historian plays.'

She hesitated. 'I was a musician at one time. Conservatoire trained. I was on the point of signing a modest recording contract, in fact,' she said, surprised at her need to impress him, to show that she was of his tribe.

'And yet you left music behind?' His expression was as

incredulous as though she had said she had chosen not to breathe.

She showed him her left hand, the stretched tendons beneath the skin of the unnaturally curled third and fourth fingers.

'I am so sorry. An accident?'

'Sort of, but we're not here to talk about me.'

A waiter arrived to pour an inch of caramel-coloured Chardonnay into each of their huge glasses then explained in detail the *menu du jour*, from which Fabien ordered for them both. As the man bowed in retreat, they waited a moment before speaking, the air thick with low conversation and the occasional clink of crystal glassware and silver on bone china.

'So you want to write a book about Sophie Clément,' Fabien said eventually, tilting his angular chin.

'I do.'

'I haven't agreed to anything other than lunch,' he said, 'but I am interested in what you have to say.' He looked at his watch. 'We have an hour before I have to leave for the conservatoire. Tell me what you know, and how you know it.'

He sipped slowly at the wild mushroom soup, listening carefully as Amy described finding Sophie's SIS file and how it had led her to Verity then Daphne, and to the discovery of Sophie's marriage to a fellow agent. She told him that no record existed of Sophie's imprisonment, nor of her death or survival, and how surprised she was to discover that Sophie's legacy remained tarnished.

'Much damage was done while the Germans were here,' Fabien said. 'She played her part well, and people suffered.'

'What do you mean?'

He shrugged. 'The Goldmanns, for instance.'

'Hanne and Max?'

'Hanne was one of the finest violinists I ever had the privilege to play with. Gunned down in the rue Ferdinand Duval like a common criminal, her husband murdered in a death camp. It took a schoolteacher in the Dordogne to rescue their little daughter, whilst Sophie seemingly watched it happen from the window seat of Maxim's over a glass of champagne.'

'But you knew Sophie was an Allied agent?'

'Not until later. I was not altogether kind to her before that. I had my own concerns about being in France under German occupation. My "type", shall we say, were not exactly favoured by the Nazis. The Goldmanns were forced to wear their yellow stars, but the pink triangle assigned to men like me . . . well, that colour has never suited me. I made my way to Marseille in early 1941. There was a rumour that an American called Varian Fry had arrived there with cash and visas for Jewish artists, musicians, actors. He helped us escape across the Pyrenees, and I spent the rest of the occupation in Lisbon.' He looked at her suddenly. 'Tell me about this pilot, the lover who captured Sophie's heart. You say he was the brother of her handler?'

'Yes, although none of them was aware of the full picture.'

'He must have been very special. She swore she would never allow herself to enter into an intimate relationship, although I knew she longed to be loved.'

'So why did she hold back?'

He hesitated. 'She had some bad experiences as a young woman.'

'And she had no lover that you knew of?'

'Certainly not. She would never have kept such a thing secret from us.'

'Who do you mean by us?'

'Myself, of course. Hanne, Inès her cousin. And Jean-Paul, naturally.'

'Who was Jean-Paul?' she asked and saw by the flash of pain that passed quickly across his expression that perhaps this was the someone Fabien had been forced to leave behind.

'Jean-Paul was a good man. The best. He worked undercover for Sophie.' He looked across at her. 'He was the love of my life.'

'I'm so sorry.'

Fabien brushed this away. 'He was not part of the Allied operation. He worked for the resistance, helping agents such as Sophie. He worked closely with her radio operator, I believe.'

'Daphne Wilson? The English girl?'

'Yes. She was arrested with him and taken to avenue Foch.'

Of course: Amy recalled Daphne's devastated account of the arrest above the print shop, and the ensuing events.

'Do you mean Jean-Paul Joubert?' she asked, recalling Verity's account of his interrogation and suicide.

'Yes. You know of him?' Fabien asked.

They paused as the first course was replaced with wide bowls of lamb cutlets and creamy celeriac mash swimming in dark, scented gravy.

'You say she didn't have a lover, but records Verity Cooper found at avenue Foch imply that she was married to Jean-Paul Joubert.'

'You are supposing that all married couples are lovers,' he replied.

'I don't understand.'

'The world is changing, probably too late for me, but there was a time when a simple certificate could protect those living outside the norms of society. Paris had always been home to men like me, but I was not safe when the Germans arrived. Sophie made sure I was.'

'I still don't follow.'

'Marrying me would have been too obvious. People recognised my name from our work and would have quickly worked out the marriage was a lie. And so she married Jean-Paul before she went to London to continue her training. Just before she met her pilot.'

'So she was free to fall in love?'

'And to marry after the war. That was the arrangement: a divorce as soon as it was safe once more. But in the end, the Germans ended the arrangement for her. Jean-Paul resisted all attempts to break him down,' Fabien went on. 'Daphne got word to Inès that Jean-Paul had given his life to protect Sophie – they shot him dead in the basement of avenue Foch.'

It was not her place to alter the better, less hurtful truth Daphne had given to Fabien and Inès, to tell Fabien that it was he Jean-Paul had saved, taking his own life as atonement for Sophie's arrest. 'I am so sorry,' Amy said instead.

Fabien sat back, his chin resting on the tips of his long fingers as he pressed his palms together. 'You are right. This has gone on long enough. The world should know what she did.'

'But the world might have: her records show posthumous commendations for the George Cross and the Croix d'Honneur, and yet her cousin refused the honours on her behalf. Why would she do that?'

'Inès is a complicated woman.'

'She is still alive? Are you in touch with her?'

He flinched slightly, as though caught out. 'On occasion.' He looked at his watch. 'I really should think about leaving. Please, tell the waiter to put it on my account.'

'Please don't leave yet. Do you think Inès would speak with me?'

'I do not believe for a moment that she would, even if I gave you her telephone number. Which I will not.' He sighed. 'Inès is not well.'

'I'm sorry to hear that.'

'She has hardly left her home since the liberation of Paris, and only accepts visits from her daughter and occasionally myself. She suffers, amongst other things, from photosensitivity and cannot manage bright daylight.'

'Maybe you could speak to her on my behalf?'

'Inès' illness is of a nervous variety. It was brought on by the war, and so I cannot imagine a conversation about the war will be welcome.'

'I understand, but she was Sophie's next of kin – she may be the only one who knows what happened to her.' Amy untied the red and gold scarf from the handle of her handbag. 'This was Sophie's – she gave it to Verity Cooper, and I would like you to give it to Inès. It might persuade her to talk to me. If I cannot find out what happened to Sophie, I cannot write this book and clear her name, and I will never be able to help Verity and Daphne find some peace.'

'I'm sorry they have suffered,' he said. 'Sophie would never have wanted that.' He took the scarf from her, smiling as he recognised it. 'I will see what I can do, but I promise nothing.'

'Thank you.'

'I appreciate what you are trying to do for Sophie.' He reached across the table for her left hand. 'You should consider playing again. I know this looks bad, but there is repertoire you could still manage. Maybe even Max's . . .' He hesitated, then shook his head.

'Max's what?'

'Nothing. I just know what Sophie would say to you if she were here.'

'She would tell me not to give up?'

'Correct: on her or on yourself.'

47

Amy had been at the end of a long day tramping the streets when Fabien's next telephone call came. She had dodged ice-cream-eating tourists as she walked the length of rue Ferdinand Duval, had stood outside Sophie's own apartment and admired the Art Deco façade of the nearby Hotel Lutetia. A few hundred metres away, on a tatty triangle of grass between the new Science University and the busy rue du Cherche-Midi, stood a tall granite memorial marking the location of the now-razed military prison where Sophie had been taken on the night of the concert, a plaque on the ground dedicated to resistants who had lost their lives there.

She had stood holding one hand over her ear as she tried to hear Fabien against the noise of the traffic. He had sounded as surprised as Amy as he passed on Inès Arnaud's invitation to visit the following morning, and he agreed to email her the address in the seventh arrondissement.

The elegant apartment was dimly lit, the bright summer's day outside blocked out by heavy velvet drapes as Inès' maid, an old retainer in every sense, brought Amy to one of a pair of frayed silk settees on either side of a low, gilt-legged table. Dust motes danced in the sliver of light that escaped from a narrow gap in the curtains and glanced off the delicate overhead chandelier dripping crystal tears. Every corner of the drawing room was stuffed with antiques and relics of a former life.

Inès dismissed the woman in French, then turned back to Amy, her eyes hidden behind large, Jackie-Kennedy-style black sunglasses. She took a long drag on her cigarette. 'Fabien tells me you wish to write a book about Sophie,' she said in English, then turned to look at a full-length portrait hanging above the marble fireplace.

'That is her?' Amy asked. 'She was so beautiful.'

The slender woman depicted wore a long white satin gown, her pale, luminescent arms and shoulders bare as she rested one hand on a piano. The artist had created a halo of the sleek blonde curls piled on her head, and the whisper of a blush sat at odds with her regal expression.

Inès laughed. 'You should have seen her in real life. She was without compare.'

'In many ways, it seems. Madame Arnaud, documents have become available that prove Sophie was not a collaborator, but an Allied spy. Her story is remarkable, inspiring. She deserves for people to know who she really was during the occupation.'

'And you think you are the person to tell her story? Because you were a pianist too?'

'Perhaps not. But I am in a position to do so.'

'Just because you are, does not mean you should.'

Amy had guessed this would not be an easy interview. 'You were her family,' she said. 'Do you not want the truth known about her?'

'You understand very little. How can you? You were not here. You did not see what we saw.'

'I heard her voice,' Amy said.

Inès looked at her. 'What do you mean?'

'I was given a recording of her last concert. She was arrested that night at the German Institute, wasn't she? And you were with her?'

Inès reached across to the coffee table and picked up a small bell, ringing it vigorously. 'It is time for you to leave,' she said. 'Celeste will show you out.'

'Please, Madame Arnaud. You are the only one who might know what happened to her. Verity Cooper found evidence of Sophie's interrogation at avenue Foch, and then she was seen boarding a prisoner convoy train. Nothing was heard of her after that – it is as though she vanished completely.'

'Then there is nothing more for me to tell you, is there?'

'No one has been able to celebrate what she did,' Amy ploughed on, 'no families able to say thank you to her memory. The Germans continued to publish photographs of her after her arrest, to confuse the Allies and maintain her sullied reputation. A reputation that has cruelly persisted, for lack of anyone speaking out. If you wish me to leave now, I will, but if you care about the world discovering what an extraordinary woman Sophie was, then please talk to me.'

The gilt-edged doors opened and Celeste appeared, immaculate in black dress and starched apron. '*Oui, madame?*'

Inès hesitated as Amy waited to be shown out. Instead the old lady gestured towards the tray of cold coffee on the table. '*Encore du café, Celeste, s'il te plaît.*'

As the maid closed the door behind her, Inès produced the red and gold scarf, holding it in her lap, where the colours sang against the black bouclé of her suit skirt. 'I gave her this myself,' she said, occasional pops of light bouncing off the heavy jewels on her bony fingers. 'Hermès 1935. How did you come across it?'

'She gave it to Verity Cooper in London.'

'Ah yes. The Cooper woman.' Inès looked up. She seemed like a tiny crow, Amy thought, her hair dyed black and set in a stiff bouffant, her straw-like legs tucked tidily at an acute angle beneath the slim pencil skirt of her suit. 'I met her myself in Paris after the liberation. She was looking for Sophie – she had been her case officer, I believe.'

'Verity Cooper was more than that. She was – is – Alec Scott's sister.'

'Alec Scott.' Inès paused as she flicked cigarette ash into the onyx ashtray. 'The pilot.'

'Sophie told you about him?'

Inès shrugged. 'She was in love. She needed to tell someone.' She looked at Amy. 'Did he survive?'

Amy shook her head. 'He was executed at Fresnes prison.'

'I'm sorry to hear that. He must have been an exceptional man to win Sophie's heart.'

'I believe he was.'

'She always believed she would find him again. It is what kept her alive for so long in that camp – the thought of their being together.' Inès' hands suddenly stopped caressing the silk scarf and the two women's gaze met as she removed her sunglasses to expose deep-set, red-rimmed eyes.

Amy was suddenly acutely aware of the oscillating tones of a police siren outside, the shifting arc of the sun pushing between the curtains to illuminate Sophie's portrait so that the ivory gown rippled in its glow. She leaned across the low table towards Inès, whose whole bearing suddenly was that of someone carrying a burden they could no longer support. 'You know, don't you?' she said to Inès. 'You know what happened to her.'

The old lady's words began to flow, carrying with them a story untold for over half a century.

Inès returned to Paris in October 1944 after months hiding out on her parents' remote estate in the hills north of Cannes. She found the city on the brink of severe malnutrition, electricity often available only for a short period each evening. Shortages of bread, milk and fuel were exacerbated by damage to the transport network by the Allies as back-up to the Normandy invasion, so that mainline train and Métro stations were often closed. The last remaining bus had been commandeered by retreating Germans, as army journalists and government officials arrived to pick through the detritus left by Hitler's men.

Parisians tried to remember who they had been before having to choose between good, bad or indifferent, and the accusations began as stories were rewritten and tracks covered over. Inès had done her best to fight, but she had also done her worst, and so she maintained a silence broken only with Fabien once he returned from Lisbon. Sophie's name had been thrown around as one of the most willing collaborators, and to her shame Inès never spoke up for her. No one who refused to prop up the occupation had heard her brave speech on the German-run radio station, but to overturn Sophie's terrible reputation would have left Inès herself open to scrutiny. Besides, she had her daughter to think of. Sophie would have wanted Inès to protect Geneviève at all costs.

In the meantime, as concentration camps to the east were emptied of survivors in the spring of 1945, Paris began to hope for reunions that had once seemed impossible. Crowds gathered outside the Gare d'Orsay to greet the buses and trains with their skeletal cargo, bearing placards with photographs and descriptions of the missing. Each day they assaulted the new arrivals with the same battery of questions: 'Have you seen my wife?' 'Were you at Buchenwald with my sister?' 'Did my father survive?' It was hard to believe that these ragged, hollow-eyed prisoners stripped of their hair and their dignity, still dressed in camp uniforms, could be their family, their friends.

By April 1945 the authorities were overwhelmed by the hundreds of returned deportees and a new whisper began to circulate: 'The Lutetia. De Gaulle has arranged for them all to go to the Hotel Lutetia.'

Inès joined the crowds now camped beneath the chestnut trees on the boulevard Raspail, opposite the beautiful Art Deco building where De Gaulle spent his own wedding night, the beloved haunt where Sophie had promised they would all drink champagne together once more when the war was over. But of that party, Hanne, Max and Jean-Paul were dead, Fabien sick with grief, and Sophie had not been heard of for nearly eighteen months.

Inès watched families post flyers on the board the hotel staff placed outside every morning, taking it in each evening so that those whose details had been posted would know someone was searching for them. '*On recherche . . .*' the posters said. 'We are looking for . . .' But the photographs pasted beneath the red headers looked nothing like the poor creatures shambling through the famous revolving doors, identifiable only by the prisoner numbers tattooed on their forearms and sprayed on arrival with white DDT powder against the lice that had hitchhiked from the hell camps. As a growing number of collaborators attempted to cover their tracks by posing as deportees and the atmosphere against those who had aided the Germans became increasingly ugly, Inès chose not to advertise Sophie's absence, relying instead on spotting her cousin amongst the returned deportees.

They became a strange kind of family of their own as they carried out their patient street vigil, and Inès began to recognise faces such as the two young girls who arrived every morning to look for their mother, whom Inès had known from the old days. 'Irène Némirovsky,' they would tell any arrivals to the hotel. 'She's a writer. They sent her to Auschwitz.' There was the old gentleman hoping to find his daughter who had run away to join the Maquis; the woman who brought her baby with her each day as she passed around photographs of her husband who had been arrested for making fake papers at his printing press; the Jewish widow hidden in an attic for a year after her son's disappearance from the street.

Once or twice an Englishwoman in uniform worked her way through the crowd with a sheaf of photographs of young women. Was this officer the one of whom Sophie had been so fond? Whom Inès had fobbed off with a letter stating she had had no news of her cousin? Would Flight Officer Cooper know how Sophie's rescue flight had come to be ambushed? Inès had handed back the photographs silently, shaking her head and turning away so that the woman would not see her tears.

April turned to May, then June, and still Inès waited. Nearly ten thousand souls had passed through the Lutetia by the time an open-topped American army truck arrived at the steps one bright August morning and a GI leapt out to open the rear gate for the dozen shaven-headed passengers huddled in the back. They stared in bewilderment at the crowd calling out for news or a whisper of hope, and at the dazzling white exterior of the hotel with its delicate carvings of angels and festooned grapevines. It was impossible to tell even whether it was men or women who were helped carefully to the ground, their striped uniforms hanging in rags from gaunt frames.

One by one they were led through the door on bandaged feet, until only one remained. Inès pressed closer to the front of the crowd as the woman turned towards them and fell to her knees, crossing herself as tears forged pale tracks along her sunken, grimy cheeks. As one of the GIs gently lifted her into his arms and carried her up the wide shallow steps, her green eyes found Inès and the two women held each other's gaze until the soldier and his almost weightless cargo disappeared inside the hotel.

'It was Sophie?' Amy asked.

Inès looked across at the portrait, at Sophie's half-smile. 'The Germans could no more contain her than any man had been able to before she met her pilot.'

The relief that Sophie had not breathed her last in a filthy death camp gave way to the question Amy had to ask. 'Her name was not on any survivor lists. How did she slip through the net?'

'These were dangerous, complicated times. Sophie had to protect herself.'

'But surely her return was recorded? Verity Cooper found no trace of her.'

'Verity Cooper did not know who she was looking for.'

48

The sun beat down on the hard, hot Paris pavements during that June day in 1945 as Inès waited for the names of the returnees to be confirmed on the daily list posted for families and friends, but Sophie's name was not amongst the Jewish and political prisoners, the Dutch, Czech and British agents of the SOE.

'My cousin is here,' she told Sabine, the young Frenchwoman reputed to have saved many Jewish lives during the war, a tough fighter now tasked with aiding the repatriation effort. 'I saw her myself.'

'I'm sorry. If the name's not on the list, she's not here. Unless she's still with the doctors and not able to communicate with us yet.' Sabine smiled gently, pushing a lock of hair from her damp brow. She looked as though she had not slept for weeks. 'I know this is hard. If we reunite just one tenth of the people waiting out here, we feel fortunate.'

'But I saw her.' She handed her a photograph of Sophie, almost entirely unrecognisable from the woman recently carried inside the hotel.

Sabine frowned as she examined the photograph. 'She's a popular one. British intelligence services are looking for her too.'

Inès hesitated. If Sophie had not identified herself, it was because she did not want to be recognised. And if Inès were to give her away, Verity Cooper would be contacted immediately and Sophie sent straight back out to work as soon as she was well enough. 'There must be a mistake. This is my cousin, not some spy. She was arrested for distributing resistance leaflets, nothing more. Could you pass around word that Inès Arnaud is looking for her?'

Sabine pressed her clipboard to her chest. 'I'll do my best. If she is here, I'll find her.'

Inès could not settle, pacing the pavement opposite the hotel as she chain-smoked the American cigarettes she had procured on the black market, barely noticing the regular stream of buses depositing yet more blinking, shattered souls as the heat of the afternoon dissolved with a fresh breeze. Nearly two hours later she was invited to pass through the doors of the Lutetia for the first time in five years.

The shell of the venerated old lady of the Left Bank had not changed, despite its passing role as headquarters of the German Abwehr. Inès even recognised some of the old staff, who had returned not as paid employees but as volunteers in the greatest operation in the hotel's history.

She took a moment to remember the last time she had been within these walls, Sophie's promise that they would meet here again one day and her heartbreaking performance of dear Max's *Song of Paris*.

The scene could not have been more different now, a queue of deportees waiting to be processed, whilst others filled the bar and restaurant, their paperwork inside waterproof pouches around their necks as they drank from silver cups, their filthy striped uniforms at odds with the luxurious setting. Some ate hungrily of the fresh bread, meat and fruit given sparingly to them, whilst others merely stared into space, their bodies removed from hell but their minds still trapped there. Very few spoke, but those who did, did so with the entire panoply of European languages. Inès was ashamed of her disgust at the smell of these wretched creatures, her fear of the residual horror that clung to them.

'We found her,' Sabine said, appearing suddenly. 'She was registered under a different name, which explains the confusion. Follow me. She is resting in one of the bedrooms upstairs.' She led Inès through the hallway past bodies sleeping on rolled mats on the ground, others preferring the bare floor after years of deprivation. Sabine hesitated as they reached the bottom of the wide stone stairwell. 'She's in very poor health. She contracted pneumonia during her incarceration – it seems they kept her in an underground cell for months, with no exercise and barely enough food and water to keep her alive.'

All along the dark, wood-panelled corridor lay more bodies, and it was impossible to tell whether some were dead or alive. Eventually Sabine opened a door into an elegant bedroom that would have had a splendid view across the boulevard Raspail had its heavy curtains not been drawn. Camp beds had been placed in every available space on the carpeted floor, and it was to one of these that she led Inès.

'Don't expect too much,' Sabine whispered. 'She has suffered considerable damage to her lungs, and she's very weak.'

She had been showered and given fresh clothing, but the deeply embedded grime would take more than one dose of soap and hot water to remove. 'Sophie?' Inès said, kneeling beside her and gently taking her roughened hands, trying not to gasp as she saw the prisoner number tattooed on her thin forearm. It was almost impossible to imagine that these broken, calloused fingers had once caressed Beethoven from a keyboard, and as she pressed one of Sophie's hands to her cheek, her tears began to fall.

Sophie stirred, opening her eyes slowly. Her cracked lips moved as she seemed to try to speak, but a fit of painful coughs claimed the last of her energy, and she slumped back into unconsciousness.

'It was two days before the doctor allowed me to bring her here,' Inès explained to Amy. 'Even then, she wasn't well enough to be discharged, but they needed her bed – over five hundred people a day were arriving at the Lutetia by then.'

'You cared for her here?'

Inès nodded. 'I did my best. Fabien had returned from Lisbon by then, and one of us was always by her bedside. I hired the best doctor I could find – not easy in those chaotic days – even though we all knew it was too late.' Inès looked at the portrait hanging on the wall. 'That's how I want to remember her.' She turned to Amy. 'She wore that dress the night of the concert. She had never looked more beguiling, more entrancing.' She smiled. 'We joked that she looked like a bride.'

'It does look like a bridal gown,' Amy said, admiring the artist's capturing of the ivory satin pooling at her feet.

'And yet she was taken not to a church, but to Fresnes prison after the ambush. That dress was all she had to wear for weeks, while they dragged her back and forth to avenue Foch. I sent her parcels of clothing and food, but each time they were intercepted. Seelman made sure Sophie enjoyed not a single privilege, other than the company of the German prison chaplain. I heard he was a good man – I hope he offered her some comfort.'

'Did she come round at all while she was here?'

'Once or twice. She wanted me to tell Verity Cooper that she would return to the field as soon as she was well enough.'

'And did you?'

Inès shook her head. 'Sophie barely had the strength to sip a glass of water, let alone answer the inevitable distressing questions. The woman had been locked alone in an underground cage for months on end, beaten and tortured – I couldn't let her relive a moment of that. And so I tried to make her last days as peaceful as possible.'

'Inès, stop.' Fabien put his hand over hers. 'You're just making it worse. She has not opened her eyes for five days now.'

'I have to try,' she said, holding the teaspoon of water to Sophie's mouth, but knowing he was right. All she had achieved was to drench the pillow, and a few drops of water could do nothing to counteract the terrible rattle in her cousin's chest. She put the spoon on the bedside table and stroked Sophie's cheek. 'My darling girl,' she said quietly.

'I'm sorry,' Fabien said, 'but you know what the doctor said. The damage to her lungs is too far advanced. She may have only a few hours now. There is nothing we can do for her other than pray.'

Inès looked up at him, rubbing angrily at the tears she did not want to shed – for all the days she had not cried, she had held out hope. And now she knew Fabien was right: the time for hoping was over, and as Sophie's hands began plucking weakly at the white linen bedsheet, Inès accepted they could wait no longer.

Fabien looked at his watch. 'It is nearly evening. If we want to find a priest before it is too late . . .' His voice tailed away, choked by his own despair.

Inès nodded, and as Fabien closed the apartment door behind him, she sat beside Sophie once more. 'I will not let you go like this,' she said to the sleeping woman. 'You are Sophie Clément, the bravest, the most beautiful of them all.'

She tore herself away for a moment, returning with a leather vanity case. She dabbed a small amount of crimson on Sophie's dry lips, a little rouge on her sunken cheeks, smiling as these tiny touches brought back a whisper of the woman who had held court at the Lutetia five years ago. Inès had sold most of her jewellery to pay for the doctor, but she clipped on to Sophie's ears a pair of paste diamond earrings, sitting back and frowning. 'But wait. There is one thing I have forgotten.' She hurried to the bathroom, returning with a tiny sapphire-blue bottle. She removed the gold lid and tipped the bottle upside down, shaking the last few drops of scent on to her fingertip then pressing it to Sophie's wrists and neck. '*Soir de Paris*. Now you are ready.'

Fabien returned with the priest, and while the elderly man quietly intoned the final blessings of the Last Rites, Inès opened the window, so that Sophie might feel the breeze on her face and hear the sounds of her beloved Paris once more. She and Fabien sat on either side of her bed, taking one of those beautiful hands each, and as Inès stroked her cousin's hair, the priest's holy oil glistening on her forehead, Fabien hummed *The Song of Paris* to her.

As he reached the final bar, a nightingale began singing outside the window. Sophie's eyes opened slowly and her lips began to move.

Inès looked at Fabien. 'Maybe she will be all right? Sophie, look at me, my darling.'

Fabien shook his head. 'Shhhh. She cannot see you.'

As the heavy incense from the priest's censer swirled around the room, mingling with the traces of perfume, they watched Sophie stare ahead of her, summoning the last of her strength.

'Alec,' she said quietly, before her eyes closed once more and the stuttering, agonising breaths that had tortured her for days eased with one final, gentle exhalation.

'I never saw her look so happy as she did in that moment,' Inès said to Amy. 'It was as though he were standing before her.'

'She was ready to go,' Amy said.

'Exactly. And in a way, that helped, to have seen her in that last moment. After she died, I went to her apartment. No one had been near it since the night of the concert. It was like she had known she would never return: everything was immaculately tidy, the grate swept clean and shutters closed, the piano lid shut. She had made her preparations months earlier.'

'Perhaps she planned to make it out on the Lysander?'

Inès hesitated. 'She may have hoped to, but it was never going to happen.'

'What do you mean?'

'She could never have left the concert hall safely – Seelman made sure of that.'

'What happened?'

'She was betrayed.'

Amy was puzzled. 'By someone in the network?'

'By me.'

'You?'

'They found my daughter at her grandmother's, and Seelman kept her at avenue Foch until I had done what he asked.'

'He didn't . . .'

She shook her head. 'He never harmed Geneviève, just kept her as insurance. He knew there was a rat, thought it might be Becker, but suspected Sophie.'

'Becker? Who was Becker?'

'Becker was the German I first introduced her to. He was always in the right place, made friends with the right people, always knew where to take Sophie. They became friends – he was a good man. I discovered afterwards that he had been working for London undercover. He was responsible for the attempted assassination of Seelman a few months later. I heard he worked with the Allies after the occupation, interviewing Nazi officials.'

Amy now remembered seeing a Becker in the paperwork surrounding some of the post-war investigations into Nazi war criminals. This man had clearly been an ally of Sophie's, whether she knew it or not. 'But Seelman didn't believe you?'

'Seelman would have arrested Sophie even if Becker had been identified as a mole. If she had escaped that night during the concert, maybe she would have been safe, but I made sure she did not. Seelman forced me to watch her, to ensure she did not leave the building. I had to believe his threats against my daughter, but I will never forgive myself.'

'You did what you had to. And in any case, she would never have left on that plane,' Amy said.

'The pick-ups were always risky, but she had a good team on the ground there,' Inès insisted. 'She would have made it.'

Amy hesitated. 'Madame Arnaud, there is something you don't know.'

'What do you mean?'

'I mean that you cannot take responsibility for her capture at Compiègne. Someone else told Seelman about the pick-up.'

'But only Daphne and Jean-Paul knew about it. Did the girl crack?' She looked at Amy, who shook her head. 'Jean-Paul?'

'They said they would hurt Fabien, just as they threatened your daughter. He had no choice. He was not executed – he took his own life.'

'And did you tell Fabien this?'

'No. It's not my secret to tell.'

'Thank you. Let him remember his beloved Jean-Paul as the hero he truly was.'

'Jean-Paul was not the only hero. You should be proud of what you did for your country.'

Inès snorted. 'It was nothing in comparison with what Sophie did, and if we hadn't let her down, she might have lived.'

'Maybe not. From what I have learned of her, she would never have stopped fighting. Even if she had escaped on that plane, she would have returned, taken more risks. At least she had the chance to be with the people she loved right up until the end.'

'But not her pilot.'

'Not her pilot.'

Inès sat up. 'Would you pull the curtain open a little? I feel the need for some air and some light.'

'Are you sure?' Amy asked.

'I have lived in semi-darkness for nearly half a century. I think it is time to see the world again. Trying to live through Sophie's punishment has done me no good – I want to look at what she has missed all these years.' Inès stood at the window, eyes wide open as she breathed in the Paris air.

Sophie's fate had finally been revealed, and for the moment there was only one more question that remained.

'Madame Arnaud?' she said, as she stood to leave. 'What was the name that Sophie gave at the Lutetia?'

As Inès answered, something from earlier in their conversation began to play on Amy's mind. She had found everything she needed in Paris, and it was now time to return to London to search the miles of documents for the one slip of paper that might confirm what she now believed possible.

49

London, 1997

'You're just in time,' Penny said. 'We exchanged contracts on the house this morning. Decided to bite the bullet and give them vacant possession as from this evening.' She laughed. 'Wish me luck trying to prise Mum out.'

'I can't imagine it will be easy for her to leave this place,' Amy said, looking around at the shell of the Cooper family home. If 72 Chalcot Crescent had looked empty last time Amy had seen it, the only visible remaining furniture now was the two armchairs and coffee table on the bare floorboards of the sitting room, where Verity sat primly, as though awaiting a taxi.

'Sorry I can't offer you a cuppa,' Penny said. 'There's not one left in the house.' The heavy tread of footsteps above them suddenly interrupted her. 'Don't touch anything. I'll be up in a minute,' she shouted up the stairs. She turned back to Amy. 'Excuse me – better intervene. I'll leave you to it.'

'So you're back,' Verity said as Amy sat in the empty armchair beside her.

'Yes. Sorry it's been a little while before I could get over to see you, but I needed to check a few facts first.'

'So you found something out about her in Paris?'

Amy nodded.

'Then you did a better job than I.'

'Not really. I just had different information.'

'What sort of information?'

'The sort given me by Sophie's cousin.'

'The next of kin?'

'Inès Arnaud. She is still alive in Paris.'

Verity frowned. 'But she insisted she had heard nothing of Sophie. We wrote to her repeatedly over the next months, in case anything had changed, but nothing had. In the end, we had to assume that Sophie had died in the camp, or in transit. Are you telling me now that Madame Arnaud knew something?'

'Yes, she did.' Amy took a deep breath. 'Sophie did return to Paris in 1945, but she was in extremely poor health. Inès brought her home to nurse her through the pneumonia that had taken hold at Dachau. The damage to Sophie's lungs was too far advanced, however, and she died that June.'

'That poor woman,' Verity said, pulling a handkerchief from the sleeve of her cardigan. 'To think I sent her away, to die like that.'

'You didn't send her away. She went willingly, determined to fight.'

'I still don't understand how Madame Arnaud succeeded in finding her where we failed.'

'Sophie was amongst the arrivals at the Hotel Lutetia in the spring and summer of 1945.'

'But we liaised with the reception committee there daily. There was no Sophie Clément admitted.' She paused. 'Nor a Sophie Joubert, her married name,' she went on quietly.

'Ah, yes. That,' Amy said.

Verity raised an eyebrow. 'More information I did not find?'

'The husband you uncovered . . . as you know, he was working for the resistance, and yes, he married Sophie in late 1940, but it was a marriage of convenience.'

'Convenience?'

'Jean-Paul Joubert was in a relationship with Sophie's friend Fabien Dupont. The marriage was a cover-up to protect the two men from German scrutiny. It was to be annulled after the war.'

Verity's eyebrows moved a little closer to her hairline as understanding dawned upon her. 'I should have guessed that was the sort of thing she would do for people she loved. And so she and Alec could have married after all.' She looked at Amy. 'I still don't see how we missed her at the Lutetia. We even gave them all her aliases, the Joubert man's name. And still nothing.'

'You missed her because you were searching for the wrong Sophie.' Amy reached down to her briefcase and pulled out a file containing a photocopied sheet of paper. 'Something Inès said made me think we had missed something. I couldn't be certain until I went through every record I could find at the Archives, but eventually I was able to confirm the information she gave me.'

'Which was what?'

'Inès told me that Sophie was kept in Fresnes prison during her period of interrogation at avenue Foch.'

'Fresnes? But isn't that where . . .'

Amy nodded. 'It's where Alec was imprisoned. And at the same time as Sophie.' She showed Verity the photocopy of a hand-typed report dated January 1946. 'This report is written by Bruno Becker, who was a captain with the German army in

Paris. He was a cultural attaché and formed a friendship with Sophie. In fact he was also working undercover for the Allies.'

Verity frowned. 'The mystery asset Tremayne alluded to?'

'Exactly. All through the occupation Becker was feeding information to Sophie and others. After her arrest, he held firm for a while, but as the Germans prepared to evacuate Paris, he led an unsuccessful assassination attempt on Seelman's life. Becker was deported himself, and after his release worked with the investigation into Nazi war criminals. He testified against Seelman in November 1946 at the High Command Trial in Nuremburg, helping secure Seelman's death sentence.'

'And what does Becker have to do with Fresnes?'

'Becker conducted the interview with the young German chaplain at Fresnes prison. Captain Paul Heinerst was a decent man, by all accounts, working with a French widow on the outside to pass messages to and from prisoners. Keen to assist the Red Cross and intelligence services, he named many of the prisoners he had encountered, describing their mistreatment by the German guards. Towards the end of his deposition he describes an event that took place at Fresnes the night before Sophie was deported.' She passed the document to Verity. 'I've highlighted the relevant paragraph for you.'

Verity shook her head. 'I'm sorry. I'm not sure I can bear to look. Would you read it out to me?'

'Of course.' Amy took the paper back and began reading slowly.

On the night of 1March 1944 I visited the cell of MLLE S. *on the pretext of performing communion for her, as I had done twice weekly with the permission of* COLONEL

KASPAR SEELMAN. It was almost midnight, but it was not unusual for my work to take place at night – God does not operate by our laws of time, and MLLE S. was to be transported to Dachau camp the next morning. When I arrived at her cell, she was dressed as usual in the white gown in which she had been arrested weeks earlier, and although she bore the marks of that day's interrogation by SEELMAN, she seemed in good spirits.

Through the network of rumours and messages, she had recently discovered the presence of a friend at Fresnes, and asked that I might find a way for them to see one another before she left. MADAME LE FAUCHEUX, my contact on the outside, had procured bottles of brandy with which to buy the silence of the guard posted outside MLLE S.'s cell in the female wing, and women's clothing with which to disguise a British prisoner who was brought to MLLE S.'s cell. I had not come across him before, as I was kept away from military prisoners, and he was, I believe, a pilot with the RAF. He removed the costume, showing himself to be distinguishable by burns damage to his right ear and cheek.

There was little space in the cell, of which most was taken up by a narrow bed, chair and desk, but the three of us managed to squeeze in, a guard I trusted keeping watch from outside the room. It was the simplest and most moving marriage ceremony I have conducted, as the bells nearby chimed midnight and I declared Mr and Mrs Scott man and wife. I was able to afford them three hours alone in her cell before SCOTT was returned to the men's wing.

The next morning MRS SCOTT was taken to Drancy

internment camp. I heard she was removed from there two days later, taken to Karlsruhe then Dachau camps.

Months later, at five o'clock on the morning of 26 July, I was called to give last rites to twenty-three male prisoners who were to be executed at Fresnes prison. ALEC SCOTT was amongst them.

'And that is why I never found her.'

'Exactly,' Amy said. 'It was Sophie Scott who arrived at the Lutetia.'

Verity closed her eyes. 'They found one another. I can't tell you how happy that makes me.'

'I know.'

She held out her hand. 'Let me see that for a moment.' She pointed towards the first paragraph of the document. 'How extraordinary. The first of March,' she said. 'The anniversary of the day of the Baker Street bomb. The day they met.' She looked up suddenly at voices in the hallway.

'Sorry, Mum, I couldn't keep him out,' Penny said, poking her head around the door. 'Can he come in now?'

Verity smiled. 'Of course,' she said, holding out her hand.

The elderly gentleman came across, standing behind her chair, his hand on her shoulder as he smiled at Amy. 'So is this the lass you were telling me about?'

'Yes, this is Amy,' Verity said, taking his hand. 'She's discovered that Sophie and Alec married in prison in Paris.'

'Married, eh? Good for Alec.' A wide, beaming smile spread across his kind face as he thrust his hands into the pockets of his corduroy trousers and rocked back and forth on his heels.

Verity quickly slapped his arm. 'Bill, I've told you a hundred times. If you tip over backwards, I'm not picking you up.'

He chuckled, leaning down to kiss her on the cheek as she stretched her face up towards him. 'Tell you what, Amy. If Mrs Cooper here had been in charge during the war, Hitler wouldn't have made it out of Berlin.'

'Don't be silly, Bill,' she replied, and Amy thought she caught a girlish blush bloom on the old lady's cheeks.

Amy stood. 'I should really let you get on. I can see it's a busy day.'

Verity turned to her family. 'Bill? Penny? Could you just give us a moment, before Amy leaves?'

They waited until they were alone, and Verity reached for a manila envelope on the side table. 'This is for you,' she said, handing it to Amy.

'What is it?' Amy said.

'Alec's medals, photographs of him with his squadron. Some older photographs of when we were children. And one of myself in uniform. You may need them for your book.'

Amy looked up at her. 'So you will let me include you in the book?'

Verity smiled. 'As long as you don't use that awful nickname they all used behind my back at Whaddon.'

Amy smiled, thinking back to her meeting with Daphne. 'I don't know what you're talking about. But Bill, Penny, your son . . . they don't know anything about Whaddon.'

'Then it's time I told them. Apart from anything else, they might finally take me more seriously. Thank you, my dear,' Verity said, 'for everything. You have given me back my peace of mind.'

'And you gave me a purpose when I needed it most. Actually, Verity, I do have one more thing for you.' Amy knelt down and pulled a small cassette player out of her bag, placing it on the coffee table in front of the old lady. 'It won't take long.'

'What's this?'

'I'm sorry it's not fantastic quality, but a friend is going to work on it. I'm hoping to make it public when my book is published. I'll send you the finished version when it's ready, but I thought you'd like to hear this before we say goodbye. It's a recording of a wartime concert in Paris.' David had isolated one of the pieces from the recital, and anxious to avoid telling Verity the circumstances of the concert at this stage, Amy pressed the Play button on the machine and stood back.

The opening bars of Chopin's Revolutionary Study shot into the room like gunfire, the tumultuous, anguished melody like a great, angry river about to burst its banks, giving way to a brief stillness before the storm erupted once more, raging until finally it was spent.

Verity looked up at Amy. 'It's her, isn't it?'

Amy nodded.

Verity shook her head. 'I never thought it would be possible. I feel finally that something has been completed – hearing Sophie play like that, I can begin to understand her, to know her a little more, if that doesn't sound strange?'

'Not at all. I have the same feeling when I listen.'

'I hope one day you decide to play again, Amy. To have music in your life is to have a true gift. Don't throw it away. Your husband knew it – let him have his own way.'

'We'll see. I already have so much. And partly because of

you.' She smiled. 'I think we've been good for one another, don't you?'

'I do. You are a different young woman to the one who arrived here weeks ago, and I certainly feel as though something has lifted from my own shoulders. Go and enjoy your life, Amy. You deserve it.'

Amy thought about the dinner party she was hosting that evening, the neglected friendships she would rekindle over home-cooked food, and the new friendship she was enjoying immensely. For the first time in a year, she was looking forward to life. 'I shall miss you, Verity,' she said.

'Then come and visit. Bring me a copy of the book when you've finished it, and that little girl of yours – although from my experience it's rather difficult to get children back to London once they've visited Shropshire!'

Bill suddenly popped his head around the door. 'Black bags, V?'

She sighed. 'Ask Penny.'

'I know you will miss this place, but I really do hope the move goes well,' Amy said.

Verity smiled as Bill came across to put an arm around his wife's shoulder. 'I rather think it will. I'm finally ready to leave,' she said.

'Be like a honeymoon over there, darling, won't it?'

'It will,' Verity replied. 'After all, we are still owed one, I believe.'

Epilogue

It felt good to have broken the social ice once more – Claire and David had been on fine form, other old friends sharing stories of Michael, and Jay had been talked into holding jazz nights at the shop. Amy had insisted on cooking everything herself, the huge, creamy lasagne and crisp green salad her first large-scale catering effort for over a year, and if the pavlova had sunk somewhat, no one cared. Amy saw the relief on the faces of those who loved her, as she took tentative steps out from the shadow of bereavement.

It had all gone on much later than she'd anticipated, and even though she had to be up in the morning for a spa weekend away with Claire, she didn't care. Besides, she suspected Claire might need a lie-in and Michael's parents were bound to be late picking up Holly.

'I should be heading off,' Jay said, wiping his hands on a tea towel as he joined her in the sitting room, where she was clearing away toys Holly had brought down to show the adults. 'Sure there's no more clearing up to do?'

She smiled. 'No, you've done it all. Thanks,' she said, coming over and kissing him on the cheek. 'You're a good friend.'

'You too,' he said, hugging her.

For a brief moment they looked at one another, and there was a slight hesitation before they both pulled back. Had Amy imagined something, or had she just had too much wine? Whatever had passed between them had been comfortable, easy, but too soon, and as she saw Jay waver, she realised he knew it too. There was no rush – they had all the time in the world.

'I'll get tickets for that play you wanted to see,' he said, heading out to the hallway to find his coat.

'Thanks, that'd be great.'

Jay muttered to himself as he dropped his coat and bent down to pick it up from on top of the shoe rack. 'Hey, Amy, think you missed some post here.' He reached behind the rack and pulled out an A4 envelope. 'Must have fallen down the back. French postmark, by the looks of it.'

Amy took it from him, examining the hand-written address on the front. 'Thanks,' she said. 'I'll open it in a bit.'

She closed the door behind Jay and stood at the bottom of the stairs, listening for Holly, then paused outside Michael's study, his desk now littered with her own papers and books about the war as she claimed the space as her own. The piano was still there, but instead of tormenting her, it acted as a connection with Sophie, even if Amy had not been able to bring herself to play it. It was going back, of course, but just not quite yet. She had a few more days before she had to confirm its return.

She sat at the desk and ripped open the envelope, pulling out a slim volume of music and a handwritten letter on thick, embossed paper, a black-and-white photograph pinned to it.

'*Dear Amy*,' she read.

It seems far longer ago than a month since you visited me in Paris. Much has changed for me in that time, and my health has improved enough that I feel ready to join my daughter and her family in the South of France. The city is far too much for a woman of my age, and besides, there are too many ghosts here.

I have begun the task of clearing my apartment and discovered the enclosed, which I know Sophie would want you to have. I believe it is the only copy in existence. Please have my blessing to play it and think of her.

This photograph was tucked inside. She and her pilot appear to be in the countryside – her hair looks unusually frightful, for which I can only blame the English climate. What a handsome couple they made, and how happy they look. Thank you for letting me know the end of their story. It is an enormous comfort to me.

With all good wishes,

Inès Arnaud

Amy looked at the slim volume of music, translating out loud the words on its front cover:

THE SONG OF PARIS

by Max Goldmann

May 1940

To Sophie Clément, friend and musician without compare

Amy opened the first page, flicking through the black, inky scrawl of Max's handwriting. She read through the score, hearing the music in her head, but it was not enough. Amy placed the music on the piano and opened the lid. She sat at the stool, adjusting the height and arranging the midnight-blue velvet skirt she had worn for the dinner party. She hesitated, flexing her fingers and rubbing at the scar tissue of her left hand, until finally she placed her hands on the keys and began to play the notes that had not been heard since they were last performed by a woman who had known her arrest was moments away.

The music was simple, elegant, with none of the flashiness that would have challenged Amy's stiff fingers and her damaged left hand. It was a stunning elegy to Paris, filling her with joy and the incredible release Michael had wanted for her.

'You really are the best pianist in the world,' a voice behind her said. She stopped abruptly and turned around. Holly was standing in the doorway in her nightdress, cuddling her toy rabbit. 'Daddy was right,' she said, climbing on to Amy's knee and leaning into her. She reached across and lifted the music from the stand, running her finger across the words on the front. 'S . . . Sop . . . What does this say, Mummy?' she said, pointing to Sophie's name.

'It says Sophie Clément. She was a very brave lady.'

'Is she the one you're writing a book about?'

'Yes, she is.'

'And she was a pianist like you.'

'Well . . .'

Holly turned to her. 'Can we keep the piano now? Daddy said if you played it, we could.'

'I don't know . . .' The year was up in two weeks' time, and already the lease firm had left an answer-machine message asking if they could arrange collection, if the lease was not to be renewed.

'Please, Mummy. I want you to play to me every day.'

Amy ran her fingers across the keys once more. It felt like coming home, like second nature. How strange that it had taken such a heartbreaking journey for her to make a natural, simple reconnection, and already her fingers ached to play more, to throw open the windows of the room she had kept closed for so long. Of course Michael had been right. Of course she had to keep the instrument. She kissed the top of Holly's head. 'OK. But only if you play to me every day too.'

'I promise.' Holly settled against Amy's chest, breathing deeply as she sucked her thumb. 'I like your perfume,' she said. 'It's pretty, like you.'

'I'm not wearing perfume, sweetheart,' Amy said.

'Yes, you are.'

Amy lifted her head. Holly was right. A delicate thread of scent hung in the air. Floral with a hint of bergamot, it smelled of silk and velvet, of champagne and diamonds. Of a woman toasting friendship beneath glittering chandeliers, a woman wrapped in the arms of her new husband as they danced together in a tiny prison cell until dawn separated them for ever.

It was *Soir de Paris*.

Author's note

Under the restrictions of a national lockdown, and wanting to write a companion novel to *The Schoolteacher of Saint-Michel*, I chose for the settings of my new book two places I know very well – London and Paris, cities that endured a very different type of war to Lucie's beloved Dordogne.

The story was fuelled partly by Oliver Sacks' book *Musicophilia*, which explores how even following neurological trauma, highly complex skills might remain intact. In particular, and depending upon which part of the brain might be affected, musical memory continues to function, as is demonstrated by the incredible work of charities such as Mindsong with dementia sufferers, and by the story of Clive Wearing, a musician with amnesia that left him with a ten-second memory, but the ability to continue playing the piano and even conducting a choir, as though nothing had happened. I exercised the fiction writer's privilege to play with the 'what ifs' of this situation to create a wartime scenario in which a stranger is adrift across enemy lines, although I make no claim to be any kind of neuropsychologist.

There has been much written and said and many films made about Special Operations Executive agents such as Odette Hallowes and Noor Inayat Khan, who were sent by Churchill to 'set Europe ablaze' by sabotaging the German occupation. Paying a visit to the National Archive and seeing their files first-hand was an incredibly sobering experience, and of the documents contained within them, it was a copy of the note with which Violette Szabo's camel-hair coat was returned to her grieving mother that has stayed with me above all.

Where it is relatively easy to research SOE agents, there is still considerable mystery surrounding the wartime activities of agents attached to the Special Intelligence Service – or MI6 as it is now known – whose role was intelligence-gathering, rather than the direct action and sabotage at the heart of SOE efforts. Many of these files remain under lock and key at the MOD.

One of the most extraordinary SIS spies operating in enemy territory was Marie-Madeleine Fourcade, head of the Alliance network in France. Sir Kenneth Cohen, head of Section VIII at Whaddon Hall and my inspiration for the character of Sir Richard Tremayne, described Marie-Madeleine as the 'textbook beautiful spy' when he finally met her during one of her rare wartime trips by Lysander aeroplane to England. Sophie's escape through the bars of her cell in the Prison du Cherche-Midi was inspired by one of Marie-Madeleine's own successes in evading capture by the Germans. *Madame Fourcade's War* by Lynne Olson provides a fascinating insight into SIS operations in occupied France and the background to this extraordinary woman who is commemorated at Les Invalides in Paris alongside many other French war heroes.

Marie-Madeleine too had a wartime love, in the form of Léon Faye, an agent who was eventually arrested and questioned at avenue Foch, before being shot on a forced march from a German labour camp at the end of the war. Faye was incarcerated at avenue Foch alongside Noor Inayat Khan, with whom he made a failed escape attempt from the attic across the Paris rooftops. Standing on the pavement outside 84 avenue Foch, now simply a beautiful townhouse, was one of the more chilling experiences during a belated research trip to Paris. Records of Noor's arrest and subsequent death at Dachau were incredibly helpful in informing Daphne's movements during my novel, and I thoroughly recommend Sarah Helm's *A Life in Secrets* for an account of Vera Atkins' efforts to find her lost SOE agents after the liberation of France.

If it seems unlikely that Sophie would be handed top-level intelligence by German officers, it was in fact Marie-Madeleine's pretty nineteen-year-old agent Jeannie Rousseau who discovered the existence of V1 and V2 rockets designed to flatten London. An employee at a trade syndicate working with the Germans in Paris, the disingenuous Jeannie simply allowed German officers to compete in trying to impress her at a drinks party, to the point at which one of them showed her blueprints for the V2 rocket being developed at the Peenemünde research station in Germany. Days later, this information was on Churchill's desk and the facility bombed. Without Jeannie's discovery, the damage to London might well have been even more catastrophic and the Allied invasion of Northern Europe significantly delayed.

Many of the achievements of the Alliance network and the SOE could not have happened without the shuttle service provided by night during the full-moon period by a secret squadron of pilots who from 1942 flew agents in and out of France in tiny single-engine Lysanders with no lights, no navigator and no defence against aerial attack. They had only a handful of moments on the ground, in which to swap incoming and outgoing agents along with supplies and intelligence. It was an absolute privilege to visit the museum at RAF Tangmere, where the black-painted Lysanders of 161 Squadron were kept during the 'moon period', out of sight of other squadrons. The more I learned about the individual pilots who performed this incredible role in the war, the more I knew one of these men had to play a pivotal role in my novel.

One staggering resource I came across by chance was the RAF flight box belonging to a friend's grandfather, a Spitfire and Mosquito pilot during the war. His logbooks, squadron photographs of horrifyingly young men, and censored letters from his fiancée brought home the extraordinary life these men led, one failed mission away from never returning back to base. The decades were eaten away as I looked through this incredibly personal piece of family history.

Unlike Bletchley Park, Whaddon Hall has disappeared from public view over the years, and is now divided into residential apartments. A short walk across the fields to the right of the church in Whaddon takes you to Windy Ridge, where all that remains of the wireless huts that formed the communication link between field and station are the concrete footings now overgrown with weeds. It is as though the whole operation never existed. The short film Amy and Eleanor watch of agents at Whaddon Hall can easily be found via a quick search of the Internet, and although you will not see Sophie or Tremayne, it makes fascinating viewing.

The scenes at the Hotel Lutetia are taken largely from fact, and whilst in Paris I stood opposite the hotel, where crowds would gather daily beneath the chestnut trees in the hope of seeing their loved ones amongst the emaciated figures returning from concentration camps. Seeing inside the hotel made it easier and yet also much harder to write the scenes based there. A small plaque on the wall outside the hotel is the only reminder of those days.

I have taken the liberty of including walk-on parts for a few real-life characters, including Stewart Menzies, who was indeed

'C', Chief of MI6, during the war, and François Mitterand, whose flight into France by Lysander is recorded at RAF Tangmere.

Captain Paul Heinerst was the German chaplain at Fresnes prison, and I discovered his existence by chance within a post-war deposition in which his kindness and his clandestine work with outsiders to improve the lives of prisoners is mentioned in passing.

The two daughters of Irène Némirovsky, the Jewish Ukrainian author, were seen daily amongst the families gathered outside the Lutetia, until eventually word came through that their mother had been murdered at Auschwitz. The manuscript for her novel *Suite Française* was discovered in a family attic decades later, and gives an incredible insight into life in occupied France.

Sabine, the Red Cross worker in my book, is in fact Sabine Ségouin, a nineteen-year-old resistance fighter who helped liberate Chartres, going on to volunteer with the refugee-repatriation programme at the Lutetia in 1945. After the war, she trained as a nurse, and as I write, still lives in France, one of the few remaining heroes of the French resistance.

Acknowledgements

There are many people I need to thank for their assistance and input into this book, not least of whom is historian and archivist Dr William Butler, who met with me at the National Archives in Kew to describe life as an archivist there and explain the process of declassification of government files. His guiding me through the several miles of files kept in the archive saved me hours of online searching.

By their very nature, the security services are pretty impenetrable to a nosy author, but I am very grateful to my friendly asset on the inside, who shall of course remain nameless. He talked me through the principles of agent handling and explained the chain of command during World War Two, from intelligence gathering to military action. A decent lunch was a small price for this gold dust.

When travel restrictions made it possible and I finally visited Paris to retrace Sophie's steps, I met some incredibly welcoming and helpful people there, including maître d's who allowed me to poke my head inside some very swanky restaurants that might have been in German officers' budgets once upon a time, but were definitely not in mine.

Very special thanks go to Nina, the Duty Manager at the Hotel Lutetia when I visited. She took a great deal of time to talk to me about the prisoner-repatriation programme there, showing me the corridors where returned prisoners slept, the restaurants where they were fed and brought back to life by staff, volunteers and doctors whilst the Red Cross helped trace their families.

I highly recommend a visit to the museum at RAF Tangmere. Curator Charles Hutcheon and Deputy Curator Pete Pitman went out of their way to make my visit as illuminating as possible, even sharing flight logs with me.

I am very grateful to Emily Lucas for allowing me to explore her grandfather's RAF records. Alec's story is much the richer for it.

Thanks, as ever, to my tolerant family and friends, who have indulged my talking at them about my research discoveries and patiently let me try out plot twists and turns.

Thanks especially to my good friend and fellow World War Two fiction writer Mandy Robotham, sharer of resources and discoveries – we were like children in a sweetie shop when we visited Bletchley Park, so thanks also to the indulgent staff there.

I would particularly like to say a huge thank you to my team at Sheil Land Associates and Headline Review: my agent Gaia Banks and her new baby boy, who has generously shared his mother with me, and Alba Arnau, who was a fantastic stand-in whilst Master Banks made his first appearance; Sherise Hobbs and Bea Grabowska at Headline are my editors without compare, and my books are so much better for their input.

Reading group questions

1. According to the Office for National Statistics, in 1940 marriages involving males up to the age of 24 increased by over 60 per cent. Living through a world war, and with an uncertain future, many young couples tied the knot in a hurry, some without even knowing one another very well. Is there a story of wartime romance or marriage in your own family? Did this relationship survive the war? How easy do you think it might have been to work through a marriage that had been conducted in haste, once the war was over?

2. Both Sophie and Amy are familiar with the phenomenon known as muscle memory. Although most of us are not concert pianists, we all experience this to an extent, whether it is in the automatic act of brushing our teeth or making a cup of tea. What complex actions in your own life do you perform without thinking about it?

3. The lives of women like Verity Cooper were changed immeasurably during the war. How difficult do you imagine it must have been for them to give up highly skilled and challenging military roles and return to being housewives and mothers? How successful were the 'homemaker' advertising campaigns of the late 1940s and '50s, designed to encourage them to be satisfied with this

return to 'normality'? Were the experiences of these women instrumental in the rise of feminism twenty years later?

4. By the end of the war teenagers were flying missions over occupied Europe. Amongst these was my own children's grandfather, who flew Lancaster bombers at the age of nineteen. Although hailed as heroes, many veterans of the RAF experienced terrible trauma, but without treatment for PTSD, how would these young men, and other servicemen and women, have coped with life after the war?

5. Many veterans of both world wars were reluctant to talk about their experiences. Is this a generational thing? How helpful is a 'stiff upper lip' in dealing with trauma?

6. One of the most harrowing aspects of researching this book was looking through the government files of SOE agents such as Odette Hallowes and Violette Szabo. I was as much moved by first-hand accounts of Violette's death as by the note written by Vera Atkins to accompany the camel-hair coat and other personal items returned to Violette's mother. Such small vignettes tell of terrible heartbreak and tragedy – what recollections of your own sum up collective pain in a tiny way, for instance a lonely care-home resident seen through a window during the pandemic, or a roadside shrine?

7. In every war there will be some considered to be collaborators. Can we forgive those who make their own lives a little easier by not sticking their head over the parapet? Is it acceptable to watch others punished, if it means your own loved ones will be kept safe by your silence?

8. Scent is an incredibly powerful repository of memory. Are there certain smells or fragrances that instantly transport you back to another time in your life?

9. Michael argued that Wagner's operas are intolerable because they were written by an anti-Semite adored by Hitler, but does and should the music stand alone? Are Coco Chanel's clothes any less beautiful because she spent the war living with a German officer at the Paris Ritz? Can art be separated from its creator?

10. As I write this, events unfold in Ukraine and history seems to repeat itself. Can any lessons be said to have been learned from two world wars?

Read on for a short extract of

The SCHOOL TEACHER *of* SAINT-MICHEL

'My darling girl, I need you to find someone for me . . .'

France, 1942. At the end of the day, the schoolteacher releases her pupils. She checks they have their identity passes, and warns them not to stop until the German guards have let them through the barrier that separates occupied France from Free France. As the little ones fly across the border and into their mothers' arms, she breathes a sigh of relief. No one is safe now. Not even the children.

Berkshire, present day. A letter left to her by her beloved late grandmother Gigi takes Hannah Stone on a journey deep into the heart of the Dordogne landscape. As she begins to unravel a forgotten history of wartime bravery and sacrifice, she discovers the heartrending secret that binds her grandmother to a village schoolteacher, the remarkable Lucie Laval . . .

Available to download

Prologue

In the peaceful pause between day and night, she steps out into the long shadows of the orchard, its treetops brushed with splashes of coral and gold. She weaves around the trees, her basket pressed against her hip, plucking the ripest cherries for her table, as she has done for countless harvests in this little corner of France.

Suddenly, like the deer in the woods beyond the stream, she freezes as dark clouds bubble on the horizon, extinguishing the last of the sun's rays. Thunderous booms echo across the soft hills as bright flashes of light dance like fireflies in the distance. Yet this strange summer storm will not bring the release of the rain the parched ground craves, nor break the crackling tension in the air. And in the meantime, life must go on, even if it is a shadow of the lives they knew not so long ago. The children must go to school, the fields must be ploughed, meals prepared, livings made, prayers said in the cool, dark church, and the summer harvest collected.

A squadron of planes flies low overhead, shaking the ground as they mimic the annual migration of geese, and she quickly fills the basket before hurrying inside. She glances back, all the grief of the world in her eyes as she searches the darkness, then pulls the shutters closed against the night. They have survived another day.

Gigi woke suddenly, her frail heart tapping out a frantic rhythm. Even after all these years, long-buried memories of the war still floated to the surface of her dreams as though it were yesterday, urging her not to forget the people she had left behind, and the debt she owed them.

She looked out of the window as a flurry of petals caught the breeze, a candyfloss cloud tumbling along the street, as blossom drifts gathered in gutters and around tree roots that burst up through the grey London pavement. How many springs had she watched the monochrome scene transform itself into a Japanese watercolour? And each spring the blossom awakened the burden that dragged on her like heavy fruit on the branch.

A group of young mothers walked past the wide bay window, babies in pushchairs in front of them and trailing toddlers behind. She watched a little boy stop at the tree outside, spinning around its trunk and laughing, and she was transported again to those long-gone days of her dreams.

She closed her eyes once more, and like an old cine film on a whirring projector, images of her beloved France flickered before her: the sun-bleached orchard and the shallow stream bouncing diamonds of light across its bubbling surface; a couple dancing beneath the trees to the strains of an old folk song while children wove around them, gorging themselves on sweet, sticky cherries, as for a brief moment the war raging across Europe was forgotten. This was how she wanted to remember her motherland during those terrible times – the memories of dark woods and dangerous city streets, damp cellars and abandoned buildings were too painful for her old heart to recall.

She looked now at the photographs on the mantelpiece: more than most, she understood the value of family, love, loyalty; knew how far it was possible to go in order to protect those one cared for. She knew too that the ties formed all those years ago had never weakened, and that those she had left behind would always be a part of her.

Again she felt her breath catch. She had become accustomed to this now: her heart was indeed broken, fighting to complete its lifetime's allocation of beats. Only difficult, invasive surgery could help her now, and she was too tired. She had lived her life as best she could, and there was only one thing left undone, one debt unpaid.

She had waited too long. She could see that now. There would be no more springs, no more time to put things right unless she gave her story to another.

She reached across to the little table beside her, and picked up a photograph of her granddaughter as a little girl. She had been lucky: of course she adored her son, but the easy friendship with dear Hannah that had grown over the years was a gift she cherished. Gigi had passed on to Hannah the arts of perfect pastry and an exquisitely tied silk scarf, the bond between them as close as mother and daughter. And now that little girl had her own life and her own love, her own pain: her dear, kind Hannah who reminded Gigi so much of someone from her distant past, the bittersweet memories of those war-ravaged times tugging at her heart.

Hannah, her *petite fille*, who understood what it was to live with something that ate away at you, and for whom she prayed this task might offer some balm.

Hannah, who might put things right for her.

She eased herself out of the chair, wincing as a pain shot down her arm, and fetched her writing paper and an envelope from the old bureau. Her arthritic hand paused over the tissue-thin paper, ink pooling at the expectant nib of her pen as she searched for the words.

My darling Hannah, she finally began, breaking off only to catch her rapidly shortening breath. And then, within a few short lines, it was done, and she folded the letter inside the delicate lilac envelope. The effort had drained her, and her beautiful copperplate handwriting wavered as she wrote Hannah's name, the final *h* trailing across the paper.

She placed the letter beside her on the table and closed her eyes once more, unable to resist the weight of her eyelids and the sleep that overcame her like a sedative, so that dreams and memories were indistinguishable as she once again stood in a shady orchard, smelling the sun-warmed grass as a sudden peace wrapped its arms around her.

She had plucked the heavy fruit from the branch and handed it to one she trusted, and at last her heart was free.